# "ABOUT LAST NIGHT . . .

I apologize for falling asleep in your bed. . . ." Maddie lost her voice suddenly.

"There was no harm done, as far as I know. Was there?" Luke asked.

Her mind momentarily lit on the memory of his hand on hers. "None that I can think of."

"Matthew," he called again. "We need to get started." This time Matthew came running and reached the wagon ahead of his father. Luke hesitated. "I'm glad we had this conversation."

"You—you are?"

"I would hate to spend the rest of my life wondering if I'd only dreamt that you were in my bed."

Maddie watched the wagon roll away and suddenly realized how much she had come to care for them both. It was no longer a matter of her wanting him to kiss her; she wanted him to love her. There was so much about them she didn't know, didn't understand. Even as frustrating as Luke's resistance was to her, she could feel herself drawn ever closer to him.

Didn't he know that whatever it was that held him captive, also held her captive . . . ?

**"Emotional, engrossing, and sparkling with touches of humor . . . A beautifully written journey."** —Raine Cantrell

**"A heartwarming example of pioneer spirit, but, most of all, it's a moving story of the redemptive power of love . . . I enjoyed it immensley."** —Jennifer Blake

# WIND SONG

*by*

*Margaret Brownley*

A TOPAZ BOOK

TOPAZ
Published by the Penguin Group
Penguin Books USA Inc., 375 Hudson Street,
New York, New York 10014, U.S.A.
Penguin Books Ltd, 27 Wrights Lane,
London W8 5TZ, England
Penguin Books Australia Ltd, Ringwood,
Victoria, Australia
Penguin Books Canada Ltd, 10 Alcorn Avenue,
Toronto, Ontario, Canada M4V 3B2
Penguin Books (N.Z.) Ltd, 182–190 Wairau Road,
Auckland 10, New Zealand

Penguin Books Ltd, Registered Offices:
Harmondsworth, Middlesex, England

First published by Topaz,
an imprint of Dutton Signet,
a division of Penguin Books USA Inc.

First Printing, November, 1994
10  9  8  7  6  5  4  3  2  1

Topaz is a trademark of Dutton Signet,
a division of Penguin Books USA Inc.

Printed in the United States of America

*To Bob, Judy, Carol,*
*Gary, Pat, and Steve*
*for making laughter*
*the wind's song.*

# Chapter 1

## 1870

The shrill sound of the train whistle pierced the early-morning air as the Kansas-Pacific slid quickly through the wind-rippled grasslands. Massive numbers of buffalo ran from the tracks, allowing the train to divide the herd as easily as a knife slicing bread.

One enormous bull lifted its woolly head toward the sky and let out a loud bellow as if to protest the intrusion.

Watching from the gilt-framed window of the Pullman, Madeline Percy rallied to the bull's plight. *You have every right to complain,* she thought, feeling an inexplicable kinship with the animal.

At first glance the buffalo seemed burdened by top-heavy bodies, their short, curving horns barely visible in the masses of dark, curling fur. Even the short, skinny tails seemed ill-conceived. But the thin legs had a deceptive strength, carrying the beasts effortlessly over the flat plains that stretched as far as the eye could see.

Maddie hadn't known such power and freedom existed, except in her own mind, and her heart fluttered with excitement as she watched the animals flee.

A deafening blast filled the air, and Maddie watched with horror as one of the magnificent animals stumbled forward, then fell, knees first, to the ground. She craned her neck and glanced back to catch a glimpse of the animal's anguished face before it was left behind by the speeding train.

Stunned by the sudden violence, Maddie required a full minute to realize that the bullet had come from the rifle of the bowler-topped passenger who sat in the seat directly behind hers.

Another shot rang out, and Maddie's shock turned to rage. Swinging herself around, she lifted her knees onto the seat and flung herself over the stiff leather back to face the man. "How dare you kill those animals!"

A startled look crossed the pockmarked face of the hunter. He lowered his rifle a few inches and gave her a dark, warning look. "It's no business of yours what I do."

"I'm making it my business," she retorted. She was so enraged that her normally firm, vibrant voice barely rose above the clackety-clack of the rails.

The man ignored her and once again aimed his rifle out the open window.

Maddie reached for her parasol and struck the offender on the shoulder. Startled by the attack, the man quickly turned, his stiff felt hat flying across the aisle. He gave an incredulous gasp and raised his free arm to protect himself against any additional blows.

"Dammit, woman! What's the matter with you?"

When she made no move to attack him further, he grabbed the end of her parasol. In the struggle that followed, he loosened his hold on the rifle and the weapon dropped against the sill with a clatter, then disappeared through the open window. With a muttered curse, the man lurched toward the window in a futile attempt to save his rifle.

Satisfied, Maddie lowered her now tattered parasol

and almost lost her balance in the swaying motion of the train.

Enraged, the man pointed a threatening finger and leaned forward menacingly. "Now look what you did, you interferin' . . ."

Maddie raised what was left of the parasol and brought it down hard upon his balding head. The man grabbed the parasol, and Maddie pressed the sole of her high-laced boot against the back of her seat to avail herself of every bit of strength during the tug-of-war that ensued.

"Let go of my parasol," she insisted between clenched teeth.

"Not on your bloody life!"

"Excuse me, sir. Is there a problem?" The porter stood looking at the battling duo as if such a shocking display of ill manners were an everyday occurrence.

Not the least bit embarrassed by her lack of propriety, and even less inclined to concede defeat, Maddie yanked hard on the leather handle of the battered parasol.

Momentarily distracted by the porter, her foe caught Maddie by surprise when he let go. Woman and parasol flew backward in a cloud of feminine petticoats. The parasol flew up and popped an English chap on the head, causing the poor man to scramble about in search of his glass eyepiece.

The other passengers, mostly men, stared at the young woman in openmouthed disapproval.

"There certainly is a problem," the victim of her attack hissed between thin white lips. "That . . . that green-eyed witch made me drop my rifle out the window."

Maddie righted herself and glared at the man. "And you made me ruin a perfectly good parasol."

"She attacked me for no good reason."

"You killed a perfectly innocent animal!"

The porter was clearly out of his element. "Perhaps you would like to change seats." He addressed the man, but it was Maddie who accepted the offer.

"That would be most appreciated. I do not wish to spend one moment longer than necessary next to this murderer."

Ignoring the disparaging looks cast by the other passengers, she reached for the leather handle of her valise and, mustering more dignity than seemed possible under the circumstances, followed the porter down the swaying aisle to the back of the car.

For the next two hours, Maddie endured the snide comments and disapproving glances of her fellow passengers in seething silence.

She breathed a sigh of relief when at long last the train screeched to a halt in front of a wooden platform.

"Colton!" the porter called out. The passengers snapped forward and back in their seats and glanced around as if to see who in their right mind would be brave enough to disembark at such a bleak, isolated stop.

Eager to make her exit, Maddie grabbed her valise and rose to her feet. All eyes followed her progress as she made her way down the aisle.

A triple-chinned woman who had boarded the train with Maddie in Washington City looked up from her knitting to glance out the window. She afforded Maddie a pitying look before lowering her eyes to resume her work.

Glaring one last time at the man whom she'd attacked, Maddie had to maneuver her valise sideways to accommodate the narrow iron steps that led down to the wooden platform.

It was May, much too early in the year, in Maddie's

estimation, for the blast of hot air that greeted her. Upon reaching the platform, she glanced around her. Not a penny's worth of shade was available to protect her creamy white skin from the relentless glare of the noonday sun.

She regretted the loss of her parasol. Freckles, which she called "sun dots" during her more charitable moments—and a most unladylike term during her least—were bound to pop out all over the place; most certainly on her nose. Still, as unsightly as she thought sun dots to be, they were a small sacrifice to make for the life of a buffalo.

Next to the platform, a swayback horse stood harnessed to a springboard wagon. The horse tossed her a long, soulful look, its owner nowhere in sight. Nor, for that matter, was anyone else.

Maddie set her valise on the platform and tucked an unruly strand of red hair beneath the brim of her hat. She had hoped for an opportunity to freshen up before meeting her employer, Mr. Boxer, Superintendent of Public Instruction. Since there was no depot in sight, nor so much as a drop of water, it appeared she had no choice but to greet her new employer in her travel-stained condition.

The uniformed porter hauled Maddie's trunk off the train and placed it on the platform, next to her valise. He gave her a polite smile and touched his fingers to the visor of his hat. He appeared no older than sixteen, seventeen at the most.

With an anxious glance around her, Maddie pulled a coin from her small change purse and handed it to him. "I didn't expect the station to be so deserted." A blast of steam shot across the platform, making it necessary to raise her voice. "Is it always like this?"

"I wouldn't know, Miss. I've only been working for

the railroad for a few weeks and this is the first time we've stopped here. We only stop here upon request."

"Are you sure this is Colton?"

"Absolutely, Miss." He pointed to a wooden sign attached to a post over their heads. "Says so right there, Miss. Colton, Kansas."

He signaled to the engineer and, grabbing the hand rail by the open door of the parlor car, jumped aboard. "Good day, Miss!"

Maddie was sorely tempted to jump aboard after him. But she stoically held her ground. She had agreed to teach for one year, and she felt obliged to live up to the agreement. Besides, after the fuss her widowed mother had made over her plans to travel westward, she could hardly go back without allowing adequate time to prove herself.

Still, she was tempted. She had never thought she would see the day that the stiff, stuffy parlor rooms of Washington would be a welcome sight. But then she'd never known a place as bleak and lonely as Colton, Kansas, existed.

The train inched forward with a clank and rattle of the socket pins that linked the Pullman cars together. The smokestack coughed up billowing black clouds.

Maddie lifted her chin in staunch resolve and plunked herself down on her trunk. Surely Mr. Boxer had only been detained and hadn't forgotten the promise made in his letter to meet her train.

She made every effort to shake off her apprehension. No doubt the man would arrive at any moment. She sat stiffly on the trunk and watched the train pull farther away, picking up speed with a long, lonely whistle.

It occurred to her that the land was so flat that if Mr. Boxer were, indeed, anywhere in the vicinity, she could pick him out miles in advance. It was not a comforting thought, by any means. For it meant she had a long wait ahead of her.

She wondered again about the owner of the horse. Despite the hot sun, she shivered at the sound of the now distant train whistle. But nothing could be worse than the silence that followed. Soon the train was nothing more than a speck on the horizon.

She'd heard about the wide open spaces of Kansas, but nothing had prepared her for the enormity of sky and land that seemed to go on forever. And never had she imagined such a dreadful smell, like ashes, that permeated the air.

The wind had picked up in the few minutes she'd been sitting on her trunk, and the air now reeked with the sickening odor. Already her throat felt parched and dry.

"Where is he?" she muttered to herself.

As if to reply, the horse gave a soft whicker and nodded its head.

Never one to sit still for long, Maddie began pacing up and down the platform. She was dressed in a blue woolen traveling dress and velvet jacket. She should have worn her trousers, she thought, which were her usual mode of dress.

That had been her original plan, but her mother had made such a fuss about the importance of making a good impression that Maddie wore the bothersome travel suit to appease her, along with the fussy concoction of lace and feathers that masqueraded as a hat.

Maddie pulled the brim of her hat lower, but the fancy headgear was designed for the sake of appearance, not service, and provided precious little protection from the blazing hot sun, no matter how she wore it.

Her traveling outfit was equally ill-suited to the sweltering heat. Yes, indeed, she should have worn her usual attire, which was so much more comfortable and functional. Maddie's fondness for her trousers scandalized her socially conscious mother, who finally conceded that the masculine garments might be acceptable attire for participating in certain ladylike sports, but she still thought they should never be worn to White House teas or church services. And most certainly not to meet a new or prospective employer.

Less than a half hour later, Maddie decided that Mr. Boxer wasn't worth the discomfort. And if he didn't present himself soon, he would no longer be an employer of hers, prospective or otherwise. She would never under any circumstances consider working for a man who did not respect time, and at the moment she wasn't willing to consider the possibility that Mr. Boxer might have a perfectly legitimate excuse for failing to meet her train.

She rummaged through her trunk and pulled out her favorite pair of trousers.

She glanced around in the unlikely event that someone might be watching her, and after assuring herself that she was indeed alone, she eagerly pulled off her worthless hat and the stifling hot layers of wool and petticoats.

She stepped into her trousers, which tied at her waist and gathered at her ankles. She topped her trousers with a short skirt that flared gracefully from her slender hips and fell to mid-knee length.

Free of the heavy fabric of her traveling suit, she felt immediate relief. She chose a simple linen waistshirt, and after carefully folding her dress and jacket, she repacked her trunk. She then traded her fashionable but otherwise useless hat for a more practical sunbonnet.

Feeling more like herself, she reassessed her predicament.

The smell had suddenly grown stronger, along with the wind. Fine, gritty sand bit into her face. Dust blew into her eyes and nose. What a horrid place!

She stepped off the platform and approached the horse. "Where's your master?" She ran her hand along the horse's rough neck, and it nuzzled her with its nose.

She noticed a disturbing absence of tracks in the dry, dusty ground. She had the uneasy feeling that the horse and wagon had long since been deserted.

Grabbing a handful of the wild oats that grew a short distance from the railroad tracks, she walked back to the platform. The horse's soft nose pressed hungrily against her palms as he chewed the dry stalks. "Poor thing. It looks like we've both been abandoned."

She eyed the wagon. The wood was old and weatherbeaten and the seat warped, but the wheels and axle, though rusty, appeared to be in good condition.

Energized by her plan of action, she dragged her trunk across the platform. It was heavy, and moving it required a great deal of effort on her part, but she managed to heave it over the slatted sides of the wagon. It fell to the wagon bed with a thump, startling the horse, which neighed and pawed the ground in an attempt to escape.

"It's all right, boy," she said soothingly, patting the horse on the rump. "Do you have a name?" She thought for a moment and decided to call the horse Rutabaga. The poor horse was certainly the color of one and, Lord knows, it had a turnip-shaped head. Yes, Rutabaga it would be.

She glanced around one more time before untying

the horse from the platform hitch and then climbed
onto the weathered seat.

Without a clue as to which direction led to the town
of Colton, she gathered the thin leather traces in her
hands, and headed south so as not to be fighting the
wind head-on.

Dark clouds of dust hugged the ground, then spiraled upward until the sky was covered in a dirty
brown film. Eventually the dust blotted out the sun,
and the cloudless sky looked dark and stormy.

Periodically she stopped the wagon and glanced
about, hoping to see a farmhouse or some other sign of
civilization. But there was nothing.

The source of the dreadful smell became apparent as
she reached a bleak flat area that was completely
charred. A fire had recently swept across this part of
the prairie, destroying practically everything in its
path. She sat for several moments staring at the black
stubble that was all that remained of any vegetation. It
was hard to believe. Never had she seen such a desolate and lonely land.

Something in the distance caught her attention. A
group of people huddled together in the wind. Feeling
a surge of excitement, she urged the horse forward.
The wagon clattered along the two ruts that passed for
a road, stirring up more dust than speed, and making it
that much more difficult to breathe. Her initial excitement turned to dismay as she drew closer to her destination.

She halted the wagon. The group of "people" turned
out to be a cluster of stone chimneys that stood like
upright coffins waiting to be buried. The ground was
covered with pieces of charred wood.

Her spirits tumbled as she hopped off the wagon and
picked her way through the ashes and rubble. A fire-
scarred sign caught her eye. Turning it over with the

toe of her high-buttoned boot, she felt a sinking feeling that reached to her very depths. Only three letters remained, but it was enough to tell her that she had found the town of Colton.

# Chapter 2

Luke Tyler stared grimly ahead as he urged his horse toward the dark cloud of dust that blew across the prairie and blurred the distant horizon until it disappeared from sight. Overhead, the sky was almost black in color. The dust and ashes from the recent fire combined to make the air thick and difficult to breathe. His throat felt parched.

Keeping one hand on the reins, he pulled the blanket over his seven-year-old son, Matthew, who was curled up asleep on the seat beside him. The boy had hardly slept the night before. No doubt he'd been worried about seeing the doctor.

Luke had heard reports that a new doctor had set up a practice in Hays. Dr. Ben Williams was his name, and he had reportedly graduated from one of those fancy Eastern schools.

It was Luke's fervent hope that the doctor could do something for Matthew. The boy had not spoken a word in two years. Not since he'd burst into the house at the age of five and found his mother dead. It was hard to believe that the boy had not said a word in all this time. Neither had he laughed aloud or made any of the sounds usually expected from a child his age. Nothing.

Maybe Dr. Williams would have some miracle cure, even though the other doctors hadn't. Luke knew his chances were slim, but at this point he was desperate enough to try anything.

Even driving three hours to a town where he wasn't wanted.

It was nearly two in the afternoon by the time Luke pulled into Hays. Matthew stirred awake as his father drove the wagon past numerous saloons, over the railroad tracks, and up to the front of a wooden building. A sign over the door swung back and forth in the wind. Dr. Williams's name was burned into the flapping shingle.

Luke patted Matthew on the leg. "Come on, son." He jumped to the ground and stretched before walking around the wagon to lift Matthew from his seat.

The boy stood perfectly rigid where Luke planted him. His face turned red, almost scarlet; his eyes began to dart back and forth.

A muscle tightened in Luke's jaw. He'd seen this particular look on his son's face far too many times to underestimate its meaning. "Matthew!" He gave the boy a stern shake. "I told you, it's all right. The doctor's not going to hurt you."

Luke knew from past experience that it was a waste of time to try to ward off the impending fit, but he had to try. "Matthew!" Matthew threw himself flat on the ground. In tortured silence, he kicked and thrashed about like a fish denied water. The young face was tight with unspoken rage and anger.

Luke struggled to control him, but the boy was focused on some inner torment and could not be reached. A crowd of shocked spectators began to gather around.

A woman whom Luke recognized as Claudia Hancock rushed across the street, her black silk skirts flapping about her ankles. She gasped in horror as she watched Luke struggle to control Matthew. "What have you done to that poor, poor boy?"

Luke had finally managed to get a firm grip on Matthew's arms and legs to keep him from hurting himself. He looked up long enough to give her a warning look. "Stay out of this, Claudia."

"I'll do no such thing!" she retorted. She glanced at the crowd. "We should all take responsibility for this boy. This is what happens when you let a child live with a murderer!"

Luke had thought he was immune to the name-calling. Lord knows, he'd heard enough of it. What was wrong with the woman? With all of them? Couldn't they see he needed their help, not their scorn?

He was close to losing control. Knowing how dangerous that could be, he gritted his teeth and scooped Matthew off the ground. The boy's frenzied fits lasted for only a moment or two, never more than that, though at times they seemed to go on forever. Today was one of those times.

Mercifully, Matthew's body finally went limp. His arms and legs stilled as he clung to his father and hid his face against Luke's chest.

"What's the matter with the boy?" someone called out from the back of the crowd.

"Crazy like his father," another voice replied.

Claudia Hancock stepped between Luke and his wagon. "Now that I have seen what you've done to this boy with my own two eyes, I intend to report you to the Child Welfare Department!"

Luke glared at her. "Get out of my way." Afraid of what he would do should he lose control, he fought against the raging emotions inside. For Matthew's sake, he must stay calm. "I said, 'Get out of my way!' "

The woman looked determined to stay, but one of the spectators interceded. "Let him go, Claudia. We don't want the likes of him in this town any longer than necessary."

Claudia stepped out of Luke's way, and he lifted his son onto the seat of the wagon.

"Don't think I'll forget, Luke Tyler! I'm reporting you!"

Heaving himself onto the driver's seat, Luke grabbed the reins and sped away. Claudia Hancock ran after the swaying wagon, screaming accusations and threats in a shrill voice for all to hear. "I won't rest until they take that boy away from you!"

Luke raced out of town as fast as his horse would go. The ugly threats faded away, but not the horror that had been instilled in him. Take Matthew away?

Could they do that?

He glanced at the son he loved more than life itself. For a man like himself, whose very emotions could mean danger, it was a love that had to be constantly guarded.

Aware that Matthew was watching him, his eyes dark and troubled, Luke gave him a reassuring pat.

"No one's taking you away from me, Matthew." Luke narrowed his eyes to the road in front of them. "No one!"

Luke supposed he should be grateful that the townfolk had not carried out their threat of long ago and hung him.

That's what the majority of them had wanted to do the day Matthew's mother had died and they found Luke dazed and confused, his clothes soaked in blood, the doctor dead at his feet.

He was convinced they'd have hung him on the spot had it not been for that do-gooder sheriff who thought it more humane to let the motherless boy grow up in the company of a murderer, isolated on a godforsaken prairie, shunned by one and all. Recalling the harrowing events of the last two years, Luke grimaced. The boy didn't deserve such a fate.

But it was the best he could do for him. He gave everything he could to the boy. It wasn't much, but it was better than being dragged off to some orphanage somewhere to be raised by strangers.

Matthew belonged with him, and nothing and no one was going to take him away.

Swallowing the fear that came with the thought of losing his son, Luke urged the beleaguered horse to pick up speed.

He remembered the day he'd first set eyes on the land known as Kansas. His wife, whom he'd rescued from a life of prostitution several years earlier, and their young son had been sitting by his side as he'd driven the Conestoga wagon along a rutted trail. It was hard to believe that it had been four years ago, in the spring of '66.

The war with the South had taken a terrible toll on his family, but not for the usual reasons. During the war years, he'd stayed at home and worked at his furniture-making business. A coward, some called him, and he suspected that, on some level, even his wife thought as much. Not that she ever said anything, of course, but he could see it in her eyes at times, especially when friends and neighbors discussed the war and the bravery of their loved ones.

Perhaps had he told her the truth, maybe then she would have understood why he refused to fight. She knew most of it: she knew his own father had been the notorious Gantry Tyler, a man who had been wanted in twenty-two counties for murder and thievery. What she didn't know, of course, is what it meant to be the son of such a man. No one could know that.

Luke was only ten when his own mother had finally revealed the horrible truth—that Luke had been conceived out of rape. As shocking as this news was, it did at least offer him an explanation as to why he and his mother had been shunned by the town. How well it explained the whispers, the strange looks, the way his teachers had overreacted whenever he'd had the ill grace to act his age or otherwise dabble in some childish mischief.

It was no easy feat growing up with the knowledge that his father was a criminal. Luke had spent the greater part of his life trying to be everything his father was not.

He had never wanted to believe that a violent streak could be passed from father to son. He resisted the idea almost all his life, even as he guarded against it. Not till the day of Catherine-Anne's death did he realize what he himself was capable of. Only then did he find out for certain what it meant to be cursed by the Tyler blood.

His mother, bless her soul, knew. She lived in fear that her son would turn out to be like his father. Every angry word or action on Luke's part resulted in swift and harsh punishment. Even a spontaneous hug from him would bring a startled look of dismay to his mother's eyes. It was as if she feared that any show of physical feeling—even love—might precipitate an attack. Perhaps that's why she never had a normal relationship with a man.

The message she gave was clear: it was dangerous to show emotion. Love, joy, anger—it made no difference—they were all feelings that must be denied or, if that failed, hidden.

Luke grew up watching his every thought and deed, repressing his feelings no matter how he ached to show them. At first he held back for his mother's sake. Later, upon reaching manhood, he held back for fear of what he might discover about himself.

As a result of this constant restraint, years of bottled-up emotions exploded in uncontrollable rage when he found his pregnant wife dead. He had little memory of what happened that day. All he could do was guess at the possible events that led up to the doctor's death. One thing was clear: his mother's worst fears had been realized; his father's evil seeds were inherent.

Luke glanced at his son. Because of that long-ago day, the boy was locked in silence. No one knew whether or not Matthew would ever speak again.

Luke gripped the reins until his knuckles turned white. Oh, Matthew. His heart filled with anguish. He'd hoped and prayed that Matthew would not inherit the same bad seed that had plagued the Tylers for at least two generations.

He'd tried so hard to ignore the signs, but he could no longer in good conscience do so. Matthew's temper tantrums were growing progressively worse. The sins of the father . . .

He blinked rapidly against the moisture in his eyes, blaming his blurred vision on the dust. He didn't dare allow himself to give in to emotion. It was dangerous to allow himself to love fully; even with Matthew he held back for fear of what could possibly happen if he hugged him too tightly or otherwise showed the full extent of his love and affection.

It angered him that circumstances made it necessary to withhold anything from Matthew. Lord knew, he had little enough to give him as it was. But anger, bitterness—all of those troubling feelings that kept simmering somewhere inside, had to be fought against at all costs. Bad feelings or good ones—they all came from the same source. To repress one was to repress them all.

The moisture in his eyes was definitely caused by the wind and the dust.

The wind, Lord, the wind. Of all the things he'd come to dislike about Kansas, the wind was the worst. His poor wife never did adjust to the elements of nature that were so much a part of the Kansas landscape.

There was a time when he'd had such wondrous dreams, wondrous plans; not even Catherine-Anne's initial dislike of Kansas had deterred him. He'd been confident that, given time, she would come to accept the raw new land as home. He promised to build her the best house in the state. He vowed to make every piece of furniture himself, provide her with every comfort.

But that was before he learned that dreams, like feelings, must be avoided at any cost.

It was late afternoon by the time Luke reached the simple one-room sod house where he and Matthew lived. He'd built the house with his own two hands soon after he and his family had arrived in Kansas. It was meant to be a temporary house. But after Catherine-Anne had died, there'd been no reason to build the house he promised her.

The wooden windmill spun in the wind as he drove the wagon to the front of the house.

"Matthew, we're home." He jumped to the ground and, keeping his head low against the wind, walked to his son's side. "We're home, son."

Luke slipped his arms beneath Matthew and lifted the boy's exhausted body from the buckboard.

Maddie's apprehension increased as the day progressed. The sun slowly inched toward the western horizon and was all but hidden by dark clouds of dust that cast the late-afternoon sky into an eerie gray dusk.

It had been hours since she'd left the station, and

she'd not seen a living soul. Not so much as a bird or a lizard. Thankfully the wind had died down, but the sickening smell of ashes filled her nose and mouth like rancid cotton.

It took forever, it seemed, to pass through the charred landscape, but when she finally reached the ankle-high green grass that now grew on either side of the rutted road, she literally cried out with joy. Surely now she would find a farm or some other sign of civilization.

She was puzzled by the dark mounds ahead. At first she thought they were boulders, but she soon realized her error. It was a buffalo herd, and the thrill of viewing a live buffalo up close made her momentarily forget her present predicament.

Before she'd spotted the buffalo from the train, her only experience with the animal was through her father, the renowned Whittaker M. Percy, chief taxidermist for the Smithsonian Institution in Washington, D.C.

All during her childhood, her father had spent a great deal of his time away on some expedition or other, capturing wild animals to be mounted and displayed in the national museum.

Maddie's mother, a woman of fine breeding who had created a scandal when she bucked convention and married the adventurer, was nonetheless appalled by the stories he told of being chased by natives in the wilds of Africa. Once he'd been treed by a wild rhino. Another time he'd nearly been squeezed to death by a boa constrictor.

Maddie had been intrigued with his adventures, and she begged him throughout her childhood to take her along on one of his expeditions. He'd promised to take her on a trip as soon as she turned sixteen. Two weeks before her birthday, he defied her mother's dire predic-

tions about his premature death at the hands of cannibals or wild animals and died peacefully in his sleep.

In the years that followed, Maddie consoled herself
with happy memories of the time she spent with him in
the laboratory. She had been with him the night they
carted in the first buffalo ever brought to the nation's
capital. Weighing in at sixteen hundred pounds, it was
an impressive sight.

But dangerous, her father had told her, and it was
those words that made her now take the fork in the
road that led away from the grazing herd.

Even so, she couldn't help but recall the look on the
face of the dying bull she'd seen earlier, and she wondered why it had never before occurred to her that her
father was first and foremost a hunter. To her, his job
had seemed exciting and glamorous; it wasn't until she
had seen that magnificent buffalo fall to its knees that
she considered the reality.

She came to a grove of cottonwood trees growing
along a creek. They were the first trees she'd seen
since leaving the train. While her horse drank thirstily
from the water that trickled over a bed of smooth white
pebbles, she filled her cupped hands and brought the
cool, sweet water to her own parched lips. After
quenching her considerable thirst, she washed the dust
off her face and hands.

She sensed a presence and, thinking she was about
to be attacked by a buffalo, spun around, ready to take
flight. An Indian, naked from his waist up and wearing
precious little below, sat upon a spotted pony not fifty
yards away. His long, black hair was shoulder-length,
and glossy strands blew across his high-boned cheeks.

Her father had told her bloodcurdling stories of being attacked by Indians. She suspected the tales were
more fantasy than fact, but just in case her father had
not exaggerated, she eyed the Indian with caution. He

didn't appear to be threatening, and if he had an ounce of common modesty he would surely refrain from doing anything that would dislodge his pitifully inadequate loincloth.

On the chance that modesty was not a consideration of his, she decided her best defense was to assert the kind of authority that worked well in a classroom. Indeed, if she could earn the respect of thirty students, certainly she could make one Indian think twice before doing her harm.

"I'm Madeline Percy," she called out in the brisk nononsense voice cultivated during her years of teaching. It was a tone that had been used with great success on students who had shown the slightest inclination toward inappropriate thought or action. She only hoped that the months away from the classroom had not lessened the stern ring of her voice, for if he were truly intent upon claiming her scalp, she wouldn't have much of a chance to defend herself. "Do you speak English?"

The Indian's face showed no expression, but Maddie was convinced he was eyeing the strands of red hair that had escaped the confines of her bonnet.

A cold chill crept along her spine. She had spent her entire life hating her flaming red hair—had, indeed, spent much of her youth devising concoctions to change its color. None of them had worked, unfortunately, and the red color remained intact, horrid as it was. At the moment, however, she was prepared to fight tooth and nail to save every unsavory red hair on her head.

Fortunately she didn't have to. For, as suddenly as the Indian had appeared, he turned his pony in the opposite direction and rode off.

"Wait!" she called. He was the only human she'd seen in hours and she had no intention of letting him

get away. Not until he had pointed her in the direction
of civilization—if, indeed, there was such a thing in
Kansas.

Besides, it occurred to her that since he was the one
trying to escape, he was obviously more frightened of
her than she was of him. Encouraged by this last
thought, she stuck her forefinger and middle finger
into her mouth and let out a bloodcurdling whistle (as
her father referred to it) that was followed by a noisy
protest as every bird within earshot squawked aloud
and took to the skies. The Indian glanced back over his
shoulder as if to check the source of the unearthly
sound.

When her whistle failed to achieve its intent, she
scrambled aboard the wagon and grabbed hold of the
traces. "Giddyup!"

Dirt and dust flew from beneath her wheels as she
chased after the fleeing Indian. "Come back. I won't
hurt you!" The wind all but carried her voice away,
and she whistled again.

Without warning, the Indian vanished before her
eyes. Startled, she slowed her horse to a trot and
scanned the area. It then became clear how the Indian
had managed to disappear from sight. This part of the
prairie was not as flat as it had first appeared. A closer
look revealed valleys and hills that could easily hide a
man.

A line of horses suddenly broke the crest of a not-
too-distant hill. Startled, she yanked on the reins.
"Jumping bullfrogs!" she cried aloud. Not only could
the terrain conceal a man, it was sufficiently generous
to hide an entire Indian tribe!

Her usual brave front deserting her, she gave the
traces a commanding shake, spun the wagon around on
two wheels and headed in the opposite direction.
Shouting a command to the horse, she drove hell-bent

for Betsy—as her father had so often described his
own narrow escapes—back the way she'd come.

Now that an Indian attack appeared imminent, the
buffalo herd seemed suddenly less threatening, commanding little more than a glance as she passed by.

Not daring to look back, she kept going until her
poor horse was winded. Fearing he was about to topple
over with exhaustion, she glanced over her shoulder.
Much to her relief, not an Indian was in sight.

She brought the wagon to a stop. Her heart beat so
fast she could barely breathe. She gasped for air and
scanned the hazy distance.

She thought she saw something ahead, a pinpoint of
light, perhaps, flickering through the dust.

Thinking it might be an Indian campfire, she proceeded forward with caution. She cast a worried glance
over her shoulder again, keeping an eye on the motionless mounds she knew were buffalo and watching for
Indians. Self-sufficient to a fault, she seldom called on
outside help. But this was no time to take chances.
"Lord Almighty," she called aloud, "if I ever get out of
this mess alive I'll . . ." She gave careful thought to
what she was willing to sacrifice. She might be desperate, but it was no reason to be foolhardy. "I'll hardly
ever again question your judgment."

She was so busy worrying about what was behind
her, she failed to see the windmill until she was practically on top of it, and even then it was the grinding
sound of the flywheel spinning in the breeze that finally caught her attention. Not far from the windmill
stood an odd-looking building with sod walls. A thin
line of smoke drew her attention to the roof, which in
the fast-fading light appeared to be flat and covered
in grass.

She left her horse by the water trough and walked up
to the house. Although a thin layer of light could still

be seen in the western sky, it was completely dark overhead, the stars blocked out by the thick layer of dust.

She concentrated on the soft light that flickered from behind the single window.

She swallowed hard and willed her heart to stay in her chest. Determined to keep her wits about her no matter what awaited her, she gave the door a brisk knock.

The door flew open so quickly, it caught her by surprise. She certainly was not prepared for the tall, dark-haired man who stood glaring at her like a bull about to attack.

His sharp black eyes could have been lances, the way they bored into her, glaring at her from a hard, cold face. "What the hell do you want?"

# Chapter 3

The thunderous, almost hateful sound of his voice would have intimated most people, but not Miss Madeline Percy. A tribe of warring Indians might have sent her fleeing, but never a lone man, not even one who towered over her by at least six inches. Given her own five-foot-ten-inch height, this latter feat was no small accomplishment.

Despite the necessity of having to look up at him, she managed to maintain the same stern look usually reserved for the most difficult of students. "I was looking for Colton."

It gave her some measure of satisfaction to see surprise on his face, though she couldn't imagine what she'd said that would bring such a reaction.

"You're not from Hays?"

"I'm from Washington. I arrived today by train."

"I see. I thought . . ." His forehead creased in a frown. "Didn't anyone tell you that Colton had burned down?"

Curious as to whom he had mistaken her for, she shook her head. It was hard to imagine that this man would have to worry about unwanted guests, considering where he lived. "I discovered the fire for myself. Do you know where I might spend the night? A hotel, perhaps?" Her voice trailed off. If there was a hotel anywhere in the vicinity, she'd be curious to know how she'd managed to miss it.

The man seemed amused by the question, and she could hardly blame him. Though he had the good grace not to laugh aloud, the harsh lines of his rugged face softened, and her earlier apprehension faded away.

He studied her with steady blue eyes. A lock of dark hair fell across his deeply tanned brow. He wore his hair longer than the city men she knew, and it curled around the collar of his unbuttoned shirt.

The shirt gave her pause. Actually, it was the glimpse of his broad, muscular chest that distracted her. She couldn't remember ever seeing a man with his shirt unbuttoned in Washington City. After encountering the bare-chested, naked-limbed Indians, and now this open-shirted man, she was beginning to think that those stuffy city men with their high-collared shirts could take a lesson or two from the residents of Kansas. She'd seen more manly flesh in the last few hours than she'd seen in her entire twenty-six years.

"The nearest hotel is three hours away."

Upon hearing this disconcerting news, she found her normally commanding voice deserting her. "Did you say three hours?" After wandering around for some six hours, she supposed three hours wasn't all that bad. If only it weren't for the dark. And the Indians and the buffalo and the . . .

"I've heard tell that a man chased by a Cheyenne war party can make it in two." He regarded her a moment before adding, "You could, of course, try to flag down tomorrow's train. The engineer has been known to stop on occasion to pick up a distressed traveler or two."

She wasn't sure she liked being called distressed. She considered it a matter of pride to keep her wits about her under trying circumstances. Particularly given the way the man's gaze slid down the length of her, she decided this was one of those situations that required rationality of mind.

She wasn't accustomed to being the object of male interest. Normally, most men took one look at her tall, slender frame and didn't bother to look further.

Not only had this man taken a second look, she had the feeling nothing had escaped his attention. Not the unruly strands of red hair that had escaped her bonnet nor the tip of her dusty boot that tapped impatiently on the ground.

His eyes did seem to linger a moment longer than necessary on the trousers beneath her skirt. As quick as it had come, the interest on his face was gone and a look of indifference took its place. She felt a moment of disappointment, which she quickly dispelled. If the man was going to discount her so easily, what did she care? Besides, a far more pressing concern was vying for attention.

"If this isn't a fine kettle of fish!" Her voice was edged with irritation and fatigue. It was late and getting later by the minute.

"You better come in." He turned and walked away from the door.

She debated whether to follow him inside. He was a stranger, and although it was all too clear that he found her womanly attributes lacking, she wasn't at all certain if he could be trusted. Heaven only knew what kind of a man he was and who he had mistaken her for. She stood firmly in place. "I'm a schoolteacher," she called to him, aware that she probably looked more like a wanton woman. "A *respectable* schoolteacher."

She peered inside the house and was surprised by the cozy domestic scene that greeted her. The room was filled with wood furniture, as fine or finer than any that could be found in the grand manors of Washington. Steam rose from a large black pot that was centered on an iron woodstove.

A delicious smell wafted out to her. Her stomach growled in response, reminding her that she'd not eaten since morning.

She was greatly relieved and more than a bit surprised to see a small boy sitting at the table. She relaxed. If there was a child, there had to be woman somewhere. That would explain the quality of the furniture.

Maddie stepped onto the dirt floor and closed the door hard behind her, causing tiny clumps of dirt to shake loose from the sod ceiling. Carefully brushing the soil from her shoulders, she looked upward and was amazed to see that the packed sod surface was supported by tree branches. Never had she seen such a dwelling. It was like a cave. "My name is Madeline Percy."

"Luke Tyler."

"I'm very pleased to meet you, Mr. Tyler." She turned toward the young boy who was looking at her so curiously. He had the same vivid blue eyes and dark, almost black hair as his father. She guessed he was around seven or eight. "And what is your name, young man?"

"Matthew," his father replied.

"How do you do, Matthew?" The boy made no reply, but he watched her through eyes sharp with interest.

Mr. Tyler spooned out a plateful of stew and set it on the table in front of his young son.

Noticing that Mr. Tyler demonstrated remarkable domestic skills for a man, she stared at the food hungrily. She wondered about the man's wife and glanced around in search of feminine belongings. But the clothes and headgear that hung from the wall on polished buffalo horns were definitely masculine in nature. So were the boots lined up neatly against the wall. But it was the clumps of dirt that competed with the dishes and condiments on the table that confirmed her growing suspicion: no woman lived here.

As if guessing her thoughts, her host brushed away the dirt before setting another plateful of tempting fare on the table. "How did you manage to get here from the train station?"

"When no one showed up at the train depot to meet me, I took the horse and wagon that had been left at the station and set out to find Colton."

"Colton burned down a little over a week ago," he explained. "Most everyone left but the Cheyennes. Most went to the next town over to arrange for loans to rebuild. They'll be back, I'm afraid."

She considered this a moment. "Who . . . who were you expecting?"

"What?"

"I had the feeling you thought I was someone else."

"Oh." He turned to the stove. "I thought you were someone from Hays."

"Hays?"

"That's the town that's three hours away."

"Unless you're chased by a war party," she added. Only his profile was visible, but she didn't miss the alluring way the corner of his mouth lifted upward. If the man ever actually smiled, he would be rather pleasing to look at, she supposed.

She rubbed her aching back. She wasn't used to sitting for such long periods of time, and the train ride coupled with the long hours spent in the wagon had taken their toll. "The Cheyennes . . . Are they dangerous?"

"All people are dangerous when protecting what is theirs." The cutting edge in his voice left little doubt that he was talking about something far more personal, but the hard look in his eyes convinced her not to probe—although probing into people's affairs came second nature to her.

"I thought that the Indians had been moving south, to Indian territory," she said.

"Some refuse to let the government decide where they can and cannot make their homes." He turned back to the stove. "Do you blame them for that?"

"No, I suppose not." Unable to relieve her stiff muscles by rubbing them, she held on to the ladder-back chair and stretched her leg upward until the toe of her boot reached above her waist. Feeling immediate relief, she touched her toes, then positioned herself behind the chair to repeat the exercise.

He turned just as she raised her other leg. He stood looking at her, his dark eyebrows arched.

"Leg cramps," she explained, lowering her leg. She smoothed the front of her wrinkled skirt. "I don't know how some people manage to sit all day, do you?"

"I don't know. Never had much occasion to sit, myself." He set the last plate of steaming hot stew on the table. "You must be hungry."

"Starved," she agreed.

She undid the ribbons beneath her chin and pulled off her bonnet, removing also the hairpins that held her bun in place. Her hair tumbled to her shoulders in a cascade of tangled curls. Her mother considered loose hair as much of a transgression as loose morals. One could surmise by the look of surprise on her host's face that his own belief in such matters was equally restrictive.

Long after the surprise left his face, his eyes continued to linger on her hair. Unable to think of a way to fill in the silence, she grew uncharacteristically self-conscious. "Is there a place I might freshen up?"

He nodded toward the door. "You'll find a rain barrel at the side of the house." He plucked a dry flour sack from a nail that had been driven into a wooden cabinet and tossed it to her. "You'll find soap on the shelf over the barrel.

"Thank you." She turned toward the door, stopping when he called her name.

"Unless you want your stew seasoned with dirt, I suggest you close the door gently."

She walked outside, taking care not to slam the door. The wind had died down completely, and the surrounding prairie was so dark and silent that she was forced to run her hand along the rough soddy walls as she made her way to the side of the house. Overhead a lone star shone through the gauzy film of dust that was still in the air.

She stood in the square of light that filtered from the soddy window and quickly washed the dust off her face and hands. Feeling refreshed, she dried herself and walked toward the wagon. She felt in the dark for her valise and pulled out the hairbrush that was tucked inside. It took a bit of determination to work the bristles through the tangled curls.

The horse nickered softly and pawed the ground.

"It's all right, Rutabaga." She patted the horse on the rump. Not wanting to keep her host and his son waiting any longer, she quickly searched her valise for more hairpins. Unable to locate the spares in the dark, she shoved the brush back into the valise.

Mr. Tyler waited until she joined them at the table, then lowered his head and said the blessing. She glanced across at Matthew, who was watching her. She'd never seen a boy his age look so somber. She gave him a friendly smile and when it was not returned, she picked up the wooden-handled fork by her plate and took a taste of the steaming stew. The meat was tasty and tender.

"This is wonderful," she said. "Chicken?"

"Rabbit."

Accustomed to the lively political debates that were such an important part of every meal back home, she attempted to engage both father and son in conversation. Her efforts to discuss current events garnered nothing more than a grunt from the father and a curious stare from the son.

She decided that Mr. Tyler might well be the only man in the States to pass up an opportunity to criticize President Grant. Certainly no such person existed in Washington City.

Wondering what people in Kansas found to talk about, she made a few comments about the weather before giving up altogether and finishing her meal in silence. The rabbit stew provided hearty fare and she soon realized she couldn't possibly finish everything on her plate.

"Why aren't you eating?" she asked Matthew. He'd hardly touched his food, nor had he spoken a word. Not only was he the most somber child she'd ever met, he was clearly the most silent. When he failed to reply, she leaned toward him. "You're about the same age as some of my students back home."

"Matthew can't talk," Mr. Tyler said brusquely.

She drew back, her head on her chest. "Oh, I'm sorry. Is . . . is he deaf?"

"He hears perfectly."

Sensing her host's reluctance to talk about the matter, she resisted the urge to ask further questions. Instead, she explained how she had accepted a teaching post in Colton.

"It seems like an odd thing for a woman to do.

Travel all the way out here alone. Couldn't you get a teaching post in Washington?"

"I was asked to resign from my teaching post there."

He pursed his mouth thoughtfully. "Why was that, Miss Percy?"

She cleared her throat. "Some people thought that my ... teaching methods were ... too progressive." Actually, she'd been asked to leave her post for misconduct, but she wasn't about to tell him that. Besides, was it her fault that the day she took her students to the Senate building was the very same day that pompous senator from Rhode Island got up and gave that horrendous speech against the idea of women having the vote?

After a half hour of listening to his shocking dissertation regarding women's lack of intelligence, she'd stood in the visitors chamber and, speaking out in her authoritative voice, told him exactly what she thought of him, his speech, *and* his ideas. Misconduct, indeed! She had done what any sensible person would have done under the circumstances.

Mr. Tyler studied her from across the table. Never had she been so conscious of her cursed sun-dotted nose and unruly red hair as she was at that moment.

He held her gaze as he reached for the bottle of wine. "So why did you describe yourself as a respectable teacher if you were asked to leave your former post?"

She wasn't usually one to blush, but now she felt her cheeks flare red. She was grateful that he was too busy pouring the wine to notice. "My teaching methods were open to debate, not my respectability." No matter what the newspapers said.

He set the bottle down. "Since Colton no longer exists, it would appear that you're without employment."

"It does appear that way, doesn't it?" The thought

was so disconcerting, she quite forgot her mother's admonishments about the unladylike habit she had of chewing on her bottom lip. She'd been so intent upon the immediate problem of finding suitable accommodations, she hadn't fully considered her plight. Until now. Not only was she without employment, she lacked even the funds to pay for her fare back home.

Mr. Boxer had sent her a portion of her advance to pay for her train fare to Kansas, with the agreement that she would receive the second half of the money owed her upon her arrival. The advance was to cover expenses until she started collecting her salary.

She took a long sip of wine. "Do you by any chance know where I might find Mr. Boxer?"

"My guess would be that he's in Hays."

"Oh, yes. Two or three hours away, depending on how much you value your life."

Humor warmed his eyes, but all too quickly the soft lights disappeared and his mouth tightened into a straight line. "At least that." He glanced at her plate and refilled her glass with wine. "Would you care for anything more?"

"No, thank you," she said, puzzled by the way her host seemed to guard every word, every look, as if determined not to give too much away. Clearly, he was a man who had much to hide. "Dinner was delicious."

He stood and cleared his plate. "You can spend the night here, if you like."

She gazed at the single bed that was pushed against one wall, and her heart started to pound nervously. "I appreciate your offer, but . . ."

He reached for her plate, his nearness bringing an unexpected warmth. His masculine smell was mixed with an earthy quality that challenged her senses to a new level of awareness.

"You aren't going to bore me with explanations of having to protect your reputation, are you?"

She pushed herself away from the table. "My reputation?"

His eyes flickered down the length of her. Now as before, her trousers seemed to give him pause, but only for the instant it took for his usual indifference to assert itself across his features. "I can assure you that you will be perfectly safe here."

That was encouraging news, though she would have preferred that he not look so thoroughly uninterested, as if he couldn't imagine anyone compromising her virtue.

"Actually, it *was* my reputation I was thinking of. You know how reputations are." She was prattling but couldn't seem to stop. "They have a way of following you wherever you go."

A dark shadow crossed his face, as if she'd touched a nerve. "In that case, I can put your mind at ease. No one but Matthew and myself will ever know where you spent the night. I can assure you that your reputation shall remain intact."

She hated feeling stranded or dependent on anyone. She lifted her chin boldly. "That's very kind of you, but I prefer sleeping outside in the wagon. If you would be kind enough to lend me a blanket and a pillow."

His gaze remained on her face as he addressed his son. "Matthew, please carry a bedroll outside for our guest."

Matthew slipped off his chair and pulled a bedroll out of a wooden trunk. He waited at the door for Maddie.

"Is there anything else you'll be needing?" Mr. Tyler's low-timbred voice suddenly struck her as too personal, too intimate in tone.

"No, thank you." Good Lord, now he had her talking in intimate whispers. "No, thank you," she repeated. This time she spoke with a loud, bold voice that brought another layer of fine dust sifting down from the ceiling. Brushing the dirt off herself, she realized that he spoke softly for practical purposes and the intimate quality of his speech was purely by accident.

Feeling foolish and a bit light-headed from the wine, she backed toward the door and purposely softened her voice to match his. "I'm most obliged to you, Mr. Tyler, for your hospitality. Dinner was delicious."

"I apologize for the way I greeted you earlier. I really did think you were someone else."

"I'm glad I wasn't ... someone else, I mean." She groaned inwardly. What a ridiculous thing to say. Evidently she was more exhausted than she had thought. "Good night."

"Good night."

She followed Matthew outside to the wagon and was greatly relieved when Mr. Tyler made no attempt to follow.

Without thinking, she slammed the door shut and grimaced. How much of the ceiling was dislodged this time, she had no idea. Furthermore, she had no intention of finding out.

# *Chapter 4*

It was pitch-dark outside, and although Maddie was having a difficult time gaining her night vision, Matthew seemed to have no problem finding the wagon. The boy might not be able to speak, but apparently, he had the keen night eyes of a cat.

The wind had died down completely, and the smell of fire was barely noticeable.

Rutabaga gave a soft neigh as they approached. "Thank you, Matthew. I can handle the rest." She took the bedroll from him and flung it over the sides of the wagon.

She would have welcomed the boy's company, but no sooner had he handed her the bedroll than he dashed back to the house.

With a nervous glance around her, she placed one foot on the wagon wheel and heaved herself over the side. Unable to see a thing, she depended on touch alone to locate the bedroll and spread it out.

What a relief it was to free her feet from the confines of her lace-up boots. She wiggled her stockinged toes and placed the boots to the side. She felt in her trunk for her linen nightgown and shook it out.

In no time at all, she was undressed and ready for bed. She longed to brush her teeth, but it was so dark, she didn't dare trek to the water barrel.

She climbed between the quilted folds of the bedroll

and focused upon the only star bright enough to shine through the layers of dusty night air.

The howl of a coyote sounded in the distance.

Sleep was a long time in coming. Her imagination tended to be active under normal circumstances, but never had it asserted such vivid control over her thoughts as it did during those next few hours.

The least sound convinced her that Indians were hiding in the shadows, ready to wage an attack on her person and to claim her scalp as a prize.

Her only comfort was the dull light shining from the window of the soddy. She felt a sense of loss when at last the light flickered out and its comforting glow was replaced with a thick black void.

She'd never felt so lonely in her life.


After turning off the gas lantern, Luke slipped into bed next to his sleeping son.

Normally he had no trouble sleeping. His work in the fields was grueling. That, along with his household duties and his parental responsibilities, required him to exert his full physical and mental capabilities on a daily basis. He usually fell asleep as soon as his head hit the pillow.

Not tonight. Tonight he found himself staring at the dark ceiling, thinking about his unexpected guest.

He tried to think of a word to describe her, but none came readily to mind. She was taller than a woman had a right to be and as slender as a sapling. Her face was neither pretty nor plain. Appealing, though. Definitely appealing. And her hair ... What a glorious head of hair she had. Vibrant red in color, it was almost identical to bird's-eye maple wood when it was polished to its highest sheen.

He wondered what she'd say if she knew he had likened her hair to a tree. She'd be insulted, no doubt, but he meant no harm by it. It was a compliment, actually. He'd been a woodworker before he became a farmer, and he felt an abiding affection for trees. The longer he lived on this wasted prairie, the more he missed the lush green woods of upstate New York, where he was born and raised. It was the only thing he missed about the place.

He should have insisted that she sleep inside. At the very least, he could have offered her the barn. As soon as that idea occurred to him, he realized why he had not thought to let her sleep in the barn.

The barn was a part of the past. He'd managed, somehow, to put the sod outbuilding so far out of his mind that he hardly remembered it was there anymore. Neither he nor Matthew had set foot in that barn for two years.

He folded his pillow in two and rolled on his side. Much to his surprise, a vision of flashing green eyes floated out of the darkness. Green as a forest in summer. His breath escaped him in a deep sigh of longing and regret. The woman wouldn't be half bad to look at if she'd pack a bit of meat on those bones of hers.

Not half bad at all.


At first she didn't know what had awakened her. She rolled to her back and listened, afraid to breathe. She tried to make sense out of the strange rumbling sound that seemed to be growing louder. Thunder, she thought, and wondered how she would ever manage to keep dry in the rain. What a fine kettle of fish!

Rutabaga snorted and began tugging at the reins. From behind the soddy came the neigh of another horse, followed by squawks of chickens and the low mooing of a cow.

The wagon began to vibrate, and Maddie fought her way out of her bedroll and sat up. The sound of thunder grew louder, but curiously enough the sky was studded with stars, the dust now settled. Puzzled, she searched the darkness for signs of lightning.

The door to the soddy flew open and her eyes blinked against the bright light of a lantern.

Mr. Tyler ran out of the house, shouting directions to his young son. He ran past the wagon to the side of the house and began swinging the lantern back and forth, creating an arc of light around him.

Watching wide-eyed through the slats of the wagon, Maddie slipped on her boots, scrambled over the splintered-wood side, and dropped to the ground.

The ground vibrated through the soles of her boots as she stumbled toward him. "What is it?" she cried. "What are you doing?"

"Here!" Mr. Tyler yanked the blanket from his son and shoved it into her hands. "Matthew, go back and get another blanket!" To her, he shouted, "Don't just stand there—start flapping!"

Not sure what it was, exactly, that he wanted her to do, she shook the blanket up and down, much like she was shaking out a dustrag.

"Damn it, woman, shake it!" he bellowed.

"But . . ." Her mouth fell open as a dark mass suddenly descended upon them. A cold terror swept through her as realization dawned. Hundreds, perhaps thousands, of buffalo were headed straight toward them.

"Shake it!" Mr. Tyler shouted, his voice all but drowned out by the sound of frantic hooves that beat the ground.

Her eyes wide with disbelief and fear, she shook the blanket up and down with as much urgency as her quivering bones would allow.

The light from the lantern reflected red in the eyes of the beasts. Long, leathery tongues hung from the an-

imals' mouths. Nostrils flared. The air was thick with
dust and the musky smell of hide and fur.

Low, harrowing bellows merged with the clamor of
pounding hoofs and clashing horns until the noise escalated into one deafening roar.

At the last possible moment, the herd split in two.
Half of the frenzied buffalo went to the left, the other
half to the right, bypassing the little sod house, but
only by a few yards.

Terrified at first, and then exhilarated by the sheer
power of the beasts that closed around them, Maddie
flapped the blanket up and down until her body was
damp with sweat and her fingers numb.

Next to her, young Matthew dragged a blanket up
and down, his arms obviously growing tired. Encouraging his son with periodic shouts, Mr. Tyler kept the
lantern swinging back and forth, creating a circle of
protection with the quick moving light.

It seemed like hours passed before the mass of
shaggy beasts began to dwindle. Finally the thunderous
sound faded behind them as only a straggler or two remained.

"You can stop," Mr. Tyler said, and when she didn't
appear to hear him, he grabbed her arm and stared
down into her damp, dusty face.

His forehead dripped with sweat, and he was breathing hard. But his eyes were soft with concern as he
looked at her. "They're gone."

She dropped the blanket to the ground and wiped her
damp brow with the back of her hand. Her heart beat
so fast, she could hardly breathe against the thick dust
that filled the air.

Mr. Tyler set the lantern on an upturned barrel and
lifted his young son in his arms. Matthew wrapped his
arms around his father's neck and buried his face. The
man was dressed in only a pair of trousers, and his

sturdy arms and back gleamed with moisture. "Don't cry, son," he said soothingly. "They're gone."

He murmured words of comfort to his son, but his eyes remained on her. "Are you all right?" His voice was so gentle, it bore no resemblance to the hard-edged voice that had greeted her earlier, when she'd first appeared on his doorstep.

She nodded, and then, thinking she heard the sound of hooves returning, she grabbed him by the arm and glanced back into the dark void that was the prairie.

"Indian drums," he explained. "The Cheyennes believe that buffalo are afraid of drums."

"They sound so . . . close," she stammered. Suddenly aware that she was dressed in her nightclothes, she quickly pulled her hand away and stepped back.

"They're not that close," he assured her. "Sounds tend to carry on the prairie."

Despite his assurance, she shivered. She wasn't certain what she found more disconcerting—the buffalo, the Indians, or the bare-chested man whose eyes seemed warm and inviting in the dying light of the lantern.

"You better try to get some sleep." His son in his arms, he picked up his lantern with his one free hand and started toward the door of the soddy. "Good night."

Her eyes wide in disbelief, she watched the bronzed span of his retreating back. "Are you going to leave me here? Alone? By myself?"

He stopped in midstride and turned. In the flickering light he looked tall and lean and ever so powerful. The lantern sputtered and went out, leaving them in darkness.

"You were the one who insisted upon sleeping outside." The softness and concern had left his voice, and what remained was the kind of voice that a reluctant host might use on an unwanted guest. "You can sleep inside if you want."

She swallowed hard and cleared her throat. Her mouth felt dry with the taste of dust. "It wouldn't be proper for a respectable schoolteacher to sleep in the same room as a man," she said, though without her usual boldness.

"It's your decision." He walked into the house, and she heard the door close gently behind him.

She was startled by an owl flying overhead, its wings a swoosh in the air. It was nearly pitch-black, but that didn't prevent her from imagining herself surrounded by buffalo, Indians, or man-eating owls.

It took no time at all to give the matter thorough consideration; she decided it would be far less proper for a respectable schoolteacher to be found dead outside the man's house than to remain in perfect health inside. Like it or not, Mr. Tyler was stuck with her until morning.

Calming the nerves that made her stomach do flip-flops, she charged inside the house without bothering to knock. It was dark inside—so dark, in fact, that she rushed headlong into Mr. Tyler.

Before she could regain her senses, he took her in his arms and steadied her. "I thought you might change your mind." His voice, soft in the darkness, caressed her ear like the tip of a feather.

Startled by the feel of warm flesh, she quickly backed away. Lordy, what was the matter with this man? One moment he was all cold and businesslike, the next warm and gentle. "Change my mind?" she stammered.

"About sleeping inside."

She was afraid to move for fear she would bump into him again. She could hear him moving about but was unable to pick him out in the dark.

When he spoke again, he was so close, she could almost feel his warm breath against her flesh. "I spread a bedroll out on the floor for you. Is that respectable enough for you?"

Feeling foolish, she was thankful for the cover of darkness that prevented him from seeing her flushed cheeks. Now that the danger had passed, she felt vibrantly alive. It was as if her body had absorbed the energy from the stampeding herd.

"I would say that under the circumstances it's most respectable." She tried to steady her racing pulse. That failing, she hoped he couldn't hear the sound of her heartbeat. The drums had stopped, which didn't help matters. In the silence that followed, every sound, from the softest intake of breath to the faint rustle of her host taking off his trousers, seemed magnified.

She quickly settled into the bedroll and hoped that the thickness of the flannel muted the sound of her fast-beating heart. It wouldn't do to let him know that at the moment respectability was the last thing on her mind.

# Chapter 5

The faint light of dawn bled through the oil paper that covered the small window set deep into the soddy wall. Not wanting to wake Mr. Tyler or his son, Maddie quietly sat up and rubbed the sleep from her eyes. Her body felt stiff, the muscles in her upper arms and shoulders sore from the hours spent shaking the blanket to ward off the buffalo.

She longed to curl up and go back to sleep, but prudence demanded that she get an early start for Hays before the major heat of the day.

That should give her ample time to track down Mr. Boxer and insist upon his giving her the second half of her advance. If she was lucky, she might make it onto the afternoon train bound for Washington City—if, indeed, there was an afternoon train heading east. If not, she would have to delay her return trip home until the following day.

Her day planned, she stretched out her muscles and massaged her neck and shoulders.

A dark, round object like a wheel lay at the bottom of her bedroll. She leaned toward it, curious as to what it could possibly be.

The coil suddenly began to unravel. Horrified, she pulled back and let out a bloodcurdling scream that brought Mr. Tyler upright in bed. Another scream and he bounded to the floor in one swift motion.

"What the hell . . . ?"

By now, the snake had stretched out to its full length and was slithering across the dirt floor. Somehow in the short time it took the snake to uncoil, Maddie had managed to jump out of bed and onto a wooden chair without having touched the dirt floor in between.

Mr. Tyler, his hair disheveled, stood staring at her as if she'd taken leave of her senses. He was dressed in ankle-length drawers that rode dangerously low on his lean hips.

Suddenly the snake seemed like the lesser problem. Her voice failing her, she had no choice but to resort to sign language to draw his attention to the retreating reptile.

There was no way to convey her concern about a waistband that was dangerously close to taking a downward dive.

"It's just a bull snake," he said. He reached over, grabbed the snake by its tail, and tossed it out the door. "There, now. It's gone." An amused look crossed his face as he regarded her. "You can come down from the chair."

She glanced around the room, checking every crook and corner in sight. For all she knew, prairie snakes were sociable creatures that traveled in herds.

"What was it doing on my bed?" she stammered.

"It just came in to keep warm. They like to do that. Don't they, Matthew?"

Matthew, who was sitting cross-legged on the bed, grinned up at his father. It was the first time she'd seen the boy smile.

Mr. Tyler turned his gaze upon her, and she was suddenly reminded that her own thin linen nightgown wasn't all that modest. Had it not been for the dimly lit soddy, she might well have been completely exposed.

Mr. Tyler wrapped his hands around her waist and

lifted her off the chair. She said a fervent prayer that the blessed waistband would defy gravity and stay on his hips.

His gaze locked with hers as he set her on the floor and released her. A shiver shot through her, but whether from the encounter with nature, the warmth of his hands, or the worrisome waistband she didn't know.

She was far too conscious of his bare torso to know much of anything at the moment, too aware of the thin, dark line of hair that started below his waist and disappeared into his drawers.

It wasn't until his gaze took a dive down the length of her that she realized she was standing in such a way that the light from the window was behind her.

In an effort to regain some measure of modesty, she sank down on the bedroll and reached for her boots. Shaken by her unexpected encounters with nature, she checked her boots for any other unwanted guests before donning them.

Her screams had dislodged more of the ceiling, and a clump of dirt fell out of her boot. Thinking it another critter, she threw the boot down with a cry.

This brought a hearty laugh from her host, which surprised her. Given the circumspect attention he paid to manner and speech, it seemed uncharacteristically spontaneous. Even Matthew seemed surprised and looked up at his father with rounded eyes.

As if to catch himself, Mr. Tyler's face grew serious, but there was still warm humor in his voice. "Between the buffalo and you, Miss Percy, we're not going to have much ceiling left."

Under normal circumstances, she would have appreciated the humor of the situation. Today, however, between her sore muscles and her unsettled future, she was in no mood for laughter. She had been in Kansas for less than a day, and it had been one disastrous event upon another. She had no intention of spending one moment longer than necessary in this dreadful sod building.

She grabbed her boots and pulled them onto her feet. Her host watched her with interest. "Where are you going in such a fired-up hurry?"

"I want to get an early start for Hays." She didn't want to sound ungrateful, but surely he must understand her desire to leave.

"No sense going anywhere before you've eaten. It's a long journey. Matthew here will get us some fresh eggs, won't you, son?"

As eager as she was to leave, she agreed to stay until after breakfast. Matthew looked so anxious to please her, she didn't have the heart to disappoint him.

Mr. Tyler tossed her a flour sack. "I'll let you have some privacy," he said. "You know where the water is. I'm going to check around to see how much damage was done by the buffalo." He glanced overhead. "We're lucky. Last time they took out the entire back wall." He nodded to the wall behind her.

"You mean that wasn't the first time the buffalo stampeded?"

"First?" He frowned. "Hardly."

Her stomach clenched into a tight knot. The knowledge that buffalo stampeded on a regular basis was yet another reason to leave Kansas as quickly as possible. *As if I need another reason,* she thought, quickly buttoning up her shoes.

Mr. Tyler grabbed a pair of overalls and a shirt and walked outside, followed by Matthew, who carried a wicker basket over his arm.

She waited until she was certain Mr. Tyler had had time to dress before cracking open the door. She stuck her head outside to check for Indians, buffalo, snakes, and any other unpleasant surprises she might yet encounter. When she saw nothing that seemed in any way, shape, or form the least bit threatening, she stepped outside, remembering to close the door gently behind her.

Luke walked around the barn. One entire sod wall and a third of the back wall had collapsed. He hesitated before stepping over the heap of dirt. He'd not been in the barn for two years, not since Catherine-Anne had died.

Shaking off the memories that suddenly assailed him, he made a quick assessment. The collapsed wall had done no damage to his workshop. It was exactly as he'd left it, except for the dust that covered everything, including his tools. In one corner stood a baby cradle, crafted by his own hands. At the center of the barn was the dining room table he had planned to give his wife for her twenty-fifth birthday.

The beautiful wood was all but hidden beneath a thick layer of dirt. Someone once said that Kansas was a state in transit, that one day it would blow away completely. In his estimation, that day was not too far in the future.

His thoughts were interrupted by a sound behind him. "Don't come in, Matthew . . ." He stopped in midsentence, finding himself face to face with the schoolteacher.

The sun at her back was far less revealing than it had been earlier that morning when light from the window had filtered through the thin fabric of her nightgown. But it was no less illuminating. Her fiery red hair was all aglow, and with her sparkling green eyes, it worked to create a vibrant presence that was hard to explain. The dull sod building seemed lighter, brighter, now that she was here. His fanciful thoughts made him frown. "Be careful. I don't know how safe it is."

Maddie glanced up at the roof that was hanging with no support over her head and stepped over the pile of debris. "It's amazing that more damage wasn't done. What do you suppose caused the buffalo to stampede?"

He shrugged. "It's hard to say. Could be anything. A bolt of lightning. Gunshot. Anything."

She stopped by the beautifully crafted baby cradle and, thinking it had probably been Matthew's, rubbed her hand along the fine wood sides. Aware that Mr. Tyler was watching her, she looked up to see a muscle tense at his jaw. She sensed his relief when she moved away from the cradle and turned her attention to the table.

Not even the thick blanket of dirt could hide the skilled craftsmanship. Curious, she brushed away a clump of sod to reveal the lovely grain of the wood. "It's beautiful." She examined one of the chairs. "Did you make these?"

He nodded curtly and opened one of the double doors.

"You do beautiful work!" she exclaimed. "I know people in Washington who would pay good money for this."

"I think we better leave. I'm not sure how safe this building is." He waited at the door for her, his face void of expression, as if he were purposely trying to keep any show of emotion at bay.

Reluctantly she walked outside, and he locked the door after them. Since one wall was completely demolished, leaving the inside of the barn exposed, it struck her as a futile gesture. Luke Tyler was definitely a man of habit.

He scanned the horizon in every direction, his eyes

narrowed in concentration as if he were waiting for something or someone.

"What are you looking for?" Maddie asked. "Not . . . not more buffalo?"

"Wildfire," he replied. "The prairie fires are the worst of it."

Startled, she followed his gaze across the endless flatlands. "What a place this is!" she exclaimed. "Buffalo, Indians, fire."

"Don't forget tornadoes, giant hailstones, and dry, hot winds. You could say we have all the thrills and action not found in Washington."

"Washington has its share of hot wind," she replied.

He regarded her thoughtfully but said nothing. He glanced at the sky with the same careful watchfulness he gave the raw prairie land. The sky was blue-gray in color, with only a few puffy clouds in sight. "In Kansas, the sky is king. I guess we can be grateful that today, at least, the king will favor us."

Matthew walked out of the sod henhouse that was some distance away. Luke waved to him. "It looks like Matthew has our breakfast. If you'd care to join us, I'll start the coffee."

"Thank you, I'd love to. But first I want to do my morning exercises."

He wrinkled his forehead. "Exercises, eh?" He started toward the house. "I'll call you when breakfast is ready."

More curious than ever about the man, she called to him, "Mr. Tyler."

He stopped, his back toward her. "Yes, Miss Percy."

"With such a talent as you have, what in the world are you doing out here?"

He turned. "You're not talking about my culinary skills, are you?"

"I was referring to your woodcrafting skills. Why

would you live in a treeless place like Kansas when you could be making a fortune somewhere else making furniture?"

"The same thing you're doing here, Miss Percy. Trying to live down a bad reputation."

# Chapter 6

The deep, rich fragrance of coffee mingled with the dank smell of sod. Waiting for the coffee to finish brewing, Luke carefully peeled down an edge of the oil paper from the corner of the blemished windowpane and squinted against the bright morning sun to peer outside.

He was not quite sure what to make of the sight that greeted him. The schoolteacher was standing by the woodpile, swinging a fairly good-sized piece of scrap lumber over her head.

She was a strange one, all right. He was struck anew by her tall, slender appearance. She wasn't a beauty in the conventional sense, but he had to admit that her flashing green eyes and flaming red hair made an intriguing combination.

He watched as she plunged forward from the waist until the wood she held touched the ground. The legs of her trousers crept up, leaving an enticing gap between the top of her boots and the hem of her pants.

The glimpse of feminine flesh reminded him of how she'd felt in his arms last night in the dark, her body firm and hard. Normally he liked his women round and soft. Maybe that's why he'd been unprepared for the flash of awareness that coursed through him when she pressed against his chest. It just proved the old saw that if you starve a man long enough, anything's likely to look tasty.

He let his gaze slide down her hard, lean body, trying to imagine the prospect of bedding such a woman. Hell, it would be like taking a piece of pinewood to bed. Didn't anyone ever tell her that a woman's body was not meant to imitate a piece of wainscoting? The thought, curious as it was, did nothing for his peace of mind; under the right circumstances even wainscoting could bend and yield.

Not usually given to fanciful thoughts, he wondered what it was about her that steered his mind so far off course. He had chores to do. Business to attend to. Yet, even as he admonished himself, he gave the fogged windowpane a quick rub with his fingers for a better look outside.

The woman straightened and lifted her arms skyward, the wood held high over her head. Her small, round breasts strained enticingly against the fabric of her blouse. He sucked in his breath and watched as she doubled over again.

Yes, she was definitely an odd one. But he couldn't deny the fact that her presence was most commanding. Yes, indeed, most commanding. Thank God she would soon be gone.

The smell of burned bacon drew his attention to the sizzling woodstove. The thin strips of smoked pork were completely charred, forcing him to scrape the iron skillet and start afresh.

Conscious of Matthew watching him, Luke pointed to the basin of water he'd set out earlier. "Better wash up. Breakfast will be ready soon."

Matthew plunged both hands into the water. Luke nodded his approval and glanced back out the window.

The woman had abandoned the woodpile. Like a wild mustang, she ran past the window and disappeared from sight. Luke was about to go to her rescue, thinking she was running from someone or something, when she jogged past the window again, coming from the opposite direction.

This time he realized she was running around the soddy, her boots but a blur beneath her.

She lifted her face toward the sky and ripped a comb from her hair. The wind lifted her hair like a bright red banner. There was nothing prim nor even proper about this schoolteacher. No wonder she had been asked to leave her teaching post.

He shook his head in amusement as he checked the bacon. A quick glance told him that Matthew was making a halfhearted attempt to wash his face. "Don't forget to wash behind your ears."

He ventured another glance out the window, catching a quick glimpse of her as she ran by for a third time. *Strange woman,* he thought, no less intrigued. *As unpredictable as wildfire.*

Between watching Miss Percy and supervising his young son's morning ablutions, it took him twice as long as usual to cook breakfast. When at last Matthew was dressed and the breakfast was on the table, he opened the door and waited for her to round the front of the soddy before calling out, "Miss Percy. Breakfast."

She stomped inside, full of vim and vigor. Her forehead glistened with moisture, and her face had taken on a warm, rosy glow. Her eyes sparkled merrily over her pretty pink cheeks, and it was all he could do to tear his eyes away from her to tend the stove.

"Breakfast smells delicious," she said, taking her place next to Matthew.

He poured two cups of coffee and carried them to the table. "Do you always run like that in the morning?"

She nodded. "I never start my day without doing my morning calisthenics. Nor do I allow my students to begin work without proper attention to exercising the body."

He had a vision of thirty or more students running around a schoolhouse in downtown Washington. "Is that why you were considered too progressive?"

"It didn't help my reputation," she admitted. "But I was right to require my pupils to exercise. As their physical condition improved, I noticed a marked improvement in their schoolwork. Every institution of learning should adopt a physical training program."

"It's an interesting theory," he said.

"I can assure you, Mr. Tyler, it's more than just a theory." Aware that Matthew was watching her intently, she asked, "Does Matthew attend school?"

"It wouldn't make sense, would it? He can't speak."

"I thought Kansas required children to attend at least twelve weeks of school a year."

"Not until they're eight. Matthew won't be eight until next year."

"Oh." She took a sip of hot coffee. "Has he ever spoken?"

A muscle tightened at his jaw, as if he were debating how little or how much to say. "He spoke until two years ago."

Maddie placed her elbows on the table and rested her chin on her folded hands. She wondered what had happened to make the boy stop speaking. Once or twice she'd had the strangest feeling that Matthew wanted to tell her something. It was the way he looked at her, his round face dark with intensity, his keen, determined eyes beseeching.

Sometimes she even imagined a word trembling on his lips, through he never made a sound. What exactly would she tell her, she wondered, if he could speak? All too aware that the closed expression on his father's face was meant to forbid any further discussion, she was reluctant at first to press for answers. Still, she couldn't seem to help herself. "What happened two years ago to make him stop speaking?"

A look of unbelievable torture crossed her host's face, and she immediately regretted the question.

"He found his mother dead."

Her throat tightened around the inadequate apology. "I'm . . . I'm sorry." She glanced quickly at Matthew, who was watching her with that same look that made her feel so terribly inadequate. "I'm sorry," she said again for the boy's benefit, and he quickly averted his eyes. Not knowing what else to say, she finished her breakfast in silence.

Mr. Tyler stood abruptly and began clearing the table. She carried her own dirty dishes to the kitchen area and slid them into the tub of sudsy water.

"I really am sorry . . . I'm used to probing into my students' backgrounds. It helps me to understand how to work with them . . . you know, bring out their best qualities and . . ."

"Matthew is not your student."

"I'm well aware of that." Resenting his curt reminder, she bit her lip, determined to say no more. She glanced at Matthew, who was staring down at his empty plate. Feeling sorry for him, she tried to break the tension that had suddenly settled in the dark, dismal room. "I'd better get started. I have a long ride ahead of me."

Mr. Tyler handed her a neatly wrapped package. "Just a bit of dried meat and some goat cheese. And here's a canteen of fresh water. You're not likely to find any that's safe enough to drink along the way."

Touched by his thoughtfulness, she took the package

and canteen from him. "Thank you. I'm most grateful for your hospitality."

Mr. Tyler walked over to Matthew's chair and laid his hands on his son's thin shoulders. "It was our pleasure, wasn't it, Matthew?"

She held out her hand. "It was nice to meet you, Matthew." She smiled as the young boy stood and politely shook her hand. With his expressive eyes and thoughtful young face, he was an appealing child. One who touched some tender chord deep within her.

Both father and son walked her out to the horse and wagon. "Stay on the road," Mr. Tyler cautioned her. "It'll take you right into town."

She hesitated. "The Indians ... won't bother me, will they?"

"They shouldn't."

She would have preferred a more positive response. "You mean they *could* bother me?"

"Don't see any reason why they should."

She tried not to think of the horror stories she'd heard involving Indians. Since they hadn't harmed her in the previous encounter, there wasn't any logical reason for them to harm her during any future meetings. "I'm much obliged to you for your hospitality."

"It was our pleasure. Are you sure it's wise to drive all the way to town by yourself? I'll help you flag down the train if you like. It should be here around noon."

Not wanting to have to explain her financial bind, she declined his offer. "I think I much prefer getting there by my own virtue. I never did like to depend on public transportation, even in Washington."

"If that's the way you want it ..." He rested his hand on his son's shoulder. Matthew lifted his hand and waved. Once again, the boy touched her on some level. It was something in his face or, more accurately, something in his eyes that seemed to call out to her. She only wished she knew what it was he was trying to say.

She gave him an encouraging smile, as she would have a student who had raised his hand to speak, only to lose his nerve after being called upon.

Much to her disappointment, Matthew dropped his head and looked so forlorn that her heart went out to him. Had she been deserting a child of her own, she couldn't have felt more guilty. It made no sense, of course. She hardly knew the boy.

She turned her eyes to the boy's father. Luke Tyler's face was without expression, making it impossible to guess his thoughts. "Would it be all right if I write to him?"

Luke tousled his son's hair. "We don't have a post office. Not since the fire, and I don't have much call to ride into Hays."

He didn't want her to write. He couldn't have stated it more clearly had he told her outright. Feeling rebuffed, she climbed onto the wagon seat and reached for the traces.

All at once Matthew fell to the ground and began thrashing about in a wild frenzy of arms and legs.

Alarmed by the sudden fit, Maddie could not help her mouth dropping open. Never had she seen such a violent outburst in a child so young. She was so stunned that she couldn't think what to do or say.

Mr. Tyler quickly scooped the boy from the ground, but his strong, muscular arms seemed challenged to the limits as he fought to control the kicking, wild fury he held.

"What's the matter with him?" she cried at last.

"Nothing. Just go."

"But . . ."

"Go!"

She flicked the traces and took off down the road. She didn't feel right about leaving, though she had no idea what she could do to help. She wasn't even certain what was wrong with the boy. Was he simply spoiled and given to temper tantrums? Somehow she doubted it. Mr. Tyler didn't strike her as the sort of man who would allow anyone, not even a child, to take advantage of him.

It wasn't epilepsy; she was certain of that, for she'd helped several students through epileptic attacks over the years. Nor was it any of the other diseases she could think of that typically caused seizures.

What, then, could have caused such a terrible fit?

Shaking off the impulse to turn back, she snapped the whip over Rutabaga's head. It had been obvious that Mr. Tyler had not wanted her to stay. It was equally evident that father and son had a lot to hide.

She'd traveled a ways down the rutted dirt road before she chanced looking back over her shoulder toward the soddy. Only the windmill was visible from this distance. The other structures blended in too well with the environment to be visible.

But it wasn't buildings she searched for; her eyes sought Luke Tyler and his appealing, though apparently troubled, young son.

Neither of them was in sight.

# *Chapter 7*

The journey to Hays seem to take forever, partly because she found a cool running stream beneath a cluster of cottonwoods and was reluctant to leave the lovely oasis.

She never saw as much as a single Indian, though she imagined them everywhere. She did pass an enormous herd of buffalo peacefully grazing on a sparkling green sea of soft, bending grass. She wondered if it was the same herd that had stampeded the night before.

At one point she caught a glimpse of a distant train heading in the same direction. Had it only been twenty-four hours since she'd arrived in this desolate land?

It grew hotter with each passing hour. Around noon, she stopped the wagon once again and poured a small portion of water from the canteen onto a clean handkerchief to mop her face and neck.

Feeling slightly refreshed, she nibbled on a piece of dry meat, more to break the monotony of the trip than to satisfy any hunger. The meat was tasty and surprisingly tender. She ate all but a small piece, which she tucked away to eat later.

By the time she reached the bustling town of Hays, she felt as limp as an old rag. It had taken her five hours.

Flimsy wood buildings lined both sides of Old North Main Street. Wagons of every size and description filled the wide dirt street and loudmouthed merchants, vying for customers, hawked their colorful wares. Farmers dressed in canvas overalls could be seen lifting bales of buffalo hides and sacks of dry corn from the wagons onto the platform of the train depot. The waiting train divided the main street in half and held up traffic.

One drummer with a brightly painted wagon took advantage of the ready-made audience that the stalled train provided and shamelessly touted the virtues of Marshall's snake oil.

Curious, Maddie stopped her wagon to watch. The drummer lifted his stovepipe hat to her. "Here's a lady that looks a perfect picture of health." He spoke loud enough for all to hear. "Tell me, Miss, do you by chance owe your good health to Marshall's snake oil?"

Maddie gave the man a dazzling smile. "Of course," she called back. "What do you think made my hair this color?"

Appreciative laughter exploded from the crowd. Maddie swung her wagon around, leaving the drummer to glare after her.

She brought her wagon to a halt in front of the Perty Hotel, which overshadowed a peanut stand and Cy Godard's Saloon and Dance Hall. Inside, the sleepy-eyed clerk stuck his pen into the inkwell and gave her a nod. Overhead, the wooden blades of a fan turned lazily in the hot, oppressive air.

"I would like a room for one night," Maddie explained.

"Sorry, Miss." He had such a slow drawl that even the fan seemed fast in comparison. "There ain't no rooms avail'ble. A recent prairie fire burned down the entire town of Colton. Haven't seen this many people since I left San Anton'o."

"But surely there must be a room somewhere? If you could recommend a place I could stay and find refreshment, I should be most obliged."

"The r'freshment part is no problem. Hays, here, has seventy-five places where a person can quench a thirst. Name your pois'n. Everything from twenty-five-cent whisk'y to five-dollar-a-bottle Madam Cliquat is at your beck and call. The room? Well, now, that might be a probl'm. Yesiree, a probl'm." The clerk thought for a moment. "My advice is to check with Widow Gray. She owns the white house on the next street. Take a right at Hound Kell'y's Saloon. I heard tell she was rentin' out rooms to stranded trav'lers. A mighty charit'ble woman, that one."

Maddie thanked him and followed the man's directions to Chestnut Street. The clapboard house was, in her estimation, more brown than white, but the lace in the windows looked warm and inviting.

A matronly woman looked up from the garden as Maddie pulled her wagon in front of the weathered picket fence.

Climbing down from the wagon, Maddie walked up to the gate. "Are you Mrs. Gray?"

The woman straightened. "Indeed I am. And who might you be?" She spoke with a thick English accent.

"My name is Maddie Percy. I'm looking for a place to stay. I was told I might find a room here." Though the rosebushes were scraggly and dry, the colorful blooms on the other bushes looked as lovely as the flowers in Washington, and Maddie suddenly felt homesick.

The woman stared pointedly at Maddie's blue cotton trousers, then gave a disapproving frown when her gaze came to rest on the mass of tangled red curls that not even Maddie's sunbonnet could hide.

"That will be a dollar a night—and there'll be no carrying on with the other guests."

"At a dollar a night, I should say not!" Maddie declared. "Do you by any chance happen to know where I might find a Mr. Boxer?"

Mrs. Gray narrowed her eyes. "That's the superintendent of schools. What business would you be having with him?"

"He's my employer."

The woman looked incredulous. "You're a teacher?"

Maddie nodded. "I was supposed to teach in Colton. Now I'm not sure where I'll be teaching."

"Oh, heavenly days, the fire." Her manner toward Maddie improved considerably. Apparently teachers were rare enough in these parts to warrant high regard. "A terrible thing. You'll find your Mr. Boxer at the law offices of Lerner and Thornburgh. They were kind enough to let him set up temporary headquarters. It's a short walk. Why don't you leave your horse and wagon here, luv? That way you won't have to fight traffic."

"Thank you, I think I'll do that. Would you mind if I freshen up first?"

"Oh, you poor thing. Come in, come in." The woman stomped her feet on the mat in front of the door to rid her boots of dirt.

Maddie grabbed her valise from the back of the wagon and followed the woman inside the house and up the narrow stairs to the second floor. The necessity room was to the right of the hallway.

"You won't find better in Kansas," Mrs. Gray said proudly. The room was complete with a dry sink and oval mirror, but was sadly lacking by Washington

standards, and any calls by nature would have to be an-
swered with a trip to the outhouse in back.

Maddie thanked the widow and as soon as the older
woman took her leave, poured water from the china
pitcher into a matching basin. It felt good to wash the
dust and grime off her face and hands, but it was only
a temporary measure at best. What she really longed
for was a bath.

She brushed her hair, braided it, and pinned it up in
cogwheel style over her ears. She debated whether to
change into more suitable attire before meeting Mr.
Boxer, but decided against it. It was far too hot to
bother. Besides, after being left stranded the day before, she wasn't feeling particularly charitable toward
the man.

A short while later, following Mrs. Gray's instructions, Maddie walked down Chestnut to Old North
Main Street. She quickly located the stone law offices
on the other side of the train tracks.

Inside, several men, including the sheriff, sat in a
semicircle facing a wall chart. A man whom she pre-
sumed to be either Lerner or Thornburgh (given the
size of his girth, possibly both) broke away from the
group of men to greet her. "May I help you, Miss?"

"I'm looking for Mr. Boxer."

The man standing closest to the chart turned and
peered over the steel frames of his spectacles. "Elliot
Boxer at your service. How might I help you?"

"I'm Madeline Percy." When he showed no recogni-
tion of her name, she explained further. "I agreed to
teach in Colton."

The man's confusion cleared. He nudged the bridge
of his glasses up his nose with his forefinger. "Oh, yes,
Miss Percy. You came all the way from . . ."

"Washington."

"Yes, yes, I remember now. As you are no doubt aware, we had a most unfortunate fire."

"So I discovered."

"Burned everything down to the ground." He shook his head, and his glasses slipped back down his nose. "Most unfortunate."

"Yes, it was." She hesitated. "I was wondering if I might have a private word with you?" She glanced at the other men, who had risen to their feet at sight of her and who were now watching with open curiosity. "If you prefer, I could come back later."

"Nonsense!" It was the sheriff speaking. "You go ahead, Elliot. We'll carry on until you get back."

"Very well," Mr. Boxer said, although he looked none too eager to leave. He walked over to her and lowered his voice. "I can only talk a minute. We're right in the middle of a very important meeting." He was a short man, his head barely reaching her shoulder.

"I won't keep you. But it's most important that we talk." She followed him to the back of the room. "I feel rather awkward bringing this matter up, under the circumstances, but I was promised the second half of my advance upon my arrival."

Mr. Boxer looked startled. "Your what?"

"My advance. You paid me the first half with the agreement that I would receive the second half upon my arrival in Colton."

"Good heavens, woman! You're not asking for more money, are you?" He spoke loudly enough to be heard by the others, and there was a noticeable silence in the room as all heads swung in their direction.

Maddie dropped her voice to a whisper and hoped he would follow her lead. "According to my contract . . ."

"Oh, that!" He waved his small pudgy hand. "That was before the fire."

Refusing to be deterred, she pulled the contract from the pocket of her skirt and unfolded it, grateful that she had thought to retrieve it from her valise, where she had put it for safekeeping. "As you can see, it clearly states that the second half of my advance would be paid upon demand."

"Miss Percy! It's obvious you have no understanding of contracts. The contract calls for you to begin classes upon your arrival."

"That's true, Mr. Boxer." She made no effort to lower her voice and, indeed, had completely forgotten the others. "But the advance was contingent upon my traveling to Colton, which, as you can plainly see, I've done. I'm fully prepared to conduct classes."

"I'm most delighted to hear that, Miss Percy. As soon as I've made the necessary financial arrangements, we shall rebuild our school, at which time classes will begin and you shall be paid in accordance with our agreement."

"And what, may I ask, am I supposed to do in the meantime? I feel that human decency requires you to pay me the money you owe me so that I might return home."

"Return home?" His glasses almost fell off his nose. "Why in the world would you want to do that?"

The ordeal of the last twenty-four hours suddenly took its toll. At that moment, she didn't care if Mr. Boxer fired her on the spot. "I can think of quite a few reasons, Mr. Boxer. I was left stranded at the train station. I came perilously close to being scalped by Indians, trampled by buffalo, blown away by a wind storm and . . . accosted by a snake."

"My word!" Mr. Boxer exclaimed. "Did you say you were accosted by a snake?"

She forced herself to control her impatience. "Mr. Boxer, I have had an extremely trying time since arriving in Kansas, and I see no point in my staying any longer."

"Miss Percy, may I remind you that a contract is a contract? And your contract spells out the terms of our agreement quite clearly. We've simply had a temporary setback."

"Is that what you call it, Mr. Boxer? A temporary setback? There is no school. There's not even a town."

"Of course, of course. No wonder you're upset. Come over and I'll set your mind at ease. Gentlemen! If I may interrupt." Mr. Boxer took her by the arm and led her to the chart. He turned to the group. "I would like to introduce Miss Percy. She has agreed to be Colton's very first schoolteacher." He pointed to each man as he made introductions. "This is Sheriff Beckleworth, Max Weedler, Cobb Hobson, and Colton's very own acting mayor, Horace Mettle." The men nodded in turn as they were introduced.

"Ma'am."

"Pleased to meet you."

Maddie responded in kind.

Mr. Boxer turned and pointed to the chart. "This, Miss Percy, is the town of Colton. We are going to do something that to my knowledge has never been done before."

The tall, skinny man with a sweeping mustache stepped forward and pulled himself up by his suspenders. "It does me proud to be the mayor of the first planned town."

"What do you mean, 'planned town'?" Maddie asked.

"You see here?" Mr. Boxer drew her attention to the carefully drawn squares that ran up and down the center of the chart. "Every business and civic building has been carefully placed. Most towns, as you must know, are built haphazardly. Buildings are placed at random like so many thrown dice. Show her, Hortie."

The mayor, showing remarkable dignity despite his name and appearance, picked up a long stick. "It would be my pleasure." He pointed to the various little squares that represented buildings. "The dentist will be next to the mortuary. That way, should any of the patients wish to show discomfort, no one else's day need be sacrificed."

The man named Cobb rolled back on his heels. "He means you can scream your fool head off and no one will hear you."

"Thank you for clarifying that," the sheriff said, frowning. He turned to Maddie. "And we've moved the blacksmith away from the church."

"Is that significant?" Maddie asked, curious.

"Of course it's significant!" the mayor declared. "The blacksmith subscribes to, shall we say, unorthodox beliefs?"

Cobb coughed. "The blacksmith is a damned atheist and insists upon working on Sundays."

Mr. Boxer sniffed with indignation and pushed his glasses up the bridge of his nose. "Couldn't hear a word the pastor said for the sound of the anvil."

The man named Max Weedler spit a stream of brown tobacco juice in the general direction of the brass spittoon. "If you ask me, that ain't such a bad thing."

Maddie bit back the urge to suggest that Mr. Weedler either give up chewing tobacco or improve his aim. "Where's the school?"

"Right here." Mr. Boxer pointed to the bottom of the chart.

Maddie leaned closer. "Next to the jailhouse?"

Mr. Boxer's spectacles slid to the tip of his nose.

"My word! She's right. The school is right next to the jailhouse."

The Sheriff heaved an impatient sigh. "Now, calm yourself down, Elliot. There's nowhere else to put the school."

"Then find a place!" Mr. Boxer insisted. "I refuse to let the school be built next to the jail!"

"Do you have something against the jail?" Sheriff Beckleworth looked positively offended.

"Don't take this personal, Mac," Mr. Boxer said.

"I do take it personal," the sheriff argued. "I'll have you know that only the best of the best stay in my jail. You won't find more mannerly prisoners anywhere than the ones you'll find in my jailhouse."

Cobb studied the chart. "We could put the school next to the general store."

"That won't do," Mayor Mettle said. "You know how Mr. Green closes his store every afternoon for a time of . . . refreshment and reflection."

Cobb rubbed his unshaven chin. "He closes his store for whiskey and a romp with that . . ."

"As I was saying . . ." the mayor continued, "Mr. Green gets downright cranky without his daily nap."

Sheriff Beckleworth concurred. "I'm always having to go over to the general store on the afternoons that old Archie misses his nap to break up a fight. He charges twice as much when he's tired, and that makes his customers madder than blazes."

The mayor nodded. "As you yourself must know, Miss Percy, it's not possible to have an uninterrupted thought next to a schoolhouse."

"We could put the buggy works next to the school," Mr. Boxer interjected.

Maddie decided that if the likes of Mr. Weedler and Mr. Cobb were permitted to put in their two cents' worth, she was certainly entitled to add her opinion.

"You don't want to put anything next to the school that would be distracting. Carriages and buggies could be driving in and out all day long."

"She's right," Mayor Mettle grumbled.

Mr. Boxer sniffed. "That means we have to start all over again."

Never one to let an opportunity pass her by, Maddie decided to try out an idea that had occurred to her on the train en route to Kansas. "As long as you have to start over, perhaps you might consider making the schoolhouse into two rooms."

Mr. Boxer looked startled by the suggestion. "But we only have enough funds for one teacher."

"I propose that the second room be used for a museum. Like the one in Washington."

"Good Grief!" Mr. Boxer gasped. "You want to build a Smithsonian Institution in Colton?"

"Not exactly. Our museum would be much smaller. *Considerably* so."

"What would you put in the museum?" the mayor asked. It was obvious by the way he rubbed his palms together that the idea interested him.

"Artifacts. Fossils. Animals."

"Animals?"

"Mounted animals that are native to the area. I've only been here one day. Even so, I've noticed a great variety of plants and wildlife."

"I think it's a wonderful idea," the mayor said. "A museum could make Colton a tourist attraction. I can see it now. Hundreds, perhaps thousands of men, women, and children lining up for a tour."

Maddie thought the mayor was being a bit optimistic about the appeal of such a museum, but she decided it was to her advantage to let the man have his dream.

"And," the mayor continued, "if we put the museum

on this side of the school, it would provide a barrier between the school and the jailhouse."

"A perfect solution," Mr. Boxer concurred. He was clearly relieved that the placement of the school had been resolved.

Everyone but Mr. Weedler, who looked bored with the idea, nodded in agreement.

Maddie was far from convinced that the problem had been resolved, but seeing that the others had agreed to the museum, she decided to let the matter drop. "How long do you think it will be before I can begin teaching?"

Mr. Boxer did some quick calculations before replying. "Shouldn't be more than a few weeks. Once the loans are approved, families should start returning to the area. As soon as we have enough workers, we can start buildings."

"A few weeks?" Maddie's spirits dropped. After paying Mrs. Gray, she had no money left.

"Wait a minute!" This was from the mayor. "What if we move the school over by the . . ."

Sensing that another lengthy discussion was about to unfold, she took her leave. She was tired and hungry. The men stood and thanked her for her contributions to the discussion.

The mayor looked especially pleased, and his checkered vest expanded outward. "Yesiree. A museum is exactly what we need."

Maddie walked the short distance back to Mrs. Gray's house.

A metal watering can in hand, the woman looked up when Maddie approached. "Did you find Mr. Boxer, luv?"

"Yes, thank you. I did find him. Unfortunately, I did not accomplish what I intended to. I'm afraid Mr. Boxer is rather mule-headed."

"Oh, dear. Reminds me of my dear departed husband, Harry. Talk about mule-headed. Why the doctor had to declare him officially dead three times before Harry would lie still."

Maddie stared at the woman in horror. "How awful."

Mrs. Gray shrugged. "Come on inside, luv. You can rest while I fix us both a spot of tea."

Maddie accepted the offer gratefully. She felt tired and discouraged.

The parlor was so filled with furniture that some sidestepping and moving of tables and chairs were required to forge a path to the dining room.

"I agreed to store the furniture of some of those poor, dear people who lost their homes in the fire," Mrs. Gray explained.

"That's very generous of you." Maddie stepped over a footstool, ducked beneath a hat rack and plopped herself on one of the Queen Anne chairs next to the table.

The tea picked up her spirits, and the teacakes were delicious. She was convinced that a hot bath and a good night's rest would restore her optimistic outlook.

"Your room is opposite the necessary room."

Thanking Mrs. Gray, Maddie took her leave. She climbed the stairs to the second floor and opened the door to her room.

It surprised her to find a man lying on the bed, snoring. A quick glance around the clothes-strewn room indicated that he'd been there for some time. She quietly closed the door. Not wanting to chance walking into the wrong room again, she hurried back downstairs to find Mrs. Gray.

The woman seemed surprised that Maddie had trouble finding her room. "It's just as I told you, luv. It's the one opposite the necessary room."

"But someone is in that room," Maddie explained.

"That would be Mr. Woolery. Nice man. His wife died just last year. Wonderful woman."

Maddie gaped at the woman. "You . . . you mean . . . I would be sharing a room?"

"Oh, dear. I do hope it's all right. Mr. Woolery is a perfect gentleman."

"I couldn't possibly share a room with . . . a man."

"Every room is taken. It was that awful prairie fire. You could stay in my room, but . . ." She blushed. "I'm afraid there is no room. Normally, you understand, I would never consider sharing my own room with anyone. But under the circumstances, I had no choice." She giggled. "It would have been most uncharitable of me to let that nice Mr. Parker sleep out in the cold."

"Perhaps Mr. Parker and Mr. Woolery would be kind enough to share a room together," Maddie suggested.

It was obvious that Mrs. Gray wasn't willing to change roommates. "I don't think so," she said vaguely. "It wouldn't be right now that everyone's settled in. You understand, don't you, how awkward it would be to start switching rooms?"

"Yes, well, I think I'd better look for accommodations elsewhere."

Mrs. Gray's hand flew to her ample bosom. "But there are no other rooms to be had."

"Maybe not, but it wouldn't be proper for me to spend the night with a stranger, being that I'm a schoolteacher. I'm sure you must understand."

"Oh, dear. You poor thing." She made it sound like being a schoolteacher was a curse. "Of course you're right. It wouldn't do for a schoolteacher to be caught sharing a room with a gentleman. Would you like me to refund your money?"

Maddie needed the money, but it seemed miserly to insist upon a refund, especially since she'd helped herself without restraint to the delicious tea and teacakes Mrs. Gray had set out.

"That won't be necessary," she said, hoping that the woman would insist upon making a refund. When it became painfully obvious that Mrs. Gray had no intention of voluntarily returning her money, Maddie took her leave, feeling more depressed than ever.

# *Chapter 8*

Maddie spent the remainder of the afternoon asking everyone she met if there was a vacancy in town. One woman with a painted face and wearing more feathers than could be found on a chicken farm, planted her fists on her hips and glared at Maddie.

"There ain't no vacant bed that I can't fill."

"I don't suppose there is," Maddie said, backing away. In her haste to escape, she almost ran into a woman who had just walked out of the mercantile shop. The woman had two small children by the hand and was clearly expecting a third.

"My apologies, ma'am."

The woman regarded Maddie with dull brown eyes. She looked tired, almost harried, but when she replied her voice was kind. "That's quite all right. No harm done."

"Would you happen to know where I might find a room?"

"I'm sorry I can't help you. I'm new in town myself. My family and I are sleeping in a covered wagon."

"Are you from Colton?"

"Yes. I guess you heard about the prairie fire. We barely escaped with our lives."

"It must have been dreadful for you." Maddie smiled at the small boy and girl, who were staring at her curiously. "My name is Miss Percy. I'm the new schoolteacher."

"So you're the new schoolteacher." The woman gave both children a gentle nudge. "Say 'how do you do' to Miss Percy." The boy did as he was instructed, but his younger sister hid her face behind her mother's full gray skirt.

"We were mighty glad to hear that we were finally going to have a school with a real teacher. My name is Lucy Eldridge. This here is Jamie and his sister, Caroline." She gazed at Maddie's trousers. As if to keep herself from staring, she quickly looked away. "What are you going to do?"

"I'm not sure." Maddie forced a smile. "I'm sure I'll find something."

A dubious look crossed Lucy's face. "I would love to stay and visit longer, but I'm afraid my husband will be wondering where we are." She looked momentarily distracted before adding irrelevantly, "My husband was a war hero."

"How interesting."

A look of desperation crossed the woman's face. Given the woman's circumstances, Maddie understood completely. She was feeling a bit desperate herself. "You must be very proud of your husband."

"We all are," Lucy said. "The whole family's proud. I'm sorry I couldn't be of more help." Lucy grabbed Caroline by the hand and hurried away, with Jamie close at her heels.

"It was nice meeting you," Maddie called after her. She hated to see Lucy and her two children leave. Mindful of the late hour and her own bleak circumstances, she peered up and down the street in search of a friendly face.

The faces around her seemed to grow more hostile with each passing hour. By the time the main street was in shadow, it was obvious that anyone wishing to survive long in this wild frontier town better have a quick fist and a ready weapon.

Maddie was forced to keep crossing from one side of the street to the other to avoid the many brawls that were breaking out as off-duty soldiers from the nearby fort rode into town, looking for a fight.

She soon realized the dangers of passing too close to the many bat-winged doors that swung out to the dirt street. At any moment someone was likely to come shooting out headfirst, followed by a mob of angry people.

It was late afternoon before a breeze picked up and the temperature began to dip. The street was packed with every kind of wagon and animal imaginable. Men staggered from one saloon to the other, shouting obscenities along the way. More than one cowhand had made the mistake of grabbing her and had received a sharp jab to the ribs or a kick in the shin in return.

"Get your hands off me!" she snapped at one drunken stranger who persisted.

A yellow-toothed smile parted a mangy beard. "I love a woman who's hard to get."

She rewarded him with a hard kick. He cried out in pain, freeing her to scramble up to the seat of her wagon. His companion lurched toward her. A hand as firm as an iron clamp gripped her ankle. The man looked up at her with blurry red eyes.

"Let go of me!" she yelled. She tried pulling her leg away, but the white-knuckled hand held tight.

She pulled her whip off the seat and struck her tormentor on the shoulder. He jumped back with a yelp and landed rump-side on the ground, his worn boots in the air.

Taking full advantage of the reprieve, she jerked on the traces and the wagon shot forward.

A group of rowdy men jumped into the street and tried to stop her. One man threw a fistful of silver at her.

"Much obliged," she called out, pocketing the coins. If the man was so foolish as to throw away his money, she wasn't going to dissuade him.

"There's more where that came from!" someone yelled. "Let's see how much you're worth!"

"With that red hair, I'd say she's worth plenty," called another.

She urged her horse around a stagecoach and drove past a mule train. The front wheel of her wagon clipped the rear of a gaudy green and yellow drummer's wagon, and her axle caught. She tried freeing the wheel to no avail. Muttering curses beneath her breath, she jumped to the ground to have a closer look.

A tall man dressed in an outlandish red-checkered suit and flashy purple vest stepped from behind the wagon.

"My wheel is caught with yours," she explained. She looked around to make certain her antagonizers had not followed her.

The drummer tipped his hat and twirled the tips of his mustache. "So it is. I would say it's providence, wouldn't you? The way we met?"

"I think it's more likely the fact that you're parked in the middle of the street."

Her ill humor seemingly had no effect on him. "I'm a great believer in giving providence all the help you can." He looked her up and down. "You look like a woman of discriminating taste. A woman who would value a genuine and authentic Indian tipi of her own."

The man had such gall, Maddie couldn't help but laugh. "What possible use would a tipi be to me?"

The man glanced down at her trousers. "I thought a woman of your discerning taste would see the value of owning something as well crafted as this." He pulled a rolled tipi out of the open door of his wagon and motioned her closer. "Genuine buffalo skin. Real rawhide lacing. No one makes a tipi like a genuine Indian. And because I have such great respect for providence I shall only charge you five dollars."

"My own respect for providence demands that I decline your generous offer. Now if you would kindly move your wagon . . ."

"Three dollars."

"Your wagon, sir!"

"Guaranteed for a lifetime."

She folded her arms. "Whose? Yours or mine?"

"Aha! That's the beauty of my offer. The customer gets to decide."

"And what happens if it doesn't last a lifetime?"

"You'll have to buy another one."

She gave him a look of disapproval. "What kind of guarantee is that?"

"An honest one." He cocked an eyebrow. "Two-fifty and that's my final offer."

Maddie was about to say she had no money when she remembered the money that had just been thrown at her and that she had stuffed in her pocket. Talk about providence! "How difficult is it to put up one of these tipis?"

"Not difficult at all. Even a child can do it."

"A dollar fifty and you have yourself a deal."

The man pursed his lips. "You strike a hard bargain."

She paid him, and he pulled out a rolled tipi from the back of his wagon and transported it to hers. The lodgepoles were longer than the wagon. The drummer lay the poles diagonally across the bed, with the ends sticking up.

"You wouldn't by chance have a gun for sale, would you?" Maddie asked.

If the drummer was surprised by her request, he kept it to himself. "You want it, I can sell it. You ever fire a gun before?"

"Never."

"In that case I have the perfect revolver." He reached inside his wagon and pulled out a small weapon that barely filled his hand. "Perfect for a tasteful woman such as yourself."

It was all Maddie could do not to laugh aloud. Tasteful, indeed. Her former employer should hear that one!

Considering its size, the gun felt heavy in her hands, but it would do. It took some skill on her part to barter the man down to where she could afford to purchase both the gun and the tipi.

"It's highway robbery, that's what it is," he mumbled. He pocketed the money and climbed onto the driver's seat of his wagon.

"It's providence!" she called back.

The sun dropped below the horizon, shading the town a sinister gray. A bearded man brandishing a knife stepped into the street. She swerved out of his way and almost ran over a towheaded youth who dodged out in front of her.

Several wild-looking men closed around her, making it all but impossible for her horse to keep moving. She snapped her whip through the air frantically trying to keep the men at bay. Someone grabbed her leg, ripping the fabric of her trousers. Another man grabbed onto the side of the wagon. She struck him across the face with her whip, and he fell backward with a grunt, taking a part of her sleeve with him.

No sooner had she gotten rid of him than another man heaved himself into the wagon and tried to wrestle the reins out of her hands. She grabbed her newly purchased gun and shoved it into his fleshy face. He laughed at her, and when she searched for the trigger she realized she was holding the gun by the barrel and pointing the handle in his face.

Seething, she tossed the gun down and it fired as it hit the footboard. The man's hat flew off his head. A look of terror crossed his face as he lost his grip and fell backward. The other men, thinking he'd been shot, abandoned their attempts to detain her and the road suddenly cleared in front of her.

Fearing the reprieve was only temporary, she wasted no time in making her escape. She flicked the whip over the head of her horse, yelling commands that proved unnecessary since Rutabaga was already going as fast as was possible given the number of vehicles in the way and the deep, rutted grooves worn into the sod by wagon wheels.

The raucous, rough voices still ringing in her ears, she drove hell-bent for Betsy past the remaining saloons.

She almost fell off the seat when the wagon cut a sharp curve out of town. Desperately gripping the traces, she held on for dear life, not daring to slow down until the shouts and curses had faded away and the town of Hays was nothing but a spot beneath the darkening sky.

Only when her safety was assured did she slow the horse to a trot. It would soon be night and she had nowhere to go.

She supposed she could go back to the soddy. The thought, as surprising as it was daring, was quickly discounted. What in the world would Luke Tyler think if she showed up on his front doorstep again? Especially in view of the incident she'd witnessed with his son, Matthew.

Still, what choice did she have? She had originally

planned to pitch her tipi outside of town and try to obtain temporary employment until the school was rebuilt. But after her narrow escape, she had no intention of ever going back there.

She was equally adamant about not returning to the Tyler soddy.

Refusing to succumb to the tears that stung her eyes, she tried to think of how her father would have acted in similar circumstances. She lifted her chin and narrowed her eyes to scan the wide expanse of dark purple prairie, determined to challenge anyone or anything that posed a threat.

She hoped to God that nothing would.

# Chapter 9

The moon cast a silver glow upon the vast grass-lands that rippled in the gentle breeze like waves on a restless sea.

The constant motion of the grass kept her on the edge of her seat. Every shadow suggested danger. She was convinced that Indians were about to attack, and if not Indians, then surely buffalo. Recalling the buffalo stampede the night before, she shivered and felt around her feet for the gun.

Relief washed over her as she located the weapon. She laid it carefully on the seat next to her. Reassured that it was easily accessible, she continued to scour the dimly lit terrain like a general in enemy territory.

The dank odor of grass and earth gradually gave way to the rancid smell left from the recent prairie fire.

Coyotes howled in the distance. An occasional owl flew overhead, but otherwise her journey, though long, was blissfully uneventful.

Although it was not all that late when she picked out Luke Tyler's windmill, probably around ten or so, the window of the soddy was already dark. She pulled on the traces and the wagon rolled to a stop.

The lively beat of Indian drums prompted her heart to pound nervously. Recalling what Mr. Tyler had said about sound traveling on the prairie, she nonetheless felt a cold sweat creep up her spine.

In her estimation, the mere fact that she could *hear* the drums meant the Cheyennes were too close, no matter how far away they might be in actuality.

She felt tired and hungry, and the cold night air was beginning to slice through the thin fabric of her clothes. Her discomfort, along with the drums, made her reluctant to continue her journey. The dark soddy called out to her like a safe refuge. She only wished she had the nerve to knock on the door and ask for shelter.

Surely Mr. Tyler wouldn't object if she spent the night on his property. If she left first thing in the morning, he wouldn't even know she'd been there.

She skirted the sod house so as not to wake father or son, and pulled her horse and wagon behind the barn. Taking her gun with her, she climbed into the back of the wagon. Between the tipi and her trunk, there wasn't much room left.

Grateful for the bedroll she'd forgotten to return, she curled up in a ball and prayed for a quiet, uneventful night without buffalo, Indians, or—heaven forbid—snakes.

The crow of a rooster coaxed her out of a deep sleep into a half-conscious slumber. She might have stayed in that dreamlike state forever had some primal instinct not snapped her into full wakefulness. Fighting her way out of her bedroll, she grabbed her gun, this time, thankfully, by the handle, and brandished it in front of her.

The boy drew back, his eyes wide with fear. He was perched on the top of her trunk.

"Matthew!" she gasped, letting the gun fall to her side. "You scared the life out of me." She carefully tucked the gun back into her bedroll. Matthew continued to watch her, his eyes wary.

She motioned him closer. "It's all right, Matthew. I'm not going to hurt you."

The fear left his eyes, but not the curiosity. She smiled at him. "You want to know what I'm doing here, don't you? Well, so do I." She scanned the area around her and was struck anew by the empty vastness of the land. "So do I."

She pulled on her boots and climbed out of the wagon. She offered her hand to Matthew and he readily accepted it. "Easy does it," she said. The sun felt warm on her back.

The hum of bees and other insects provided a bass harmony for the melodious song of the yellow-breasted meadowlarks. Suddenly the horrors of the last two days seemed like a bad dream.

Thrilling to the early-morning symphony, she took a deep breath, inhaling the earthy smell of damp soil and dew-sweetened prairie grass. Moving away from the shade of the barn, she caught a whiff of the wildflowers that grew in incredible abundance all around.

A prairie dog sat upright before dodging headfirst into a mound of dirt.

"Interesting animal," she said, pointing for Matthew's sake. "We don't have those back home." A jackrabbit raced past them, and she laughed in delight. "We don't have jackrabbits either. We only have cottontails."

It suddenly occurred to her how many opportunities the prairie offered for exploration and discovery. Despite her still unsettled future, she felt a sense of anticipation.

Mr. Tyler's voice floated toward them. "Matthew!"

Maddie swore silently beneath her breath. She had hoped to make her escape before anyone found out she was there. Since escape was impossible and there was no time to do anything about her disheveled appearance, she heaved a sigh and braced herself.

Mr. Tyler walked around the barn and stopped in midstep. A look of surprise crossed his face as he gaped at her. "Miss Percy!"

"Mr. Tyler," she said briskly. Why hadn't she thought to brush her hair instead of watching the wildlife? Or at the very least change her bedraggled clothes?

He walked toward her, his brow creased. "Didn't you find Hays?"

"Yes," she said, her voice weak. "It was exactly where you said it was. The problem was I couldn't find a place to stay."

"I'm sorry . . . I . . ." He stared at her torn sleeve and his eyes narrowed in alarm. "What happened to you?"

"Nothing," she said, feeling self-conscious.

His gaze lowered to the tear in her trousers. "Nothing?"

"I ran into a group of drunks. I doubt that they meant me any real harm . . ."

His eyes quickly met hers. "I should never have let you go to Hays by yourself." The soft lights of concern quickly left his eyes, and his face grew dark with a sudden flash of anger. Thinking his anger was directed at her, she drew back and was about to jump into her wagon and take her leave, when he surprised her by inviting her to breakfast.

"Well . . . I . . ." She was starved, and this was probably the last chance she would have to eat for who knew how long? Accepting his offer was a matter of survival. "If you're sure it's no trouble . . . ?"

"No trouble at all. Coffee's ready." He glanced at Matthew. "And as soon as this young man gathers the eggs and milks the cow, breakfast will be ready."

"That's very kind of . . ." Before she had a chance to

voice her thanks, he had already walked away, his long strides carrying him effortlessly over the packed sod ground.

After Matthew left to do his chores, she stood behind the barn and quickly changed into pretty blue trousers and a matching skirt. She topped this outfit with a white blouse. The clothes she'd worn on the previous day would require some skillful repair. Just thinking of the way those men in Hays had attacked her filled her with renewed indignation and fury. Never had she been treated so shabbily in Washington!

She touched her toes fifty times and stretched her arms overhead, as was her usual habit. But it took more than her normal exercise routine to dispense with her outrage and concentrate on her current situation. It took a vigorous run, followed by more bending and stretching.

Her exercises completed, she walked briskly to the water barrel at the side of the soddy. The sparkling clear water was icy cold but invigorating. She dried herself with a clean flour sack and pinned her hair up in a no-nonsense fashion.

Ready to face her host, she walked toward the door. She was nervous, and her hand shook as she knocked. Lordy be! What was the matter with her?

Matthew opened the door, but it was his father who invited her in. "Come in, Miss Percy."

She stepped inside and remembered to close the door gently. "Breakfast smells delicious."

Matthew hurried to take his place at the table. Once seated, he pointed to the chair next to his. There was no sign of anger in his expression or manner, nor anything to suggest he was capable of the kind of fury she had witnessed a day earlier.

"Thank you, Matthew." She brushed a fine layer of dirt off the chair before sitting down.

Luke filled two cups of coffee, then set the pot down on the stove before sitting down opposite her. "You look amazingly fit, given your ordeal."

She wondered what ordeal he referred to. She'd been through so many in the last forty-odd hours since arriving in Kansas, she was beginning to lose count. "Hays is not a fit place for man nor beast."

Again she noticed the hard look in his eyes, the tightening of his strong, firm jaw. A shiver shot through her, and she wished she'd thought to bring her wrap. "If Sheriff Beckleworth was doing his job instead of attending meetings . . ."

He shot her a look of surprise. "You know Sheriff Beckleworth?"

"I met him briefly."

"Beckleworth is Colton's sheriff. He has no authority in Hays."

"As far as I could tell, no one has authority in Hays. I thought there was a fort nearby."

"That's part of the problem, I'm afraid. Many of the troublemakers were probably off-duty soldiers. There's not much to do at the fort. So the men ride into town during furlough and get drunk."

"Was Colton as rough and lawless as Hays?"

"Colton was a family town. We had a few troublemakers, but nothing like you'll find in Hays." After a while he asked, "Did you find Mr. Boxer?"

"Yes, for all the good it did me." She described the unsatisfactory meeting she'd had with her employer. "He insists that I keep to the terms of the contract before he'll pay me the money he owes me. So that's what I came back to do. Teach school."

A look of thoughtful contemplation crossed her host's face. "I'm not sure I understand what you're saying. You can't teach without students, and as I'm sure you've already noticed, students are pretty hard to come by around here since the fire."

"Mr. Boxer insists that the school will be built in a few weeks' time, and that all the original families will return. He says the entire town will be rebuilt soon. They have the plans already made up." She smiled at Matthew, who had not taken his eyes off her during her entire discussion with his father. "Meanwhile, Matthew can be my student."

"I need Matthew in the fields with me." It was a simple enough statement, and she would have accepted it at face value had it not been for the obstinate narrowing of his eyes.

"I just wanted to help. Your son needs an education, and I thought since I have nothing much else to do with my time . . ."

"Matthew *is* getting an education. He's learning to farm. One day this land will be his. One more year and I'll be eligible to prove up."

"Prove up?"

"The homesteaders act requires me to live on this land for five years. Next year, I'll get the deed and this will all be mine. Mine and Matthew's."

Maddie glanced at Matthew, who was watching a tiny white grub inch its way up the dirt wall. "As I'm sure you'll agree, a farmer needs to know how to read and write."

"Have you forgotten, Miss Percy, that my son cannot talk?"

She took a deep breath. Conscious that the boy had lost interest in the small insect, she chose her words carefully. "No, I have not forgotten that. But it seems to me . . ."

"I can't discuss this any further." Her host grimaced and ran his fingers through his hair. The hardness left his eyes and was replaced by a look of regret. "I didn't mean to be rude in any way. I know that you're trying to help."

Not sure how to answer him, she accepted his apology with a quick nod. "I *am* trying to help and you're right, I had no business interfering."

He held her gaze for a moment before he stood and reached for his straw hat. "Please accept my apologies for having to leave you. Matthew and I have work to do."

Taking his cue, Matthew stuffed the last of his flapjacks into his mouth and grabbed his own straw hat.

His father waited at the door until Matthew had scooted past him and raced outside. "Feel free to stay here until you're able to find more suitable accommodations."

"That's most generous of you," she said. "But I couldn't impose."

"You wouldn't be imposing. In any case, it doesn't look like you have any choice in the matter." He placed his hat on his head, pulled the brim low on his forehead, ducked his head beneath the doorjamb, and walked outside.

Maddie wasn't certain how she felt about staying with the Tylers. She treated herself to another cup of coffee and considered every possible option. The idea of pitching her tipi near the Colton site was even less appealing than it had been when she first conceived of the idea. After crossing that prairie at night, she had no desire to pitch a tent on empty land, with no neighbors in sight.

She wasn't even certain if staying with the Tylers was an option; her being a respectable schoolteacher and all and him being an eligible man. Not that anything could ever develop between them. He was far too serious-minded for her taste, and he probably considered her too frivolous for his.

This probably explained why he didn't want her to get close to Matthew. He no doubt thought her a bad influence; in that regard, he wouldn't be alone. But of all the parents who had objected to her unorthodox ways, Mr. Tyler's decision was the most puzzling. He knew very little about her, had no knowledge of her teaching abilities. So what was he judging her by? Appearances? Or was there some other reason for his objection? A reason that had nothing to do with her?

Grateful to have the house, such as it was, to herself, she finished her coffee and washed up the breakfast dishes. It was the least she could do to show her appreciation.

She gave the table a good scrubbing and cried out when a splinter sank into the side of her palm. Grimacing, she squeezed the sliver of wood out and wrapped her hand in a flour sack.

By the time the bleeding stopped, the table was already covered with a fine layer of dirt that had sifted down from the ceiling.

The table, with its uneven legs and rough surface, was a curiosity compared to the rest of the fine-crafted furnishings. She recalled the beautiful table in the barn and wondered why it hadn't been brought in and put to use.

She walked around the room, studying the ceiling. Lordy be, what a strange dwelling this was. She wondered what her mother would say if she knew her daughter was a guest in a house with dirt walls, a dirt floor, and one inadequate window.

It was exceedingly hot by the time she stepped outside. She stood by the motionless windmill and scanned the surrounding area in hopes of finding shade for her tipi. Not a tree nor as much as a bush grew anywhere in sight. With no hope for shade, she decided to choose her location based on other criteria.

Safety, for one. She made a wide circle around the tiny sod house, eyeing the distance and estimating the length of time it would take to dash inside should a buffalo, Indian, or snake show its unwelcome face.

She decided it was better not to take chances. For this reason, she decided to pitch her tipi as close to the soddy as possible, without being too obvious, of course.

She wondered if five feet was enough space to leave between Mr. Tyler's house and the tipi. Much closer and he might get the wrong idea. A sudden vision of his bronzed chest came to mind. Shaking the thought away, she decided that ten feet was close enough.

She pulled the tipi off the back of the wagon and unrolled the gleaming white cover that was made of several buffalo hides and wrapped around twenty wooden poles.

She held a pole in each hand and looked for a clue as to how they could possibly fit together. Undaunted, she unfolded the skins, and stood several of the poles on end to form a triangle. This left at least a dozen more poles that she had no idea what to do with. It also posed another problem: how to lash the poles together.

Pitching the tipi was turning out to be more difficult than she had anticipated.

*So simple that a child could put it up.* Indeed! If she ever got her hands on that drummer, she would make him eat every one of those words.

Frustrated, she tossed the poles to the ground and was startled by the sound of laughter behind her.

Whirling about, she was horrified to discover an audience of no less than three scantily dressed Indians watching her from atop white-spotted ponies. Her alarm soon gave way to indignation upon realizing that she was the object of their mirth.

Not knowing what else to do, she decided to ignore

them. She turned around and continued to work her way through the confusion of lodgepoles and bleached buffalo hides. The laughter grew louder.

Let them laugh, she fumed. See if she cared. But despite her cavalier appearance, she kept a wary eye on her unwelcomed guests and almost stopped breathing when the three Indians dismounted and approached.

Cursing herself for leaving her gun in the wagon, which was still parked behind the barn, she straightened and willed her fast-beating heart to stay put.

The tallest of the three Indians spoke in his native tongue. She had no idea what he was saying, but just in case he was issuing instructions to scalp her, she glared at him and shook her head vigorously. She sincerely hoped that wagging one's head from side to side held the same meaning for the Indians as it did for her.

The tallest of the three raised a hand as if to halt the others. She felt slightly encouraged, if not altogether relieved. If she could so readily make them understand how thoroughly she detested the idea of being scalped, who knew what other meanings she could convey?

A second Indian spoke. The scar that ran down the side of his face gave him a menacing look, though he didn't sound particularly threatening.

He pointed to the tipi, then stabbed his finger into his own chest. Studying him intently, she tried to think of every conceivable thing he might be saying. *Maybe he wants the tipi for himself,* she thought. If so, it might not be prudent to deny his request.

Tentatively, she nodded, hoping she wasn't inadvertently giving her permission for him to help himself to more than just the tipi.

The scar-faced Indian picked up a pole, and his two companions followed his example. The tall Indian pulled a piece of rawhide from his waist and lashed the three poles together, making a tripod.

The tips of the remaining poles were arranged against the tripod, the opposite ends forming a wide circle. Maddie watched in amazement as the top of the impressive framework rose skyward, standing high above the prairie and dwarfing the little soddy house.

The three Indians took turns weaving a length of rope in and out of each pole until the frame of the tipi was secured. Once the rope was in place, it was pulled tight.

The buffalo canvas was heaved upward with the help of a lifting pole, dropped into place on the frame, then unrolled until the two ends met between the door poles.

She pointed to the flap of the door, which she wanted to face in the direction of the soddy for maximum security. But the Indian shook his head and waved his hand sideways. He pointed to the door, then extended his finger toward the east.

Using his same motions, she pointed to the flap, then to the soddy. If she was able to understand his intent to make the door face east, then certainly she should be able to make him understand that she wanted the door to open toward the soddy.

It was obvious that he understood what she was saying, but he wasn't in any mood to give in to her wishes. He shook his head and spoke in a harsh voice that left no doubt as to who had the upper hand. The flap would face the direction he said it would face!

She stepped back. Why he cared which direction her door faced, she couldn't imagine. Still, she wasn't about to argue with him. She decided it might be wise to allow the three men to continue their work unimpeded.

The tipi, outlined against the flat prairie and the clear blue sky, was an impressive sight. When the Indians had completed the task, Maddie did her best with gestures and smiles to convey her appreciation.

Laughing among themselves, the Indians mounted their saddleless ponies and rode off.

Maddie watched them until they were out of sight, then walked inside her tipi. It was light inside and surprisingly spacious. At least she didn't have to worry about the ceiling falling down every time she raised her voice above a whisper.

It wasn't the sort of home she'd imagined when she accepted the teaching post in Kansas. But it would do until she was able to obtain more suitable accommodations.

She set to work making the tipi more homey. She found an empty wooden crate in the barn that would serve double duty as a cupboard and table. She drove the wagon as close to the tipi as she could manage, so she wouldn't have far to drag her trunk.

It was while she was searching the barn for more empty crates and other discarded items that might be useful that the baby cradle once again caught her attention. The polished wood of the headboard felt smooth beneath her fingers. She knelt down to examine the intricate designs carved into each rung.

On impulse, she reached for a rag on the workbench and dusted off the sides. The mattress was covered by a quilted baby blanket. She gathered it up and shook it outside until it was free of dust.

Tiny water marks like raindrops marred the blanket. She glanced upward and searched the ceiling for holes in the roof. But not a single speck of sunlight filtered through the sod-covered roof.

Tears? she wondered. Is that what had caused the pearl-sized water marks? But whose tears? Luke Tyler's? It was hard to imagine. The man seemed so rugged and strong, his broad shoulders capable of supporting weights that would break most men's backs. But he did have an air of sadness, despite his strength. Could these really be Luke's tears?

Feeling that she was intruding on something personal, she drew away from the cradle and, as she did, backed into the table.

She ran her finger across its edge, exposing a small area. Noting the lovely grain, she wiped her rag across the wood until the layer of fine dirt had been brushed away. What a beautiful table. It seemed like such a waste for a sturdy piece of furniture like this not to be put into service.

Her hand still throbbing from the splinter, she set to work rubbing the cloth over the table and chairs.

It took a lot of energy and much persistence to drag the old table out of the house and replace it with the new one. By the time she'd carried each chair and set it in place, rivers of perspiration were rolling down her face and back.

She felt hot and irritable, but no less pleased with the results of her efforts. She could hardly wait to see the surprise on Mr. Tyler's face when he saw the difference the table made to the otherwise dreary room. If only there was a way to prevent the dirt from falling onto the smooth surface.

She stood looking up at the ceiling, her hands at her waist. Suddenly an idea occurred to her. Forgetting the heat, she dashed back outside to her tipi.

# Chapter 10

Luke looked up from his plow. The red globe of the sun hovered just above the horizon. He decided to finish the row he was plowing and call it a day.

The buffalo stampede two nights earlier had trampled the soil and exposed what few seeds he'd managed to plant since the fire to the perilously hot rays of the sun. This latest episode was one of many such disasters that had befallen him in the four years he'd been farming this land, and the second time this spring that he'd been forced to start anew and replant.

Since he had come to Kansas, his crops had been ruined in turn by droughts, floods, fires, and once by a great sweeping cloud of grasshoppers. Some said the land could never be farmed. It was known by others as the wastelands. More than one discouraged farmer had called it the Great American Desert.

Luke was beginning to think that the naysayers might be right.

He lowered the plow. The wooden handles were damp with sweat, making them hard to grip. He wiped his arm across his brow. It would take another three days' worth of work to finish plowing the area. Replanting this late in the spring decreased the chances of a successful harvest.

That could mean yet another difficult winter on the

bleak Kansas prairie. He unharnessed the oxen and led the huge animals to the corral that had been fenced with railroad stakes. It was Matthew's responsibility to keep the trough filled with fresh water drawn from the nearby creek. Luke checked to see that the job had been done, then dragged the gate closed and wired it shut.

"Let's go, Matthew," he called. "It's time to go home." Heaving himself onto the seat of the wagon, he grabbed the reins. Matthew came running across the field and scrambled up the side of the wagon to take his place next to his father.

Luke nodded his approval at Matthew for his promptness. The boy usually dawdled at this time of day, unwilling to go home. Today, in contrast, Matthew seemed anxious to leave the fields and head for the soddy.

As Luke drove the wagon along the narrow dirt trail, Matthew craned his neck as if searching the horizon.

What was he looking for? Luke wondered. Miss Percy? Was that it? Not that he blamed the boy. She certainly did liven things up. In fact, he admitted, he felt a surge of anticipation, too. He had never thought she'd come back. What a fool he had been to let her go to Hays by herself. If anything had happened to her, he would never have forgiven himself.

The woman struck him as so capable, she made it easy to forget how vulnerable her sex could be on this wild frontier. He only hoped that her recent encounters would not discourage her free spirit.

The fatigue that normally gripped him at this time of day seemed to fade away as the memory of her running around the soddy came to mind. The bright, almost scarlet color that spread across the sky reminded him of the way her glorious red hair caught the sun as she ran, dancing upon her shoulders like quick burning flames.

He wondered how it would feel to be caught up in the passion of the moment. To act freely, without having to consider every possible consequence of one's actions. He tried to imagine himself running without restraint, laughing, feeling. On all accounts he failed.

Matthew tugged on his arm. "What is it, son?" he asked gently, reluctant to let the vision of her fade from his mind.

Luke's gaze followed Matthew's finger. He was still dazed by the fanciful thoughts he was not willing to let go, and it took him a moment to comprehend what he saw. "What the . . ."

He squinted to get a better look. No doubt about it. An Indian tipi stood next to his soddy. What in the world? With all the land around here, why would the Cheyennes want to park themselves on his doorstep?

"Giddyup!" he shouted to his horse. If there was a problem, by George, he wanted it solved before nightfall!

Miss Percy was standing in front of the soddy when he pulled the wagon up. Her red hair was brushed back from her smooth forehead and cascaded in gentle waves down her back.

She didn't look the least bit perturbed by this latest intrusion upon his property. This lack of concern on her part struck him as odd, even for her. If anything, she looked like a soldier who had conquered the enemy. He hoped to God she hadn't messed with the Cheyennes.

He gave her a wary nod. "Miss Percy."

She greeted him in kind. "Mr. Tyler."

He swung himself to the ground and pushed his hat

back from his forehead. "Could you explain why there is an Indian tipi on my property?"

"I would be most happy to explain," she said, looking indignant. "Mr. Boxer insists that I live up to the terms of my contract, and that's exactly what I intend to do. As soon as Colton is rebuilt, I most certainly shall fulfill the terms of my contract."

He lifted his hat, brushed his hair back, and settled the hat back on his head. He wanted to know about possible trespassers, and she was talking about contracts. "Your difficulties with Mr. Boxer hardly explain the tipi."

"I need some sort of shelter."

His scowl deepened. "This is *your* tipi? Are you saying that you're going to *live* in this tipi?"

A worried frown crossed her face. "You don't mind, do you? You said I could stay here ... It wouldn't be proper for me to ..." She was talking so quickly, it was hard to keep up with what she was saying. "... And the wagon offers no protection against the weather and ... I promise you that I won't pose a problem."

"Well ... I ..." He cleared his throat and began again. "It hardly seems proper for a woman to live in a tipi."

"It's my understanding that Indian women find them quite comfortable. Besides, it will only be for a short while. Mr. Boxer said that as soon as he has acquired the appropriate funding, building will begin. I really don't have much of a choice."

He studied the tipi with dubious regard. He'd never before seen one this close. Lord, the thing was tall. Stood out like a sore thumb. Made his own soddy look like a pittance.

Still, size aside, it struck him as a strange abode, and for reasons he couldn't fully understand, he felt responsible for this woman's welfare. Certainly it wasn't an appropriate dwelling for the likes of Miss Percy, even if she was the most unconventional woman he'd ever met. Not that the soddy was that suitable, either.

"Of course, I expect to pay my way," she said.

"I wouldn't feel right accepting money from you."

"I'm mighty relieved to hear you say that. I have very little money, I'm afraid. But I do expect to pay my way nonetheless. I'm a rather good cook—or at least I was in Washington. I do suppose you can substitute buffalo for venison, don't you think? And rabbit for chicken?"

"I suppose so but . . ."

"And I really don't mind doing household chores, though I must admit, I've never seen so much dirt in all my born days."

"If you insist upon helping out, I suppose it would be all right." He wasn't at all certain he liked the idea of this eccentric woman taking over his house. Instinctively he knew that's exactly what she would do. Take over.

He tightened his jaw. The truth was, it wasn't his house he was worried about. His real concern was protecting Matthew. It had been a mistake to invite her to stay, though admittedly he had little choice in the matter.

If she stayed for very long, she would soon learn the awful truth about Matthew and himself. She had already witnessed one of Matthew's fits and was bound to witness more.

He walked around the tipi to where Matthew stood by the open flap, peering inside. Luke looked over his son's head. "Are you actually going to sleep in this thing?"

"That's my intention. Believe me, Mr. Tyler, you

won't even know I'm here. I won't be any problem to you at all."

She sounded sincere enough, but somehow he doubted that he would so easily be able to forget her presence.

He laid a hand on Matthew's shoulder and walked his young son toward the water barrel to wash up.

He handed Matthew the bar of lye soap. "Don't forget to wash behind your ears." Setting his hat on the wooden shelf, he cupped his hands and drew the cool and refreshing water to his face. He scrubbed his face and arms and grabbed a towel.

"All the way up to the elbows," he reminded his son absently, his eyes on the tipi. Maddie was nowhere to be seen, and he assumed she was inside. Leaving the towel behind, he quickly walked around to the front of the house.

He walked inside and froze in his tracks. Squinting against the dim light of late afternoon, he stared up at the bewildering display of ruffles and lace that covered the ceiling. Petticoats, he thought, baffled. Why would the woman tack her petticoats to his ceiling? He hardly had time to ponder the question before he noticed something even more startling. The table he had intended to give Catherine-Anne for her birthday filled a third of the tiny room, its lovely smooth surface polished to a glossy high sheen.

A bouquet of wildflowers spilled over the brim of a chipped china cup, filling the room with a sweet fragrance that all but obliterated the usual dank odor of wet sod. He forgot the dark, grim surroundings, but only for the moment it took him to shake off the dreamlike spell that momentarily captivated him.

It was dangerous for men like him to stray from reality. Dreams were a luxury he could not afford.

Nor could he afford the feelings of loneliness and

despair that surged from some previously unexplored part of him. He closed his eyes in an attempt to regain control, but this only made him more aware of the deep longing that welled up from somewhere within, awakening the dark recesses that were normally numb.

His senses spun in confusion. He tried to understand the emotions that assailed him but soon realized it was futile. He so seldom allowed himself to feel, he could barely put a name to the emotions that churned inside. Without a name, the emotions were impossible to fight.

He opened his eyes to the pretty white petticoats overhead, and dug his fingers into his palms. Feminine they were, intriguing, just like the woman.

He tightened his jaw. Now she'd done it. Made him feel things he had no business feeling.

He blinked against the vision that suddenly came to mind, a vision of her running free as a colt. *Made him think things he damned well better not be thinking.*

How dare she interfere with his life? Intrude in his thoughts? Rearrange his living quarters? What gave her the right?

He stormed outside, slamming the door shut behind him. What did he care if the ceiling collapsed?

Matthew barreled into him suddenly. Luke grabbed him by the shoulder and shook him once before releasing him. "Why don't you look where you're going?"

Matthew looked up with startled eyes. His freshly scrubbed face had such a worried expression that Luke fell back, crushed.

"I'm not angry at you, Matthew." He wrapped his arms around Matthew and hugged him, fighting against the cautionary voice that warned him to hold back. As always, the inner voice won. Quickly withdrawing his arms, Luke let his hands fall to his side. "Go in the house, Matthew. I'll be there in a few minutes."

Matthew ran inside, leaving the door ajar. Luke stood for a moment, struggling with the demons that still churned inside. He couldn't even say what he was angry about. Not the table, certainly. What then? Not that it made any difference. Anger might be a normal emotion for most people, but to him it was akin to a lethal weapon.

Falling back on years of practice, he took deep breaths until he felt his body relax. He forced himself to think of other things, mundane things, things he didn't care about, things that were far removed from Maddie or the past, or even Matthew.

It was only after he was convinced he had regained full control that he trusted himself enough to walk around the tipi and call her name. "Miss Percy."

Maddie stepped from her tipi, and he took another deep breath. "How dare you meddle in my affairs?" Realizing that his anger was beginning to flare again, he forced himself to lower his voice. "Why did you move that table from the barn?"

She studied his face for a moment, as if trying to puzzle something out. "It seemed like an awful waste . . ."

"That wasn't for you to decide . . ."

"I'm sorry, I . . ."

"Sorry? Do you actually think an apology will excuse your behavior?"

"My behavior?" Her eyes flashed with indignation. He had never known that eyes could be so green. "You make it sound like I committed a crime. I merely moved a table."

"Which you had no business doing!"

"I was thinking of Matthew . . ."

He stiffened, as if suddenly wounded. "What's Matthew got to do with this?"

It gave her some small measure of satisfaction to

watch the look of surprise cross his face. The surprise, at least, was spontaneous. She was disappointed to see his usual bland expression settle quickly back in place, for she could no longer read his emotions. At that moment she would have welcomed even his anger, for anything had to be better than the cool, detached look he now gave her.

"The old table was dangerous. I cut myself on it." She held up her hand and indicated the small wound on the side of her palm. "I was worried that Matthew might hurt himself too."

"Is your hand all right?"

"It's fine. Just a splinter."

He studied her face. "From this moment on, I must insist that any decision regarding my household or my son be cleared through me."

She lifted her chin. "As you wish."

"Then we understand each other."

"I don't know that we could go as far as to say that, Mr. Tyler."

A look of uncertainty and confusion fleeted across his face. He wasn't as much in control as he would like to think, and for reasons she couldn't begin to define, knowing this gave her great pleasure. She couldn't help but wonder what other emotions she could provoke in him.

For reasons she didn't understand, she had the most overwhelming need to find out.


The dining room table was hard to ignore. Not only did it take up more space than the other table, it stretched between them at suppertime like a chessboard during a high-stakes competition. Both made a gallant effort to make polite conversation, but it was hard to ignore the underlying current that seemed to punctuate their every word.

"Are those your petticoats, Miss Percy?" he asked finally. "Up there on my ceiling?"

Maddie had nothing but disregard for the bother-some garments that her mother had insisted she bring to Kansas.

"I'm glad to put those pesky things to good use," she declared. The yards of soft cotton fabric had worked better than she had hoped. For once, not a speck of dirt marred the table or seasoned their plates.

"I would like to . . ." His unspoken words hung be-tween them and she wondered why he felt the need to watch every word, every action, every smile, even. ". . . thank you."

"Does that mean you forgive me for the table?"

He met her gaze. "I was thanking you for the . . . ceiling."

*But not the table,* she thought. Not that it mattered. *She* thought it was a beautiful addition to the dreary dirt room, and she was convinced that once Luke had gotten used to the idea, he would agree.

The warm, rich wood glowed beneath the light of the lantern. Even Matthew seemed awed by the table. He kept rubbing his hand along the wood as if he couldn't quite believe he could do so safely.

At one point his father glanced up and frowned. "Eat your supper, Matthew."

When his father's admonitions failed to get Matthew to eat, Maddie tried to divert his attention from the ta-ble. She pointed to his untouched plate. "This recipe was given to me by Julia Grant, the wife of the presi-dent."

Maddie had devised a substitute for each of the orig-inal ingredients, and what resulted was unlike anything she'd ever tasted. Apparently buffalo required more cooking than venison, and the roots she found were a poor alternative for potatoes. The stew definitely required a great deal of chewing, but it was hearty, and the gravy, though thicker than she preferred, tasted quite good.

"You do know that Ulysses S. Grant is the president of the United States, don't you, Matthew? Nice man. He was once a farmer, just like your father." She met Luke's steady gaze. "Just shows that you never know what the future has in store. That's why it's important for *even* a farmer to have a good education."

"If I recall, Grant wasn't much of a farmer," Luke remarked. "If he'd given more attention to farming, he might not have had the misfortune of being in politics."

"Some people consider politics a noble profession," she argued.

"Some people think stealing land from the Indians is noble."

Conceding that he had a point, she continued to give Matthew a lesson on government. She explained the functions of the House and Senate, punctuating her discourse with lively comments and humorous anecdotes.

Matthew hung on to her every word, which only confirmed her earlier belief that the boy was intelligent and eager to learn

Luke made no further comment throughout the meal, but his gaze continued to travel from her to the ruffled ceiling and back again, as if he were trying to reconcile the two.

After they had finished eating, he stood. "I thoroughly enjoyed your *unbiased* explanation of how our government functions. I hate to bring this to an end, but I do have work to do."

"That's quite all right," Maddie said. "I think we've had enough talk of politics for one day."

Luke lit a lantern and carried it the short distance to

the barn. He hoped to finish putting up the wall that had toppled during the buffalo stampede.

He hung the lantern on a nail. A stack of lumber that had been left over from the table needed to be moved before he could begin hauling the sod blocks into place. Once the wall was replaced, he would be able to lock up the barn and he would no longer have to deal with the ghosts of the past.

He picked up a piece of lumber, then stopped to run his hand along the board's unfinished surface. He'd forgotten the satisfaction that came from taking a rough piece of wood and turning it into something beautiful and useful. He'd heard farmers express a similar sentiment about land. If that were true, then he wasn't cut out to be a farmer. He had poured his heart and soul into that land, and what did he have to show for it? Calloused hands and little else.

The furniture in the soddy, including the table and chairs, had been crafted from bird's-eye maple that he'd carted all the way from New York. This particular wood was so hard that it was near impossible to remove rough chips from its surface by conventional methods. It required the skillful use of a chisel.

He'd spent countless hours working on the table. Every night for weeks before Catherine-Anne's birthday, he'd locked himself in the barn. She pleaded with him to let her see his latest project, but he refused. It was to be a surprise, he told her. How could he possibly have guessed that she wouldn't live long enough to see her birthday, let alone the table?

Damn the table! He should have burned it. Maybe if he had, the ghosts would not have come back to haunt him.

He abandoned the wood and began heaving the heavy blocks of sod one on top of another. Nothing cleared the mind like hard physical labor. He had cut fresh sod earlier that day to replace the blocks that had crumbled during the stampede.

He worked until the wall of sod blocks reached the roofline. All that was left to do was to fill in the cracks with clay, and that could wait until tomorrow.

His body soaked with the sweat of his labors, he ached, literally ached, with exhaustion. He'd had trouble sleeping since his trip to Hays. But he would sleep tonight.

He doused the lantern and walked outside. He leaned his head against the barn door for a moment before slipping the rusty lock back into place.

His way lit by starlight, he turned to walk the short distance to the barrel of water to wash. Still distracted by thoughts of the past, he suddenly found himself jolted into an even more disturbing present.

The golden glow of a candle flickered inside the tipi, casting the shadow of the schoolteacher's feminine form against the buffalo sides as she undressed.

He was rendered breathless by the beautiful shapes that danced upon the tipi walls. His startled gaze traced a line along the soft swell of her lovely, round breasts. Her hips flared from her tiny waistline. He'd had no idea she had such long, shapely legs.

He felt a stirring in his loin, an answering cry from that same lonely and previously numbed part deep within that had made its presence known earlier. He closed his eyes, but when that failed to block out the lovely vision of her, he opened them again and stood mesmerized and overwhelmed by all that he saw.

He had no right, no right at all to intrude on her privacy. And even less right to give in to primitive desires and feelings. The last time his feelings had gone unchecked, a man had lost his life. Never again would he take the chance. Not as long as Gantry Tyler's cursed blood ran through his veins.

With this silent vow, he tore his gaze away from her loveliness and hurried to the rain barrel where he plunged the upper part of his fevered body headfirst into the frigid water.

# Chapter 11

The sound of gunfire ripped through the early-morning stillness. Luke's eyes flew open and focused on the feminine ruffles overhead. As always, his first thought was for Matthew, and he quickly checked to make certain the boy was still safely asleep by his side.

It was cold inside the soddy, and he was tempted to roll over and go back to sleep. But it had been his experience since coming to Kansas that the sound of gunfire was best not ignored. Not if a man valued his life or his property.

By the second shot he was on the floor and running. He grabbed his trousers and pulled them on as he did a one-legged hop across the room. With his trousers in place, he grabbed his hat, not bothering with a shirt. His senses alert, he listened a moment before inching the door open.

Another shot sounded and he ducked back against the wall, waited a moment, then slipped outside. He quickly scanned the area. His back against the front of the house, he edged forward and peered around the corner.

Miss Percy stood not twenty feet away, aiming a pistol at the pile of wood scraps. Her head was turned away from her target as she fired, her eyes closed. The blast hit the ground amid an explosion of dirt, causing a stir in the nearby chicken coop. Her horse, Rutabaga, shook its head and gave a low whicker. The cow bellowed from behind the soddy.

Dropping his arms to his side, Luke stepped away from the house.

He walked toward her, shaking his head, half in amusement, half in disbelief. He rested his bare foot on the splintered fence railing and leaned his elbow against his thigh.

Maddie opened her eyes and grinned at him. "What do you think?"

Luke lifted his hat, pushed back his disheveled hair, and let his hat drop back in place until the brim covered his forehead. "Unless you were aiming for the ground, you missed."

"I wasn't aiming for anything," she said. "I was simply preparing myself in the event of an unfriendly attack."

Luke let his gaze linger on the spot where her bullet had hit the ground. "I've been here for four years, and I've yet to see the ground attack anyone."

She gave him a cool, appraising look. "I was talking about Indians or wild animals. I have no intention of letting a man or animal lay a hand ... ah ... paw on me." Her rosy cheeks seem to grow a shade darker as he took in her figure. He couldn't help himself. Not after last night. Not after seeing the smooth, hard lines of her body exposed.

She blew on the barrel of the gun. "Nor do I intend to allow myself to be scalped!"

Luke's gaze flickered over her gleaming red hair before he realized he faced mortal danger. The barrel of her gun was pointed directly at a part of his anatomy that was second only to the heart in terms of where a man least wanted to be shot. Some said they'd rather get shot in the heart.

"I do believe, Miss Percy, that you have found a most effective way to safeguard your virtue."

A puzzled frown crossed her face. She looked down at her gun and followed an imaginary line from the barrel to the spot beneath his waist. "Oh!" she exclaimed. It amused him to see her look so flustered. She moved the barrel in another direction.

Feeling greatly relieved, he let his foot drop and hooked his thumbs into his pants pockets. "Of course, you still have the scalping problem to worry a . . ." Her gun fired, exploding in a loud blast. Luke's hat blew off his head. Something ripped across his scalp.

Paling, he grabbed his head with both hands. For a long moment, he and the schoolteacher stared at each other, neither one able to speak.

When Luke finally managed to convince himself that his brains were still in their rightful place, he lowered his arms, slowly. Praise the Lord, he was still standing. He reached over and picked up his hat. A clump of shiny black hair fell to the ground at his feet.

"I do believe you have everything covered, Miss Percy. Scalp the Indians before they scalp you. It's so damned simple, it might just work."

Maddie dropped her arm to her side, the gun pointing at the ground. "I apologize, Mr. Tyler," she said in a tremulous voice. "I had no idea these weapons were so sensitive."

"They aren't half as sensitive as my head." He examined his straw hat. Normally, he gave his hat a good whack against his thigh whenever it flew off, either by design or accident. But thinking the hat had enough abuse for one day, he gingerly brushed it off. The bullet had left a hole at the base of the brim. A half inch lower and it wouldn't have mattered that his manhood remained intact.

"Do you suppose I would do better with a different type of gun?"

"I think you'd do better with no gun," He put on the hat, adjusting the brim to make certain no further damage had been done. He then seized the weapon from her. "Where did you get this relic?"

"From a gentleman in Hays."

"Would that happen to be the same *gentleman* who sold you the tipi?"

"The very same one," she admitted. "Would you like to try it?"

"What?"

"The gun. Would you like to see how it works?"

He'd never touched a gun in his life until he came to Kansas. He hadn't dared to. Not with his family background. He learned to use a gun that first winter. It was either that or let his family starve to death. His family pretty near starved to death anyway, but he gave it his best effort. Since that first disastrous winter, he preferred trading corn and dairy products for his meat, leaving the hunting to others. Now he aimed the gun at the woodpile and fired. A chip of wood flew upward, a good six inches from his intended target.

"Not bad." She looked impressed. Obviously, she had no idea what a bad shot he was, and he wasn't about to tell her. She hesitated a moment. "Perhaps you would be kind enough to give me some instruction?"

"I could try, I suppose."

Her gaze lingered momentarily upon his bare chest. As if aware that he was watching her, she quickly averted her eyes.

Although he often worked shirtless in the fields, he felt oddly exposed. The outline of her naked body flashed into his mind's eye, but he quickly pushed it away. When that failed to work, he purposefully inventoried her deficiencies. Tall and skinny. Almost tawdry in appearance. Definitely not his type.

However, tallying her negative traits made it perfectly clear that the parts did not add up to the whole. She was altogether pleasing to the eye. Too gosh-darn pleasing.

"I didn't have time to finish dressing," he explained apologetically. "If you like, I could . . ." He motioned toward the soddy.

Her eyes met his. "You needn't bother on my account. I was concerned that you might catch cold."

He wasn't feeling cold. Not a bit. "I'm used to it. You . . . you weren't cold, were you?"

Cold?"

"Last night. In the tipi . . ." Dammit, why did he have to mention the tipi? He tried to think of a way to cover his error. "Did . . . did you have enough blankets?"

"Yes, thank you. I was most comfortable."

A moment of silence stretched between them. She was the one who broke it. "You were going . . ."

"Yes, yes, of course." He felt strangely awkward and self-conscious.

He stood behind her. Lord, he'd never stood by such a tall woman. As tall as he was, there was only five, maybe six inches difference between them. No wonder her legs had looked so damned long last night. You couldn't tell normally. Not with the ridiculous, though admittedly fetching, outfit she wore.

He was aware of the energy that seemed to flow from her. Her movements were brisk and confident as she took the gun from him. Considering her lack of skill, he had no idea what she had to be confident about. He was a fine one to talk. He had no business teaching anyone how to use a weapon.

He slipped his hand around her slender waist and

lifted her arm upward until it was even with her shoulder. By George, she was as thin as a pole and just as firm. Hadn't anyone told her that men liked more substance to their women? More roundness?

"Now target something." Still, she had a lovely, fresh fragrance, and she didn't feel all that bad in his arms. "See that piece of wood? Aim for the knot."

He tightened his hand against hers. Come to think of it, she felt mighty nice. "Fire!"

She did as she was told, and a chunk flew off the targeted spot. He narrowed his eyes to make certain he wasn't seeing things. The target was gone, all right.

"See?" he said, trying to sound as if shooting came easy to him. "That wasn't so hard now, was it?" She glanced back over her shoulder, and for an instant he couldn't breathe.

"You're hurting me, Mr. Tyler."

He blinked. "What?"

"My hand . . ."

His mouth went dry, and he quickly loosened his hold on her. "I'm sorry. I didn't mean to hurt you." He swallowed hard and fought the sudden urge to flee. "Do . . . do you want to try again?"

She nodded slightly and turned her head toward the woodpile. Head against her shoulder, he tried to focus on the gun. "Pick out your target."

"I want to hit that L-shaped piece of wood," she said.

"Fire."

This time she missed the target by a mile.

"Try it again!" he insisted. "And this time keep your eyes open."

She moved away from him and looked straight into his eyes. She was something, all right. Proud and high-spirited. The two qualities one would look for in a horse. Hell, if she were a horse, he'd think she was purebred Arabian. With this thought came the memory of her running in carefree abandon around his house, her hair streaming behind her, her face lifted toward the sky.

She shoved the gun in his hand and brushed her hands together as if relieved to be free of the worrisome weapon. "It isn't right," she declared.

"What . . . isn't right?"

"The gun. I don't feel comfortable using it. Should I have occasion to meet any unfriendly Indians, I shall just have to use diplomatic tactics."

"I'm sure the Cheyennes will be greatly relieved to hear of your decision."

She let out a gasp. Thinking she'd seen another snake, he quickly checked the ground around his bare feet. "What's the matter?"

No sooner had he asked the question than he realized they were no longer alone. A short distance away, a group of Cheyennes sat watching them from atop their ponies.

"What do you suppose they want?" she stammered. She dug her fingers into his bare arm.

"I have no idea," he said. The Indians had previously kept their distance from him—although he had heard of occasions when some of them had visited other farms in the area.

"They're pointing at something," she said.

He narrowed his eyes from beneath the still dusty brim of his hat. "They're pointing at your tipi. I just hope that damned drummer who sold it to you didn't steal it."

The Indians rode closer. "What should we do?" she whispered.

"I'm not sure," he whispered back. "But whatever those diplomatic tactics are that you talked about earlier, I hope you're prepared to use them."

There were nine Cheyennes in all. They kept their distance, but it was clear that Maddie was the object of their interest. The Indians pointed at Maddie and the tipi, and their laughter rang out.

Resenting their derision, she balled her fists at her sides. "What is the matter with them? What's so funny?"

"I suspect they find it amusing that a white woman is living in a tipi."

"Humph," she sniffed. "If you ask me, it's most unmannerly to laugh at someone. Actually, it's downright rude."

"Laughing may be rude, as you call it, but it's a lot more preferable than some other behavior I can think of."

As quickly as they had appeared, the Indians rode off, leaving a cloud of dust behind them.

Maddie glared after them. "Of all the nerve."

"Now that our visitors have gone, I'd better see to Matthew. Would you like some coffee?"

"In a while. It's time for my morning exercise. Would you mind taking that gun? I don't think I'll be using it again."

"Yes, of course." Gun in hand, he headed toward the soddy, but he couldn't resist glancing back at her when he reached the door.

What he saw brought a smile to his face. There she was, walking with her usual urgent stride, her arms swinging back and forth, her back so straight she looked like she had swallowed a stick. Commanding was what she was. Most commanding.

Earlier, she'd looked vulnerable with that damned weapon in her hand. But at the moment she looked plain formidable. It was a paradox the way she looked helpless with a weapon and formidable without it.

Fortunately her back was toward him, so she couldn't see the laughter on his face.

One, two, three. She counted silently as she picked up her pace.

Handsome, two, three. Too conventional for her taste, though. One, two . . . his arms around her waist had felt good.

She slowed to almost a standstill before she realized she'd lost her stride. Muttering, she forced herself to concentrate. "One, two, three. Nice . . . chest . . . Three."

Great eyes. Her mind wandered for a moment as she tried to think of a way to describe their deep blue color. Where was she? Oh, yes, one, two, three . . .

She circled the soddy the twenty-five times she had allotted herself, then glanced in the direction the Indians had gone. Satisfied that no prying eye remained, she began her morning calisthenics. Touching her fingers to her toes, she tried to reconcile the contradictory opinions that kept popping into her head about one Luke Tyler.

# Chapter 12

Luke filled the coffeepot with newly ground coffee beans, water, and eggshells and gave his sleeping son a gentle nudge. "Come on, Matthew. Time to get up. We have a full day of work ahead of us."

Matthew stretched and yawned, then rolled over and pulled the blanket over his head.

Shaking his head fondly at the boy, Luke walked over to the stove to start breakfast. He couldn't resist taking a look out the window. He peeled away the oil paper at the edge of the glass pane and narrowed his eyes in the direction of the woodpile.

She was doing her exercises, just as she'd said she would, and he watched her bend gracefully at the waist, then stretch her arms over her head. Her tall, lean body was as supple as a young sapling swaying in the wind. Again he was reminded of the vision of her naked body on the walls of her tipi. Suddenly he couldn't breathe.

He replaced the oil paper and turned. Matthew stood peering out the door toward Maddie, a smile on his face.

The smile warmed Luke's heart, but only for the instant it took for him to realize the worrisome implications. It wouldn't be good for the boy to form an attachment to the eccentric schoolteacher. Matthew had already suffered one loss. Luke didn't want to think what another loss could do to his son. To them both.

"Matthew!" His voice, coming from some deep-rooted fear, was far more harsh than the situation warranted. He felt immediate remorse when the boy turned to him, the smile gone from his face. He wanted so much to take the boy in his arms and explain.

*Explain what?* he thought bitterly. *That we are two of a kind? That neither one of us can ever allow ourselves to get too close to anyone because of who we're related to.*

Luke's voice grew hoarse with regret. "Breakfast will be ready in a few minutes."

It seemed so much lighter in the room than usual. It was the petticoats, he decided. It was something in the way the frilly white material reflected the otherwise inadequate sunlight that filtered through the window. He reached above his head to finger the soft fabric, yanking his hand away when the door flew open.

Maddie stomped into the room, and the last of the lingering shadows seemed to dissolve in her presence.

All during breakfast, Maddie used every possible opportunity to work a fact of historical interest into the conversation. She did it so glibly that at first Luke thought it was only by chance.

But he soon realized that Miss Maddie Percy did nothing by chance. She knew exactly what she was doing. She was giving his son a thorough education in the War between the States. She cited so many facts and figures, Luke's head began to ache. How in the world did she remember all those statistics?

"Did you have occasion to fight in the war, Mr. Tyler?"

"No," he said, his voice a sharp edge, "did you?" The question was meant in jest, but she treated it seriously.

"Unfortunately not," she replied, and much to his surprise, her voice was filled with regret. "It had something to do with my equipment."

Thinking he'd not heard right, he blinked, only to find her looking at him with undeniable challenge in her eyes. Equipment? Like the kind he'd seen reflected upon the tipi walls . . . ?

Lord Almighty, was she flirting with him? It was hard to know. In any case, he had no intention of pursuing the topic she'd introduced, no matter how intriguing or tempting. He pushed his chair away from the table and stood. "It's time we got to work, Matthew."

It was all he could to keep from running out the door. Once outside, he took a deep, steadying breath.

The sky was blue, with only a few white clouds skimming lightly overhead. The prairie stretched peacefully in every direction. There was no sign of fire. Equally important, there was no sign of the dust that would indicate visitors.

Since his trip to Hays a few days earlier, Claudia Hancock's threat remained very much on his mind. His greatest fear was that someone would come and take Matthew away from him. Would Claudia carry out her threat? He didn't know, but just in case, he intended to keep Matthew in sight at all times.

With a deep sigh, he slipped the bridle over his horse's head and led the animal toward his wagon.

Matthew and Miss Percy walked out of the soddy hand in hand, and they appeared to be enjoying a private joke. He envied the easy rapport that had developed so readily between the two. His own relationship with Matthew, though loving, was of necessity less demonstrative.

Damn, how he hated the man who was his father! He had never met the man, but he hated him nonetheless, and bile filled his mouth as he recalled the many reasons why.

Luke couldn't so much as hug his own son without questioning his own worth. He was afraid to love a woman like a man was surely meant to love one. Not that he had any interest in loving a woman, of course. None.

Seeing her shadow fall by his side, he asked, "What are your plans today, Miss Percy?"

"I'd feel much better if you would call me Maddie."

He'd never known a Maddie before, but it suited her in some odd way. "Very well, Maddie."

A silence stretched between them, and he sensed her waiting for him to ask her to return the favor. Well, she would have to ask him outright, and he doubted that even she would be that forward.

"Do you mind if I call you Luke?"

He stiffened, but he kept his back toward her as he checked the harness. "If you wish."

"It seems less formal, don't you think? Since we're living together."

He glanced back over his shoulder, hoping she had the good grace to blush. She didn't. Lord, were there no limits to what the woman would say or do?

He swung up onto the seat of the wagon and waited for Matthew to climb aboard.

"Luke . . ." His name tripped off her tongue smoothly, as if it had every right to be there. "If you would like, you may leave Matthew with me for the day. I shall be more than happy to teach him his letters and finish our little history lesson." She smiled and patted Matthew on the leg as he climbed into his seat.

Matthew turned his face toward his dad, his eyes bright with eagerness. Luke felt like a heel having to deny the boy's unspoken request, but he had no choice.

"That won't be necessary, Miss . . . Maddie."

"But I have all this free time on my hands . . ."

"Which I'm sure you'll put to good use." With that, he drove away.

Matthew looked so disappointed as he waved to her, she almost regretted having suggested the idea in the first place.

Almost, but not quite. As a teacher, she believed it her right to speak up in a child's behalf.

She hoisted herself up on an upturned barrel and wondered what she was going to do with all the time on her hands.

A cloud of dust in the distance drew her attention away from her thoughts. She jumped to the ground and shaded her eyes against the sun, then cast a quick glance in the direction Luke had gone. His wagon was no longer visible. It was up to her to handle the visitors.

She watched the approaching horses with increasing anxiety. Even though she couldn't really tell from this distance, she was convinced the Cheyennes had returned. It wasn't long before her suspicions were confirmed.

Whether they were the same Indians who had made an earlier appearance during her shooting lesson was hard to determine.

One of them, who appeared to be the leader, left the others behind and rode his pony toward her. His long black hair fell to his shoulders in two thick braids. He dismounted his pony and spoke to her in his native tongue.

Maddie was more curious than frightened. He didn't seem to be threatening. She made an attempt not to stare at the inadequate loincloth or the dark, naked thighs. The Indian made no such attempt to keep from staring at her trousers.

He pounded on his chest with his hand, and it occurred to her that he was trying to tell her his name. He spread his arms outward and looked to be imitating a bird in flight. Feeling a surge of excitement, Maddie thought of something. "Wait!" She held up the palm of her hand to indicate what she wanted him to do, then dashed inside her tipi.

Dropping to her knees in front of the trunk, she rifled through her belongings until she found a portfolio of drawings of wildlife that she used in her classroom.

In the time it took her to find what she was looking for and rush back outside, the remainder of the Cheyennes joined their leader and were standing together in a small knot.

She laid her portfolio on the ground next to their moccasined feet and searched through the pictures. Upon finding the one she wanted, she held it up for all to see. It was a picture of a hawk. The leader snatched the picture out of her hands and began stabbing it with a finger.

"Your name is Hawk?" It was more of a statement than a question. Then remembering his arms, she spread her own arms outward. "Flying Hawk."

The Indian repeated after her. "Flying Hawk."

She held up each picture in turn. The deer brought an immediate reaction from one of the other Indians, who nodded his head vigorously and pointed to himself.

"Your name must be—" she glanced at the picture "—Deer. Or is it Running Deer?" She ran in place to demonstrate.

The Indian followed her example. He was surprisingly light-footed. "Running . . . Deer."

Gradually, she was able to put a name to the remaining Indians through use of the pictures. The elephant caused much laughter and discussion among them. She could only assume that they had never seen such an animal.

Flying Hawk handed her the pictures and pointed to her. "My name is Maddie," she said. "And I have no picture to show you." She pointed to herself. "Maddie."

Flying Hawk stabbed the photos and barked out something that sounded threatening. "No picture!" she barked back, refusing to let him intimidate her.

The Indians looked disbelieving, and the one she now called Running Deer grabbed a picture of an ostrich and pointed to its long, skinny legs, and the balloonlike bulk of its body. He then pointed to Maddie's trousers and her short, full skirt. Obviously he saw a comparison.

Maddie conceded with a good-natured grin. "Have it your way." She held up the ostrich for all to see and said the word with distinct emphasis.

"Ostrich!" they repeated in unison.

She'd been called many things in her life, but never an ostrich. The little group of Cheyennes were so childlike in their delight that the last of her fears left her, and instead of taking offense, she was soon laughing along with them.

For Luke, it had been a long, hard day in the fields. The buffalo and grama grass were less tall than grasses that grew further east. In this part of Kansas the grasses grew thick and the roots went deep into the sod, requiring much in the way of man and machinery to conquer.

Luke usually waited until the sun set before heading for home. Today, however, the sun was still fairly high in the sky when he called to Matthew and motioned him to the wagon.

Matthew looked surprised and glanced westward as if to check the time. He then tossed the handle of his hoe over his shoulder and started toward the wagon.

"You did a good job, son." Luke gave his son a gentle pat on the back.

Matthew rewarded him with a lopsided grin, threw the hoe into the back of the wagon, and began chasing a butterfly.

Luke stood watching his son and fought back the urge to grab him and hold him close. *Be careful,* Luke's mother had cautioned him whenever he'd given in to any childish need to be close to her. *Mustn't show your feelings.*

Damn it! He wanted to show his feelings. Did she know how it had felt to be constantly rebuffed by her? His father was the criminal, not him.

As if he guessed Luke's tortured thoughts, Matthew abandoned the butterfly and tugged on Luke's hand. Luke knelt down and wrapped both arms around Matthew, resisting the urge to hug his small son with complete abandon.

*Be careful.* Today, as always, his mother's words echoed from the distant past. *You must never forget who your father was and what he was capable of doing. You must never allow his evil ways to come out in you.*

He cradled Matthew's face gently between his

hands. "Why can't you speak, son? Why can't you tell me what's in your heart?"

It was a question he'd asked himself more times than he could remember.

According to the doctors Luke had consulted shortly after Catherine-Anne's death, it was quite possible for the vocal cords to stop functioning after a severe shock to the system.

Although the doctors couldn't tell him if his son would ever speak again, they did say that the longer he remained mute, the less his chances for a full recovery.

It had already been two years. Two long, interminably long, years. How he longed to hear his son's voice again. He couldn't remember the last time he'd heard Matthew laugh aloud. At this point, he would settle for a grunt. Anything would be better than the unnatural silence.

His heart heavy, he released his son, hopped onto the wagon, and grabbed the reins. He was tired, he told himself. That's why he'd called it a day so early. It had nothing to do with Matthew, nothing at all to do with that nightmarish trip to Hays three days before. It had even less to do with the schoolteacher.

Still, he didn't feel tired. His body felt alert and more energetic than it had felt in months, maybe years.

*Wonder what she's up to?* Not that it mattered to him, of course. But there was so little diversion in his life these days. And she was indeed a diversion. A mighty interesting one, at that.

If he hadn't been straining his eyes to catch sight of her, he wouldn't have noticed anything amiss from such a long distance.

Thinking he must be seeing things, he stopped the

wagon and stared across the flat prairie land to where his soddy stood.

His eyes wide with disbelief, he could do nothing but stare. Unless he was seeing things, the whole Cheyenne tribe was camped on his doorstep!

# Chapter 13

He forced himself to calm down as he waved his arms to get her attention. "Miss Percy . . . Maddie . . ." He rose on tiptoe, his arms over his head. "May I have a word with you?"

She was standing amid a group of half-naked Indians. At the sound of his voice, she looked up. "Yes, Luke, what is it?"

He stared at her incredulously. "What is it?" Fifty or more tipis stood on his property, and she asked *What is it*? He couldn't even locate his own soddy for all the tipis and ponies. "If you will afford me a moment of your time, I shall be more than happy to enlighten you!"

She said something to the Indians, made some exaggerated gestures with her hands, and left amid a roar of laughter.

His eyes widened. Since when had she learned sign language? He'd been gone for little more than eight hours. How in the world had she managed all this in such a short time?

He waited for her to join him, then took her by the arm and led her behind the barn, where they could speak in relative privacy. "What is the meaning of this?"

"You mean the Indians?" she asked. "They're attending school."

She spoke so matter-of-factly, one would think that teaching Indians was a normal, everyday occurrence. "You're teaching school? To all these Indians? Here? On my property?"

A look of concern crossed her face. "Is that a problem?"

He glanced over her shoulder to the gathering of Indians, who were obviously waiting for their teacher to return. "Of course it's a problem. Whenever a hundred people move onto one's doorstep, it's a problem."

"If you like, I'll explain that they can't camp here."

"That's downright thoughtful of you."

"I'll insist that they come during the daylight hours only. I'll make certain they're gone by the time you return from the fields."

"Yes, well, make certain that you do." He turned and, motioning for Matthew to follow him, zigzagged his way around several tipis in search of his soddy. He finally found it, but was obliged to walk around a young eagle attached to a rope before he could enter.

Inside the house, he dipped the ladle into the bucket of water and drank. He was thirsty and his head ached. What, he wondered, would be next?

Matthew walked in, carrying a bucket of buffalo chips he'd gathered earlier in the fields.

"Thanks, son." Luke stoked up the fire in the woodstove and put a kettle of water on to boil.

No sooner had the water come to a boil than a knock sounded at the door, and Maddie's voice filtered into the room. "They're gone."

He opened the door and glanced outside. It was astonishing how quickly the Indians had disappeared, taking their tipis, ponies—everything—with them. "So they are."

"I planned to cook dinner," she said.

"That won't be necessary."

"We agreed that I would cook and do light house-keeping to pay my way."

In no mood to argue with her, he nodded in assent and she followed him inside.

Watching her at the cookstove, he had to admit that the woman, with all her eccentricities, could cook—though she had a terrible time keeping the fire going.

"You have to keep adding fuel," he explained. He grabbed several dried buffalo chips from a wooden barrel and tossed them into the fire well.

Maddie lifted a chip from the barrel. "I've never seen firewood like this. What kind of tree is it?"

"A bison tree," he said.

"A bison . . ." She looked at him suspiciously. "You mean . . . ?"

"We don't waste anything out here, do we, Matthew?"

He ruffled his son's hair and in so doing accidentally brushed against her arm. She quickly turned her head to look up at him. The heat from the stove brought a faint flush to her cheeks.

His eyes flickered involuntarily to her soft pink lips before he stepped back. "The chips burn quicker than wood," he explained.

She turned her attention to the steaming black pot on the stove. "So I noticed. They also burn hot and make a lot of ashes."

She overcooked the rolls, but the boiled buffalo meat smelled delicious, and somehow she managed to make the table, chipped dishes and all, look inviting.

"I have another petticoat in my trunk," she said as she stirred the stew. "If you like, we can hang it on the wall over the bed."

He almost knocked over the lantern.

"It'll keep the dirt from falling onto your pillow," she added.

He lifted his eyes to meet hers. "Perhaps it would be better to hang it on the wall by the stove. To keep the dirt out of the food."

"That's a good idea," she agreed.

Her gaze traveled involuntarily toward the bed. She wondered which of the two feathered pillows was his. Not that it was any business of hers, she thought, quickly pulling her eyes away.

"Next time I go into town, I'll pick up some muslin. We could cover the walls like you did the ceiling." He glanced around the room, seeing it perhaps for the first time in years. "You must think this house . . . ugly."

"Ugly?" Her luminous eyes grew round. "I don't think it's ugly. Actually it's rather interesting and makes me think of home."

"Home?" He'd never been to the nation's capital, but even so, the idea struck him as ludicrous. "Home as in Washington?"

"Come here and I'll show you what I mean." She ran a finger along the sod wall next to the stove. "Do you see those white veins running through the sod?"

He leaned forward. "Those are the roots from the buffalo grass. That's what makes this sod so tough."

"It might look like roots to you, but to me it looks like marble. Prairie marble."

He laughed. "Prairie marble, eh?"

Their eyes met, and it suddenly occurred to him he was blocking her way. He cleared his throat and took a step backward.

She picked up a platter of meat and set it on the table next to the bowl of greens. "Matthew, did you wash up?"

Matthew nodded and slipped into his seat.

Luke held her chair out for her before taking his own place.

"I never realized that Indians were so interested in

learning!" she said. "But I have never in my life seen so many obese people. Do you know how thoroughly unhealthy it is to be so misshapen?" She forked a small piece of meat onto Matthew's plate before passing the platter to Luke. "Do you suppose it's the buffalo meat that makes them so ponderously overweight?"

Luke heaped his plate high with meat. "Even if it is, you aren't going to change their diet." He studied the bowl she handed him, and tried to put a name to the stringy vegetable.

"Dandelion greens," she explained.

He made no comment as he took a heaping spoonful. "I've heard many people complain about the Indians, but you're the first I've heard show concern for their health."

"Maybe it's high time someone did show a bit of concern." She lifted her chin determinedly. "I think I'll conduct a class in nutrition and health for the Cheyennes."

Luke put a forkful of the dandelions in his mouth and grimaced. If this was her idea of nutrition, the Indians had best play hooky.

After the supper dishes were washed and stacked on the shelves, Luke went outside to work on the barn wall.

Maddie considered withdrawing to her tipi, but she felt reluctant to leave the boy alone. Obviously, Matthew was able to put himself to bed, but she remembered the bedtime rituals of her own youth, especially when her dear father was home, and it saddened her to think of Matthew's lonely existence.

"Would you like me to tell you a story?"

Matthew nodded, and she tried to think of a suitable bedtime story to tell. It suddenly occurred to her that the stories her father had told her when she was Matthew's age inevitably involved his narrow escapes from cannibals and other savage tribes in Africa.

She had never questioned the appropriateness of such stories, and indeed had begged for more. The more gruesome, the better. She was hard-pressed to think of a story that didn't involve danger or death-defying escapes.

"Have you ever seen an elephant?" she asked.

He shook his head.

"Here, I'll draw you one." She picked up her notepad and pencil and proceeded to sketch a picture of the animal.

Matthew was totally absorbed in the picture that was taking shape on the paper. "My father captured one of these for the Smithsonian," she explained. "I bet you never saw a kangaroo either, did you?" She drew the animal. "Strange animals. They have a pouch to carry their young ones."

She pushed the notepad in front of him. "Why don't you draw something?" When he appeared reluctant, she nodded encouragement. "You can do it."

Matthew took the pencil from her, but had trouble holding it properly.

"Like this," she said, moving his fingers into the proper grip. "Now try it."

He drew a simple but excellent picture of a buffalo. "That's very good," she said. "What else can you draw?"

He thought for a minute before drawing a windmill, identical to the one outside. He impressed her with his attention to detail. "Are you able to write your name? Can you write Matthew?"

He shook his head.

"Let me show you." She took the pencil and wrote his name out in bold letters. "M-A-T-T-H-E-W. Now you do it."

Matthew took the pencil and tried to copy the letters she'd written for him. When it was obvious he was having trouble, she took his hand and helped him to make the various shapes in the air. "Now try it on paper."

This time he managed to write the letter "M" without difficulty. She felt a surge of excitement. "That's wonderful, Matthew. Now try an 'A.' " She held her breath as he worked.

When he was finished, he glanced up at Maddie, seeking her approval. "Oh, Matthew." She squeezed him tight and planted an exuberant kiss on his forehead.

He looked so startled by her spontaneous display of affection, she couldn't help but laugh. "Don't tell me you're getting to that age when you don't want to be kissed and hugged," she said. "Well, never mind. You'll get over it soon enough. What do you say you try the letter 'T'?"

Matthew did as she asked him. Much to her delight, he insisted that she give him another hug before he proceeded to repeat his efforts and write the second "T."

While Matthew labored over his name, Maddie's mind raced with all sorts of wonderful possibilities. If he could write his name, then perhaps he could learn to write other words. If he could write, he could tell them what he was thinking. Perhaps offer a key as to why he couldn't talk. It would truly be a miracle!

"Oh, Matthew!" She flung her arms around him and hugged him tight. He greeted this latest show of spontaneous affection with a startled look before hugging her back.

Luke had planned to spend the evening troweling clay into the crevices between the sod blocks. He had never intended to work on bookshelves. But it seemed a shame to waste the stack of maple left over from the table and chairs.

He'd almost forgotten the satisfaction that came from working with wood. Any imperfections could be overcome by jack-planing a board, rough edges smoothed away by sanding. Why couldn't life be that simple? Have a moral weakness? Whack! An ill temper? Gone!

He recalled that during the years of his youth spent learning his trade, he used to pretend that if he made a scrap of wood perfect, it would reflect upon him in some favorable way. He never could achieve perfection, of course, but he never gave up trying. That was the challenge of working with wood.

He'd been at work for almost two hours when the barn door behind him squeaked open. His hand stilled on the wood plane and he glanced over his shoulder. Thinking it was Matthew come to say good night, it surprised him to find Maddie standing in the doorway. "Is something wrong?"

She shook her head. "Matthew's asleep."

"So soon?" He felt a surge of guilt that he had not gone inside to tuck his son in bed.

"He was tired." Her eyes took in the piece of wood he was working on. "I was just curious as to what you were doing."

"Working on bookshelves."

She ran her hand across the smooth, unfinished wood. Her hand was large for a woman's hand, but as gentle as it was capable. "They'll be beautiful."

"Not too practical, I'm afraid. Matthew and me ... we only have two books."

"I brought some with me," she replied. "Books I use for teaching." After a moment or two of silence, she added, "It seems a shame that you don't utilize your woodworking skills more. I mean it, Luke. You really are talented."

"I used to own a woodworking shop."

"What made you give it up to come here?"

"I had my reasons."

She sensed the change in him immediately. It was like clouds that suddenly blotted out a sunny sky. She forced a light tone. "Now I remember. You're trying to live down a bad reputation. Same as I am."

Their eyes locked. "Not much call for furniture out here," he said at last. "Finding wood is a challenge. I carted this piece all the way from New York."

"New York? Is that where you're from?"

He nodded, then leaned over a plank of lumber that was supported by two barrels and ran the plane across the surface.

"Luke . . . I . . ."

He glanced up.

"May I speak openly with you?"

He straightened. "Have you ever spoken less?"

So already he had learned that about her. "Not intentionally. It's about Matthew." A look of wariness crossed his face, as if he might fear what she had to say.

"I think your son is exceedingly intelligent." The lines on his face softened, and she sensed his relief. So this isn't what he thought she'd come to say. What, then?

He wiped his arm across his forehead. "You'll get no argument from me on that score."

"He needs a proper education."

"And you think you can give it to him?"

"Yes, I do."

"Can you teach him to talk?"

"I don't know."

He raised an eyebrow. "You don't know?"

"All right, maybe not."

"What about farming? Can you teach him to farm?"

"No, I can't teach him to farm. But I can teach him to be a better farmer. I can teach him to write."

"You want to teach him to write?"

"And to read."

"My son has a low frustration threshold. The doctors have advised me against putting him in situations that are too difficult or too challenging for him."

"Are you saying that he's not to be challenged?"

"I'm only telling you what the doctors told me."

"I do not frustrate my students. My intention is to teach Matthew only that which he is ready to learn."

"I think I have a better understanding as to how much Matthew is capable of learning." A sigh so deep and urgent as to be almost a sob escaped him. "Maddie . . ." It was the first time her name sounded natural on his lips. "I appreciate your offer, but I'm afraid it's out of the question." He resumed working on the bookshelves, a clear indication that the subject was closed.

She took a deep breath and, taking her cue, walked out into the dark prairie night.

# Chapter 14

The following morning Luke rolled over in bed and tried to make sense of the insistent voice that had roused him from a deep sleep. Once he determined the source, he groaned and rubbed his forehead. Now what? What could she possibly be doing at this ungodly hour?

"One, two, three . . . Breathe in. Breathe, I said."

He sat up. Was someone having trouble breathing? Next to him Matthew was still asleep. Who, then, could be having trouble?

He slipped out of bed and plodded the short distance to the door.

"One, two, three . . ."

Cracking the door open, he peered outside. The sight that greeted him made his heart skip a beat. Maddie was doing her usual morning calisthenics, with one small exception; the entire Cheyenne tribe was exercising along with her. Or so it seemed to his sleep-dazed eyes.

Shaking his head in disbelief, he stepped outside to have a better look. He rubbed his eyes and watched as she led the Indians through the most unbelievable contortions imaginable. With her usual supple grace, she stretched her arms skyward, then bent over to touch her toes.

The Indians tried to follow her lead. But they were

neither graceful nor supple, and the loud grunts reminded Luke of a hog farm he had once had occasion to visit.

Maddie was obviously not impressed. "Breathe!" she called, her voice stern yet encouraging. "You can do it!"

Luke clenched his fists by his side. He supposed he should be grateful that no one's life was in danger, but he wasn't feeling particularly charitable at the moment. Irritated. Annoyed, perhaps. He had been denied an hour's sleep—and for what? For some potbellied Indians, that's what. He was tempted to work his fingers around that pretty neck of hers and . . . kiss her!

The thought, coming out of nowhere, did nothing for his already surly disposition. What was he thinking of? The annoying woman was not even his type. He preferred his women demure and ladylike. There was certainly nothing demure or the least bit ladylike about this loudmouthed, interfering schoolmarm. Nothing!

With this last thought firmly in place, he stomped back into the soddy to begin breakfast. In his haste he forgot to close the door gently, and a clod of dirt fell upon the stove. Cursing beneath his breath, he woke Matthew and then started the coffee.

Maddie was still leading the Cheyennes through a series of stretching exercises a short while later when he and Matthew prepared to leave for the field.

Matthew stood by his father's wagon and took in the sight with grave interest.

"Come on, Matthew." Luke climbed up on the seat, but Matthew stayed behind. "Matthew!"

The boy glanced up, but didn't move. Luke felt a sense of dread as he noted Matthew's rigid face begin to grow red. He knew the signs by heart. Had come to dread them.

He hopped to the ground and kept his voice gentle but firm. "Matthew, we need to go. Come on, son."

Matthew's face twisted.

"Son . . ."

Clearly, Matthew was past the point of reason. His arms flung out wildly as if to ward off an attack by an invisible monster. Luke caught him by the wrists, but that only seemed to make matters worse. Matthew twisted and turned violently until he was fully on the ground, kicking his feet.

It took all of Luke's strength to lift the writhing body in his arms. The boy continued to thrash about wildly as Luke set him upon the seat of the wagon.

Standing in front of the group of Cheyennes, Maddie's eyes were fixed on Luke, who continued to struggle with his young son long after he'd managed to pick him up and carry him to the wagon.

"Ostrich not exorcist," Running Dear complained.

"Exercise." Maddie corrected him without thought.

Upon realizing that twenty-five pairs of eyes were staring at her, she drew her attention away from Luke and stretched her arms upward. "Breathe!"

It was the second time she'd seen Matthew throw such a fit. She was no less startled today than she had been the first time she'd witnessed his uncontrollable rage.

Luke impressed her with the patient way he handled Matthew. Most parents might well have been tempted to give the boy a proper flogging for such behavior. She, for one, would not have been as tolerant as Luke, though she had never found the need to resort to physical punishment.

Still, as shocking as the tantrum was, she'd had enough experience with troubled children to recognize it as a symptom of a deep, possibly serious, disturbance, not the result of a spoiled child denied his own way.

This new insight might explain why Luke was so protective of his son. Would this be why he was so reluctant to let her teach Matthew?

Matthew sat quietly by his father's side, staring into space. The dazed look on his face indicated that the boy had escaped to some inner sanctum. Luke doubted that Matthew was aware of his surroundings.

Matthew's frenzied fit ended as quickly as it had begun. It was like all the others that had occurred in recent months.

The tantrums had started six months after his mother's death and had gotten progressively worse. They usually occurred no more than once a week, but this was the third one in five days.

The violent streak in his son filled Luke with grave concern. Hardly a moment went by that he didn't ponder the implications.

Dear God, did his beloved Matthew have to suffer the same inescapable curse he himself had lived with all these years? How he hated knowing that the son he loved more than life itself showed such violent tendencies at so tender an age.

It took a strong hand to control him. Luke feared that if Matthew were left in Maddie's care, she could be injured should a tantrum occur.

It was for this reason that he was against her idea of teaching Matthew. He seldom let Matthew out of his sight and would certainly never consider doing so for an entire day while he worked in the fields.

He glanced at the boy and knew the worst was over. For now. Matthew sat perfectly still, his eyes gazing into space. Sometimes Luke wondered which was worse, the tantrum or the unnatural stillness that followed.

At least when Matthew was kicking and lashing out, it was a form of communication. But whenever Matthew escaped to that inner place, Luke felt even more inadequate as a father than usual. He felt shut out from his son's life just as he was shut out from society as a whole.

Matthew kept to himself for the rest of the day. Not once did he come over to his father to show him some new insect or other discovery, as was his usual habit.

Luke did notice, however, how many times Matthew stood and stared in the direction of the soddy. Luke was willing to bet it wasn't home that Matthew was thinking about. It was Maddie.

He considered telling her about the streak of violence that ran in the Tyler family. But almost as soon as he thought it, he changed his mind. If he told her who his father had been, he would have to tell her the rest; he would have to tell her that he himself killed a man with his own two hands. He would have to tell her how his father had raped his mother ... how many lives the elder Tyler had taken before he was caught and hung.

He would have to tell her that Matthew's tantrums indicated that he had inherited the same violent tendencies.

Even if he could bring himself to tell her about his own dark deed, telling her about Matthew would be impossible.

He recalled the softness on her face each time she looked at Matthew, the gentleness in her voice. Luke could not remember anyone ever looking at him with such unconditional approval. Certainly not his mother. No one.

He couldn't bear to think of the look of horror that

would surely cross Maddie's face if she knew the truth—the fear he would see in her eyes whenever she looked at Matthew.

His first concern was for his son, but he couldn't forget his other responsibilities. He owed it to Maddie to try and discourage her interest in the boy. For her own safety, if for no other reason.

And that's exactly what he intended to do. In fact, he left the fields early for that sole purpose. He couldn't bear for Maddie to judge him for the way he would handle things. He'd explain that he didn't want Matthew to grow too attached to her. She was a teacher; she'd understand.

He should have known better than to think he could march home anytime he felt like it for the purpose of having a serious conversation with her. The truth was, there was so much going on, he had trouble finding her. He couldn't even get into his soddy for the Indians who were packed inside and blocking the doorway.

"What the hell . . . ?" He pushed his way through the mass of nearly naked bodies, shouting her name.

"I'm over here," she called gaily from the direction of the woodstove. "What is it?"

What *is* it? Gritting his teeth, he peered over the feathered roach on the head of one of the Indians. If she hadn't been so tall, he wouldn't have been able to pick her out.

The tribesmen turned to look at him as if he had no right to be in his own house.

"Would you mind telling me what is going on?"

"We're having a nutrition class," she called.

A Cheyenne brave next to him grinned. "Dandelions, good." The Indian held out a plate that was heaped with the wilted greens, which Luke declined.

"That's the end of our class," Maddie announced. When no one made a move toward the door, she mo-

tioned with her hands, and when her students still refused to leave, she appealed to the Indian nearest her.
"Flying Hawk, please explain that class is over for today. Tell them to come back tomorrow."

Flying Hawk spoke a few Cheyenne words, and everyone started pushing and shoving out the door, their
moccasins shuffling against the dirt floor.

"One at a time!" Maddie called out, and presumably
the garbled words from Flying Hawk were the Cheyenne interpretation. In any case, there was less pushing
and shoving, and Luke, finding himself pinned against
the wall, was grateful.

After they were gone, Luke heaved a sigh and
pushed the door shut.

Maddie motioned him to the table and handed him a
glass of cool water. "I apologize. I didn't know you
would be home so early. Where's Matthew?" He could
see the worry in her face. "Is ... is he all right?"

"He walked off by himself. He'll be back." He lowered himself on the chair, just as Matthew walked in
the door.

Maddie greeted him with a warm smile. "There you
are, young man. Would you like a cold drink?"

Matthew nodded. His gaze followed her every move
as she ladled water into a clean glass and handed it to
him. It was clear that Matthew was growing extremely
fond of Maddie. As dangerous as it was to let the boy
form such close attachments, Luke wasn't certain he
could stop it even if he wanted to.

"Why did you come back early?" Maddie asked
again. She was watching Matthew closely, and Luke
could guess what she must be thinking. He couldn't
blame her.

"I was worried about Matthew," he said simply. A
moment of understanding passed between them, and as
if by mutual consent, the subject was dropped.

Right or wrong, he simply couldn't bring himself to deny his son what he himself had been denied.

Later that night, after the supper dishes had been washed and put away, Maddie sat at the table sewing a patch on a pair of Matthew's britches.

Luke had planned to work in the barn, but for some reason he didn't want to be alone.

He sat at the table across from her, oiling his hand tools. Although neither of them said much, he appreciated the companionship. It was still fairly early when she stood and gathered up her sewing supplies.

"I think I'll turn in," she said.

"I'll walk you outside."

She accepted his help with her shawl and walked out ahead of him. She paused in front of the soddy. The voice that floated to him out of the darkness was vibrant, yet soft. "I don't think I'll ever get used to this sky at night. It's incredible."

He gazed upward and watched as a shooting star fell toward the southern horizon. "Don't you have stars in Washington?"

"Not like this. Not where I can see the stars touch the earth on all four sides of me."

He couldn't see her face in the dark, but he could feel her eyes upon hm.

"It must be difficult raising a child by yourself."

His first impulse was to change the subject, but the compassion and understanding in her voice touched some inner need, and he momentarily dropped his guard. "It's very difficult."

"What was Matthew's mother like?"

"I . . . I don't want to talk about his mother."

His clipped voice would have discouraged most people, but he should have known that once Maddie had something on her mind, it would take more than a few cold words to discourage her.

"Has it ever occurred to you that your refusal to talk about her could be the reason for Matthew's tantrums?"

"Tantrums?" He couldn't believe his ears. "Is that what you think they are? Temper tantrums from a spoiled child?"

"I never said he was spoiled, Luke."

"His tantrums have nothing to do with his mother's death."

"How can you be so certain? Think about it. He can't talk about her. You won't. Where do you think his rage is coming from?"

"You know nothing about this."

"I know a great deal about children."

"More than medical doctors?" When she didn't reply, he gave a grim nod. "I thought not. According to the doctor I consulted, the tantrums are inherent."

She wasn't a doctor, but one couldn't live in the nation's capital for long without learning a thing or two about so-called experts. "Feelings are inherent. Anger. Frustration. How one handles those feelings is learned."

"I think in this instance you are out of your element."

"Is that why you refuse to let me teach Matthew? Because of his tantrums?"

"It requires much physical strength to hold him down."

"I've never had difficulty handling children. In fact, I'm of the opinion that it's parents, not children who are difficult to handle."

"Is that why you were asked to leave your earlier teaching post? Because of your low opinion of parents?"

"For your information, one of the reasons I was

asked to leave was because I told a United States senator exactly what I thought of him."

"One of the reasons? What was the other?"

"I told the father of one of my students that he was letting his own prejudices interfere with his son's education."

"It appears that meddling in other people's affairs comes second nature to you. You will, however, from this point on, refrain from interfering with my son's life." Hating the sound of his own rough voice, he tried to soften the harshness of his words. "Maddie, please try to understand . . ."

"I understand perfectly."

Brittle silence stretched between them. Then, unexpectedly, the tension broke and he pulled her into his arms. He held her close for a moment, his lips pressed to her forehead, then released her. With a muttered oath, he spun around, and all that was left was the sound of the closing door.

# Chapter 15

The brief but puzzling encounter left Maddie shaken and confused. She barely remembered stumbling into the dark tipi. Her fingers trembled as she undid her buttons, her heart still beating wildly. When the dratted task was done, she flung herself upon the bed-roll. What in the world was she to think? One moment he's accusing her of meddling and the next . . .

Not even the night air could cool her fevered brow. She pressed her hand against her chest. Her heart was beating so fast, she could barely breathe. Somehow, she had to make sense out of all that was happening.

Matthew needed a friend.

Lord, so did his father, for that matter. Just thinking about the loneliness she sensed in Luke defused her anger, if not her confusion.

Lonely. Yes, that certainly described the look so often seen in his eyes. That also seemed like a pretty apt description of the yearning she so often saw on his face. It would certainly explain the intensity by which he listened every time she spoke. It was as if every word she uttered gave much-needed nourishment to his soul.

The truth of the matter was that she had never seen more lonely and wanting souls than Luke and his son. She longed to make things right for them, to fill their lives with laughter and music and all that was good.

She pounded her fists upon her pillow in a futile attempt to change the course of her thoughts. Had it been only loneliness that made him hold her close for one brief moment tonight?

Maybe, maybe not. But she did know one thing. She could do nothing for the father or his son. She couldn't be the one to rescue them, if indeed they could be rescued.

Whatever had happened to disillusion father and son about life was out of her realm. She was a teacher, not a miracle worker. Her job was to teach, not to heal broken hearts and wounded spirits.

But she wanted to. Lord, how she wanted to. If only she knew how.

She felt so inadequate. She pushed herself upright and stepped back outside. The lonely cry of a coyote shattered the silence. The sound made her shiver. She hugged herself and ran her hands up and down her arms.

Overhead, countless stars glittered in the velvet black sky. But the stars for once held no interest for her. It was the small lighted window that caught her attention, beckoning to her like a lighthouse in a stormy sea. It was all she could do to resist the invitation.

Feeling as restless as the wind that so often blew across the plains, she felt the need to run.

She bolted into the darkness and ran around the soddy like a colt in a meadow. The pins flew from her bun and she shook her hair free, then lifted her face to the starlit sky to feel the cool air against her fevered brow.

What she was running from, she couldn't say, but she ran until she gasped for breath and could run no more.

\* \* \*

In the days that followed, the Cheyennes' eagerness to learn continued to amaze her. Some of the Indians already knew a few words of English, which they had learned from soldiers at Fort Hays, and they quickly picked up more words from Maddie. They also took great delight in teaching Maddie their own language and laughed uproariously at her efforts.

One brave in particular won her heart with his friendly antics. Through a series of hand signals, she was able to determine that his name had something to do with his being left-handed. The other Cheyennes were constantly pointing out how he favored his left hand, leading her to believe that such an occurrence was rare among Indians.

His Cheyenne name was difficult to pronounce and seemed to have no simple English derivative. For this reason, she called him Lefty, and he offered no objection.

"Me Lefty. You Wildfire." He pointed to her hair and did a graceful dance on moccasined feet, imitating the way prairie fires swept across the grasslands.

Jokes made about her hair had, in the past, brought an immediate retort to the offender. But the inhabitants of Kansas did not seem to place as much value on conformity as those back home. For the first time in her life, she laughed at the jokes made at her expense. In this land of buffalo and Indians, and various social misfits who traveled here to find a home, she felt like she belonged.

This feeling of belonging increased as she learned more about her new home. She spent hours walking the grasslands, searching for plants and abandoned bird nests to display in her museum. The seemingly endless prairie had originally struck her as barren, but no longer. For she now knew that a myriad of treasures awaited anyone willing to take a closer look.

She found a discarded snakeskin from a rattler, a

fish fossil from the bottom of a dry creek, and any number of bird nests.

It was astonishing how many varieties of wildflowers grew among the prairie grass. She could identify many, but by no means all. She decided to send samples of the ones she was unfamiliar with to her father's friend at the Smithsonian for identification.

While gathering flowers on that first day in June, she was pleasantly surprised when Matthew joined her. Luke was nowhere in sight, and she wondered if he knew of Matthew's whereabouts. It wasn't like Luke to let Matthew wander away from the soddy unsupervised.

"I'm gathering specimens for the museum," she explained. "Would you like to help me?"

His eyes bright with interest, Matthew hunched by her side and watched as she pointed to the wide diversity of flowers that bloomed among the grass. "This is blue indigo, and I believe this flower belongs to the phlox family." She studied the little orange flowers of another plant that was all but hidden next to a clump of buffalo grass. "I don't know what this one is called, but I think that one is a spiderwort."

She took in a deep breath, enjoying the fragrance of sun-warmed grass and wildflowers in the air. A bee hovered close, and Matthew drew back, a look of fear on his face.

"It's all right, Matthew. The bee is trying to gather the pollen." She explained how bees, butterflies, and even birds helped to pollinate the flowers.

How she loved to take her students on nature walks. She found the elements of nature a useful tool in teaching many subjects, including arithmetic and even grammar. Her methods had come under numerous reviews by the school board, but it wasn't until Johnny Wychoff's mother fainted in the lab of the Smithsonian at the sight of blood that Maddie was forbidden to take her students outside the classroom. What a pity that was, and as she gave Matthew a lesson in botany, she vowed never again to let a school board dictate to her how to teach.

Matthew seemed to absorb everything she said, and when another bee hovered near, this time an enormous black bumblebee, he stood perfectly still and watched the bee flit from blossom to blossom.

Once the bee had moved on, he ran ahead of her and stopped to point eagerly at any flower that she had not previously collected. His eyes sparkled at every new discovery. On one such occasion, Maddie let out a squeal of delight. "Wild strawberries, Matthew."

She fell to her knees and quickly set to work plucking the ripe red fruit. The strawberries were sweet to the taste and juicy.

"Let's pick some for supper." She glanced around for something to put the berries in. "Let me have your hat, Matthew." Matthew pulled off his straw hat and handed it to her.

"Perfect." She dumped a handful of berries into the tightly woven crown.

His face wreathed in smiles, Matthew fell to his knees by her side, and together they started picking the lush red berries. More fruit ended up in their mouths than in the hat, and conversation was done mostly with smiles, but it was enough, and eventually the hat was piled high with the tempting red fruit.

"Oh, look, Matthew, a baby rabbit."

Matthew crept near the little animal. The rabbit hopped away, and a merry chase ensued as Matthew ran behind in hot pursuit. "Be careful, Matthew. There might be snakes."

Matthew kept running and Maddie's concern increased. Fingers in her mouth, she let out a shrill whistle that made Matthew stop and turn. She motioned to him with her arm, and this time he ran back to her. "That's a good boy."

He tugged on her arm. "What is it, Matthew?"

He pointed to his ear.

"I'm not sure what you're trying to tell me."

Frustration crossed his face as he kept pointing to his ear. She cradled his face in her hands. "Don't get angry, Matthew. I'm trying to understand. You have to help me. Now tell me. Does your ear hurt?"

He shook his head. He pointed to her and then to his ear, and when she still couldn't understand, he started to tremble.

Fearing that he was about to have one of his fits, she gave him a gentle shake. "Matthew! Stop it!" He pulled away and started to run. She whistled, and he stopped and turned.

"That's it!" she shouted in delight. "You wanted me to whistle." She ran to him and fell to her knees by his side. "Is that what you were trying to tell me?"

He nodded, watching her closely. She stuck her fingers in her mouth and whistled again. She couldn't help but laugh at the look of admiration on his face. The ungodly sound usually brought horror to people's faces, not admiration.

Matthew stuck his fingers into his mouth and tried to imitate her.

"Like this." She demonstrated again.

He tried again, with no more success.

"That's right, Matthew. Hold your fingers together." She hadn't been much older than Matthew when her father taught her how to whistle. She'd been so delighted to learn such a wondrous new skill, that she rushed home to show her mother, who had been entertaining some important guests at the time, including the wives of two senators.

Maddie would never forget the look of dismay on her mother's face when she filled the elegant parlor with a loud, high-pitched shrill that caused a prized crystal vase to crack and the guests to cry out in alarm.

Matthew kept trying until he managed a faint sound.

It was the first sound she'd heard him make and, judging by the look on his face, probably the first sound he'd made in a long time.

"Thataboy, Matthew. Now, again." She whistled, and the clear shrill sound traveled across the miles of prairie.

# Chapter 16

Luke heard the strange, high-pitched sound and changed directions. Dammit, where was he?

He'd been searching for Matthew for the last half hour to no avail. Had they come for him? The Child Welfare Department. Had they taken him away? The very thought made his throat grow tight with dread and his stomach ache. Despite the warm afternoon sun, a cold sweat broke out on his forehead.

He'd sent Matthew outside for water, and when he failed to return, Luke went looking for him. He found the bucket, but no sign of Matthew. It wasn't like Matthew to stray. And where was Maddie? Was Matthew with her?

And what in the name of God was that godawful sound?

He ran up a slight incline, and when he saw Maddie and Matthew he felt relief wash over him. He'd been so afraid—so terribly afraid—that his son had been taken from him.

"Matthew!" It was anger in his voice, not fear. Anger at himself for letting fear color his judgment. "I've been looking all over for you. I told you not to wander away from the soddy!"

Matthew's smile faded and his chin dropped to his chest. The change in his son was so drastic, from joy to despair, that Luke felt immediate remorse.

Maddie stood and faced him. "I'm sorry, Luke, it's my fault. We were gathering things to display in the museum, and I didn't realize how far we'd gone."

Luke glanced at the bucket of flowers and the hat full of strawberries. He lifted his eyes. He wanted to explain himself. But how could he? What kind of father would she think him if she knew what Claudia had threatened to do?

"Matthew has something to show you," she said. She placed a hand on Matthew's shoulder. "Show your father."

Luke gazed at Matthew. "Go ahead, son."

Matthew glanced up at Maddie, who nodded encouragement, then stuck his two fingers in his mouth. The whistle wasn't much, more air than sound, but to Luke's ears it was the most wonderful thing he'd ever heard.

He dropped down by Matthew's side and gave him a gentle hug. He wanted so much to squeeze the boy, to pull him close and never let him go. But today, as always, the knowledge of who and what he was held him back. He squeezed his eyes tight and could almost see the look of horror that had been in his own mother's eyes whenever he'd made the mistake of throwing his arms around her. Would he ever forget how she looked at him? The fear that he saw on her face whenever he wanted to hug her?

He gazed over Matthew's head and was startled by the radiance on Maddie's face as she watched. He had always wondered how it would feel to see caring in another's face directed at him, to see love, true and unadulterated love in another's eyes. Never could he have imagined anything like he felt at that moment. He felt perfect in her eyes, whole.

Like a drowning man, he held on to the vision of her, and for one magical moment, he was able to block out memories of the past long enough to tighten his hold on Matthew and plant a firm kiss on the boy's smooth forehead.

The surprise on Matthew's face made Luke ache with shame and regret. He wanted so much to make Matthew understand that the quick perfunctory hugs of the past had not been by choice. Lord, never that.

Damn his mother. Damn his father. Damn all the people who had robbed him of such a precious gift— the gift to love freely and without fear. Damn all of them!

Shaken by his thoughts, he straightened and met Maddie's questioning look. "I had no way of knowing that Matthew was with you." His voice was husky, but not from anger, not this time.

She studied him a moment as if trying to puzzle something out. "It ... it won't happen again, Luke." She laid her hand on his arm. "Are you all right?"

He stared down at her hand, so soft and white next to his suntanned skin. He wanted desperately to thank her for helping him to silence the voices of the past, if only for a short time. For once he had held Matthew as a father was surely meant to hold his son, without fear or restraint, and without all those disapproving voices from the past to remind him of all the reasons why he shouldn't. And if he never managed to drown out the voices again, he had this one time to cherish and remember.

Oh, Maddie ... his heart fairly sang her name. He lifted his eyes to hers. He wanted to tell her what she'd given him today, but he couldn't. If he told her, he'd drive her away.

"Luke?"

"I'm perfectly all right," he said, pulling his arm away. His rejection hurt her. He could see the hurt in her eyes, watched achingly as it spilled across her face.

He hated causing her pain. Hadn't he caused enough pain in his life? His mother, his wife. Lucy Eldridge. Matthew.

Just thinking of the long list of names that came to mind toughened his resolve. What's one more hurt? "I caught a prairie hen for supper." At that moment he felt that changing the subject was not only necessary, but a matter of survival.

"That's wonderful," she said. "I'm growing a bit weary of buffalo meat. I'll stuff it with dandelion dressing and . . ."

He frowned. "Dandelions?"

She gave him an arch look. "Unless, of course, you have an objection to dandelion dressing."

"I can't imagine what objection I could have." He winked at his son. "Unless Matthew can think of one."

Matthew shook his head and tried another whistle.

"Very well," Maddie declared, "dandelion dressing it shall be."

She gave a long shrill whistle that made the prairie dogs dive for cover. Matthew clapped his hands in glee, and Luke covered his ears. "What are you trying to do, Maddie? Make me deaf?"


The next morning Maddie rose early to work on the various wildflowers she and Matthew had gathered. It promised to be a hot day, and she was anxious to finish her chores before the heat became unbearable.

She covered the various blossoms with cornmeal and set them out in the sun to dry. It would take a few days for the moisture to be absorbed from the stems and blossoms. Once the flowers were dry, she would attach them carefully to a wooden board for display, with an identifying tag.

She turned at the sound of a galloping horse. Recognizing the horseman as Lefty, she wiped the cornmeal from her hands and hurried to greet him.

He swung down from his spotted pony and patted his chest. "Want Wildfire's hair."

She stared at him in confusion. Was he talking about scalping her? Or was this a simple matter of miscommunication? "My . . . my hair?" she stammered.

Lefty nodded his head. "Me want hair."

"You can't have it," she said, scowling. "It's mine."

Lefty drew back in surprise, as if it had never occurred to him that she would object. "Me want!"

Maddie took a deep breath and tried to recall the diplomatic tactics that she had thought to employ in such situations. She placed her hands on her waist and glared at him as she had on so many occasions glared at an unruly student. "You may not have my hair."

Clearly offended, Lefty said something in Cheyenne that sounded like an insult, mounted his pony, and rode away.

Breathing a sigh of relief, she placed her hand on her chest to try to still her pounding heart. She felt on edge for the rest of the day and kept a wary eye focused in the direction of the Cheyenne village.

That night she brought the subject up at the dinner table. Not wanting to cause undue alarm, she tried to talk in general terms.

"Have you had any trouble with the Cheyennes?" she asked.

Luke looked up from his plate. "Not personally. Most of the trouble stopped when the majority of Indians were relocated. Why do you ask?"

"No particular reason." She glanced down at her own plate. "But I have heard a few stories about . . . scalping." She glanced up to find his gaze resting speculatively on her hair. For a moment, she imagined warm approval in his eyes as he gazed at her hair, and it occurred to her that no one had ever looked at her in quite the same way that Luke looked at her. A flow of warmth rushed through her, and she quickly forgot her earlier concerns.

The following morning Lefty was waiting for her when she emerged from her tipi, a big smile on his face. Despite his friendly demeanor, she felt a moment of panic until she noticed his hair.

"Like Wildfire's hair," he explained, turning his head from side to side so she could see how he'd done his hair in cogwheel fashion.

He hadn't been completely successful in imitating her own unique style, but it was close enough. Feeling a profound relief wash over her, she smiled her whole-hearted approval and clapped her hands together. When he said he wanted her hair, he hadn't meant it literally.

"I like it," she said. "It makes you ... look most distinctive." She supposed the others would think his new hairstyle looked odd, but in her opinion it seemed no more odd than the layers of bone beads draped around his neck.

In the days that followed, a bond of friendship developed between Maddie and the left-handed Indian. Lefty never seemed to grow weary of explaining his culture to her, and she often listened to him for hours on end.

Lefty's English was extremely limited, but combining it with the sign language and quickly drawn pictures that he scratched on the ground, she was eventually able to understand all that he tried to tell her about his people.

She learned that Running Deer's squaw recently had what he called a *moksiis*. Maddie was soon able to determine this meant a little girl. Little boys, he explained, were called *moksois*. "Mean 'potbelly.' "

Enchanted by all that he told her, she laughed aloud. "What a thing to call a baby."

He grinned and pointed to his own potbelly.

"Why do your people insist that my tipi flap face east?" she asked, after he had explained how Cheyenne drew pictures of great hunts and other memorable occasions onto their tipis.

"So that the wind does not blow tipi down," he explained.

It made perfect sense, of course, and she began to understand that everything the Cheyenne did was in perfect harmony with the world around them.

"And the drums," she asked. "Why do they beat?"

He was unfamiliar with the word "drums," and she acted the word out.

"Tom-toms," he said, nodding, using a word he'd learned from the soldiers. "Tom-toms keep time." He demonstrated by slapping his thigh quickly, then slowly. "Make happy sound when papoose enter world."

Maddie's enchantment grew. "All that drumming I hear is to help a mother give birth?"

"Not only births," he told her. "When man take squaw." He held a finger from each hand together to indicate.

"For weddings?" She thought of all the times she had listened to the drums and felt anxious. "What about war?" she asked. "Do the drums ... tom-toms ... beat for war?" He looked confused by the question, and she pretended to fight an imaginary foe.

Understanding crossed Lefty's face. "War." He nodded.

"How does a person know what the tom-toms are trying to say?"

He looked surprised by the question. "Ears tell," he explained.

While they talked, she happened to notice a lone horseman watching them from the distance.

"Who is that, Lefty?"

"That Red Feather. He son of Chief Talks to the Sun."

"Why doesn't he join us?"

Lefty traced a stern finger in front of him. "Red Feather think white woman's school bad thing."

"But why?"

"He says this is Indian land. White man should . . ." He moved his hand to indicate the word he was looking for.

"Leave?" she suggested.

He nodded. "Leave."

"There's so much land out here. It seems there's room enough for us all."

Lefty's eyes followed the thin line of smoke that moved across the distant horizon as the Kansas Pacific—or the Iron Horse, as he called it—raced westward. He pointed away from the train, to the east. "My people live here . . . how say . . . many moons."

She followed his finger. There was no indication of inhabitants in the direction he pointed, only flat prairie, serene sky, and the perfect harmony of nature.

His people had roamed the land for hundreds of years, and yet there was no trace of them anywhere; the land was left intact.

"Then your people come and everything change."

"Is change so bad?" she asked.

"Some change good." He pointed to his hair, but his smile quickly faded away as he added, "But some change not so good."

Lefty left her by the windmill, and she watched him race his pony across the grasslands until man and land became one.

Behind her, Red Feather remained on his horse and

kept watch. Outlined against the sky, he looked time-less and noble, like the bronzed statues that were be-coming so common in Washington.

Feeling faint from the blazing-hot sun, she walked to the soddy, taking care to bolt the door after her.

It was much later that she looked outside and found him gone.

# Chapter 17

She debated whether to mention Red Feather to Luke, but finally decided against it. She didn't want Luke to think that Lefty and his friends would pose a problem for him or Matthew. In any case, Red Feather had done nothing wrong.

There was yet another reason why she hesitated in sharing her concerns. Luke maintained a cordial, yet guarded, demeanor toward her. He was willing to discuss the running of the farm, but Matthew and anything pertaining to his own personal life were clearly off limits. This in turn made her less inclined to share many of the mundane, everyday things she might normally have shared with someone with whom she was so closely associated.

Despite his reserve, she found herself an unwilling opponent in some sort of game that felt as intense as any game played for high stakes.

At odd times—as she put the Indians through their early-morning calisthenics, or worked on her museum displays, or went about her many chores—the strangest feeling would wash over her.

She invariably found Luke watching her at these times, though he tried to pretend otherwise by quickly looking away.

What was wrong with the men of the prairie? she wondered. First Red Feather, then Luke, both watching her like she was an animal to be stalked. Was it some sort of strange courtship ritual? Unique, perhaps, to Kansas? No sooner had the thought occurred to her then she burst out laughing.

Few men had thought her worthy of courtship in Washington. She doubted that even the severe shortage of women on the prairie would make her that much more appealing here.

Still, the possibility that Luke might be interested in her romantically was a thought she was reluctant to discount. The truth was, she became obsessed with the idea and soon found herself going out of her way to search him out, as if to prove how ridiculous the idea truly was.

Twice that same week she rode her horse out to the fields to take Luke and Matthew a cool drink.

On both occasions Luke was so intent on his work that he failed to see her at first, which allowed her time to watch him at her leisure. She sat on the spare saddle Luke had loaned her and feasted her eyes upon his shirtless back. Muscles that looked as hard as iron rippled beneath his gleaming sun-bronzed skin, and his sturdy thighs strained against the canvas fabric of his trousers. Despite the heat, his actions were swift and his powerful body moved with fluid grace.

It was Matthew who always spotted her first, and as much as she regretted that her secret observations were interrupted, it filled her with pleasure to see the joy on his face at sight of her. Indeed, his face lit up brighter than a lantern, and he stopped whatever he was doing to signal Maddie's arrival to his father with a piercing whistle that brought a loud protest from nearby birds and prairie dogs. His strong little legs quickly cleared the distance as he ran into her open arms.

Luke joined them and he always seemed pleased to see her, but never as pleased as she'd hoped. Or maybe she was expecting too much from him; he wasn't a particularly demonstrative man, not even with Matthew.

She came away from both these brief encounters more confused than before. It suddenly occurred to her that not only did she seek him out to satisfy her curiosity, but she *wanted* her suspicions to be true. It was a startling thought, one that took her breath away.

It took her three days to come to terms with it. Once she did, she wondered why Luke was taking so long to make his intentions known. If this game they played was some sort of courting game, than maybe there was something she was supposed to do in return, perhaps send him a signal of encouragement.

Most of the men in Washington had been rather boring. She had allowed one or two of them to give her a chaste kiss, but had never felt the need to have the kiss repeated; indeed, when one man, a senator's son, made the mistake of trying, she firmly pushed him away and gave him a piece of her mind.

She was never one to engage in flirting—not like her friends who made fools of themselves by flitting their fans and batting their eyelashes. Certainly Luke wouldn't be waiting for her to carry on so, would he? She wondered if she could even bring herself to bat her eyelashes. Surely the Cheyenne women didn't resort to such a ridiculous pastime.

Lefty laughed when she asked him. "No bat eyes," he said, after she demonstrated.

"How does a woman show a man she likes him?"

Lefty grinned. "Warrior steal woman band . . ." He indicated something that was worn around the wrist. "If woman like, she let him keep."

"And if she doesn't like him?"

"She send someone for band."

"I like your ways," Maddie said.

Lefty looked pleased. "I like your ways too." He thought for a moment. "But not bat eyes."

Matthew began the practice of joining her each morning as she led the Indians through their calisthenics, and he and Running Deer became fast friends. He even taught Running Deer how to whistle, and the two could be heard trying to outdo one another.

At the end of every day, after returning from the fields with his father, Matthew quickly came to find her and together they spent a pleasant hour before she prepared supper searching through the grass for things to display in the museum. By the middle of June, the prairie grass was still green but had grown knee-high, making it more of a challenge to discover the treasures that were hidden beneath.

She enjoyed the boy's company and, despite his lack of speech, felt so in tune with him that she quite forgot she was the one who did all the talking.

She sensed Luke's anxiety whenever she and Matthew spent time together. At such times, the door of the soddy remained open, even when the wind was blowing. It wasn't unusual for him to stand on the steps watching them do their morning workout, his forehead creased and his face grim. At other times, his vigilance was more discreet, but no less noticeable.

It seemed to her that Luke was always waiting for disaster to strike. He was constantly on the lookout for prairie fires, and it was his habit every morning and every night to stand a distance from the soddy to scan the horizon. He monitored the sky, studying every cloud as if it spoke to him. Even the slight creak of the windmill would send him running outside to investigate.

One didn't have to live in Kansas for long to understand such vigilance, but she sensed that his watchfulness went beyond environmental concerns. He appeared to be waiting for someone, and every time the train whistle sounded in the distance, he tensed and quickly sought out Matthew.

Who was he waiting for? And what did it have to do with Matthew?

It was a question she put to him that Friday morning as he helped her spread the laundry across the grass to dry.

"No one," he said, his back to her. "I'm not waiting for anyone."

He was a man who kept many secrets, and it was hard to know if his refusal to look at her meant he was keeping yet another one from her now.

"Then it is just me you don't trust with Matthew?"

This time he did turn to her, and the look on his face told her that she had touched upon some deep, abiding pain. "Trust has nothing to do with it. There're things about him . . ."

"What do you mean, 'things'? Are you talking about the tantrums?"

"You know I am. You don't know what he's capable of."

"And you don't know what I'm capable of!" Frustrated that he had such little regard for her vast experience with children, she turned and spread a sheet over the grass to dry.

"Maddie . . ."

The sound of her name on his lips made her heart leap. She turned, and the uncensored look in his eyes touched every womanly cell in her body. It was clear that he wanted to take her in his arms, kiss her. It couldn't have been more clear had he said it aloud— which he didn't and probably never would.

The silence stretched between them, and she watched helplessly as desire faded from his eyes and the usual cool indifference took its place. She realized the next step would be up to her. Somehow she must let him know that she wanted him to fulfill the promise she had seen reflected in his face moments earlier. The promise of a kiss ...

Oh, Lord, she wasn't good at this. She wished now that she had paid more attention to the parlor games played out by the others. At the time, she much preferred to spend her time in her father's lab or up to her chin in books borrowed from his extensive library.

Her heart pounded and her knees felt soft as mush. Shaking now, she held her breath and blinked rapidly.

Luke knit his brows. "Is there something wrong with your eyes, Maddie?"

"Wrong?" She had never felt more mortified in her whole life. "There ... there's nothing wrong." Eyes stinging with humiliation, she bent over and pulled a newly laundered flour sack from the wicker basket.

"About Matthew ... Don't fight me on this."

Cheeks burning, she watched him walk to his horse and mount with easy grace. Soon he was galloping along the trail leading to his crops.

Matthew joined her moments later. Watching his father, he tugged on her arm as if to ask where he was going. She fought off her depression for Matthew's sake.

"He'll be back soon." Luke wasn't likely to leave Matthew long in her care. She rubbed her eyes quickly. She had no patience with tears and certainly had no intention of feeling sorry for herself. She had only herself to blame for what had happened. When was she going to learn that it was the male's prerogative to pursue a woman or not, as he chose? Probably at the same time she came to accept that the male also was at liberty to take his own sweet time in the process, if that was what he wanted to do.

It was yet another example of how the mores of society were undeniably stacked in favor of men. She had hoped to escape such rigid customs and traditions upon leaving Washington. It had not occurred to her that some things remained the same no matter what the location.

There didn't appear to be any way to make her feelings known to Luke without rebelling against firmly established traditions.

Not wanting Matthew to know something was wrong, she tried distracting him by pointing to the little prairie dog that she had named Prince.

Prince popped his little round head out of the hole next to a mound of dirt and regarded them with small, beady eyes. Maddie never tired of watching the little creatures who flitted in and out of the numerous mounds like friendly neighbors stopping in to chat. They were interesting animals, and seemed especially suited to the prairie.

Matthew whistled as Maddie had taught him, and countless little feet flashed upward as hundreds of prairie dogs dived for cover amid a chorus of startled yelps. Matthew clapped his hands in delight, his eyes shining with mischief.

Maddie couldn't help but laugh. "Now look what you've done."

Prince was the first one to emerge. The little prairie dog sat up on hind legs and made little barking sounds as if to keep his friends apprised of what was happening above ground.

"He's a brave one," she said. "One day I'm afraid that little fellow is going to get himself into trouble."

She slipped her hand into the deep pocket of her apron and pulled out the kernels of corn she'd found stored in an Indian rubber sack in the barn. She squatted and held out her hand, palm up. The rodent sniffed and eventually crept forward until he was close enough to grab the food out of her hand.

Matthew had previously watched her feed Prince from afar, but on this particular morning he stooped beside her, and she could feel his intensity as he watched. "Would you like to feed Prince?"

Matthew kept his eyes focused on the little animal. She took his hand in hers and gently unfolded his closed fingers. "It's all right." She gave him an encouraging smile and placed a kernel in his palm. "Now hold it out so Prince can reach it."

Cautiously Matthew followed her instructions.

Prince's nose wiggled as he crept up closer. Matthew stiffened next to her. Fearful that he would have one of his tantrums, she slipped an arm around his shoulders. "It's all right, Matthew. Prince won't hurt you."

The animal grabbed the corn in his mouth and ran back to his hole like a little thief, his feet flashing in midair as he disappeared.

"See? What did I tell you?" She looked into Matthew's face, and his wide smile chased away her depression.

"Oh, Matthew," she whispered. She wrapped her arms around him and hugged him tight. She was touched deeply when he hugged her back. She wished his father were as open and giving. There were a lot of things she wished about Luke.

In the days that followed, Matthew grew brave enough around the prairie dog that she no longer had to prod him. Soon he began a daily practice of feeding Prince with no help from her.

It had occurred to her recently that she needed to put more structure into her day. Earlier she had driven to Colton to check on the progress of her school; she felt restless and eager to begin full-time teaching.

While in Colton, she met Reverend Moser, who told her his plan to begin Sunday worship services on the site of the new church. He was a kind, humble man who was so unlike the fire-and-brimstone preachers she knew back home, she took an instant liking to him.

"You'll come, won't you?" he asked.

"Of course I'll come," she promised.

Her promise to Reverend Moser required her to cancel her exercise classes on Sundays.

Lefty took great offense at this. "You don't want me to be flat," he said accusingly. He pointed to his flabby stomach.

"One day isn't going to make that much difference," she explained. "And it will only be on the Sabbath Day."

He frowned. "Sabbath?"

She pointed upward. "Great Father's Day."

He nodded solemnly. "Great Father."

She should have known it would not be that simple. Lefty had no concept of the white man's calendar. No matter how many times she explained and showed him on charts and counted out the days with sticks, he never failed to ride his horse over each day before dawn and stand outside her tent demanding to know if it was the "Great Father's Day."

He was greatly relieved on the six days of the week the answer was no. On such days, he rode off happily to tell the others. He returned a short time later, shouting and waving his hands as he led the others to the grassy area that had been set aside for their calisthenics class.

By contrast, on Sundays, after she explained what day it was, he rode away looking forlorn and confused. He did not understand the Great Father's Day.

It was a warm Friday morning that third week in June when she next noticed Red Feather watching her from the distance, long after the other Cheyennes had left for the day. It was wash day and she was hanging the wet clothes on the rope that Luke had recently stretched from the windmill to the side of the barn for her.

Matthew was so eager to give Prince his breakfast, he tugged impatiently at her arm. "Just a minute, Matthew."

Unwilling to wait a moment longer than necessary, Matthew reached into her pocket and pulled out a handful of dry corn.

Maddie laughed at his impatience. "Prince has got you well trained, hasn't he?" Matthew ran off in search of the little prairie dog, while Maddie hung the last of the wash to dry.

Watching the Indian between the flapping sheets, she saw him turn and ride off. Something about Red Feather's sudden retreat put her senses on alert. Normally, he left so unobtrusively that she hardly noticed.

Shaking off the uneasy feeling that washed over her like the shadow of a cloud, she picked up the empty laundry basket and started for the house.

She turned to call to Matthew. Something in the way he held himself made her stop in her tracks. He stood too rigid, too still. "Matthew?"

His arms and legs began to flail around his body. Alarmed, she dropped the basket and raced to his side. "Matthew? What is it?"

By the time she reached him, he had already flung himself to the ground. Feet kicking, he pounded the ground with his fists. "Stop it, Matthew!"

She grabbed an ankle, but he thrashed about so violently, she was forced to jump back.

Luke seemed to appear out of nowhere, his face grim. He shoved her away and grabbed Matthew by the shoulder. With a skill that could only have come from experience, he lifted Matthew in his arms and carried him to the soddy.

Shaken, Maddie followed Luke and was hurt when he slammed the door shut in her face. She was tempted to follow, but thought better of it. There was nothing she could do for Matthew. She wasn't even sure if there was anything she could do for Luke.

She scanned the distant prairie. A cloud of dust hovered in the distance, blocking out Red Feather and his horse.

She lowered her gaze and froze at the sight of a red feather sticking out of the ground. Her stomach clinched into a tight knot, she moved toward the feather until she could see the small furry mound beneath the arrow's shaft.

With a cry of protest, she dropped to her knees next to Prince's motionless body. So that's why Red Feather had raced away so quickly.

Filled with anger and grief, she pulled the arrow from Prince's body and tossed it aside. Poor Matthew. No wonder he'd been so upset. Unable to speak, he had no other way to show his feelings but through rage.

Tears blurred her eyes as she scooped the still-warm body in her arms and carried it away from the soddy. She chose a spot among a colorful array of wildflowers and lay the body on the ground. After retrieving a spade from the side of the barn, she set to work digging a hole.

It was hot and the air was still. Not a prairie dog could be seen, nor a bird's song heard. Maddie couldn't remember a time that the prairie had seemed so still and quiet. It was as if the whole world were in mourning.

She drew her arm across her damp forehead and

glanced back at the soddy. Recalling the dark, grim look on Luke's face, her heart ached for him.

After laying Prince to rest, she covered the small grave with dirt and planted wildflowers upon the mound.

She thought of the many times she had seen dead animals in her father's lab and wondered why she had never been affected previously the way she was today. Indeed, there had been a time when she had wanted to follow in her father's footsteps. She'd made the decision while her father was away on one of his expeditions, and she recalled how impatiently she'd waited for his return to tell him.

She had expected her father to embrace this news with the same support he showed for everything else she did. Something as insignificant as announcing that she was going to learn to play the piano would bring a round of hugs and joyful exclamations from him. That's why it hurt so much when he rejected her idea. For the first time in her life she had been angry with her father, and hurt by him.

"It's because I'm a girl!" she cried accusingly. "You don't think I can do the magic!" The magic is what she had called her father's ability to display animals so realistically that people often thought at first glance they were alive.

"You can do the magic," he told her. "It's the other thing . . . I would not want that for you."

"What other thing?" she persisted, but she didn't get an answer that day; she would have to wait until years later before she got her answer. She would have to wait for the day she stood on a hot Kansas prairie at the grave of a little prairie dog.

Never once during her childhood had she considered how her father acquired the animals he brought to the museum. Her father was first and foremost a hunter.

That was a necessary part of the job. The part of the job that she had no heart for. That was made painfully clear to her the day she had witnessed from the train window the shooting of a buffalo.

And now this senseless killing of an innocent animal. For what reason? she wondered, as she stared across the shimmering hot prairie toward the Cheyenne camp. For what reason?

# Chapter 18

It was late that same afternoon before Luke emerged from the house. Maddie followed him into the barn. "How is he?"

"He's ... asleep." Luke sounded tired, and his face was lined in weariness.

"Is there anything I can do to help?"

"No." He grabbed a hoe and started for the door.

"Don't do this," she pleaded.

He stopped for a moment, then pivoted to face her. "Do what?"

"Shut me out. I want to help ..."

"I told you, Maddie. There's nothing you can do."

"I can try."

He turned his back.

"Please," she persisted.

Her plea was followed by a long silence. She touched his arm, and he covered her hand with his own. For a moment, he squeezed her hand so hard it was as if he were trying to pour himself into her. Abruptly he dropped her hand and moved away.

"There's nothing you can do. There's nothing anyone can do."

"But ..."

"Leave it alone, Maddie. For all our sakes." He reached out and grabbed her arm. "Please."

She lifted her eyes to meet his and wondered what it was he was really asking her to do.

The following morning when Lefty rode up on his pony to inquire as to whether there would be classes that day, Maddie was waiting for him.

"This Great Father Day?" he asked.

She shook her head. "It's not the Sabbath, Lefty, but we're not having class today. I have something important to do. I want you to take me to your village."

Lefty slid from the back of his pony. "Why Wildfire want to go village?"

"I wish to speak to Red Feather. He killed a little prairie dog that Matthew had adopted as a pet. Red Feather shot him with an arrow."

Lefty looked undecided. "Not wise go village."

It was the second time in less than a day's time that she had been denied the right to speak to someone. "If you don't take me, I shall go by myself."

"Heap bad idea."

"Then I suggest you do as I ask." She mounted her horse and waited. Lefty hesitated for a moment, then nodded his head in assent before mounting his pony and racing off. If he meant to outrun her, he failed, for his pony offered no challenge for Rutabaga, who seemed to love nothing better than the chance to race across the grasslands.

It was less than a five-mile ride to the Cheyenne camp. The camp was concealed by a hill and it surprised Maddie to look down from the crest and see numerous tipis scattered below them along a winding creek.

Lefty led her along a narrow path that cut through the grass. "Buffalo path go north, south," he told her.

"If you follow path long enough, you always find water."

Despite the heat of the midday sun, the camp was bustling with activity. A young woman, her raven hair streaming down her back in two thick plaits, was on bent knees, scraping a buffalo skin that was stretched upon a wooden frame. A small infant lay strapped to a fur-lined carrier by her side.

A group of robust Indians were strapping skins to a travois that was attached to a horse. Various campfires blazed beneath heavy iron pots. On the outer limits of the camp, a dozen or so dark-skinned youths took turns casting spears into a willow hoop.

One by one, the Cheyennes looked up from their activities to glance at the two on horseback. Work and play were halted as the Indians caught sight of the white woman in their midst. Soon an eerie silence swept through the camp.

Maddie gripped the reins of her horse with damp hands. Her heart pounded as she rode past the stoic Indians. Intent upon proving she came in friendship, she tried to smile, but her mouth felt so wooden she could only manage a tightening of her lips.

She was greatly relieved when one young warrior whom she recognized from her calisthenics class raised his hand in greeting. But even he looked more surprised than friendly.

Lefty led the way to a small gathering of elderly men. No sooner had Lefty dismounted and joined the group than a lively conversation ensued. One of the men, with gray plaited hair and a granitelike face carved with deep lines, spoke in a thick, harsh voice. Maddie didn't need an interpreter to tell her that he objected to her presence.

After the older man had finished his barrage, he angrily stalked away. A warrior wearing a red-dyed roach upon a clean-shaven head pointed to a tipi that stood a distance from the others. Maddie recognized him as one of the Indians who had helped her put up her tipi. Since he gave no indication that they had met previously, she thought it best to follow his lead. She looked for Running Deer and Flying Hawk or any of the other Indians she knew by name, but they were nowhere in sight.

Lefty motioned for her to leave her horse and follow him on foot.

They were several yards away from the tipi when the Indian she recognized as Red Feather stepped outside, his arms folded across his chest. She had the feeling he was expecting them.

"Tell Red Feather that I come in peace. I do not wish him harm."

"If you are sincere in not wishing to do us harm, you will refrain from teaching my people the white man's ways."

Red Feather's command of the English language was a welcome surprise. Encouraged, she glanced up at Lefty. "I wish to speak to Red Feather alone."

Lefty's disapproval was evident, but he made no attempt to dissuade her. "Me wait by your horse."

He turned and walked away, leaving Maddie alone with Red Feather. "In my classroom, we teach each other. Lefty is teaching me your ways, and I am teaching him and his friends my ways."

"Your ways!" Red Feather grated out. "Is that why he walks around with hair looking like white woman?" To demonstrate, he spun his wrists in circles at both sides of his head. His every action radiated contempt.

"It's by teaching each other and coming to understand each other's ways that we can become friends."

"We will never be friends with white men! They make promises they do not keep. They lie."

"I do not lie, nor do I break promises."

"But you live with a murderer."

Shocked to hear Red Feather suggest such a thing, she quickly denied it. "I live with no one. I stay on Mr. Tyler's property, and I can assure you that he is no murderer."

"If you believe what you say is true, then you are the worst kind of liar, for you are lying to yourself."

Stunned by his rebuke, she could only watch in silence as he turned and ducked into his tipi. She was tempted to follow him, but thought better of it. She was not going to change Red Feather's anger toward white men in one day. That much was apparent. It was obvious to her that his feelings were too deep-rooted to be changed by talk alone.

She turned and found herself face to face with a sharp-featured Indian. Along with the usual inadequate breechclout, he wore a deerskin vest. Recalling Red Feather's unfair accusations, she folded her arms across her chest. If she really wanted to change the Indians' ways, she would persuade them to exchange their breechclouts for a decent pair of trousers!

The Indian grinned and grabbed a handful of her hair, which he rubbed between his thick fingers. Startled, she cried out and tried to free herself, but he refused to let go of her hair.

Fighting panic, she called to Lefty, who immediately came running to her rescue. "Quick, tell him he can't have my hair!"

Despite Lefty's attempts, the man refused to let go. She had no choice but to stand motionless while Lefty tried to persuade him to unhand her.

Lefty switched to English. "He say your hair color of red sunset."

"Lefty, listen to me carefully. You must explain that I will not take kindly to being scalped."

Lefty interpreted or at least she hoped he did. It was hard to know what was going through her captor's mind. He did, thankfully, let go of her hair, but his interest in her seemed no less ardent as he studied her from head to toe. He raised his hand parallel to the ground to indicate her exceptional height. He then held his hands parallel to each other to indicate her slender frame.

Maddie watched him with growing horror. She was convinced he was measuring her for a cooking pot, and if that indeed was the case, it didn't much matter what plans he had for her scalp. "Why is he looking me over like that?"

"He never see such high and narrow squaw."

"You mean tall and slender." She corrected him without conscious thought, then immediately chastised herself; her life could be in danger, and all she could think about was the correct use of the English language.

The Indian continued his open assessment of her. "What's his name?" she asked.

It took much pointing and hand movement for Lefty to convey the name. After several wild guesses, she finally determined what Lefty was trying to tell her. "His name's Shooting Star!"

Lefty nodded his head, his mouth curved in a wide grin. "Shooting Star."

She turned to Shooting Star, who was still appraising her. "It's very nice to make your acquaintance, but I really must be going." She tried to step around him, but he blocked her path and continued to hold his hands this way and that to indicate her measurements.

Irritated by his rude assessment, Maddie decided to give him a bit of his own medicine. She moved her hand in front of her to indicate his large, rounded stomach.

Much to her surprise, Shooting Star laughed aloud and said something that sounded like he had a mouthful of rocks.

Lefty grinned. "Shooting Star joyful that you admire him."

"Admire . . ." She burst into laughter. She couldn't help herself. Unfortunately, her laughter seemed to please her admirer all the more.

Suddenly Shooting Star's face grew serious, and he said something to Lefty. A lively discussion followed that sounded to Maddie suspiciously like an argument. Since Shooting Star and Lefty kept pointing at her as they shouted at each other, she could only assume that she was the subject of their discord. A crowd of Cheyennes started to gather around, glaring at her as if she had done something wrong.

Suddenly Lefty spun on his moccasined heel and walked away. Shooting Star tried to block her own departure, but he was accosted verbally by an old woman whose head was covered by a red woven blanket.

As the woman's voice escalated, Maddie used the distraction to make her escape.

It was all she could do to catch up to Lefty. "What was all that about? What did Shooting Star want? What were you two arguing about?"

"Nothing you want to know," Lefty took the reins of her horse and shoved them into her hands. "Follow trail to main road."

She mounted just as the old woman came charging after them. She raised a gnarled hand toward the sky and glared at Maddie with glistening eyes, her voice crackling like fizzling firecrackers as she spoke. Mesmerized by the woman's rage, Maddie had no clue what she had done to incur such wrath.

Maddie gripped the reins in an effort to keep her horse from bolting. "What's the matter with her? What does she want?"

"She wants you to go," Lefty explained.

"Well, holy blazes, why doesn't she just say so?"

# Chapter 19

Supper that night was smoked meat, goat cheese, and fresh-baked bread. Maddie had finally learned how to use the stove, but she held little hope of ever learning how to manage the fuel so that the fire would last until an entire meal was cooked.

Earlier she'd gathered a small bouquet of wildflowers and arranged them around a buffalo-tallow candle. Despite the chipped dishes and dented silverware, the table and centerpiece brought a dignity to the simple meal. Unfortunately, it did little to break the tension in the air. Luke said nothing, his full attention centered on his son, as if he expected another fit.

She looked across the table to where Matthew sat, his untouched plate in front of him. He held himself unnaturally still, as if moving would shake loose whatever he held inside. Her heart went out to the boy, and she longed to take him in her arms and make up to him in some small way for all the terrible things that had happened to him.

She decided if she could divert Luke's attention away from him, maybe Matthew would relax enough to eat his supper. "Did you know that the Cheyenne village is only five miles away?"

Luke lowered his fork and lifted his gaze to meet hers. "How do you know that?"

"I was there."

His eyes widened in astonishment. "You were there? At the Cheyenne village? Are you out of your mind?"

She lifted her chin. "What else was there to do? Red Feather can't be allowed to go around killing . . ." She glanced at Matthew, who kept his eyes focused on his plate. "He can't be allowed to go around doing anything he pleases to other people's property!"

"And what do you propose can be done about it?"

"We can discuss our disagreements like civilized people."

"Spoken like a true diplomat." He surprised her with a smile that softened the harsh lines of his face. Lord, she hadn't realized until now how defenseless she was against his smile.

"So what did you and this Red Feather talk about? And how did the two of you manage to communicate in the first place?"

"He spoke English," she said. "He called white men liars. He said we made promises we did not keep."

Luke thought about this a moment. "I remember now. Red Feather spent much time in Colton trying to assure the citizens that he and his people wished to live in peaceful coexistence. Catherine-Anne . . ." He stopped.

Her breath caught. "What about your wife?"

His eyes locked with hers. "She was frightened when that band of Cheyennes returned to the area. It hadn't been that long since the Indian raids. Some of the homesteaders in Colton had lost homes or family members in those raids."

"But Red Feather and his band were allowed to stay?"

"The town was divided. Some, including the mayor, were violently opposed. I wouldn't be a bit surprised if some blame the Indians for the recent fire."

"You don't believe that, do you?" Maddie asked.

"It doesn't matter what I believe. What else did Red Feather say?"

Maddie glanced down at her plate. Red Feather had called him a murderer. She'd been shocked at the time, but now she was convinced that it wasn't Luke he'd called a murderer, but all white men. It was the only explanation that made sense. "That was all."

She glanced up to find Luke looking at her and she tried to read his expression. But now, as always, it was difficult—mainly because he took such care to keep his thoughts to himself.

"He did make it clear to me that he has a low regard for white men. He claims they lied to him."

Luke nodded. "The government made many false promises in order to persuade the Indians to move into Indian Territory." He leaned forward. "Maddie, please be careful. You don't know what he . . . what Red Feather might be capable of."

"Do you think he'll resort to violence?"

"It appears he's already resorted to violence."

Maddie shivered. She'd been cold ever since finding Prince's body. "Do you think . . ." She glanced at Matthew. "What happened to Prince . . . do you think it was a warning?"

"Maybe."

She met Luke's gaze. She didn't want to think about the possibility that Lefty and Flying Hawk and the others might turn against them. "Is Matthew going to be all right?"

Luke's face looked grim, but he nodded his head.

"Did you talk about it?"

"Talk about what?"

"Prince's death?"

A muscle tightened at his jaw. "Some things are best not talked about."

"But . . ."

"Please don't fight me on this, Maddie. I know what's best for my son. Discussing something that is obviously very upsetting to him can only do more harm."

She clamped her mouth shut. He was wrong about how he handled Matthew. She was positive of it. But she had no right to go against his wishes.

After he'd finished his meal, Luke pushed his empty plate away and excused himself. He stopped by her chair as if to say something, then apparently thinking better of it, he heaved a deep sigh and walked outside.

Maddie set to work washing the dishes and tidying up the soddy. When she had finished, she sprinkled fresh hay upon the dirt floor. Matthew normally helped her, but tonight he sat on the edge of the bed and stared into space.

He looked so distant and forlorn, she didn't have the heart to scold him for neglecting his chores. She dried the last dish and stacked it with the others on the shelf. She wiped her hands on the flour sack tied to her waist for an apron and walked over to the bed.

"It's bedtime," she said gently. Without meeting her eyes, he lay his head on the feather pillow. She sat on the edge of the straw mattress and rubbed his back. The boy held himself rigid seeming almost oblivious to her presence. She wanted so much to talk to him, to talk about Prince, about his own mother. But she couldn't in good conscience go against his father's wishes.

Still, she fervently believed that loss and sadness needed expression. She pulled off his boots. "My father died when I was sixteen," she said softly. The candle next to the bed flickered, and for an instant it appeared to her to grow brighter as thoughts of her father came flooding back.

"You would have liked him, Matthew. His job required him to travel a lot, and I hardly saw him as a child. But when he came back to town ... oh, did we have fun." She smiled as the warm memories of her childhood filled her heart.

"His favorite pastime was to race by the White House in his carriage." She glanced down at Matthew and was surprised to find him looking up at her, the blank expression gone. "The White House is where the president of the United States lives," she explained. "And my father was certain that the president stopped everything he was doing just to come to the window and wave at us as we raced past."

She fell silent a moment to savor the memory, before adding, "I was very sad when my father died. I cried for days, and my heart felt like it was going to break inside my chest. And right here ..." she ran a finger along Matthew's throat ... "I felt a lump that wouldn't go away."

Matthew couldn't say anything, of course, not verbally. But his face, his eyes, the hand that found hers, spoke to her on so many levels, she could almost hear his voice. *That's how I feel,* he seemed to say, and his eyes filled with tears.

She wrapped her arms around him and held him close. "Let it out," she whispered. His body shook as the tears ran down his cheeks and dampened her blouse. She never knew that one so young could shed so many tears.

It was quite some time before his body grew still and she released him. Matthew obviously thought she was going to leave him, for he grabbed her hand and looked at her with panic-filled eyes.

She squeezed his hand and leaned closer to reassure him. "I'll stay until your father returns. I promise." Kissing him on the forehead, she helped him to undress and put on his linen nightshirt. "If you move over, I'll lay by your side."

His mouth softened. It wasn't exactly a smile, but it was close enough to make her heart lilt. He moved away from the edge of the mattress, and she lay her head on the pillow next to his and sang him a song that her father used to sing about drunken sailors and tipsy horses. What a song to sing to a child, her mother used to scold. What a song indeed.

But it did the job, and soon Matthew's eyes fluttered shut.


It was nearly ten o'clock before Luke doused the lantern in the barn and stepped outside. The tipi was dark, and for that he was grateful. Still, the memory of the schoolteacher outlined against the hide walls of her tipi came to mind, and he was momentarily taken aback.

Why did that particular vision of her keep coming back to taunt him? And why was it that at odd times during the day when he was in the fields working, he kept seeing her in his mind's eye, bolting through the tall grass like a wild young colt, her red hair streaming behind her?

No, she wasn't his type. Not physically. Not even intellectually. What in the world was to be done with a woman who had the audacity to call the president of the United States a drunken swindler and who knew the personal strengths and shortcomings of every senator? She understood things he had no knowledge of, confound it! And where in the world had she learned all those statistics about the war? It didn't seem right, somehow, for a woman to be so knowledgeable about military strategy.

She wasn't his type, praise the Lord for that. A

woman with such a mind of her own could drive a man to drink.

He tiptoed passed the dark tipi so as not to wake her and walked quietly into the house.

The candles had burned down to the stub, and the flickering light was so dim, he could barely find his way around the room.

He peeled off his shirt and pants down to his underwear. Not wanting to wake Matthew, who preferred to sleep on the outside edge of the bed, he crawled onto the mattress from the bottom of the bed. Halfway up he froze. The light flared as the last bit of wick gasped amid a puddle of hot melted wax.

In the instant before the light went out altogether, he caught a glimpse of glowing red hair, and his heart practically stood still.

Maddie was sound asleep on his bed.

# Chapter 20

During a span that lasted mere seconds, no more than a moment of time, Luke's heart stopped, fluttered, and then beat so quickly that he could barely breathe. The world seem defined, suddenly, by her presence. His senses were so attuned to her that even the gentle sound of her breathing seemed like a roar to his ears.

For the longest time he remained in place, frozen on hands and knees, afraid to move for fear of waking her, for fear of waking himself from what surely must be a dream.

His mind raced with a bewildering profusion of sensation. It was all at once dark and light, hot and cold, noisy and quiet.

He forced a deep breath, clearing his head. The hard muscles in his back relaxed and the knots began to dissolve. At long last, reality took precedence. It was cold, dammit. And uncomfortable. He had to do something.

He supposed he could sleep in her tipi. It wasn't a very appealing option, though, and he quickly discarded it. Besides, he was likely to wake her up if he started to bump around in the dark. Relieved that he'd found a justifiable reason to crawl into his own bed, he inched his way along the length of the mattress and took his place next to Matthew.

There wasn't room in the bed for three people. He would have to sleep sideways, with his back pressed against the wooden board, next to the wall.

He could sleep on the floor, he supposed. It would be the gentlemanly thing to do under the circumstances. But he wasn't feeling particularly gentlemanly. Come to think about it, he wasn't feeling particularly tired, although scant moments ago he'd felt exhausted.

His senses were focused on her, alert to the sweet flowerlike scent—even the warmth—of her body.

It had been so long since he'd slept with a woman. Not that he was sleeping with one now, of course. Not in the traditional sense. If he ever did have occasion to take a woman to bed, it certainly wouldn't be a brash, tall, skinny woman with ... warm, soft, loving eyes that could melt butter, whose hair was so shiny and bright that even the dimmest of lights danced upon its lovely, silky strands.

He pressed his heated body against the wall and tried to erase the memory of her naked form upon the walls of her tipi. *A shadow,* he told himself, *that's all it was. Just a shadow.* Even so, his mind had had no trouble filling in every glorious detail. Not then. Not now.

Lord, if it weren't for Matthew, he'd have her in his arms so fast she wouldn't have a chance to object. He would devour her lips with his own, make her body sing until all of her fiery sparks and boundless energy were focused solely on him.

Just thinking of it made his own body sing.

Just thinking of it made his own body ache.

Just thinking of all that he would do to her made his heart fight the tight constraints he had put on it. If only Matthew weren't between them.

The fantasy was wiped out by another thought, this one a grim reminder of the past. Even if Matthew weren't between them, Luke could not give into his feelings, not completely. He must maintain control, hold back, never let himself love fully. That was the Tyler legacy.

He felt a stiffness in his shoulder. He was cramped, and something—Matthew's elbow, it turned out—was poking him in the ribs. Gingerly, he moved his son's arm. He then flung his own arm across Matthew's waist, stiffening when his hand found hers. He held his breath, and when she didn't move, he relaxed and let his own fingers curl around hers.

Her skin felt warm and silky soft beneath his. *Soft.* He chuckled silently. Now that was a word he had never thought he would use in regards to Maddie. And here, tonight, already, he had used the word twice to describe her.

Reminding himself not to feel too much, he held on to her hand like a drowning man held on to a life raft.

It was much later that he felt her pull her hand from his and leave the cabin. He was tempted to ask her to stay. But she left so quickly—as if she was fleeing from some danger—that she was gone before the dreamlike state of his mind could form the thought.

The bed felt empty without her, the room void of life. He should have asked her to stay, dammit. Should have.

The tipi was dark and cold when she slipped inside and felt for her bedroll. His bed. Lord, she'd never forget waking up and finding *his* hand on hers.

He hadn't known he'd had his hand in hers.

He probably thought it was Matthew's. Of course. That was it. And it had been dark when he entered the soddy; maybe he hadn't realized she was there. Was that possible? Could someone actually not know that a third person was in a bed that size? Not likely. But if he had known . . . why hadn't he waked her so that she could return to her own bed?

He didn't know.

He did!

Shaken by the womanly feelings that stirred within her, she sank to the ground and scampered like a frightened child into the protective warmth of the bedroll.

It was a poor substitute for the warmth and fullness of his bed, knowing he was but a child's width away from her. If it hadn't been for Matthew . . . holy Jupiter. Her heart thudded at the thought of what might have happened, could have happened, would surely have happened had it not been for Matthew.

She left early the next morning to check on the progress of the school, driving her wagon along the dirt road leading to Colton as fast as poor Rutabaga could go. She'd left before Matthew or his father had made an appearance, before the smell of coffee told her that they were awake, before Lefty had made his morning trek to inquire if it was the Great Father's Day.

Not that she had any reason to avoid anyone, she told herself. She had nothing to feel guilty about. She had simply fallen asleep. In Luke's bed. Luke's and Matthew's bed, she amended. It was a perfectly innocent act.

She was anxious to begin her classes. That was why she woke that morning feeling like someone had built a fire beneath her. In her.

She was . . . bored. She wasn't used to so much free time, and that certainly would explain the way her mind had been working lately. She'd never been one to harbor such wanton thoughts. She was far too practical.

So why had she lain in bed in the wee hours of the morning, staring at the darkness and trying to ignore the heat of desire that kept her twisting and turning? She was feeling the same disarming warmth just thinking about it.

Fortunately she caught sight of Mr. Boxer, and the effect was similar to being doused with ice water.

He was studying a set of plans, along with Colton's sheriff and mayor and the man called Weedler, who from the first moment she met him in Hays had made her feel uneasy. All four men turned toward her as she drove her wagon alongside them.

Mayor Mettle was the first to greet her. "Good morning, Miss Percy. What brings you here so early?"

"I thought I'd check to see how things were coming along. When do you think the school will be finished?"

"No time at all," Mr. Boxer replied. "The only thing holding us up is manpower. But the problem is about to be resolved. Several families will be arriving at the end of the week. Leaving Hays by caravan. Isn't that so, Sheriff?"

"Sure 'nuf is. And you'll be able to meet some of your students."

At the mention of students, Maddie's interest perked. "I can start classes then?"

Mr. Boxer looked dubious. "I doubt that the school will be ready for another couple of weeks or so."

"But we could still begin classes." She glanced around in search of shade. If she ever had occasion to see another tree, she would be inclined to hug it. A short distance away, the eastbound train whizzed by in a cloud of dust.

Mr. Boxer offered to give her a walking tour of the town. "That would be most generous of you," Maddie said.

They left the other three men discussing the plans.

Mr. Boxer pointed out the staked ground. "As I told you previously, most towns are built at random. A shop here, a shop there. But this town has been planned precisely so that we don't have two incompatible businesses next to each other."

They walked a full circle along what would become Main Street and headed toward the plot of land designated for the schoolhouse. "Right there will be the jailhouse," he said.

Maddie frowned. "It's seems awfully close to the school." It was in fact adjacent to the play yard.

"Close, you say?" He adjusted his glasses. "It will be the museum that will be adjacent to the jailhouse."

"Even so," she protested. "I expect the children to spend a lot of time in the museum." She glanced at the row of stakes behind her. "Isn't there somewhere else?"

"We can't put the school at the other end of town because then it would be right next to the church."

"I don't see why not. School is not in session on Sundays."

"But there are times during the week that the church may be used. For example, the ladies of the quilting bee might wish to meet at the church."

"I see. But couldn't we move the school down a few doors?"

"Down a few doors?" He looked positively startled. "That would mean we'd have to move the saloon and . . . Come along. I'll show you the plans."

They rejoined the other men. "Miss Percy is still of the opinion that the school is too close to the jailhouse."

While the men discussed the problem and made notations on the plans, she noticed an Indian sitting on his horse, watching them from a distance. It was Red

Feather, she was sure of it, although he was too far away for her to see his face.

As if he sensed her eyes on him, the horseman suddenly raced off, leaving a cloud of dust in his wake. She felt a cold chill as she recalled the last time he had raced off in such a conspicuous manner.

Boxer and the mayor were so intent upon studying the plans, they seemed oblivious to anything around them. Only Weedler seemed to notice the intruder, and the look on his face made her wince. It was not idle curiosity Maddie saw, but hatred and contempt. Aware, suddenly, that she was watching him, Weedler managed to compose himself and turn his attention back to the plans, but she couldn't forget the look of hatred she'd seen a moment earlier on his face.

It was mid-morning by the time she pulled the wagon up in front of the soddy.

Matthew ran outside to meet her. He held out his hand to show her a flat rock. Maddie jumped down from the driver's seat and took the rock in her hand. A faint outline of a fernlike leaf had been captured in the limestone rock.

"It's a fossil," Maddie explained. "This leaf was probably from a plant that grew here many thousands of years ago." She handed it back to him. "Where did you find it?"

He pointed in the direction of his father's fields.

"Do you think you can find more rocks just like it?" she asked. "They would be perfect for the museum."

Luke walked from behind the soddy. He seemed pleased to see her. "We missed you at breakfast."

Not wanting him to think that last night had anything to do with her absence, she hastily explained. "I drove out to check on the progress of the schoolhouse.

Do you by any chance know a man by the name of Max Weedler?"

"Only that he drifted into town a year or two ago and started a gambling hall. Why?"

"I was just curious."

"Come on, son." He called to Matthew, but his eyes remained on her face as if he were trying to read her thoughts even as she tried to read his. Any hopes she held that her presence in his bed had escaped his notice were immediately dashed.

There was nothing left to do but to bring the matter out in the open and be done with it. "About last night . . ."

"Last night?"

"I apologize for falling asleep in your bed . . ." She lost her voice suddenly and was forced to clear her throat before she could continue. "Matthew was still upset by what happened yesterday and asked me to stay." Even though he still couldn't speak, she felt confident in her ability to understand him.

"There was no harm done, as far as I know. Was there?"

Her mind momentarily lit on the memory of his hand on hers, and by the time she'd shaken off the surge of warm blood that coursed through her veins, she'd forgotten the intent of the question. "Was there what?" she stammered.

"Harm done."

"None that I can think of."

"Then I can't think of any reason why you should apologize."

Nor could she, and in actuality, her apology had only been a ruse to bring up the subject that seemed to be creating a barrier between them.

"Matthew," he called again. "We need to get started."

This time Matthew came running and reached the wagon ahead of his father.

Luke hesitated. "I'm glad we had this conversation."

"You ... you are?"

"I would hate to spend the rest of my life wondering if I'd only dreamt that you were in my bed." Judging by the look on his face, this was hardly the kind of comment that came easy to him. Not like some of the men she knew in Washington, whose conversations were often rife with provocative innuendos. Still, he managed an air of composure as he walked away, something that she was momentarily, unable to achieve herself.

Maddie watched the wagon roll away, and suddenly she realized how much she had come to care for them both. It was no longer a matter of her wanting him to kiss her, she admitted to herself. She wanted him to love her.

The thought filled her with warmth at first, but it was soon replaced by an unsettled feeling. Matthew couldn't talk and Luke wouldn't. There was so much about them she didn't know, didn't understand. Even as frustrating as Luke's resistance to her was, she could feel herself drawing ever closer to him.

Didn't he know that whatever it was that held him captive also held her captive?

# Chapter 21

Luke's wagon was but a spot of dust on the distant prairie. Wanting to hold him in her vision for as long as possible, she shaded her face with her hand and narrowed her eyes.

It wasn't until a shadow crossed her path that she knew she was no longer alone.

Startled, she turned and was surprised to find herself face-to-face with the old Indian woman who had accosted her at the Cheyenne village.

Maddie's hand flew to her chest. "You scared me."

The woman tossed her head in what looked like disgust and shuffled toward Maddie's tipi.

Maddie followed her. "Is there something I can do for you?"

Ignoring the question, the woman spread the blanket she carried on the ground in the shade of the tipi and lowered herself down. Once settled in place, she pulled a red woven shawl around her thin shoulders and glared at Maddie with eyes as black as obsidian.

"What can I do for you?" Maddie asked again. She glanced in the direction of the Cheyenne village. Holy blazes, where was Lefty when she needed him? "How may I help you?" She punctuated each word with broad gestures but received no response. She might as well be talking to a wall.

The woman continued to glare, but said nothing. Maddie made several attempts to communicate with her. Eager to start her morning chores, she finally gave up.

When Maddie walked to the well for water at noon the woman was still sitting in front of the tipi, and remained there for the remainder of the day. As the day grew hotter, Maddie began to worry about the woman. She took her some water and offered her dry meat and cheese. The woman ate, but refused the water.

The old Indian was still by the tipi when Luke and Matthew returned from the fields. The sun had disappeared behind the distant horizon, leaving a ruby-red glow in its wake. A slight breeze brushed over the land, gently rippling the grass.

Matthew jumped from the wagon and ran to Maddie. She greeted him with a smile, and he surprised her by handing her a wooden bucket that held a dead cardinal.

Startled, she glanced at Luke, who looked as puzzled as she was. "He found the bird today and insisted upon bringing it home."

Maddie stooped down to look Matthew in the eye. "What do you want me to do with this?" she asked softly.

His face remained expressionless, but she sensed some struggle within him. He was trying to tell her something. "Matthew?"

He reached into the pocket of his overalls and pulled out his fossil rock.

Understanding dawned, and she straightened. "Oh, I see. You want me to put the cardinal in the museum." She took the bucket from him. He smiled up at her, and she didn't have the heart to explain that the body of the dead bird would decay and not make an appropriate display.

She carried the cardinal back to her tipi, while Luke and his father washed up.

Red Shawl, as Maddie now called her, gave Luke a hard, glaring look before gathering her blanket and shuffling away.

Maddie set the bucket down and ran after the woman. "Wait!" She pointed to the wagon. "I'll take you home."

The woman shook her head and kept walking. Not knowing what else to do, Maddie walked to the rain barrel where Luke and Matthew were drying themselves with the clean flour sacks she had set out for them earlier.

"Who was that?" Luke asked.

"I'm not really certain. I met her when I went to the Cheyenne village."

"What was she doing here?"

"I don't know. She showed up this morning, but I have no idea why." Maddie scanned the distance. It worried her that the old woman was traipsing across the prairie by herself.

"Something smells good," Luke said.

"Rabbit stew," she explained. "I never saw a jack-rabbit before coming here." It surprised her that during her father's trip to the prairie in search of buffalo, he had not thought to capture any of the less impressive, but no less interesting, prairie animals for display.

During dinner, Maddie talked about the things she had observed during an earlier walk. "It's the most amazing place, this prairie," she said, breathless with excitement. "I saw a hawk approach the nest of a mourning dove, and the dove pretended to be lame."

Luke listened in the way he had of listening to her,

his head inclined slightly, his eyes warm and alive, as if she nurtured some vital part of him. "Pretended? Why?"

"So that the hawk would think it had itself an easy catch. And you know, it worked. The hawk followed the mourning dove, and the nest was saved."

Matthew greeted this news with a wide grin.

Warmed by the joyful look on his young son's face, Luke asked, "What about the mourning dove?"

"She returned a while later without the hawk." Feeling shy before the intensity of his gaze, she turned to Matthew. "Isn't that wonderful news, Matthew?"

Matthew nodded his head, his eyes aglow.

Luke watched his son from across the table. He'd never seen the boy look so happy as when he was in Maddie's company. He watched her every move, seemed to hang on to her every word. Luke couldn't blame Matthew for that.

Lord, she made the prairie sound like some magical place filled with the most wondrous creatures. It amazed him to think how blind he'd been to his surroundings.

"Maybe the prairie wouldn't be so bad if it weren't for that infernal wind," he conceded.

"Oh, but that's the amazing part!" she declared. "I've been studying the wind, and I've noticed something. Most of the plants out here depend on a certain wind velocity for the seeds to pop open. Some seeds scatter in the gentlest wind; others require a gale."

Luke gazed at her in wonder. Seen through her eyes, even the wind earned respect, if not complete tolerance.

Lord, the wind, the endless grass, the glaring sun— all of it took on new meaning for him because of Maddie.

After dinner, the three of them washed and dried the dishes. Matthew indicated he wanted Maddie to tell him a bedtime story.

"Maybe your father will tell you one." She glanced up at Luke. "I have to work on Matthew's little bird."

Luke looked puzzled. "Work on it?"

"Matthew wants me to display the bird in the museum. Before I can do that, I must prepare it for display."

"You know how to do that?"

She nodded. "I used to help my father in the lab."

She gave Matthew a hug, lit a lantern, and carried it outside. It was dark and still warm, the earlier breeze giving way to the softest whisper of moving air.

She hung the lantern from a stick that stuck out of the side of the sod house. Standing in the circle of light, she balanced a board upon a keg to use as a work table. She then laid the tiny bird gently in the center of the table and, with knife in hand, made a careful incision beneath the wing.

The knife had been a gift from her father, along with the bottle of arsenic that was used as a preservative. She kept both in a leather case. She had never thought to use the knife or the arsenic until tonight, and it surprised her how much her hand shook.

She needn't have been concerned, for her confidence grew after the first incision, and she could almost hear her father's booming voice echoing from the past, guiding her through the many steps that would preserve—without compromising—the beauty of nature.

It was late before she completed the task. Too late to show Matthew what a wonderful addition to the museum the bird was going to make.

She buried the innards and then scrubbed down her work bench and tools.

She then plunged her hands into a bucket of clean water and scrubbed them with lye soap. The light had been turned off in the soddy an hour earlier, and she suspected Luke and Matthew were already asleep.

Nevertheless, she doused her own lantern before stripping off her clothes and lowering herself into the tub of water that she'd set out earlier for her bath. The water was tepid, and she tried not to think of the hot baths back home. Water temperature aside, there was something magical about taking a bath beneath a star-studded sky.

A sound unlike any she had ever heard before floated out of the darkness. Her heart beating fast, she sat up in the tub and listened intently. She soon realized that the soft, reedy sound was coming from a flute.

She reached for a towel and stepped out of the bath. Wrapping the towel around her, she hastened to the tipi.

Shivering, she dried herself briskly and quickly donned a nightgown. The flute stopped playing, and after a while she fumbled in the dark until she found a candle and tinderbox.

Once lit, the candle flickered softly, casting shadows onto the tipi walls. She stood at the door of her tipi and stared out into the darkness. Only the usual sounds of night could be heard.

Who was it? she wondered. Who would wander about at night, playing music beneath the stars? Smiling to herself, she dropped the flap of the tipi in place and reached for her hairbrush.

Upon hearing the flute, Luke climbed out of bed and slipped on his boots. He stood at the door of the soddy and listened to the clear, melodious tune. All too soon the music stopped. Wanting it to continue, he stepped outside and stared into the darkness.

The sound of a horse galloping across the prairie told him it was probably one of the Cheyennes. White men would follow the road. Indians, however, seem to have no qualms about cutting through the grasslands and following the natural trails, even at night.

Spotting the glimmer of light from the side of the house, he closed the door softly behind him and walked toward her tipi. Maybe Maddie would know the name of the musician.

He stopped in midstep when he saw her shadow play across the walls of the tipi. She was brushing her hair.

He'd not been able to sleep. He kept thinking about the night she'd shared his bed. How she changed everything. How the endless lonely prairie, the ugly sod house, the ever-threatening sky had suddenly become treasures to cherish.

And Matthew—oh, God, Matthew. Even he had changed. How it did Luke's heart good to see his son smile again and laugh, to see color in Matthew's bright young face and excitement in his eyes.

If he loved her for no other reason, he loved her for what she had done for Matthew.

Love. The word hugged him in a cocoon of longing and need. But it was a fleeting warmth at best. He feared love as he feared hate. Both could be dangerous to a man like him. Isn't that what he had been brought up to believe?

Still, as he stood watching her brush her hair, it was hard to conceive that anything he felt for this woman could be the least bit dangerous. Certainly not the love he felt. No sooner had he put his feelings into words than he was overcome by disbelief.

Lord, it can't be love. All these warm, puzzling,

wonderful, frightening feelings ... can't be love. He could never—must never—allow himself to love.

At least not the kind of love she deserved—would surely demand. A woman of extremes, yes, she was that, all right. He couldn't imagine her settling for the kind of love he'd shared with Catherine-Anne. The kind of respectful and protective love, dispassionate and undemanding love that was so safe and sane.

Knowing Maddie, he realized she would demand more—far more—than he could dare give her.

He took a step back. He had no right standing outside her tipi, intruding on her privacy, thinking thoughts that were meant to stir a man's blood, not make him retreat.

Unable at that moment to return to the lonely soddy and the even lonelier bed, he stood watching her, cursing the circumstances that kept him from giving in to the full depths of his feelings.

Kept him from going to her.

Kept him from loving her.

A moment later, he had yet another reason to curse her. For she had tossed the brush aside and lifted her arms to pin up her hair. The action allowed the full loveliness of her body to become more clearly defined. Her nipples budded freely from the delicate mounds of her lovely, round breasts and pressed against her gown.

A deep, anguished sigh escaped him. Unable to withstand the torture a moment longer, he spun on his heels and hastened back to the soddy.

Shortly afterward, he lay in bed and stared into the dark void of the night.

Matthew's soft breathing was the only sound that broke the silence, but Luke was unaware of the peacefulness of the night. He was haunted by too many ghosts. His troubled thoughts kept him tossing and turning, until his body felt like a ship battered by stormy seas.

The fact that he could no longer control his thoughts, let alone his feelings, worried him. He could not afford the luxury of losing control of his emotions. He had lost control following Catherine-Anne's death, and that had proven every bit as lethal as his mother always told him it would be.

And now he was losing control again.

He couldn't let himself care for someone. He was a damned murderer; he should have told her that in the beginning.

Before she had begun looking at him with the softness he had seen in her eyes earlier.

Before he had felt his limbs pulse with desire for her.

Before his heart had started its annoying habit of lurching whenever she came into sight.

Who would have thought he would fall so hard? She was unlike any other woman he'd been attracted to. Tall and willowy, she was, loud and bossy. Given to strange ways.

Oh, but those eyes, those lovely green eyes that seemed to fill the room with hidden messages. And her hair, her lovely, lush hair that was obscenely, yet gloriously, red.

He wanted her.

But he was a murderer, and she had the right to know that about him.

He closed his eyes. He could hardly breathe for the want and need that possessed him. He wanted so much to go to her.

But she deserved so much better. And as he lay there in the darkness, he wondered if this was to be his true punishment for taking another man's life, this unfulfilled need for a woman he could never hope to have.

The sins of the father . .

# Chapter 22

The next day, Matthew ran into the house and stopped dead in his tracks. His eyes were focused on the little cardinal that was perched upon a piece of scrap wood Maddie had found in the barn, its tiny beak parted as if in song.

"Do you like it?" Maddie asked. She had taken great pains to create the illusion of a natural environment. The bird stood next to a tiny nest in a field of buffalo grass. Tiny eggs filled the nest, made from real eggshells.

It was the kind of display or "magic" for which her father was known. Before he had begun his work, museums had made little, if any, effort to display animals in their natural environment. But Whittaker M. Percy had changed all that.

Matthew's eyes shone with excitement as he looked up at her and nodded. He reached out and stroked the soft feathers.

She gave him a hug. "This is going to make a wonderful addition to our museum. Meanwhile, I'll set it on the shelf by your bed."

Luke's voice drifted through the half-open door. "Hurry, son."

"You better go," Maddie said.

Matthew stroked the bird one more time before racing back outside. Maddie cleared a place on the shelf next to the bed and set the bird in place.

She then busied herself washing the breakfast dishes and spreading fresh hay upon the dirt floor. On impulse, she lifted Luke's pillow to her bosom and squeezed it tight. Her mouth went dry as she got a whiff of his manly fragrance.

Shaking herself, she put the pillow back on the bed. What in the world was she thinking? The last thing she needed was to fancy herself in love with a man obviously so at odds with himself. He was simply too serious-minded for her. What she needed was someone to laugh with. Luke Tyler didn't laugh much. But when he did, oh, Lord, when he did . . .

After she finished her morning chores, she walked out to the tipi and found Red Shawl sitting on her blanket, as she had on the previous day.

The old woman said nothing as Maddie approached. It had taken many years of sun and wind to carve the deep lines into that rough, dark skin. But nothing had dimmed the bright eyes that seemed to judge Maddie anew every time they looked her way.

"Good morning," Maddie said. She was not certain how much the woman understood. "Would you like something to drink or eat?"

The woman made no reply. Maddie tried out a few of the Cheyenne words she'd learned, but these only brought more suspicious glares.

Lefty rode up later that day and walked into the soddy without knocking, startling Maddie as she prepared supper.

"You startled me, Lefty," she scolded. "Don't you know you're supposed to knock?"

Lefty looked confused. "Knock?"

"On the door. Like this." She wiped her hands on her apron and demonstrated.

He folded his arms across his bare chest and glowered at her. "Me no drumming bird!"

"Drumming bird?" She thought for a moment. "You mean woodpecker?"

"Me no woodpecker!"

"It's only polite to knock," she explained. "Don't you knock when you visit another tipi?"

"Not woodpecker!" he repeated. He looked offended, and she tried to think of a way to restore his usual sunny disposition. "Where have you been, and why haven't you and the others come for your exercises?"

Lefty was not so easily distracted. "Great Father's Day."

Maddie folded her arms across her chest. "It is not the Sabbath."

"No Great Father's Day?"

"No. Now would you mind telling me what Red Shawl wants?"

"Red Shawl?"

"Whatever her name is. The woman who sits by my tipi all day. What does she want?"

"That Picking Bones. I'll ask her." He walked toward the door and knocked before opening it. Maddie was tempted to explain that one only had to knock *before* entering, but she decided to let the matter drop. Outside, Lefty and the old woman had what seemed to Maddie a rather spirited conversation.

Hearing the voices rise, Maddie watched from the window. When Lefty and the woman finished their conversation, she motioned him inside. Even though she held the door open, he made a point of knocking before entering.

"Like woodpecker," he mumbled.

Ignoring his complaint, she made him sit down. "So what did Picking Bones say?"

Lefty frowned as he struggled to find the proper English words. "Picking Bone's daughter, White Blossom, wants to be Shooting Star's squaw." He grinned proudly. "That's why Picking Bones sit in front of tipi."

Maddie puzzled over this. "I don't understand."

Lefty looked surprised. "No? Me no say words right?"

"The words were fine. You just didn't say enough of them. What does White Blossom's wanting to be Shooting Star's squaw have to do with me?"

"Ah." Lefty nodded. "Me understand. You no understand."

"That's right. I don't understand. You tell me."

"Shooting Star like Maddie."

Maddie recalled how the brave had looked her up and down like she was a piece of meat to be bartered for. "I still don't understand."

Lefty thought for a moment. "Shooting Star like ..." this time he emphasized the word with gestures that could leave no doubt to his meaning ... "Maddie."

Maddie's eyes widened. Not wanting to believe what he was telling her, she lowered herself into a chair. "You mean he ... *likes* me?"

Lefty looked puzzled. "Heap like," he added helpfully, nodding his head to emphasize.

It was hard to believe. Shooting Star had only laid eyes on her once. Of course it would explain the argument between Lefty and Shooting Star at the Cheyenne camp, she supposed, but she still wasn't convinced. "Shooting Star doesn't know me."

"He talk about you."

"This is terrible. You must tell Picking Bones not to worry. Shooting Star and I can only be friends."

Lefty shook his head. "No friend. Shooting Star want squaw."

"No squaw!" Maddie declared adamantly. "Now go and tell Picking Bones what I said. I'll go with you."

Maddie marched Lefty to the tipi with the same sense of urgency she would employ upon escorting an errant student home to his parents. "Tell her."

While Lefty talked to Picking Bones, Maddie paced back and forth in front of them. It was her opinion that Lefty didn't sound forceful enough when representing her viewpoint. In contrast, Picking Bones sounded most assertive. Whenever the woman spoke, Maddie stopped pacing and demanded to know what she said.

"She stay here so that Shooting Star not come."

"This is ridiculous." Maddie walked back and forth, thinking. She stopped in front of the older woman. "How long does she plan to stay here?"

Lefty bent over Picking Bones and, after he exchanged a few terse words with her, straightened. "Picking Bones stay here until White Blossom is Shooting Star squaw, or she die of thirst."

"I offered Picking Bones water," Maddie said, feeling defensive.

"Picking Bones say you give her dead water."

"Dead water?"

"My people do not drink water that stand all night. My people drink living water."

"I'll fetch her some fresh water," Maddie promised. "But what about the other? What if Shooting Star doesn't want to marry White Blossom?"

Lefty frowned. "Marry?"

"What if Shooting Star doesn't want White Blossom as his squaw?"

"Then Picking Bones no go."

Maddie sighed. What a fine kettle of fish!

For the first few days that Picking Bones kept guard, Luke paid little attention to her. The woman was only one of a growing number of strangers who had begun to loiter on his property. Maddie seemed to attract Indians, drummers, stray astrologers, and all matter of strangers like a sugar bowl attracted so many flies. Strange as it seemed, he was beginning to get used to the idea of coming home and finding what surely seemed like the whole tribe of Cheyennes parked in his front yard.

One day he discovered his soddy surrounded by the members of the Astronomical Society pointing their strange-looking telescopes toward the heavens. A short time later, he opened his door and found a brightly colored wagon on his doorstep that belonged to a traveling salesman who sold pots and pans.

How in heaven's name did Maddie manage to attract such a strange assortment of visitors? Before her arrival, he'd not seen a soul on his property for six months!

He'd begun to expect the unexpected from Maddie. Nothing surprised him. Almost nothing.

Still, Maddie's announcement that night during supper that the woman was to be a permanent figure was not particularly welcome. Of all the strangers that had made themselves at home on his property, he had to admit that the old woman was the most annoying, especially since she made no attempt to hide her dislike for him.

"Does this mean the woman has moved in with you?"

"She hasn't exactly moved in with me," Maddie explained. "She leaves after sunset and arrives at dawn."

"What is she doing here?" Luke asked.

"She's . . . protecting my virtue."

Luke's eyes widened in astonishment. "From . . . from who?"

"Shooting Star."

Luke turned and in doing so accidentally knocked over a rabbit, the latest in the growing number of mounted animals that were beginning to clutter up the soddy. He gritted his teeth. Since Maddie had stuffed that damned cardinal, Matthew insisted upon carting home every carcass he found.

The place was beginning to look like a damned morgue! Why couldn't Maddie take up needlework or soapmaking like other women?

"This is the last straw! I won't have it, Maddie. The woman has got to go!"

"I tried to tell her that," Maddie explained. "I asked Lefty to translate."

"Then I shall tell her. And believe me, I won't need anyone to translate." Luke stormed outside. The woman looked up at him, clutching her shawl.

His exasperation left him. He simply didn't have the heart to scold an old woman, no matter how much she provoked him. "You can't stay here," he said gently. She glared at him, but remained steadfast in her demeanor.

"You . . ." He pointed at her. "Can't . . ." He shook his head. "Stay here. You must go home." He pointed in the direction of the Cheyenne encampment.

There was no response. He ran his fingers through his hair. "I said, 'Go home!' " The voice he used was intended to be understood.

The woman jumped to her feet with a youthful energy that surprised him. He drew back, thinking she was going to strike him. She did attack, but not physically. Instead, Picking Bones screamed at him, spewing words like venom. He had no idea what she said, but it sounded downright hostile, maybe even threatening. By the time the tirade had ended, she had earned his grudging respect.

He was more than a bit relieved when she shuffled off.

He turned at the sound of musical laughter behind him and watched in amusement as Maddie tried to control her mirth.

"I would say that you're not exactly her favorite person," she said, and in the soft glow of the setting sun, she looked radiant.

"I got rid of her, didn't I?"

"For the time being."

"That might not be such a good thing," he said softly. "For that means you'll have to protect your own virtue."

"You needn't concern yourself about that. Most men take one look at me and run the other way."

He considered this a moment. He didn't feel much like running. If anything, he felt drawn to her like a moth to a lantern. "Why do you suppose that is?"

"My mother says it's because I'm not ladylike enough."

"Is that so?"

"Yes. She says a lady never runs except to protect her virtue."

He laughed at this.

"And a lady should never lift objects over her head. Nor should she raise her voice."

He thought about the loud, commanding voice he woke to each morning, so different from the silky softness of her present voice, and smiled. What a sight it was to see her leading the Indians, and any other visitors who had the misfortune to be in the vicinity, in her brisk calisthenics class.

Her mother was right. "Ladylike" was not an apt description of Miss Madeline Percy.

He swallowed hard in an effort to dislodge the lump that had suddenly risen to his throat. "I'm glad."

"What?"

"That you're not a lady."

"Why . . . why would you be glad about that?"

"I know from experience that a lady can't survive out here in this hostile land. Why? What did you think I meant?"

"Nothing," she replied. "Nothing at all." After a moment's silence, she added, "I better go back inside. I . . . I promised Matthew to tell him a story."

His impulse was to keep her there, to take her in his arms and hold her. He took a step forward, but the clamor of angry voices from his past prevented him from reaching out to her.

"If I don't see you, have a good night."

He usually spent his evenings in the barn. "You too," he said.

She stood for a moment longer. Then, without warning, she threw her arms around his neck and planted a hard kiss on his mouth.

Startled, he gasped and pulled back. "What the . . . ?"

Her arms dropped down to her side. "I'm sorry, Luke. I didn't mean anything . . ." She sounded hurt, and he chastised himself for overreacting.

"Don't apologize . . . you surprised me, that's all." He straightened his shirt. He'd never known a woman could be so demonstrative. He didn't know what to do, what to say.

She stood motionless. He wouldn't have thought her capable of standing so still.

"I just wanted to tell you how obliged I am to you for letting me stay here," she said.

"I'm the one who should be thanking you. For everything you've done for Matthew . . . for me."

"That's very kind of you to say."

Damn, he hated this. Hated the polite talk, being constantly on guard. "Maddie . . ." Her name was barely more than a sigh on his lips. He reached out to her, but she'd already turned and was walking away.

"Good night," she called softly over her shoulder. He heard the door to the soddy open and close—and then, silence.

Picking Bones continued to show up like clockwork every morning.

The stoic and intrusive presence of the old woman was beginning to get on Luke's nerves. What right did she have to plant herself on his property and glare at him every time he had occasion to raise his voice at Maddie—which seemed to be every day lately?

Not that he meant to raise his voice, but Maddie brought out the worst in him. If it wasn't one thing, it was another.

Ruminating on the perplexing situation he was in, he walked into the soddy and found himself face to face with a fiercely snarling bobcat. Gasping in horror, he dropped to his knees and grabbed a chair in an attempt to defend himself.

Maddie turned from the stove, her face aghast. "My word, Luke, what is it?"

He held the chair in front of him, staring through the rungs at the yellow fangs.

The bobcat hadn't moved, and now he realized it was the latest in the growing number of mounted animals that filled the room.

"Damn it, Maddie!" he bellowed, unable to curtail his anger. "A man can't even walk into his house anymore without being scared out of his wits." Then knowing how dangerous his anger could be, he threw down the chair and quickly left the soddy. He mounted his horse and raced across the prairie in an effort to calm down. But it wasn't only the anger he feared; there were other feelings far more terrifying.

He rode for hours before he felt it was safe for him to return home. By the time his anger was spent and his other emotions under control, it was late, almost midnight, and the lights in both the tipi and the soddy were out.

He fell asleep as soon as his head hit the pillow and didn't wake up until her strident voice told him it was morning.

*Lord,* he thought as he lay there staring up at the frilly petticoats on the ceiling, *she sounded like a general, putting those poor Indians through their early-morning drills.* He did have to smile, though, as he recalled the group of potbellied astronomers running around the soddy, trying to keep up with the Cheyennes. He hadn't heard so much huffing and puffing in his life!

He couldn't seem to remain indifferent anymore. He was either smiling or frowning. Mostly frowning. Wanting her to leave. Wanting her to stay. Cursing her. Praising her.

It was with these same ambivalent feelings that he prepared to leave for the fields early that Thursday morning in July.

Matthew had dawdled more than usual. He'd taken forever to eat his breakfast and twice his normal time to dress.

When it was time to leave, Matthew was nowhere in sight, and Luke was forced to search for him. He walked around the barn and stopped in midstep. The word *Matthew* was scratched into the dirt. A short distance away, Matthew was hunched over, his back toward his father.

Luke moved closer and watched quietly as Matthew finished writing his name once again in the dirt.

Luke bent down by his son's side, a lump in his throat. Matthew dropped the stick and started for the wagon, but Luke stayed him. "I didn't know you could write your name, son. That's wonderful. God, it's the most wonderful thing in the whole wide world!" Luke wrapped his arms around Matthew and gave him a quick hug. "What else can you write?" He picked up the stick and handed it to Matthew. "What else, son?"

Matthew took the stick and, with his father's encouragement, scratched out the word *school*. He then looked up his father, his beseeching eyes as blue as the sky overhead.

Luke rubbed his chin. He knew full well what Matthew wanted; he wanted to attend Maddie's school.

That part was clear. What was not clear was how to answer him. What if he had one of the tantrums?

Consideration for Maddie's and Matthew's safety was uppermost in his thoughts. Even so, he regretted having to deny the boy something that obviously meant so much to him.

"What else can you write, son?" It was as if he'd suddenly been given access to a boarded-up house. He wanted to throw open every door, every window, expose every room to the sun, until every shadow had been chased away.

Matthew scratched the dirt with his stick. He took painstaking care to form each letter perfectly. The words *I love you* took shape, and Luke wiped away the moisture that suddenly blurred his vision.

He wrapped his arms around Matthew and pressed his cheek against Matthew's smooth young face. "I love you, too." He squeezed his eyes tight to keep the tears at bay.

He couldn't remember saying those words without feeling apologetic, as if he had no right. Today, he kept saying them over and over, as if to make up for all the times the words had gone unsaid.

But it scared him. It scared the hell out of him. What if he felt too much? What if he lost control . . . ?

Before his worst fears could be realized, he took Matthew by the hand and led him to where Maddie was sitting on a box.

Several Indians sat cross-legged around her. Their gruff voices lifted in unison as they repeated various phrases after her.

"The sky is blue," she said. "Now, your turn."

The voices rose in unison. "The sky is blue. Now, your turn."

"Again."

"Again."

When Luke and Matthew walked up to the gathering, Maddie dropped the pictures on her lap and raised her eyes above her students' heads to look at him.

"Do you have room for another student?"

He absorbed the softness that touched her face when she looked at Matthew, and he was again reminded of how much he'd been denied in his youth because of who he was.

"I think we can find room."

"Are you sure?" he asked. She knew how violent Matthew's tantrums were. She knew the dangers. What he was really asking was if she could handle it.

She lifted her chin. "I'm quite sure, Luke."

"Wildfire sure," Lefty added with a toothy grin.

Luke nodded and released Matthew's hand. With childish enthusiasm, Matthew ran around the Indians and fell knee first in front of her.

Luke headed back toward his wagon, but it was a

difficult moment, one that was filled with a combination of hope and dread. For two years, he'd been Matthew's sole protector. It was hard to let go. His only hope was that he hadn't let go too soon.

# Chapter 23

A hot wind swept across the prairie, tossing dust clouds over the turbulent sea of grass. The wind blew so hard on occasion that one corner of the roof lifted during the strong gusts, and Maddie feared the whole roof would be blown away.

Though she had spoken eloquently on the wind's behalf, in reality the wind was the one thing that Maddie most disliked about Kansas. That and the dust it dislodged, which seemed to fill the air for days after the wind had stopped.

Matthew glanced up at the ceiling, his eyes round with concern. "Finish your work, Matthew," she said. Noting that he had written the letter *b* backwards, she took his finger and helped him to trace *b*'s in the air.

"Try again."

At first Maddie thought the sound she heard in the distance was the windmill. But the sound grew louder and when she finally looked out to determine its source, she was surprised to see a covered wagon on the road.

The wind lifted the wagon's canvas cover until it billowed upward like a large white balloon ready to take flight. Dirt swirled from beneath the wheels as the wagon lumbered along the dry, dusty road.

She reached for her sunbonnet and stepped outside

just as the wagon came to a halt by the windmill. Struggling to tie the bonnet to her head, she fought the wind and rushed to greet her visitors. A man struggled from the driver's seat and called out, his voice barely audible above the wind. A young boy hurried to his side to hand him a pair of crutches.

"Would you be kind enough to give us water?" The man, who had managed to step down from the wagon unassisted, tucked the crutches beneath his arm pits.

"Of course," Maddie called back. Head lowered against the wind and dust, she went back to the soddy to fetch clean cups. "We have company, Matthew."

She dashed back outside, eager to make her guests as comfortable as possible. The man and his two children were standing by the well. The little girl's dress billowed out, and the wind playfully tugged on her long blond hair.

Maddie passed out the cups and carried a cupful of fresh water to the woman who remained on the wagon. Maddie was surprised to recognize her as the woman she had met in Hays. Had the wind not been blowing the children's hair in front of their faces, she would probably have recognized them as well.

"It's Lucy, isn't it? Lucy Eldridge?"

Lucy held the flapping brim of her bonnet, and her eyes widened in surprise. "Why, yes." She lifted her voice against the wind. "Fancy meeting you again, Miss Percy."

"Call me Maddie."

"Maddie. May I ask what you're doing here?"

"I live here."

The woman's expression went from friendly to hostile. "Here? With that . . . that horrible man?"

"You don't mean Luke . . . ?"

The woman's face darkened with scorn. "I didn't

want to stop here. I told Peter I'd rather die of thirst than stop here. But he insisted."

The woman's hatred and anger made the otherwise dramatic prairie look bland. Even the wind seemed to have lost its stinging presence. Maddie was so startled by the unexpected outburst that she could only stare at the woman in bewilderment.

"Peter!" the woman called to her husband.

"Would you like some water?" Maddie asked, holding up the cup.

"No, thank you!"

Maddie guessed that the woman was at least seven months along in her pregnancy. It didn't seem wise for Lucy to deny herself water, no matter what the reason.

Peter hobbled up to the wagon on crutches, the children behind him. Jamie held his sister's hand, and both kept their heads down to ward off a sudden funnel of dirt that blew by.

Peter said something to Jamie, who then held a canteen up to his mother.

"I'm most obliged for the water." Peter shouted to make himself heard.

Maddie battled with the ribbons of her bonnet. "If you want to come inside, I'll fix you something to eat."

"We don't have time," Lucy snapped.

Peter gave Maddie a look of apology but said nothing as he took his place next to his wife, shoved the crutches behind him, and picked up the reins.

Maddie helped Jamie and Caroline into the wagon. The two children waved to her from the canvas opening, and Maddie lifted her hand in return.

It was a puzzling and disturbing encounter and one she thought about for the rest of the day.

The wind died down late that afternoon, except for

occasional gusts. The air remained thick with dust, preventing her and Matthew from taking their daily walk.

She waited until they were seated around the table for supper before mentioning the Eldridges' visit.

Luke's face grew as dark as a thundercloud. The knuckles of his hand turned white around his fork. "What did they want?"

"Nothing," she said, her voice suddenly deserting her. "Only water. I offered them food but . . ."

He rose abruptly, his plate barely touched. "I have work to do in the barn." He quickly left the soddy. The door slammed shut with a loud, dull thud that tore another lay of dirt off the ceiling onto the petticoats.

Matthew stared at the door, a worried look on his face. Maddie leaned across the table and squeezed his hand. "Eat your supper, Matthew."

*So they were back.* Luke pressed his hands against the sod wall of the barn and tried to steady himself. Lucy and Peter Eldridge were back.

He had never thought they'd return to Colton. Not after losing everything they owned in the fire.

Luke had known Peter since they were both ten. They'd grown up together in a little town outside of Buffalo. They were practically brothers, although out of necessity the boys kept the friendship a secret. Peter was the only friend that Luke ever had. Peter's parents would have been shocked had they known that their oldest son was friends with the Tyler boy.

When the war broke out between the states, Peter didn't hesitate to enlist, and he failed to understand Luke's refusal to do likewise.

"It's our duty," Peter had argued on that long ago day.

"You know why I can't fight," Luke had said.

"Because of your papa? You don't have to worry about that anymore. The damned war is going to make murderers of us all."

"Not me," Luke insisted. "No one is going to make me a murderer."

Luke had been certain that he would never see Peter again, and indeed he did not hear a word from him all during those war years.

Peter returned after the war, minus a limb. Whether it was the missing leg that made him restless and unable to settle down or something else, Luke couldn't say. But he did know that the man who returned was not the same one who had left. It was as if some essential element of his character had been lost on some distant battlefield.

Maybe that's why Luke had found it so surprising when Peter approached him with the idea of pulling up roots and heading out west to stake a claim in Kansas. "Give us both a chance to start fresh, where no one knows us." It was a strange statement coming from Peter. What did he care who knew him? He had nothing to hide.

At first Luke resisted the idea; he wasn't a farmer, he was a woodworker. The fact that he had been successful in his business until the war was a tribute to his skills as a carpenter. Even the most righteous pillars of society were willing to overlook Luke's notorious family background long enough to obtain one of his superbly crafted tables or chairs—so long as he made no attempt to sign his work as was the habit of many artisans, or to leave an identifying mark of any kind.

Who knew how successful he could be if he moved to a place where no one knew him, a place like Kansas? The more he thought about it, the more he was tempted.

Matthew was only two at the time, but already there had been several unpleasant episodes that convinced Luke his son would have as little chance of living down the past as he had had.

Kansas offered Matthew a chance to grow up away from the gossip and recriminations that had plagued Luke as a child and that continued to haunt him until the day he packed up his family and left.

The two families, including Lucy's brother, a medical doctor named George Stanford, traveled to Kansas. It was a relief not to have to hide his friendship with Peter. Equally gratifying was meeting people who had no notion of who he was. For the first time in his life, he was not condemned by the past. He was accepted as just another homesteader trying to make a better life for his family.

Despite the hardships that awaited them on the plains, Luke felt confident it would work. If Catherine-Anne hadn't died ... If he hadn't killed the man responsible ...

He looked up at the sound of the barn door opening.

Maddie stood watching him, a look of confusion and uncertainty on her face. "Did I say something wrong earlier?"

He dropped his hands from the wall and shoved them into his pockets. "No."

"About the Eldridges ..."

"I don't want to talk about the Eldridges."

"Very well." She turned to leave.

"Wait."

She hesitated at the door, turning her head to glance at him over her shoulder.

Suddenly he didn't want to be alone. He wanted her company. Wanted to be near her. Damn it! Why didn't she do something annoying, like shout out orders or touch her toes? Why did she have to stand there looking so damned desirable? He averted his head and closed his eyes. "Good night," he said roughly.

He listened for the door to close, then picked up a scrap of fine-grained wood and held it to the light.

The irony of having to spend his life on a vast tree-less wasteland did not escape him. For a man who loved working with wood, it was a cruel fate.

Even more cruel was having to push Maddie away.

The following day, Luke was repairing a broken plow when Peter Eldridge rode up in a wagon. Maddie and Matthew had driven into Colton earlier to check on the progress of the school and museum.

Luke wiped his greasy hands on a rag and walked over to the wagon so that Peter wouldn't have to struggle with his crutches. "Peter."

Peter nodded. "I came to ask your help. The army tent is too hot for Lucy. We need to build a sod house. I figure the two of us can build one in a day."

"Does Lucy know that you're here?"

"Leave Lucy to me. What do you say?"

Peter didn't have to ask twice. "I'll be there first thing in the morning."

Maddie drove her wagon toward Colton with Matthew by her side. The hazy covering of dust from the recent windstorm tinted the sky more gray than blue. Touched by the pale sun, the prairie grass rippled in the soft breeze like the gentle rolls of a silvery sea.

A jackrabbit sat on the dirt road ahead, then scampered into the grass as the wagon rolled by.

The town of Colton was beginning to take shape, and the wooden spire of the church came into view as they followed the road over a slight rise.

Mr. Boxer emerged from the wooden frame of the schoolhouse to greet Maddie. Behind him, several men dressed in canvas overalls hammered and sawed. "What do you think?" He lifted his voice above the racket.

"It's wonderful!" Maddie exclaimed. She swung down from the seat of her wagon and picked her way around the stacks of lumber. She stopped to caution Matthew not to step on the nails that were scattered on the ground. "I didn't know the school would be a wood building."

"Had the wood brought in by rail," Mr. Boxer said proudly. He led her up the wooden steps. "As you can see, nothing but the best for the good citizens of Colton." He pointed to the floor. "Most of the school-houses in Kansas have a dirt floor, but I insisted that we provide our citizens of tomorrow with a sound foundation." He laughed at his own joke.

Maddie had taken hardwood floors for granted prior to coming to Kansas. Never again, and today she gazed around her feet with full appreciation. "It's going to be beautiful. Isn't it, Matthew?"

Matthew ran his hand along the wooden frame of the door, his cheeks flushed with excitement. The look on his face, the way he held himself, reminded her so much of his father that for a moment she could hardly breathe.

It wasn't until Mr. Boxer motioned to her from the doorway leading to the other room that she was able to recover enough to breathe normally again. "This is the museum you requested."

The rough-framed room was smaller than the class-room, but Maddie thought it was the most wonderful room she'd ever seen. Her mind fairly danced with ideas. "Come and look, Matthew." Two small windows allowed the afternoon sun to spill its warmth across the floor.

"We'll display the animals along this wall. And

maybe your father will make us some shelves for over there, and . . ."

The ideas fairly bubbled out and by the time she ran out of breath, Mr. Boxer and the workman were staring at her with glazed looks. Feeling somewhat embarrassed, she gave them a sheepish look and grabbed Matthew by the hand. "Come along, Matthew. These men have work to do."

During the trip home, Maddie's mind whirled with new ideas for the museum. "Our museum is going to be wonderful." She gave Matthew a quick smile. "You wait and see."

A horse and wagon was parked in front of the soddy. "I do believe we have company. Probably another family returning to Colton."

She pulled alongside the wagon. Luke stood in the open doorway of the barn talking to Sheriff Beckleworth and a woman who was dressed from head to toe in black. The woman had a cane that she kept jabbing into the ground as she spoke.

Maddie couldn't hear what was being said, but it was obvious that Luke and the woman were having a heated argument.

The woman turned and quickly strolled toward Maddie and Matthew, with Luke and the sheriff at her heels.

The woman stopped next to Maddie's wagon. Shading her face with a gloved hand, her bright black eyes lit into Matthew. "What is your name, young man?"

Matthew pressed against the back of his seat and turned to look at Maddie.

Maddie jumped down from her seat and walked around the wagon. She was extremely conscious of the grim look on Luke's face. "I'm Madeline Percy. I'm Colton's new schoolteacher. Who might you be?"

The woman appraised Maddie with a sharp look.

"I'm Miss Alberdeen. I'm with the Child Welfare Department." She studied Matthew, who had climbed down from his seat and was tugging nervously on Maddie's skirt.

Miss Alberdeen bent over, and practically thrust her long, pointed nose in his face. "You *are* Matthew Tyler, are you not?"

Matthew stiffened by Maddie's side. Maddie slid an arm around him and pressed her hand on his shoulder to steady him.

Luke was standing a short distance behind the woman. She had never seen him so filled with rage. Maddie spoke in a calm voice in an effort to defuse the tension. "Matthew is not able to speak."

The woman straightened and looked Maddie in the eye. "Not speak?" She gave the sheriff a triumphant look. "This is worse than I thought."

Maddie glared at her. "I would think someone from the Child Welfare Department would employ more tact. He can't speak, but he can hear. Perhaps you would be kind enough to explain your interest?"

Miss Alberdeen's stance grew more stern. It was clear she did not take kindly to being chastised. "We received a complaint that the boy was being raised . . . eh . . . in a somewhat irregular manner."

"Irregular, Miss Alberdeen? Would you care to define what you mean by 'irregular'?"

"The report said that the boy acted like a wild animal."

Luke tore his gaze away from Matthew's face and stepped between the sheriff and the woman. "The report is wrong. Now if you'll get the hell off of my property . . ."

The sheriff rested a steadying hand on Luke's shoulder. "Calm down, Luke."

Luke pulled away. "Calm down? She threatens to

take my boy away from me and all you can say is 'Calm down'?"

"It's not my intention to take your son away, Mr. Tyler. As I told you earlier, I am required to investigate any complaints received by my office. The boy will have to come with me. We'll take the train to Kansas City, and I'll have a doctor evaluate him. It will be up to the doctor to decide if any action need be taken."

"And what is a doctor going to base his decision on? He knows nothing about me, nothing about Matthew."

"I'm required to consult with a professional and . . ."

The voices grew louder, and Matthew began to tremble. Maddie glanced at Luke and knew by the horrified look on his face that she had every right to be worried. The eyes that met hers were dark with desperation. She fought to keep her own rising panic at bay.

She gave Miss Alberdeen a cool appraisal. "If you'll excuse us a moment, I want to talk to Matthew in private."

Her heart pounding, she tried to pull Matthew toward the house. Perhaps if she got him inside, she could calm him. Matthew resisted her efforts, forcing her to tighten her hold.

The woman might have noticed had Luke not stepped in front of her, blocking Matthew from sight.

"My son stays here!"

"If you refuse to let . . ."

Sheriff Beckleworth cut her off. "Let me handle this, Abigail. Luke, I think you know that I have always given you a fair shake . . ."

Grateful that the sheriff and Miss Aberdeen were too occupied to notice Matthew's strange behavior, Maddie tried to lift him in her arms. She had almost succeeded when suddenly he pulled away and threw himself to the ground. She positioned a foot on either side of him, grabbing him by the wrists. "Write, Matthew." She kept her voice low so the others could not hear her, but firm.

She pulled a fossil rock from her pocket and forced it into his hand. "Tell me what you're thinking."

Matthew's legs grew still as he stared down at the stone. She moved her legs and lifted him to an upright position. "Write," she urged. "You can do it."

Holding the rock between his fingers, Matthew scratched something in the dirt. The argument escalated, and Maddie chanced a glance over her shoulder. Luke's face was almost purple with rage.

"I'm not letting my boy go anywhere!"

The sheriff appeared to be sympathetic with Luke. "I have no choice, Luke. We've got to take the boy in. It'll only be for a short while."

Miss Alberdeen sniffed. "You don't know that for sure, Sheriff. It'll depend what the doctor decides." She stalked past Luke and slammed the tip of her cane into the dirt next to where Matthew had written *I want to stay with my Pa.*

Miss Alberdeen was clearly surprised. "You write very well, young man."

"He's also very good at arithmetic," Maddie said proudly. She scratched a column of numbers into the dirt with a stick. "Show Miss Alberdeen how well you can add."

Matthew wrote out the answer without hesitation.

Sheriff Beckleworth hooked his thumbs on his belt. "That's mighty impressive, son. I never did cotton much to numbers, myself."

Maddie stood. "Matthew lost the ability to speak from the shock of losing his mother two years ago."

The woman's eyes filled with sympathy. "How sad."

"It *is* sad," Maddie agreed. "But I can assure you,

that in every other way, he is a perfectly normal seven-year-old boy."

Miss Alberdeen nodded. "I'm inclined to agree." She turned to the sheriff. "I believe I've seen enough to write my report. There's no need to pursue this any further."

The sheriff scratched his head. "I thought you were required by the state to consult with a professional."

Miss Alberdeen scowled at the sheriff. "For goodness' sakes, Sheriff. Where have you been? Miss . . . what did you say your name was?"

"Percy."

"Miss Percy is a schoolteacher. A teacher *is* a professional." Miss Alberdeen stalked past Maddie and took her place on the driver's seat.

Sheriff Beckleworth tipped his hat. "Sorry to trouble you, folks."

The wagon was no sooner out of earshot, when Luke grabbed Matthew and hugged him. It did Maddie's heart good to watch the joy on Matthew's face. But nothing compared to her own joy when Luke wrapped his arms around her waist and swung her around as easily as petals in the wind. "They aren't going to take Matthew away from me!"

She flung her arms around his neck and laughed aloud. She'd never seen him so filled with joy. "I know, Luke. I know!"

He lowered her until her feet touched the ground, but he kept his hands at her waist. "Maddie, I . . . Matthew was about to have another fit . . . How did you stop him?"

"Those aren't fits, Luke. Not the kind of fits you think. They're caused by frustration and anger because of his inability to let people know what he's feeling and thinking. But he's learning. Oh, indeed he is. He can now express his feelings through writing and drawing."

The look Luke gave her took her breath away. "You . . . you mean he's not . . . dangerous?"

"Dangerous?" She drew back from the circle of his arms to look him square in the face. "Mercy me, Luke. How could you think such a thing?"

# Chapter 24

*M*atthew *was a normal seven-year-old boy!* Maddie's words echoed in his heart for the re-mainder of that day.

That night Luke stood next to the bed and watched his sleeping son. *Normal.* What more could a father possibly want for his son?

Aware that Maddie had put away her mending and was watching him, he pulled the blanket over Matthew's shoulders and joined her. He took her by the hand and pulled her out the door and away from the house.

It was a clear, warm night. The stars stretched over-head for as far as the eye could see.

"It's beautiful," she whispered.

Standing behind her, he slipped his arms around her waist and buried his face in her sweet-scented hair. He didn't have to look at the sky to know that what she said was true. Kansas, the prairie—everything was beautiful. How could he have lived here for four years and not noticed the beautiful nights? The beautiful days?

"Maddie . . ."

She turned in his arms. He couldn't see her face, but he could feel her warm breath and hear her soft sigh as he ran a finger along her smooth, warm cheek.

A melodious tune floated out of the darkness. It was the same flute sound he had heard on previous nights.

She pressed her fingers into his arm. "Listen," she whispered. "Who do you suppose the musician is?"

"I don't know."

"It's a love song," she said.

"How can you be so certain?" he asked, intrigued.

Her throaty laugh warmed him. "I just know." They listened in silence for a moment, before she whispered in his ear, "Do you know what I want to do?"

He groaned. "Don't tell me you have the urge to do calisthenics."

"No."

"Run?"

"I want us to dance."

"Here?"

"Don't you want to?" she asked.

He smiled. "I'm not much of a dancer."

"Nor am I . . ."

"I step on my partner's toes . . ."

"I always want to lead . . ."

He laughed. "I can believe that." He hadn't danced in years, but the magic of this night made him believe that anything was possible. "I'm willing to try if you are." He took her hand in his and slipped his right arm around her waist. He led her around the soddy in a slow waltz. After some initial clumsiness on his part, he felt confident enough to increase the speed. Soon, they were whirling and twirling, their feet nimble and quick.

There was no sense of who was leading, who followed. It was as if the two of them had become a single entity. They were like two leaves caught together in the wind. Together, yet free, and the voices—those constant reminders of who he was—had been replaced, temporarily at least, by her laughter.

They were forced to stop dancing to catch their breath. "Listen," Maddie said, her voice breathless. The flute had stopped playing. "When do you suppose the music stopped?"

Luke couldn't answer. For him, the music had not stopped. If anything, the music reached a crescendo as he lowered his head and found her warm, sweet lips.

His mouth was warm, tender, but nowhere near as satisfying as she imagined. He was kissing her like she was a fragile china doll! She stood on tiptoe in an attempt to deepen the kiss. When that didn't work, she held her breath for the count of three, then quickly thrust her tongue in his mouth.

He drew away. "My God, Maddie!"

He was shocked by her forward behavior. No doubt about it. His voice, everything suggested he thought her a common hussy. Lord, why couldn't she remember that it was the man who was supposed to determine how much or how little a woman should be kissed?

Flushed with humiliation, she stood frozen in place, willing herself to drop through the ground. But before she could think what to do next, she was suddenly in his arms again, crushed against his chest.

His mouth slammed against hers, taking her breath away. This time he needed no encouragement; his tongue bulldozed through her lips, invading every recess of her mouth and sending shock waves to every part of her body.

His hand left her shoulder, and a fiery thrill shot through her as he cupped her right breast in his hands. Tenderly, lovingly, he kneaded first one breast, then the other, until they both tingled with warm pleasure. Shamelessly, she pressed against his male hardness.

He moaned aloud and gasped her name between impassioned kisses. Finally, he lifted her in his arms and pulled her tight against his chest. His mouth never leaving hers, he carried her quickly into the tipi and somehow managed to find the bedroll in the dark.

He lay her down and joined her, his body pressing against hers as he struggled with the hooks and eyes of her blouse. She wondered if it would be too forward of her to help him. The seconds seemed to stretch into eternity, and she could no longer hold back. Abandoning propriety, she pushed his hand away and quickly tore off her blouse and chemise.

He chuckled softly. "My little wildfire." He caught a swollen nipple in his mouth, and she arched against him in sweet ectasy.

He explored the soft lines of her waist with his fingertips, and her breath caught between her ribs as he inched the waistband of her skirt and trousers downward.

Unable to breathe, she waited for him to touch the most intimate part of her. The small part of her brain that was still sane was shocked that she would want such a thing, but her heart sang that this was right. It seemed to take him forever to caress her there. Impatiently, she took his hand and drew it between her legs, bringing first a chuckle from him and, finally, a gasp.

"Are you all right?" he whispered.

"Oh, yes!" she said, not bothering to keep her voice low. She was about to become a woman in the fullest sense, and she didn't care who knew it.

He quickly undressed and then slipped on top of her, his mouth pressing into hers. Reminding herself that it wouldn't be ladylike to put her hand around the hardness that pressed against her thigh, she resisted for less than a moment before giving in to her impulse.

Lord, it felt like fire. She felt like fire.

His breathing quickened at her touch and his body trembled. He moaned her name. "I can't wait any longer, Maddie." He spoke with an urgency that matched her own need for some unnamed fulfillment she didn't understand but was driven to attain. She wrapped her arms around him and spread her thighs.

The tip of his manhood was poised in place. She felt moist and wet and, more than anything, ready for him. It seemed as if she'd waited a lifetime for the moment that even now remained just outside her reach. What was taking him so long? Why wasn't he as eager for her as she was for him?

Lord, he felt eager enough. Never could she imagine that a man's organ would be so hard. She lifted her hips upward and felt a thrill as he pressed against her.

She pressed harder, but it soon became obvious he was having trouble entering her. Oh, Lord. Was there something more she was supposed to do?

"Easy," he whispered in her ear. "I don't want to hurt you." And then, "Relax."

Relax? How was she supposed to relax? She wanted him so much, her whole body ached with need. What if something was wrong down there, something that prevented her from taking a man?

He was massaging her now with the warm, throbbing tip. Waves of passion spiraled through her, but instinctively she knew there was more awaiting her. There was something . . . something wonderful. Something powerful.

Whatever it was, she wanted it and she wanted him to be the one to give it to her.

She gritted her teeth and pressed against him, hard at first, then harder still.

He plunged into her, ripping her apart. She cried out in pain, but the pain left as quickly as it had come, and a burning sweetness took its place.

He froze in place at the sound of her cry, and the body that had seconds earlier seemed so wondrously hard now seemed rigid and unyielding. "Maddie? Oh, my God, what have I done?"

"It's nothing," she whispered. She moved her hips to prove to him she was all right, and fresh waves of desire shot through her, leaving her every nerve wanting more.

He pulled away from her, and she felt as if someone had wrenched away some vital part of her. "Dammit, Maddie. How can you say it's nothing?"

His hard, angry voice was so unexpected, her senses spun. Before she could make sense of what was happening, he rolled off her.

"Luke?" She could barely find her voice.

He said not a word, nothing. He was so quiet that even his breathing seemed to stop. Not wanting to believe that he was going to leave her without some word of explanation, she held her own breath and waited. She was stunned when he grabbed his clothes and left.

She felt humiliated and confused. She had always known she was lacking in feminine ways. The teasing interplay that she'd witnessed between men and women during all the fancy balls and socials in Washington had never come naturally to her.

But never once had it occurred to her that a man might find her lacking in bed.

She searched in the dark for something to use as a cover. Finding her nightgown, she held it up to her and ran to the open flap. "Luke?"

The only sound she could hear was the thundering hooves of Luke's horse as it raced away.

*Your father raped me.* He'd never forgotten his mother's words to him or the grim, almost hateful look on her face when she'd first told him. She'd cried aloud as if the mere act of telling him was enough to bring back all the pain.

He remembered thinking to himself at the time that he would never hurt a woman like his father had hurt his mother.

Until tonight, he never had. He'd made damn sure he never had!

He spurred his horse onward, until he fairly flew along that dark, lonely road.

It had been easy to keep his promise with Catherine-Anne. If the woman had had an ounce of passion or desire in her, he certainly never saw it. She once told him that the only way she had been able to lie with all those men had been to remove herself emotionally and pretend she was someone else during the actual act. Old habits never die, apparently.

Knowing how she hated the intimate part of marriage, he never felt compelled to do more than fulfill his needs as carefully and quickly as possible. He had married her to rescue her; he imagined it his duty to rescue every woman who had ever been hurt by a man. But maybe there'd been another reason for marrying her. He knew things could never go much beyond the chaste kisses and perfunctory lovemaking stage. If the voices of the past failed to keep him under control, he could always depend on Catherine-Anne to remind him.

The taste of Maddie was still on his lips, and his hands still held the womanly scent of her. The farther away he rode, the more she seemed to beckon him.

"Oh, Maddie." Her name was an anguished cry that escaped him to become a part of the night. *Will you ever forgive me?*

He had tried to be so gentle. He should have known better. Maddie was a woman of extremes. She would never settle for anything less than the whole. He knew this about her, and that was why he'd fought so long

and so hard to prevent what occurred tonight from happening.

God almighty, he'd hurt her, hurt Maddie.

His heart was filled with pain so excruciating that it
felt like a knife had been plunged through his very
center. It was hard to breathe, harder still to think.

All during the long, anguished hours that followed,
only one thing was clear: he would make damn sure
never to hurt Maddie again.

# Chapter 25

Early the next morning, Luke hurried into his clothes and tiptoed from the soddy so as not to wake his sleeping son.

Outside he paused to watch Maddie lead Lefty and his friends through their morning exercises. He absorbed the sight and sound of her like the earth absorbs the sun and rain. The voice that had once sounded so strident today touched his ears with the sweetness of a song.

Suddenly, he remembered how that same voice had sounded when she cried out in pain.

He staggered to his horse, but it took a while before he could ease himself into the saddle and start toward the Eldridge camp.

Maddie said something to one of the Cheyennes and then ran toward him.

"Luke, about last night . . . I . . ."

He grimaced inwardly. "I don't want to talk about last night."

She looked up at him, and he hated the confusion and hurt on her face, in her voice, in her lovely green eyes.

"I think the least you owe me is an explanation." She spoke calmly, but he had the feeling she was anything but calm inside. Her eyes were too bright for calm; her cheeks too flushed. "Why did you pull away from me . . ."

"I'm sorry, Maddie. I never meant to hurt you. You have to believe that." He jerked the reins hard and galloped off. No matter how much he apologized, tried to explain, it could never be enough.

Peter was waiting for him. The two men exchanged a brief greeting and then set to work.

A slight breeze rippled the brown prairie grass as they harnessed Peter's oxen to what was commonly called a grasshopper plow or sod cutter. While Luke guided the team, Peter stood on his crutches and supervised young Jamie in clearing the grass away. Little Caroline packed down the ground to form a tough earthen floor. At the age of five, she had more enthusiasm than ability, but she gave it her best.

Luke cut the strips of sod into individual blocks one foot wide by two feet long. It took a full acre of prairie turf to provide enough blocks for a sixteen-by-twenty-foot dwelling.

Each block weighed fifty pounds, much too heavy for Peter to manage with his one leg. Peter could do little more than watch as Luke struggled with each block in turn.

Peter looked grim as the sod walls began to rise. "I never thought I'd see the day I would live in a dirt house." He had refused to live in one when he first came to Kansas. It cost him his entire savings to have lumber shipped by rail to Colton. But the house he built had been the envy of his neighbors, and soon many of them began to abandon their soddies for houses similar to the Eldridge home.

The citizens of Colton could never have guessed what a mistake it was to build wood houses. The recent wildfire, buffeted by the strong prairie winds, had swept across the land, devouring every wooden structure in sight. Only the sod houses had survived.

Luke wiped the sweat off his face. "Don't think of it as dirt," he said. "Think of it as prairie marble."

Peter grinned. "Prairie marble, eh? I wonder if Lucy will accept that?"

No sooner had Peter mentioned his wife's name than Lucy could be seen walking toward them. The two children ran to greet their mother, but she seemed not to notice their presence.

Peter frowned. "She shouldn't be out here in the hot sun. The baby is due soon."

"You better go and see what she wants," Luke said.

Peter positioned his crutches beneath his armpits and hurried to meet his wife. She ignored her husband and kept walking toward the site. "What are you doing here?" she demanded of Luke.

Luke straightened. "Peter asked me to help out."

"Now I'm asking you to leave." She planted herself directly in front of Luke.

Luke studied her pale, pinched face. The hatred and contempt he saw in her eyes were no surprise. It was a look he'd seen all his life, from his mother's family, his teachers, neighbors, even his customers. In the past, he had accepted such a look as his due. But no more. After seeing the love in Maddie's eyes as she looked at him, looked at Matthew, he never wanted to see hatred or contempt again.

"Maybe it's time we talked."

"I have nothing to say to you."

"I think you have plenty to say, and I think it's time you said it."

"Very well. I hate you, Luke Tyler. I'll never forgive you for murdering my brother. My only regret is that they didn't hang you. Now get off of my property."

"I'm sorry about your brother, Lucy. You've got to believe that. If I could change the past, I would."

"Sorry? You're sorry? Do you think that makes up for what you did? Well, it doesn't! There's nothing you can say that will change my feelings. Now get off my property!"

"I'll leave as soon as we've completed your house."

She glanced down at the neat row of sod blocks with contempt on her face. "I'll not live in a dirt house like some animal!"

Peter's jaw tightened. "Be reasonable, Lucy. A wood house isn't safe. If there's another fire . . ."

"Find a way to make it safe!" She glared at Luke. "Furthermore, I won't live in a house that was built by the hands that murdered my brother!"

Luke was about to say something, but upon seeing the strain in her face, he bit back his angry retort. The woman was obviously feeling the effects of her advanced pregnancy. He had no intention of causing her further distress.

"I'm sorry you feel that way, Lucy." He glanced at Peter, who made no effort to argue with his wife. Luke dropped the handles of the sodcutter, spun on his heel, and walked away.

Maddie's stomach gripped into a tight knot as she drove the wagon along the rutted road leading to the Eldridge camp. Even Matthew seemed to sense her anxiety, and he sat by her side watching her, his eyes full of worry.

In an effort to ease his concern, she smiled at him. "See if you can see your father."

It was a bad idea, this seeking Luke out, with the purpose of trying to pretend that nothing had happened between them. Lord, what *did* happen?

One moment he was making love to her, and the

next ... Even if he found her lacking in some way, surely he had to know it was her first time. She tried not to think of last night. For Matthew's sake, if not her own.

She pointed to the little prairie dogs that stood upon their endless mounds and yipped at the wagon wheels. Matthew in turn pointed to the two hawks that circled overhead.

Matthew had been entrusted with the wicker basket that contained smoked meat and fresh bread, and he held the basket on his lap, shifting it from time to time as if to distribute the weight from one leg to the other. She smiled approvingly and then directed her gaze to the road ahead.

Her stomach fluttered nervously as they drew near to their destination. Her head began to ache. She pulled on the traces until the wagon rolled to a stop. She couldn't face him. Not now. Maybe later.

"I've changed my mind, Matthew. I don't think it's a good idea to bother your father while he's working."

Disappointment crossed Matthew's face, and she felt guilty for spoiling his fun.

"I know what we'll do. We'll find ourselves a spot and have a picnic. Just the two of us. I think there's a stream not far from here." She gathered the traces in her hand. "Giddyup." They traveled a short distance up the road. "Look for a buffalo trail. Lefty said the trails always lead to water."

She and Matthew were so busy watching the herd of buffalo grazing peacefully on either side of the road, they failed at first to notice the Eldridge camp to the right, almost hidden behind a grassy knoll. Neither was prepared for the sudden appearance of a horseman thundering toward them.

Maddie pulled the wagon to the side of the narrow road to let the horse and rider pass.

It wasn't until the horse veered off and galloped in another direction that Maddie realized it was Luke. He was riding so hard, she feared something might be wrong.

She called to him and when he kept going, she shoved her fingers into her mouth and whistled. Matthew covered his ears to block out the high-pitched sound. All around them, hundreds of prairie dogs yipped in protest and dived for cover. A large buffalo lifted his head and bellowed. Even Rutabaga whinnied and pawed the ground.

Maddie had been so busy watching Luke, she failed to notice Lucy. It wasn't until Maddie heard the woman's hateful, angry voice that she was aware of Lucy's presence.

"Murderer!"

Startled by the woman's rage, Maddie glanced anxiously at Matthew. The boy's face paled. He turned to Maddie, his lower lip quivering. It was obvious he was trying to say something.

Maddie ran her hand across his forehead, hoping to wipe away the shadow of frustration that was centered there. "I know, Matthew. You don't like people saying unkind things about your father. Don't pay any attention to what they say. You and I know that your father is not a murderer, and that's all that matters, right?" She coaxed a faint smile from him, before tugging on the traces to pull the wagon forward. "Lucy! May I talk to you?"

Lucy turned and trudged, head down, toward the covered wagon and tent that made up the Eldridge camp. Maddie was about to give up and turn back when she noticed Lucy stumble.

"Stay here, Matthew." She jumped to the ground and raced to Lucy's side. Peter, who had been standing next to the unfinished soddy, hurried toward his wife, but Maddie reached her first. "Are you all right?"

Lucy was on her knees, her hands on her middle. "It's just a sharp pain. They come and go."

Peter reached his wife's side and, balancing himself on his one leg, tried to comfort her.

"We better get you back to camp," Maddie said. "Do you think you can walk?"

Lucy nodded. "I think so. The pain is gone."

Maddie helped Lucy to her feet. "Hold on to my arm."

By the time they reached the tent, Lucy was almost faint with exhaustion. Peter watched as Maddie helped Lucy into bed. She then stepped outside the tent to quieten the children, who had seen their mother being helped to the tent.

"Your mother's going to be fine. She just needs to rest. Where's the drinking water?"

Jamie pointed to a wooden bucket beneath the wagon. Maddie found a tin cup and filled it. "Stay outside now."

She ducked through the canvas opening of the tent and handed Peter the cup of water. Lucy was lying on a cot. Peter sat on a camp stool and lifted the cup to his wife's mouth.

Maddie waited for Peter to leave Lucy's side. "How do you feel?"

"The pain is gone. I'm tired, is all. The baby isn't due for another month."

"If you'd like me to stay, I'd be happy to."

Lucy glanced away. "That won't be necessary." Her voice had a definite edge, and Maddie decided not to press.

Still, she was reluctant to leave. There were so many questions Maddie wanted to ask her. Lucy seemed to hold the key to Luke's past. Even so, she couldn't take

the chance of upsetting her further. Her questions
would have to wait until she saw Luke.

Luke was nowhere in sight when Maddie and Matthew arrived home later that afternoon. Since his horse
was gone, she assumed he was in the fields.

Picking Bones sat in her usual place in the shade of
the tipi. Despite the heat of the day, the old woman had
her red shawl wrapped around her. Maddie knew it
would be a waste of time to question her about
whether she'd seen Luke. Other than an occasional
outburst, the woman still refused to communicate with
the three of them.

"Take her some water, Matthew. That's a good boy.
Make sure it's fresh from the well."

Picking Bones's tireless vigil never failed to amaze
Maddie. It had been nearly a month since the old
woman had first appeared. She had become so much a
permanent fixture that Maddie and Luke had grown
quite accustomed to her presence.

Before entering the soddy, Maddie stopped to puzzle
over a dark cloud in the distance. She'd heard stories
of the Kansas cyclones. But there was no wind; in fact,
the air was so still it seemed like the entire earth held
its breath.

*What a strange land this is,* she thought. Shrugging
off her concern, she walked inside the soddy to finish
the chores she'd put off earlier. So many confusing
thoughts crossed her mind, it was hard to concentrate
on what she was doing.

*Murderer.* The word kept hammering at her. Lucy
had called Luke a murderer. But so had Red Feather,
although at the time she thought he was talking of
white men in general. Now she wasn't so certain.

*Murderer.*

It couldn't be true.

*Murderer.*

Not Luke. Not the man she had come to love.

She covered her ears in an attempt to drown out her thoughts, and when that failed to work, she busied herself with chores, rushing about the little soddy like a one-woman cyclone.

She was so absorbed in trying to keep busy that at first she failed to notice how dark the room had suddenly become. It wasn't until a strange humming sound filtered through her consciousness that she flew to the window to investigate.

She peered outside, but couldn't see what was causing the strange noise.

Matthew ran into the house, his eyes wide, his mouth opening and closing in a desperate effort to speak.

"What is it, Matthew?" She ran to the door and stared at the huge, humming cloud that swooped across the land, extending as far as she could see.

She rushed outside and looked straight up. Hail began to fall, pelting the ground all around her. She raced back to the house, but the crunching sound beneath the soles of her boots made her halt in midstep and stare at the ground in disbelief and horror.

# Chapter 26

Grasshoppers! They were everywhere. Thousands upon thousands of grasshoppers!

Dazed and disoriented by the swarm of darting insects, Maddie staggered toward Matthew, who stood frozen in place, his eyes wide with fear.

"It's all right, Matthew."

She waved her arms to ward off the insects, then pushed Matthew inside the house and slammed the door behind them.

Her apron was covered with grasshoppers. With a cry of alarm, she quickly pulled her apron off and tossed it out the door.

Matthew stood rigid. His body started to tremble. Desperate to prevent the impending tantrum, she quickly pulled him to the table, grabbed the writing tablet used for his sums and shoved it in front of him. "Write, Matthew!"

Matthew took the pencil from her.

"Write!"

He had no words for his fear. Somehow she knew this, and taking the writing implement from him, she drew a grasshopper. She handed him the pencil. This time, he needed no further encouragement. He drew one grasshopper after another until the page was covered. The look of fear and wildness had left his eyes, and Maddie knew the danger had passed.

She nodded her approval as he scribbled over his picture, then began erasing the grasshoppers. In his own small way, he had found a way to control his fear.

No sooner had the one problem been resolved, than a worrisome thought occurred to her. The crops. Lord have mercy. What would the grasshoppers do to the crops?

"Stay in the house, Matthew. I'm going to look for your father." His head snapped up and he grabbed her arm.

"Don't be afraid." She hugged him and dropped a kiss onto his forehead. "The grasshoppers won't hurt you if you stay inside." He searched her face, and apparently satisfied that she spoke the truth, turned back to his drawing.

She reached for her shawl and wrapped it over her head, leaving only enough of an opening to see. "I'll be back soon."

The humming sound was almost deafening as she stepped outside. The air was filled with darting insects. Picking Bones rushed by, the red square of fabric over her head. Maddie ran after her and grabbed her by her frail arm. "Go inside the house. You'll be safe there." She pointed to the soddy, but the woman shook her head and continued on her way.

Thinking it pointless to argue with her, Maddie ran to the wagon and, swallowing her distaste, brushed her arm over the seat to rid it of the moving mass of grasshoppers.

Flying Hawk galloped up on his pony. "Where Picking Bones?"

Maddie waved her hand frantically to keep the insects away from her face. "She's heading back to camp." It was necessary to shout to be heard over the sound of flapping wings and dropping bodies. "How do you get rid of these things?"

Flying Hawk grinned. "Cook over fire. Taste good."

Maddie grimaced. "I'm serious, Flying Hawk. The crops. We've got to save them."

"No save crops." He raced off in one direction, Maddie in another.

Luke stared in disbelief and horror at the hordes of grasshoppers that dropped from the sky like hard-driven hail. Before he could fully register the significance of what was happening, the ground around his feet was covered.

Running between the rows of cornstalks, he pulled off his straw hat and waved it. The horde of insects continued to drop around him, latching on to every blade of grass, every leaf, every last square inch of sod. He tossed his hat aside and pulled off his shirt. He whipped the shirt back and forth through the air in an effort to save his precious stalks.

He soon realized the futility of it. There were simply too many of them and too much ground for him to cover.

Winded, he stumbled to a halt and watched with a combination of awe and incredulity as the fabric in his hand began to disappear beneath a mass of grasshoppers. Cursing, he discarded the shirt. He covered his face with his hands in an attempt to block out the horrible, destructive force around him. But there was no escaping the dreadful drone that filled the air, nor the sting of flying insects against his flesh.

He'd survived the invasion of grasshoppers that had demolished this land in '67, but that was nothing compared to this. These grasshoppers were eating everything in sight, the stalks, the sod, even the wooden handles of his tools.

There was not a thing he could do but go home.

Brushing the insects away from his face, he searched

for his horse, but the animal had evidently panicked and run off. There was no sign of the horse, only Maddie's wagon, racing toward him. His heart lilted at sight of her, a habit he seemed to have no control over. But reality soon took hold, and his only thought was to protect her from the horror that surrounded him.

What was she thinking of, anyway, to come out here? His only hope was that she didn't have Matthew with her. He waved his arms over his head. "Go back, Maddie. Please, go back!"

The wagon kept coming, and he realized she probably couldn't see him through the cloud of grasshoppers. Despite his annoyance at her, he was amused to hear that godawful whistle of hers. Even the incredibly loud drone of the grasshoppers couldn't drown out the shrill, clear sound of Maddie's whistle.

No sooner had the whistle sliced through the air than the flapping sound of grasshopper wings grew louder. Suddenly the top level of soil lifted upward and took flight. The sky filled with darting black spots that seemed to move in a frenzied spiral but were, in reality, moving south. Luke stood and watched in utter amazement as the dots came together overhead to form a dark, whirling cloud.

The droning sound began to fade away as the cloud drifted off.

As quickly as it had come, the ravenous swarm left. All that remained was a few dying insects.

Luke watched the cloud until it was but a tiny spot in the distance. Overcome with relief, he threw his fist into the air and yelled with joy.

Like a child on Christmas morning, he ran between the cornstalks, his heart beating out a song of thanksgiving. The leaves had been chewed, but the damage was nowhere near what it could have been. The crops had been saved!

He turned as the rumbling sound of wagon wheels drew near. Maddie waved and pulled up by his side, tearing the shawl from her head. "Luke! Are you all right?"

"All right? My God, Maddie, I've never been more all right in my life. What are you doing out here?"

"I wanted to see if you needed any help with the crops." She jumped to the ground and examined one of the cornstalks.

He pulled her into his arms. "Do you know what you did? You saved the crops!"

She looked up at him, thoroughly confused. "Oh, Luke, that's wonderful. About the crops, I mean . . . But . . . I don't understand. How did *I* save them?"

"You really don't know, do you? When you whistled . . . the grasshoppers left." He threw his head back and laughed at the absurdity of it all.

"Are you sure that's what did it?" Maddie gazed around her. "I didn't think grasshoppers could hear."

"I don't know if they can hear or not. All I know is that when you whistled, they left. To tell you the truth, I don't blame them."

She slapped at him playfully, and he drew her nearer. At that moment he felt like the happiest man alive. "I thought I was about to lose everything again. Oh, Maddie . . ."

He pressed his lips to her forehead, but when he felt her stiffen in his arms, he pulled his mouth away.

Still clinging to him, she lifted her lashes and searched his face. He felt himself drowning in the lovely green depths of her eyes.

"I'm so sorry, Maddie." The apology was ripped from the very depths of him, and the next words came out in a muffled sob. "I never meant to hurt you."

Her eyes widened. "You didn't hurt me . . . not that much. It was my first time . . ."

He looked at her in astonishment. "Your first? But you seemed so . . . at ease. As if making love was the most natural thing in the world to you. I thought . . ."

They stared at each other.

"Is that why you pulled away? Because you thought there had been others before you?"

"My God, Maddie. Is that what you think?"

"What else can I think?"

"I was wrong to leave you like that. But when I heard you cry out . . . I thought I'd hurt you. I mean *really* hurt you. I couldn't bear to think that I brought you pain . . ."

"And you don't think that leaving me without a word of explanation . . . you don't think that caused me pain? I thought I'd done something wrong. I thought you didn't love me . . ."

Hearing the word *love* on her lips made his heart pound that much faster. He wasn't use to hearing that word spoken aloud. He'd been taught to fight such feelings, not talk about them.

"You don't . . . do you?" she whispered. "You don't love me. Last night meant nothing to you."

He tightened his fingers around her upper arms. "Last night meant everything to me, Maddie. And . . . I do love you."

"You don't have to say things, you know, that you don't mean."

"I mean every word."

She searched his face and looked unconvinced. "I know I'm not the kind of woman who's easy to love. So don't feel you have to say things to make me feel better. I'm not good at . . . womanly things. I'm never quite sure how to act around men."

"You know how to act around me, Maddie."

"I . . . I do? I mean, you're not just saying that . . ."

"I mean it," he said hoarsely.

He dropped his hands to her waist, then slipped his arms around her. When she offered no resistance, he crushed her to him and covered her mouth hungrily. Her lovely, lithe body molded against his as easily as the Kansas sky met the prairie land.

She pressed the hardening tips of her breasts against his bare chest. Her arms around his neck, she ran her fingers through his hair, and her warm, sensuous lips seemed to melt with the touch of his tongue.

He pulled his mouth away and touched his hand to her cheek.

"Oh, Maddie," he whispered. "I would never forgive myself if I did anything to bring you pain."

"It ..." The open, honest look she gave him made him feel even more of a fool because of all the things he kept from her. "It should be easier the second time."

He drew away from her. "Maddie, there can't be a second time."

She couldn't have looked more stricken had he slapped her—and indeed, he felt that he had. "Why ... why not?"

He closed his eyes so he wouldn't have to see the look of devastation on her face. "Because I love you too much." He reached over and picked up his hat. After giving it a good whack against his thigh, he pressed it on to his head.

"Wait!" she called, as he turned away. "You can't just say something like that and not explain."

He gazed across the prairie. The cloud of grasshoppers had disappeared. But the cloud that was his past remained. "We'll talk about this later."

"Now, Luke. I want to talk about it now."

He met her eyes. "I don't think we should leave Matthew alone any longer."

Something seemed to drain out of her. She looked like a soldier who had suddenly surrendered in defeat.

Finally, she let her head dip in a stoic little nod that nearly broke his heart. "You're right. Matthew will be waiting."

Luke drove the wagon home with Maddie by his side, her back as straight and rigid as a pole. Neither spoke, not in words, but they talked to each other with imploring glances and silent pleas until the air between them hung thick with unspoken messages.

No sooner had Luke pulled the wagon in front of the soddy than Matthew ran outside to greet them. He pointed in the direction the grasshoppers had gone.

"You're right, son. They're gone. Thanks to Maddie." Luke jumped to the ground, then stooped down to let Matthew onto his back, carrying him piggyback into the house.

Maddie stood watching father and son until they disappeared from sight. Then, throwing her shawl over her arm, she followed them into the soddy.

It seemed necessary to immerse herself in domestic chores. It was not the horrors of the day that haunted her, but the memories of the night. As long as she kept busy, she could keep the threatening tears at bay.

"I'll have to check out the well," Luke said. He, too, seemed to need to focus on domestic chores, as if to distance himself from the night. Or from her. "Make sure it's not contaminated." He drank a glass of water and set the glass down on the table. His actions seemed hesitant, as if every movement had to be thought out in advance. "I just hope they didn't get into the dairy cistern or the smokehouse."

"I'm sure they didn't." She glanced out the window, but all she could see was clear blue sky. It looked like a perfectly normal day on the outside. How amazing. Inside, she felt anything but normal.

Matthew opened the door cautiously, but when one

of the dying grasshoppers hopped inside, he jumped back.

"It won't hurt you." Maddie stopped to pick up the grasshopper from the floor and held it up for Matthew to see. "I've never seen such tiny grasshoppers."

Barely longer than an inch, it was half the size of the grasshoppers back home. "It's interesting," she continued. "Look at the unusual colorings." The red and yellow colors were beginning to fade. "We definitely need to exhibit this in our museum." She carefully placed the insect into one of the jars she used for specimens.

That night, after Matthew was asleep, Maddie and Luke sat at the table, drinking coffee. Luke looked tired, his face etched with lines of fatigue.

The three of them had walked around the property earlier, assessing the damage.

As bad as the damage was, though, it was nowhere near as devastating as it could have been. The chickens were bloated with grasshoppers, but the well had escaped, and that was the most important concern. The water that was kept by the side of the house had to be dumped and the barrels scrubbed, but even this was minor compared to what could have happened.

"More coffee?" she asked.

He shook his head no.

"I better let you get some sleep."

"It's been a hard day," he admitted. "But I don't want you to go. Not yet. I know earlier . . . I said some things that you might have misunderstood."

*I love you* is what he'd said, and he was right—she had misunderstood. But no longer. "You don't have to explain."

The lines deepened at his brow. "It was selfish of me to let this happen. I never meant for it to. I hope you can forgive me . . ."

"Forgive you? Luke, this is ridiculous. I wanted us

to be close. I'm the one who forced . . . I practically threw myself at you."

"I don't think you did that, Maddie. Lord, I've wanted you since the first day you arrived on my doorstep. That's what makes it so hard for me."

"It doesn't have to be hard, Luke. Just don't lie to me. Don't tell me you care when obviously that's not true. I may be ignorant in matters of the heart, but I know that a man can want a woman and not have any special feelings for her."

"This isn't about want . . . not in the sense you mean. I love you, Maddie."

She took a deep breath, savoring the sound of his words, even though she knew them to be false. "Please, don't, Luke."

"It's true."

He looked so sincere that her heart skipped a beat. "Then why . . . ?"

"You heard Lucy. You heard her call me a murderer."

Maddie swallowed hard. This introduction of the past was every bit as threatening as the grasshoppers had been. She didn't want to think about what Lucy had called him. "Some people don't need much of a reason to call a person names."

"She has every right to hate me." He sighed deeply and ran his fingers through his hair. "If you knew who I am . . ."

The look he gave her was so full of anguish that her breath caught between her ribs. "Who . . . who are you, Luke?"

"You don't want to know, Maddie. Please don't make me tell you."

"Does . . . does it have something to do with last night? With why you pulled away?"

He didn't answer her; he didn't have to. The look of

despair in his eyes was answer enough. She knew she was battling an unseen enemy, and somehow knowing it was a formidable one made it that much more difficult to fight.

"Can't you at least tell me something about your background?" She wanted—needed—to know everything about him. She leaned forward, her face troubled. Earlier she had wanted to forget the past and complete what they had begun the night before. But during the most intimate of moments, something had come between them, and it was painfully obvious that whatever that something was, it stood between them now. Maybe it always would.

"Help me to understand." Sensing his reluctance, she started with something she thought might be relatively simple for him to answer. "Why did you come here? Why did you come to Kansas?"

But even that question seemed to cause him distress, and she sensed a silent war being waged within him.

When at last he spoke, his words were muffled. "Peter asked me to come."

"Then you knew Peter prior to coming to Kansas?"

"Peter and I were childhood friends." He spoke in a flat voice that was so low, she was forced to lean forward so as not to miss a single word. "Our friendship became strained when the war broke out."

"Is that how Peter lost his leg?"

He nodded.

"You once told me you didn't fight in the war."

"I didn't."

"Why not?"

"It was a personal reason. I assure you, it was not an easy decision to make, and it was an even harder one to live with." As was far too often the case, his face remained impassive, but his eyes once again betrayed him. For there was agony there, and maybe even self-loathing.

She pulled her shawl around her shoulders, but not because she was cold. What she needed was protection, and even something as tenuous as her wrap made her feel more secure, better able to combat whatever was keeping her and Luke apart. "It must have been hard to make such a decision."

"It was. It would have been easier had my best friend understood. Or even my wife."

At mention of his wife, she held her breath, hoping he would continue. Maddie was curious about the woman who had once won his heart. For all she knew, Catherine-Anne was responsible for Luke's leaving her bed last night. "Why . . . was it so important to you not to fight in the war? Was it fear?"

"No!" He spoke so sharply that she jumped, and he immediately regretted his harsh response. It was fear, of course, but not the way she meant it. He wasn't afraid of dying.

His only fear was not knowing what he was capable of doing should he take up arms. He still didn't know. When he was with Maddie, it was so easy to imagine he could be capable of love—not the carefully controlled love he had allotted his wife and young son but the kind of love that knew no bounds.

Last night, he had thought such a love possible. But when she'd cried out, it all came back to him, the past, his father, his mother.

He glanced toward the bed where Matthew slept and thought of the many times during the preceding years that he had longed to pick him up, hug him, love him without restraint, without fear, without having to worry about unleashing the sleeping monster within. He felt ashamed now for letting himself be convinced it was wrong to love—wrong to feel love, taste love, show love. He felt ashamed and guilty. He wanted to make it up to Matthew for all the times he'd held back.

He shifted his gaze to meet her eyes, and he wondered, as he had so many times in recent days, if he was even capable of giving such unrestrained love. He wanted to. Lord, he wanted to. But he just didn't know how.

Poor Catherine-Anne. Had she ever suspected how little of himself he actually gave her? Had she ever known how necessary that holding back was?

"It wasn't fear," he said at last.

"Why did Lucy call you a murderer?"

He stood abruptly, and when she drew back he froze. He hated the look of fear that suddenly flashed in her eyes. The look sickened him; it was the same look he had seen on his mother's face whenever he went to hug her.

He clenched his fists at his side. "Why don't you ask Lucy?"

"I want it to come from you. I want you to tell me who you are and what happened to make Lucy hate you so. I want you to tell me why, if you love me, you keep pushing me away."

They stared at each other across the table. Maddie was as unrelenting in her need for answers as he was in protecting her from them.

Even so, it took a great deal of determination on his part now to walk outside, leaving her questions unanswered.

# Chapter 27

She stared at the closed door, resisting the urge to follow him. His failure to share his past with her was proof enough that he had no intention of sharing his future or anything else with her.

Feeling weary and disheartened, she checked on Matthew. He was sound asleep and looked like an angel with his long, dark lashes fanning across his soft, rounded cheeks. She ran her fingers lovingly across his smooth forehead. His lids lifted, and his mouth turned upward at the sight of her before his eyes flickered shut again. "Sleep tight, sweetie," she whispered, dropping a kiss on his temple.

She tiptoed outside, closing the door softly behind her. She searched the darkness for Luke and strained her ears for the sound of his footsteps, but all she could hear was the melodious sound of the flute drifting out of the darkness.

All through that long, seemingly endless night, she was haunted by things she didn't understand. What could have happened to put such a look of anguish and despair on his face? So much hatred in Lucy's? And how much of what had happened was responsible for Matthew's inability to speak?

All she had was bits and pieces, and the more she tried to fill in the missing links, the more the questions outnumbered the answers.

Adding to the confusion was the memory of his kisses and the warm, secure feel of his arms around her. Maybe the truth was here, somewhere, staring her in the face, but she didn't want to see it. Maybe love really *was* blind.

She was tremendously relieved when the first glimmer of dawn announced the end of night, and Lefty's horse could be heard galloping across the prairie. Soon his familiar voice sounded outside her tipi. "This Great Father's Day?"

She stepped outside to greet him. "Not today, Lefty."

He grinned. "Me be back."

"Don't go yet. I need to talk to you." She walked beside his pony. "Do you know anyone who plays a flute?"

Lefty frowned. "Flute?"

"Musical instrument." She tried to think of other words he might know that would convey her meaning, and when none came to mind, she pretended to play a flute to demonstrate.

Lefty nodded. "Flute." He said the word as she said it. "Love flute."

Her heart skipped a beat. "I knew it was a love song," she whispered. "But who?" A sudden thought stopped her in her tracks. "Oh, no! Not Shooting Star."

"Shooting Star like Wildfire. Call you Ostrich. Flute magic. Make . . . how say? Drop in love."

"Drop? You mean fall . . . fall in love? The flute makes people fall in love?"

Lefty nodded. "Flute make Wildfire and Shooting Star drop in love."

"Listen to me, Lefty. You must tell Shooting Star no more love flute."

Lefty rode off, and all she could do was hope that he would make her wishes known to Shooting Star. As she turned back, something red caught her eye. Picking Bones was walking toward the tipi to begin her day-long vigil. Maddie shuddered to think what the woman would do if she found out that Shooting Star was playing love songs to her.

Following her early-morning workout with the Cheyennes, Maddie rode out to the Eldridge camp. Peter emerged from the tent. Tucking his crutches beneath his armpits, he hobbled out to greet her. His haggard appearance shocked her. It seemed that he had aged ten years in a single night.

"Lucy? Is she . . . ?"

"She had a hard night. The grasshopper raid upset her. Jamie and Caroline had nightmares. I'm afraid none of us got much sleep." He regarded her thoughtfully. "Looks like you didn't get much sleep yourself."

"I didn't."

His gaze traveled across the prairie. Only yesterday the area had been covered with wildflowers and tall grass. Today, in contrast, the ground was bare, stripped of every blade of grass or plant, anything green, or even brown. Even the canvas on the wagon had been devoured, and little more than tiny strips of fabric hung from the steel frame. It was obvious that the Eldridges had suffered far more damage than Luke had.

"How much crop damage did you have?" Peter asked.

"We . . . were lucky. For some reason, the grasshoppers moved on before doing too much damage."

"You *were* lucky. It was all I could do to save the tent. They were all over the thing. As it is, I'm afraid that when it rains, we'll be in for some problems."

"Is there anything we can do to help?"

"That's mighty generous of you to offer. If we think of anything, I'll let you know."

"We have quite a bit of meat in the smokehouse and plenty of dairy products."

He looked surprised by the offer. "We're pretty well stocked with tinned goods, and I just sent the children down to the stream for fresh water. I'll boil it to be on the safe side."

She dismounted and Peter took the reins from her. She walked by his side, marveling at the ease with which he maneuvered his crutches. "Luke told me that you lost your leg during the war."

"I don't like to talk about the war. What happened, happened." He wrapped the reins around a wagon wheel. "Lucy's inside."

Maddie found Lucy lying on the cot inside the tent. She looked pale, but otherwise healthy enough. After they had exchanged a few pleasantries, and talked about the horror of the grasshoppers, Lucy told her about the new house Peter was going to build.

"He rode over to Colton this morning and made arrangements for the excess lumber to be sent over here. The workers said they would help Peter put up a house and barn. It won't take more than a few days."

Maddie remembered Luke telling her that prairie fires made him question the wisdom of wood houses. "Do you think you'll have your new house in time for the baby?"

"Perhaps not. But soon afterward." Her face softened. "Peter is truly a hero. There's nothing he can't do, even though he's missing a leg."

The look of love and adulation on Lucy's face brought a pang to Maddie's heart. She wondered if Lucy knew how very lucky she was.

"Lucy, yesterday, I . . ."

"You want to know why I called Luke a murderer?"

"I find Luke to be a very gentle and caring man. I

can't imagine why you would make such an accusation . . ."

Lucy gave her a knowing look. "Don't let your heart blind you from the truth."

Maddie bit her lower lip; she remembered that Red Feather had accused her of the same thing. "What is the truth? Please, Lucy. I need to know."

Lucy looked up from her pillow and nodded. "I guess you do. I'm only telling you this because I'm fond of you. I hardly know you, but I admire the way you conduct your life. With no regard to what anyone thinks."

Maddie laughed at this. "That's the first time anyone ever said they admired me for anything."

"It's the truth. My father was a minister, and we couldn't breathe without worrying about what the community would think." She paused for a moment to adjust the pillows at her back.

Maddie assisted her, then sat on the camp stool. "If you're not up to talking, I'll come back."

"I'm all right." Lucy's face grew dark as she considered the past. "You probably know Luke's wife died in childbirth."

"I wasn't sure how she died. Luke won't talk about it much except to say that Matthew has not spoken a word since."

At the mention of Matthew's name, Lucy's face softened. "Poor child."

"About Luke's wife . . ."

"My brother George was her doctor. He was a brilliant man and a dedicated doctor. Everyone in Colton idolized him. He did everything he could to save her. I know he did. That's the kind of man he was."

"Was? You're not saying that . . ."

"That's exactly what I'm saying. Luke killed my brother."

Maddie covered her mouth with her hand to hold back the wave of nausea that suddenly overcame her. It was certainly true that Luke was a brooding, perhaps even moody, man, but his gentleness and patience with his young son made it impossible for her to believe he was capable of such a heinous crime. And would a man guilty of murder be concerned about hurting a woman while making love to her?

"I can't believe this, Lucy. Are you sure? I mean, if he really did kill your brother, why wasn't he arrested?"

Lucy made a bitter sound. "It was because of that Sheriff Beckleworth. He said it was all circumstantial evidence."

Maddie felt a surge of hope. "Then it's possible he's innocent."

"Nobody believes that, Maddie. Not even the sheriff. Luke even admitted it. What else could he do? He was caught red-handed, you might say."

Maddie stiffened. Everything in her fought to rally to Luke's defense. "Luke told the sheriff he killed the doctor?"

"He didn't actually say it. But he didn't deny it either." Lucy dropped her head to her shoulder. She looked completely drained.

Not wanting to tire Lucy more than she already had, Maddie took her leave and rode home, hardly aware of her surroundings.

She and Matthew spent the rest of the day raking up dead grasshoppers. She'd never seen anything like it in her life. The dried bodies of the insects were stacked up against the barn like snowdrifts.

After raking the grasshoppers into a neat pile, she sprinkled kerosene around the mound and set it afire.

Maddie stepped back from the hot flames and was surprised to see Picking Bones racing toward her. The red shawl flew off the woman's thin shoulders as she ran. With youthful energy, she waved her hands and shouted a steady stream of Cheyenne obscenities. At least, that's what the harsh words sounded like to Maddy.

Showing more agility than care around the fire, the woman stomped her feet and shook her fists at Maddie.

Luke rushed from the barn and gaped at the fire in horror. "Good God, Maddie. You can't start a fire out here. The least bit of wind and the whole prairie would be on fire."

"There isn't any wind," Maddie said stubbornly. "Besides, how else do you get rid of this mess?"

"Next time, bury them." He turned and headed back to the barn.

"I don't intend to be around for next time!" she shouted after him.

Picking Bones mumbled under her breath as she continued to stomp around the dying flames with moccasined feet.

The blaze died down, leaving an odd smell in the air, and the woman gave Maddie a look of contempt as she shuffled back to the tipi.

Maddie threw water on the dying embers, then spaded dirt on the ashes. Satisfied that no danger remained, she scrubbed her hands and face, changed her clothes, and headed into the soddy to prepare the noonday meal.

When Luke didn't join her and Matthew for lunch, she carried a pitcher of water and two glasses out to the barn.

Luke wiped his arm across his forehead. "Fortunately no grasshoppers got in the water supply."

"That's good news," she said, though her mind was far removed from grasshoppers and any of the problems they might have caused.

He drank a full glass without stopping. "Thank you. I needed that."

"I thought you might." She set the pitcher down on his workbench and picked up a wooden frame.

"It's going to be a writing slate for Matthew. He can carry it around with him. That way he'll always have something to write on."

"It's a wonderful idea," she exclaimed.

The soft caress of his gaze felt like a lover's touch. It was easy to believe at that moment that he really did love her.

Was it possible for a man capable of such softness also to be capable of murder?

"When I varnish it, it'll be the exact same color as your hair." He reached out to take a handful of her hair and held it as if it were a strand of precious jewels.

"Oh, no! Not red!"

He arched a dark eyebrow. "Why do you make it sound like there's something wrong with the color of your hair?"

"It's a terrible color. I tried so hard as a child to get it to fade. I even washed it in lemon juice."

He looked incredulous. "Where did you ever get such a ridiculous notion?"

"Lemons are supposed to lighten stains . . ."

"I was talking about . . . your hair."

"My . . . my hair?"

"Do you know the trouble I went to to get this wood sent all the way from New York because of its distinctive rich color?"

Disarmed by the way he looked at her, she watched him run his long, sinewy fingers lightly across the wood and was reminded of how wonderful it had felt when he touched her bare flesh.

She felt a warmth spread down the length of her as if it were her own body his fingers were exploring. She remembered the girlish blushes of the young women back home when a man so much as looked at them. No wonder Luke had thought her experienced. Why hadn't she felt the same sort of embarrassment? And why, now, did she feel an almost uncontrollable urge to kiss the small square of taut, tanned flesh that his partially unbuttoned shirt revealed? Lord Almighty, wouldn't he be shocked to know what she wanted to do to him at that moment?

She only wished there weren't so many questions begging for answers.

Turning her back to him, she waited until she had regained her usual composure before tackling the subject that was most on her mind. "I saw Lucy this morning. She was having some pain yesterday, and I wanted to make sure she was all right. As you might expect, the grasshoppers upset her."

When he made no reply, she chanced a glance at him. He was no longer caressing the wood. He was attacking the wood with a plane.

She took a deep breath. His face looked grim, his expression etched in forbidding lines. Normally, such an expression would have prevented her from pursuing a subject that was obviously off-limits. But she knew, perhaps better than anyone else, that the hard stone mask would dissolve in an instant if Matthew walked in the door. Knowing that the soft, caring side of him was so close to the surface gave her courage, and she pressed on.

"Why, Luke? Why did you kill her brother?"

His hand stilled and he raised his eyes to hers. For the longest time, the question hung between them like an ugly, open wound.

Slowly, he straightened. His eyes flickered, and for a fleeting second he looked like a man betrayed.

Betrayed by whom? she wondered. Certainly, he

didn't think she was betraying him for asking him outright. Lucy, perhaps? Somehow she doubted that Lucy had anything to do with this. In any case, she wasn't even certain if she saw what she thought she saw. For the look had been replaced by a hardening of the eyes that let nothing in, and let even less out.

"Did you?" she probed, hating the doubt that made her demand an answer.

This time there was no hesitation. "Yes."

She felt a strange inertia as her usual boldness was overcome by heartache. She had wanted so much to believe that what Lucy had said was not true.

"I murdered him," he said, almost cruelly. "Are you satisfied? Would you like to know what else I'm capable of doing?"

She hated that raw look on his face that left no doubt he spoke the truth. Unable to speak, she ran from the barn.

*How long will it take her?* he wondered. *How much longer before she packs up her things and leaves?* Two hours had passed since she'd stormed out of the barn. For two long hours he'd dreaded the moment of her departure like a man who was about to hang dreaded the final walk to the gallows.

How would he get through the days knowing she was gone? Knowing he would never see her again? How would he get through the nights?

And Matthew? Dear God, how would he explain her absence to Matthew?

Dammit! He should have told her the truth from the start. Before he had started feeling the things he felt for her.

But how the hell was he supposed to know that he was going to come to care for her? He would never have guessed it in a million years. In those first days, when he was just getting to know her, he thought her eccentric, obtrusive, loud, overbearing, as tall and skinny as a rail—everything he hated in a woman.

Everything he'd come to love.

He pushed against the barn door and peered outside. Her wagon was still parked next to the windmill. He pulled the door to and resumed his pacing. What was taking her so long to leave?

She *was* going to leave, wasn't she?

Of course she was! What woman in her right mind would continue to live practically under the same roof with a murderer?

A footstep outside made his senses leap. He spun around to face the door, hoping against hope that she had come to tell him she would stay.

He tried not to look disappointed when Matthew stepped inside. Lord only knew how much the boy needed him at that moment. For it was painfully clear from the stricken look on Matthew's face that he knew something was seriously wrong.

Luke motioned his son closer. He wrapped his arms around the slender shoulders and was startled when Matthew pushed him away.

Luke kept his voice calm. "It's all right, Matthew. You and I . . . We're going to be all right."

Matthew's face grew still, and Luke saw the same wild look that had preceded each of his son's tantrums. Luke reached for his arm. "Calm down, Matthew."

Matthew threw himself face down on the ground. He kicked and pounded with his feet and fists, completely out of control. Not a sound came from his mouth, but his face was twisted in anguish and rage. It was the first tantrum that Matthew had thrown since he'd been attending Maddie's classes.

Desperate to stop his son's violent outburst, Luke grabbed a screwdriver from his workbench and dropped to his knees by Matthew's side. He clamped a hand around Matthew's wrist. "If you have something to say, then say it!" He tried to force the screwdriver into Matthew's hand, to no avail. "Write!"

Matthew seemed oblivious to anything but the tortured feelings inside that he could not express.

"Matthew!" Luke's voice was loud and sharp, sharper than he would normally allow himself to talk. But he had to reach Matthew, some way, somehow.

Out of fear that Matthew would hurt himself, he forced himself against his son's writhing body. "Do you hear me? Write it down like Maddie showed you!"

Matthew's body went limp. Luke rolled Matthew into his arms and rocked him until the wild look had left his eyes. But the tears that followed were just as devastating to Luke as the rage, and he held his son tight, battling his own tears, his own rage.

The voices from the past issued the usual dire warnings, but Luke's grief over losing Maddie was so great that he clung to his young son with all his heart and soul.

After a long while, Matthew's tears stopped, and though the rage was gone, his face was still shadowed with frustration and despair.

Luke took his son's hand in his own and placed the handle of the screwdriver in the small, damp palm. He sat Matthew up and pointed to the hard dirt floor. "Write it, Matthew." His voice was gentle this time. "Tell me what's inside."

Matthew turned the screwdriver over, fingering it.

"Go on, son. Write like Maddie showed you."

His lower lip quivering, Matthew leaned forward and pressed the tip of the tool into the ground. The letter *M* took shape in the dirt. Hesitating, Matthew looked up at his father as if to say he didn't know how to write the rest.

Luke nodded. "*M* for Maddie. I understand. Keep going, son."

Matthew scratched out each letter with careful precision. After he completed a word, he looked up at his father as if to seek reassurance, before writing the next word.

Matthew wrote *M is going away.* Once the sentence was completed, he threw down the screwdriver and covered his face with his hands. Luke pulled Matthew into his arms once again and rocked him. He remembered thinking that if his son ever spoke again, he'd be the happiest man alive.

Well, Matthew was speaking to him in a dozen different ways, and each way only added more pain to Luke's misery.

Luke buried his face in Matthew's hair and squeezed his eyes shut. "I don't want her to leave either, son."

# Chapter 28

Maddie packed the last of her belongings into the trunk. She planned to leave first thing in the morning. Her hope was that the Eldridge family would let her stay with them for the week or two it would take for the hotel in Colton to be completed. Lucy could certainly use the help.

Of course, it would depend on whether they were willing to put up with Picking Bones standing guard all day.

How she hated leaving Matthew. But it couldn't be helped. Her only hope was that he understood how very much she cared for him.

She closed her eyes and shivered at the memory of Luke's confession. *I murdered him.* The words spun like wheels in her head, growing louder with each passing minute until she thought she would lose her mind.

Rubbing her hands up and down her arms, she tried to justify Luke's behavior. Was it possible he'd been out of his mind with grief? Maybe it had been an accident . . . Maybe . . .

A dozen other possibilities came to mind, but none that made much sense.

There had to be more to the story.

But what if there wasn't more? What if he truly was a cold-blooded murderer?

The thoughts continued to plague her for the rest of that day and throughout the evening. She fixed a light supper for Matthew and tried to offer him reassurances. At one point, he threw his arms around her and sobbed on her shoulder.

"I'm not going that far away," she explained. "I'm just going to help Mrs. Eldridge. Maybe you can come and visit me and play with Jamie and Caroline."

She waited until he was asleep before tiptoeing outside and quietly closing the door behind her. She stood watching the light that fanned out from beneath the barn doors, tempted to go to him, to ask him for more ... what? Details, perhaps. Something that would help her to understand what could make someone take the life of another.

It was fear that kept her in place—fear of what he might say. After a while, she abandoned any thought of confronting him. Dreading the hours until morning, she ducked into her tipi and began undressing for bed.

The sight of her outlined on the walls of her tipi brought him to a halt. It was still fairly early. She didn't normally prepare for bed this early.

He stood frozen in place. Looking at him, no one would have guessed that he was fighting a bitter, though silent, battle between doing right by her and giving in to his own selfish need to go to her.

He reminded himself of all the reasons why he shouldn't feel the things he felt. He was in no position to offer a woman anything, least of all himself. Never had been. Never could be.

Oh, how he longed to hold her again. To feel that wild streak of hers, that same sweet passion she'd showed him the night his past and his present collided. Lord, to think it had been her first time.

A deep, abiding sigh escaped him as he watched her

slip first her skirt, then her trousers down her soft, rounded hips. He imagined running his hand down the long line of her back to the gentle flare of her buttocks.

He ached, literally ached, as he watched her lift her arms and work her nightgown over her head. He rubbed his chin. It had been a difficult day and promised to be an even more difficult night. He wiped the moisture off his forehead with his arm.

It was a relief to him when she doused the lantern and he could no longer see her. But the relief was only minor, for the vision of her naked loveliness continued to torment him for the remainder of the night.

It was still dark when Maddie awoke to the sound of wagon wheels. The wagon was traveling fast, and sensing that something was amiss, she quickly felt for a candle and lit it with shaking hands. She carried the candle in its holder to the front of the soddy just as the wagon pulled up.

She recognized the driver at once as Peter. He looked visibly relieved to see her. "The baby's on the way."

"Give me a moment," Maddie called. Cupping her hand around the flickering flame, she hurried to the tipi to dress. She was back outside in record time. "Has anyone gone for the doctor?"

"There's no time . . ." Peter's voice sounded strained.

"We don't know that for sure. I think someone should go for him."

"Maybe you should go to Lucy alone. I'll head for Hays."

"I should be the one to go," she said. "I can make better time." Peter would have to take the wagon because of his leg.

"I . . . I don't know if that's such a good idea, Maddie. I know nothing about delivering a baby . . ."

"I'll go." It was Luke's voice floating out of the darkness.

"That will be a great help, Luke," she called, grateful for his offer.

"I don't think there's time to get a doctor," Peter said worriedly.

Luke stepped into the circle of flickering candlelight. He was buttoning his shirt. "If I reach Hays early enough, the doctor and I might be able to catch the train to Colton. That would save a few hours' time."

This seemed to relieve Peter's mind, and after waiting for Maddie to climb onto the seat next to him, he urged his horse through the misty darkness.

The silver light of dawn spilled from the east as they reached the Eldridge camp.

The buckboard rolled to a stop next to the army tent. Maddie jumped to the ground and hurried to Lucy, leaving Peter to struggle with his crutches.

A lantern burned inside the tent, casting shadows against the dark canvas walls. Lucy looked greatly relieved when she saw Maddie. "Thank you for coming. I thought after our talk yesterday . . ."

Maddie dropped to her knees by the woman's side. "Of course I would come. How long has it been?"

"The pains started around midnight. They . . ." She broke off with a moan.

Maddie offered her hand to the woman. "Squeeze tight," she said. Lucy's hand grew limp, and Maddie sponged off her forehead. "Don't worry," she said. "I know what to do when the time comes."

Lucy looked hopeful. "You've delivered a baby before?"

"As a matter of fact, I've helped deliver seven." What she didn't say was that they had been kittens. Still, the principle was the same, and thanks to the time spent in her father's lab, she was educated in the field of anatomy.

Despite Peter's concern, the baby didn't seem to be in any hurry to make an appearance. For the next few hours, all Maddie could do was to make Lucy as comfortable as possible.

Lucy slept between contractions, and Maddie took advantage of one of her catnaps to step outside the tent and splash cold water on her arms and face. Not a bit of breeze moved the stiflingly hot air.

Peter, whose crutches had poked a series of holes in the sod outside from his constant pacing, searched her face. "Is she all right?"

"She's having a hard time."

"She didn't have this hard a time with the others."

Maddie wanted so much to say something that would relieve his worry. She wished she'd spent more time listening to her mother's friends and their whispered talk of childbirth, and less time focused on the adventures of her father and his colleagues.

"It doesn't necessarily mean that anything's wrong." She tried to sound encouraging for Lucy's sake, as well as the sake of the two small children who were watching her with fearful eyes. She tousled Caroline's hair and chucked Jamie under the chin. "This baby is probably larger than the other two were."

"I hope you're right."

Upon hearing a groan from Lucy, Maddie met Peter's eyes briefly, gave the children a wink, and quickly ducked through the open flaps.

She spent the rest of the morning trying to keep Lucy calm and cool, while Peter entertained Jamie and Caroline outside. At ten-thirty, Peter drove the wagon to the train depot to pick up Luke and the doctor.

Maddie heard the train whistle in the distance as she sponged off Lucy's hot forehead. *Please let the doctor be on board,* she prayed.

It was close to forty minutes later when Jamie stuck his head through the tent opening. "I think I see them."

Maddie rushed outside to see for herself. A dust cloud rose in the distance. It was coming from the direction of the depot. It had to be the doctor!

Maddie and the two children stood watching the wagon grow closer. At last, the wagon was close enough to reveal the welcome news that Peter was not alone. Next to him sat a rather pompous-looking man in shirtsleeves. The wagon rolled to a stop, and Luke jumped down from the back of it. He turned to lift Matthew to the ground, then handed the doctor a black bag.

"This way!" Maddie called.

The doctor ran the short distance to the tent, his bald head gleaming in the glare of the late-morning sun. "I'm Doctor Williams." He drew a handkerchief from his pocket and mopped his brow.

"Are we glad to see you!" She led him to Lucy's side, then withdrew, leaving him to examine his patient in privacy. Matthew greeted her with a hug, then ran off to join Caroline and Jamie, who had been sent to the stream to fetch fresh water.

Maddie stood outside the tent with Peter and Luke. Both men looked tired and worried, though Luke looked more haunted than anything else. Try as she might to make eye contact with him, he refused to look directly at her.

Peter offered Luke some whiskey. "Do you want some?" he asked Maddie.

She shook her head. Whatever happened, she would need a clear head.

Dr. Williams stepped out of the tent. The serious look on his face made her heart sink. She had been so certain that once the doctor arrived, their worries would be over.

"The baby appears to be tied up in the cord," he explained.

Peter took a quick gulp of the whiskey he'd poured for Luke. "It sounds serious."

"It is serious. I recommend a surgical birth."

Peter paled. "You mean . . . cut her open?"

"It's the only way."

Luke grabbed Peter by the arm, his face ashen. "Don't do this, Peter. I beg of you, don't do this!"

The doctor looked stunned by Luke's outburst, but he was no more surprised than Maddie.

Peter grimaced in uncertainty. "What . . . what choice do I have?"

"You have no choice," the doctor said firmly. He frowned at Luke, then turned back to Peter.

Luke ignored the doctor's warning look. "Think about it, Peter. How many men in the war survived surgery? You were one of the lucky ones."

"This is different," Peter said. "This is childbirth, not gunfire."

"How do you think Catherine-Anne died? It was because your damned brother-in-law cut her open!"

"He did what he could to save her!" Peter yelled back.

"Stop it, both of you!" Maddie cried. "Lucy needs us. This is no time to bring up past history."

Her anguished plea was met with a moment of strained silence. From inside the tent came Lucy's cries. Her moans were like a knife cutting through the tension.

The doctor glanced from one man to the other and then disappeared through the flap of the tent.

"I don't know what to do," Peter said. He sank down on the ground, his crutches falling, and covered his face with his hands. Maddie was tempted to tell him in no uncertain terms that it was no time to be weak, but sensing the anguish behind his muffled sobs, she resisted the urge. Instead, she dropped to her knees beside him and wrapped her arms around him.

"You have to be strong, Peter," she said gently. His body shook as she held him. "Lucy needs you to be strong."

The doctor joined them moments later. "Well? What's it going to be? Surgery or not?"

"Peter?" Maddie nudged him gently.

Peter looked up into her face, his cheeks streaked with dust and tears. "You decide, Maddie."

Her heart closed in protest. "It's not my place to decide. Lucy's your wife."

"I can't." He reached for his crutches and stood. He quickly hobbled away and headed for the wide open prairie.

"Peter!"

From behind her, the doctor cursed. "I can't perform surgery without permission."

Maddie turned, her eyes on Luke. This time he met her gaze. There was no denying the closed look he gave her. *Don't do this, Maddie,* he seemed to say. She looked away from him and took a deep breath.

She faced the doctor and prayed for strength and courage. "You have permission to do what must be done."

The doctor wiped his forehead with his arm. "Permission must come from the next of kin."

"You heard Peter. He told me to make the decision."

"I have to have written proof."

Maddie's anger flared. A woman's life was at stake, and they were arguing over legalities. "In case you've not noticed, Dr. Williams, her next of kin is not here. Nor is he in any condition to make decisions. Certainly you can make allowances under the circumstances."

The doctor glanced in the direction that Peter had gone. "I could lose my license for performing surgery without proper permission. The Medical Society is quite clear on that."

"Should you not perform surgery and something happens to Mrs. Eldridge, I am fully prepared to write to Dr. Coswell and tell him you failed to comply with Mr. Eldridge's wishes and perform surgery."

Surprise crossed the doctor's face at the mention of Dr. Coswell's name, whether because she knew the name of the man who headed the Medical Society or because of her bold declaration, it was hard to say.

In any case, the doctor recovered quickly, and his anger flared. "The patient's husband expressed no such wishes!"

"Are you quite certain about that, Doctor?"

The doctor turned to Luke, obviously looking for support. But although it was clear that Luke was against her decision, he said nothing to contradict her contention.

The doctor paled, but he nodded in defeat. "If something happens during surgery . . ."

She lifted her chin. "I think it would be best for everyone if the surgery is a success."

The doctor rolled up his sleeves. "I'll need an assistant."

Luke uttered a curse and spun on his heel. He covered the short distance to Maddie's wagon with long, angry strides, stopping only long enough to call to Matthew.

She hated to go against his wishes. But what choice did she have? Lord, what choice? She turned to the doctor. "Tell me what to do."

# Chapter 29

The doctor took great pains to prepare for the surgery. Every instrument was sterilized, and he insisted that Maddie wash Lucy's abdomen with hot water and lye soap. By the time Maddie had completed the task to his satisfaction, Lucy's skin was red.

While she worked, Maddie did her best to soothe Lucy's fears. "Dr. Williams is very knowledgeable." She wiped away the perspiration from Lucy's forehead. "Your baby will be fine."

"Where's Peter?" Lucy whispered, her parched lips barely moving.

Maddie glanced toward the doctor, who was methodically washing his hands. It seemed to her he was taking an inordinate amount of time to prepare for this surgery. She couldn't help but wonder if he was hoping for some miracle that would prevent it altogether. "Peter's outside," she lied.

Lucy clutched at her hand. "I need to see him. Please."

Maddie covered Lucy's hand with her own. "I'll . . . fetch him."

She pulled open the flap, hoping that by some chance Peter had returned. She motioned to Jamie with her hand. "Have you seen your father?" She kept her voice low so that Lucy couldn't hear.

Jamie shook his head.

Maddie walked away from the tent and scanned the sweltering, airless plains in every direction. There was no sign of Peter. Where in the world was he? And what was the matter with him? How could he run off and leave his wife at such a difficult time? Lucy always referred to her husband as a hero. Some hero. If Maddie ever had occasion to see the man again, she intended to give him a thorough tongue-lashing!

Maddie walked back to the tent. "Your mother is going to be all right," she told Jamie, but he looked unconvinced. Behind him, Caroline sat clutching her rag doll and sucking her thumb. "Take care of your sister and if you should see your father, come and get me." Her heart heavy, she ducked into the tent.

Lucy lay quiet, her eyes closed.

Maddie whispered the bad news to the doctor. "I can't find her husband."

The doctor held up a white cloth. "It's ether," he said softly. "She won't feel a thing." He placed the cloth over Lucy's mouth, and a quiet repose spread across her face.

The problem of having to explain Peter's absence had been postponed, but the enormity of what they were about to do gripped Maddie's heart with cold dread. If anything should go wrong, she knew that she alone would have to accept the blame.

The doctor took his place by Lucy's side. He was prepared to make the first incision. Over his head, the white globe of the hot afternoon sun burned through the canvas.

Maddie watched the tip of his scalpel score the white flesh of Lucy's swollen belly and was surprised by the dizziness that suddenly came over her. She had watched her father perform any number of dissections in his lab, and as she had recently proven, she herself was rather adept with a knife. But none of her past experiences had prepared her for surgery, nor for the life-and-death gamble she now faced.

She knew enough about anatomy to know that one slip of the knife would mean the end for Lucy and the baby.

She appreciated the importance of a steady hand, and Dr. Williams certainly impressed her with his. She kept herself busy as he worked, handing him various instruments, wiping away the excess blood, mopping the perspiration away from his forehead. And always she kept an eye on Lucy's still, porcelainlike face.

The doctor lowered his hands to the open wound. She closed her eyes until she heard the marvelous sound of a baby's thin cry.

Her eyes flew open to gaze at the wondrous sight. She felt all at once like laughing and crying, but she did neither. She was too filled with relief and joy to move, too overcome with gratitude. The baby was so tiny it hardly filled the doctor's hands.

"It's a girl," the doctor said, smiling. "Come and hold her while I cut the cord."

The baby felt slippery to the touch, not at all like the furry bodies she was used to working on. Terrified that she might drop the precious bundle, Maddie stood frozen in place, with the baby in her hands.

The doctor threaded a needle and began to work on the mother. After a while, when it was apparent that Maddie was not going to act of her own accord, he motioned to the chest of drawers with a nod of his head. "You can clean up the baby."

Maddie chanced a glance at Lucy, whose face was so white it seemed she must be dead, or close to it. It was a shocking thought. Shaken, Maddie moved toward the dresser and lay the infant onto a clean flour sack.

The baby found her tiny fist and sucked. Watching

her, Maddie fought back tears. "What a beautiful baby you are."

She rinsed a clean rag in a basin of water and gently washed away the blood and mucus. As she worked, she marveled at the tiny hands and feet, so perfectly shaped.

The infant sucked her little fist so furiously, Maddie was convinced that anyone with that much vigor had to be healthy. "And to think we worried about you surviving."

She dabbed the precious child dry with a clean towel, then wrapped her in a soft blanket. Lifting the baby in her arms, she turned to the small wooden cradle. She pressed her lips gently against the downy hair on the baby's head before lowering her onto the hay mattress with its cover of soft cotton ticking.

Feeling the strain of the last few hours, Maddie wiped her own heated face with a wet cloth. It was so hot and sticky, her clothes clung to her body.

Dr. Williams finished sewing the wound together and cut the sinew thread. He motioned to Maddie, who rushed to his side with a basin of clean water and a fresh cloth.

The doctor squeezed the cloth with one hand, then wiped away the blood before covering the wound with a clean gauze. Maddie glanced worriedly at Lucy's face. She'd never seen anyone look so pale. "Is she going to be all right?"

"She should be. If no infection sets in."

Infection was the real enemy. Luke had been right to worry. Dr. Williams had done everything possible to make the environment sterile, but this was Kansas. They worked in cramped quarters with dusty canvas for walls. The very air was thick with dust.

The doctor dropped his scalpel and surgical scissors

into the basin of bloodstained water. "I think you'd better go and find that man of hers."

Maddie checked on the sleeping baby, then opened the flap of the tent. Not a bit of breeze stirred the air. "Doctor, I'm much obliged to you. If she lives, she owes it all to you."

Outside, Jamie and Caroline were lying in the shadow of the tent. Caroline sat up, her dark eyes huge with worry. "We heard a baby cry . . ."

"You have a little baby sister," Maddie announced. "And she's beautiful."

Caroline clapped her hands in delight. "Can we see her? Please, please, please?"

"Of course you may see her, Caroline. But not yet. The baby is asleep."

Jamie tugged on Maddie's arm. "Is Mama . . . ?"

"Your mother's fine." Maddie gazed over Jamie's head. "Have you seen your father?"

Jamie shook his head and tugged on his sister's hair. Caroline threw a blade of grass at him, and the two ran off in a merry chase.

Maddie left them to their game and borrowed one of the horses that was tethered nearby.

She rode the horse hard across the prairie in the direction Peter had gone. It wasn't difficult to follow the tiny round tracks left in the buffalo sod by his crutches.

She found him lying face down next to a trickle of water that had once been a creek. "Peter?"

When he didn't move or otherwise respond, she feared he'd fallen ill. She quickly dismounted and ran to him. "Peter?"

"She's dead, isn't she?" he moaned.

"No, Peter. She's going to be fine. Just as your little girl . . ."

"It's a girl?" He sat up, revealing a face streaked with tears and dirt. "We had a baby girl?"

"Yes, and she's beautiful and healthy. No thanks, I might add, to you!"

Her angry voice didn't seem to register. He was almost childlike in the way he looked at her, and she suddenly had no heart to scold him.

"Lucy . . . Is she . . . ?"

"She needs you, Peter. It's going to take time for her to recuperate."

He dipped his fingertips into the trickle of water and rubbed his face. "Luke is right, you know." He looked past her, to some distant place not visible to her. "Hardly anyone survives surgery. I saw countless men die in the war after having a limb cut off. The fact that I survived . . . I was one of the lucky few. No one expected me to live."

"Doctors know a lot more about what causes sepsis than they did during the war. I watched Dr. Williams, Peter. The man's a fanatic. He sterilized everything."

"You think Lucy'll be lucky like me? Is that what you're saying?"

"What I'm saying is that she'll have a lot better chance of survival with you by her side." She picked up a crutch that had been carelessly tossed aside. "Come on. I'll help you onto the horse."

# Chapter 30

It was dark by the time Maddie returned home. She felt exhausted, drained. She wanted nothing more than to take a bath and collapse in bed.

Light shone from the window, but when Matthew failed to run out and greet her as was his usual habit, she assumed he was asleep.

The look on Luke's face earlier still haunted her, as it had all day. She'd never known it possible to see so much pain and torment etched on a single face. He had shown genuine concern for Lucy's welfare. It was not the kind of look one would expect to see on the face of a cold-blooded murderer.

She knocked twice, and when there was no answer she turned the handle and opened the door. Matthew was sound asleep on the bed, just as she had supposed. She pushed the door open another notch. It sighed against its worn leather hinges.

Luke sat at the table, a half-empty bottle of whiskey in front of him. In the flickering shadows of the room, his face looked dark, grim, almost demonic.

Swallowing hard, she stepped inside, closing the door softly so as not to awaken Matthew.

"Lucy had a healthy baby girl. Mother and baby are fine."

She waited for his reaction, but his expression never changed as he took another swallow of whiskey.

"Did you hear what I said?"

"You should feel proud of yourself."

"I'm relieved and happy." She pulled out a chair and sat opposite him. "You should have seen Peter when he held his baby for the first time. I've never seen a happier man."

She could tell by the absent look on Luke's face that her words didn't register. He appeared to be focused on the private demons that resided in that part of him that still remained a mystery to her.

He reached for the bottle and she stilled his hand, wrapping her fingers around his. Suddenly his eyes cleared, and he peered at her as if seeing her for the first time.

"I tried to save her," he said, and his words sounded muffled.

She kept her voice low. "Who? Who did you try to save?"

"Catherine-Anne."

"Your wife? You tried to save your wife?"

As if he suddenly realized who and where he was, he shook his head and pulled back his hand. Elbows on the table, he rested his head in his hands. "I didn't know about surgical births. George was always trying out some newfangled idea."

"And you thought that when he tried to save your baby, he was experimenting."

"I don't know what I thought at the time. All I remember is walking through that door and seeing Catherine-Anne on the table. I never saw so much blood in my life."

Maddie closed her eyes to blot out the horror that he described. "Where was the doctor?"

"I don't know. I still don't know why he left her alone. Even if she were dead, wasn't it his job to stay with her until I returned?"

"It would seem so. Where was Matthew?"

He met her eyes, and for once the guarded look was gone. "I had gone to Hays to arrange for the delivery of lumber. I thought it was time to build a proper house for my family. Catherine-Anne wasn't due for another two months. Matthew stayed home with his mother. He wasn't at the house when I arrived, and at the time I had no idea where he was. I went looking for him. Someone told me that George was at the saloon. He was there, all right. All I could think about was that he'd left my wife to die in her own blood and that my son was missing." He shook his head. "I don't remember the rest."

"How did you . . ."

"Murder him? They told me I did it with my bare hands."

"Don't you remember?"

"I remember the anger and rage I felt . . . God, Maddie! He left her. He left Catherine-Anne."

She squeezed his hand tight. "I know, Luke. I know."

"I remember feeling frantic at not knowing Matthew's whereabouts. I searched everywhere for him before finding George. After that . . . I don't know . . . I don't remember what happened next. Only what they told me."

"They?"

"The sheriff, the Eldridges, the townspeople. None of them saw me attack the doctor. But they saw the rage in me. Knew what I was capable of doing."

"Luke . . ." She drew his hand next to her cheek. "Isn't it possible that you never meant to kill the doctor?"

His gaze sharpened as he looked at her. "Don't, Maddie. Don't try to justify my actions with pretty words."

"I want to understand the truth, Luke. That's all. Just the truth."

"The truth is that George is dead because of my actions." Despite Luke's tragic loss, the townspeople's sympathies were with the doctor, who had been revered by locals as a miracle worker. Luke was but a stranger in these parts at the time—a man who refused to speak of his past. That fact alone made him suspect.

"If you really are a murderer, why weren't you arrested?"

"The sheriff said there wasn't enough evidence that I actually meant to kill the doctor. But that didn't change anyone's mind any. Then when a reporter from the *Colton Press* found out . . ." He stopped and took a mouthful of whiskey.

"Found out what?" she prompted.

"Never mind. It's not important."

She sensed that it was extremely important, but fearing he would clam up altogether if she forced the issue, she let it drop. "Where was Matthew during this time?"

"Chad Spencer, the owner of the general store, found Matthew hiding in his storeroom. He was obviously in shock."

"Was . . . was he with his mother when she died?"

"I don't know. I know nothing about what happened that day. Matthew hasn't said a word since. Soon after the funeral, I took him to a specialist in St. Louis. The doctor said that a severe shock can paralyze a person's vocal cords. He didn't offer much hope for Matthew's recovery."

What he would give to hear Matthew's voice again, to hear Matthew laugh aloud. Lost in his thoughts, he was surprised to feel Maddie's arm around his shoulder.

"I wish there were something I could do," she said

softly. She pressed her cheek against his, and he breathed deeply to absorb the nearness of her.

Then, with a muttered curse, he turned his head away. Confused, she drew back, and the eyes that met his were filled with hurt.

He hated knowing he was the cause of her pain. The guilt he felt at that moment was strong, but he no longer had the strength to push her away.

He felt shaky. He had never cared much for alcohol and never built up much of a tolerance for it. Even so, it surprised him how much he was affected by the relatively small amount he'd had to drink. "Don't look at me like that."

"Like what?"

"Like a schoolteacher dealing with a wayward student."

"I . . . I didn't mean to. Were you drinking that day? When your wife died?"

He narrowed his eyes in thought. "I'd had a few drinks. Someone gave me some whiskey at one of the saloons when I was looking for the doctor. He said I looked like I needed a drink." He studied her for a moment. "Does it matter?"

"I'm just trying to understand everything that happened that night. Why you have no clear memory of it. Before today, I never saw you drink alcohol much, except for an occasional glass of wine."

"I don't handle the stuff well." He pushed the bottle away. "My father was a drunk."

"I'm sorry," she whispered.

He lifted a hand and caressed her cheek as he so often caressed any fine wood whose beauty required more than a visual appreciation. A soft light flared in the depths of her eyes, contradicting the stubborn jut of her jaw.

Intrigued, he traced her lips with the tip of a finger,

feeling her mouth soften beneath his touch. He slipped his free hand around her waist and held her gaze until he saw the full extent of his own need and desire mirrored in her eyes.

He brushed a gentle kiss across her brow, but it wasn't until he captured her mouth with his own that he knew for certain that she still wanted him, even now.

He pulled his mouth away from hers and wondered if he could really trust his instincts. "Are you sure you want this?" he asked. "After knowing what I've done?"

"I don't know that you've done anything, Luke. What happened that day was a tragedy, but it's over. You've got to put it behind you. Behind us."

"It was a mistake for me to make love to you the other night. Before you knew the truth. Maybe that's partly the reason I pulled away. There was so much you didn't know about me. Still don't know . . ."

She looked at him in disbelief and wonder. Most men would have put their own needs before honor. Now the love she felt for him only grew deeper. She threw her arms around his neck, openly and freely, and this time he accepted her flamboyant show of affection without protest.

Desire flared into passion as he deepened his kiss and plunged his tongue into the velvety depths of her mouth. Wrapping his arms around her, he pressed his heated body against hers, forgetting the legacy that forbade him to give in completely to his feelings.

He was ready, more than ready, to take her right there. Had it not been for Matthew, he might well have done so. But fearing that Matthew would awaken, he tore his lips away from hers, even as his body moaned its loss.

Matthew was a potent reminder of the dangerous

ground he was treading on. "You better go to your tipi." It was an order, a plea.

A deep, abiding pain radiated from his loins. An aching need that was as great as the wide expanse of prairie outside his door.

She tugged on his arm. "Come with me."

"No!"

His loud declaration caused Matthew to stir, and they drew apart like two guilty adolescents afraid of being caught. Neither spoke until the boy had rolled over and it was clear he'd fallen back to sleep.

"Do . . . do you find me lacking in some way?" she asked.

"Dammit, Maddie! Do I look like a man who finds you lacking?"

"Then why won't you come outside with me? Luke, listen to me. What happened to the doctor . . . it was an accident."

He shook his head. "Violence runs in the family. My father was a brutal man who was finally and, I might add, justly hung. You've probably heard of him. Lord knows, everyone else has."

A sudden wrenching thought held her in its grip. Tyler. *Gantry Tyler.* How often she had seen that name in headlines, heard it spoken at social gatherings. The name had become synonymous with all that was evil. There had even been legislation dubbed the Gantry Tyler Bill introduced in Congress. Her father vehemently opposed it. The bill, which was defeated, would have placed too much restriction on the way local law enforcers gathered evidence. Had it passed, Gantry Tyler would probably still be alive to continue his reign of terror.

Luke watched her face. "So now you know."

"What difference does it make who your father was?"

He looked at her incredulously. "What difference? How can you possibly ask such a question, Maddie? Violence runs in the family. Why do you think I was so worried when Matthew had those fits of rage?"

"But now we know the truth, don't we? Matthew is a gentle, loving child who gets angry and frustrated on occasion because he can't talk."

"That might be true of Matthew, but you have no way of knowing that's true of me."

"I know you're not a murderer, Luke. I know that much."

"If I thought for one moment that were true ... oh, Maddie." He touched her hair, her lovely red hair that seemed to hold warming rays of sunlight even at night.

"Is that what the reporter found out? Who your father was?"

He nodded. "Once the word got out, I was no longer welcome in town. I only wish ..."

"What, Luke? What do you wish?"

"That I could remember that night. Everything that happened." He looked deep into her eyes. "When I'm with you, it's so easy to believe that I'm incapable of murder."

"That's because you are ..."

"Listen to me, Maddie. There's no way any of us can be sure. It's the uncertainty that's the worst of it. I look at you and I see a man mirrored in your eyes who I don't recognize ... a man who's good and incapable of doing anything wrong."

"It's you who's mirrored in my eyes," she whispered.

"I want it to be, but I can't be sure. And until I am ... until I know for sure what kind of man I am, I'll always feel that I'm giving you less of me than you deserve."

She inhaled, and her breath caught somewhere between her ribs. "There's no way to be sure," she whispered. "Unless . . ." A thought suddenly occurred to her. "What about Matthew? Now that he can write, maybe he can tell us something that will help put the pieces together."

Luke shook his head. "No, Maddie. Leave Matthew out of this."

"But he might know something . . . Please, Luke. It's possible, isn't it?"

"We don't know that for sure. In any case, I don't want Matthew to relive such a tragic day. He's shown real progress in recent weeks. I don't want to do anything that would prevent his progress."

"We won't let that happen, Luke. All I'm asking you to do is to talk to him about the day his mother died. Ask him to write down what he remembers. If he becomes upset, you can stop . . . Please, Luke, it's the only way that you will ever be free from the terrible burden you carry."

"I can't take the chance, Maddie. I'm sorry." He grabbed hold of her arms. "Promise me, Maddie, that you won't question Matthew. You've got to promise me."

"You have my promise." It was the hardest promise she'd ever made.

# Chapter 31

It was obvious the following morning that things between them would never again be the same. They could never again act neutral in each other's company. Knowing the truth, as horrible as it was, made her feel that much closer to him. She only hoped that the love they shared would be enough to conquer any doubts that Luke still had about himself.

She accidentally brushed against him as she reached for the coffeepot. Their eyes locked.

"Thank you for last night," he said. "For . . . for understanding and . . ."

Luke didn't have a chance to finish what he'd been about to say, for at that moment Matthew threw his boot across the room. Luke's jaw hardened as he turned to look at his son. Doubt and self-loathing played their deadly games across Luke's face.

She lay a hand on his arm. "It's nothing. He's just frustrated . . ."

"You can't know that for sure!" He spun around and stormed outside.

Maddie retrieved Matthew's boot and unknotted the rawhide shoelace. "You mustn't throw things, Matthew," she admonished gently. "When you're upset, you must write it down." She handed him his slate and pointed firmly to the surface. "Write!"

Matthew snatched the slate from her and scribbled

all over it. He tossed the slate aside and gave her a de-
fiant look. He was clearly surprised when she nodded
in approval.

"Good for you. That's how you express your anger,
Matthew. Not by throwing things."

She knelt on the floor next to him. "Matthew, look
at me."

The boy lifted his eyes. She stroked his neck, starting beneath his chin and working her finger downward
to the hollow at the base of his throat. "See if you can
make a sound. Try it." She grunted to indicate what
she wanted.

Matthew's body tensed as he tried to follow her
lead. She gently pressed her fingers against the area
around his vocal chords. "Relax now. Don't try so
hard."

His face clouded in frustration. Fearing he was about
to have a tantrum, Maddie removed her fingers from
his neck and handed him his slate. "Write something,
Matthew."

This time, instead of scribbling, he wrote, *I have no
words*. He looked so devastated, she almost regretted
that she'd tried to get him to speak. She wasn't even
certain that her motivation was all that pure. There was
no denying how much she might gain personally if
Matthew regained his speech, how much they all stood
to gain if he could tell them something that would ab-
solve Luke's guilt.

"You have words, Matthew." She pointed to the
slate. "These are your words. They are quiet words,
that's all. But there's nothing wrong with quiet words.
I have quiet words, too. Everyone does. Sometimes we
speak with our hands." She touched his cheek gently to
demonstrate. "Like Lefty and Flying Hawk and all the
other Indians do. Sometimes we speak with our eyes.

Look . . ." She gave him a dazzling smile. "Now you tell me what my words are."

Matthew studied her face and wrote a single word on the slate. *Papa.*

She puzzled over the word for a moment. Then she realized that Matthew understood more than any of them gave him credit for. "You're absolutely right. I was thinking of your papa. That's why I was smiling. See? What did I tell you? There are all kinds of ways that we speak to one another."

After breakfast, Maddie took Matthew with her and drove to Colton to check on the progress of the school. To her delight, the two-room building was complete.

"As soon as the desks arrive, you can start holding classes," Mr. Boxer said.

She was tempted to tell him to cancel the desks. She found desks too confining. Children needed movement, and she much preferred to have her students march in a circle around the room while she quizzed them in spelling or multiplication. She was tempted, all right, but she thought better of it. Mr. Boxer was bound to find out soon enough that her teaching methods were far from conventional, and often controversial.

Later that night she approached Luke with the idea of making slates for her class. "Could you make them light in weight so that they can be easily carried?"

"That won't be a problem," he said. "When do you need them?"

"Mr. Boxer said the desks should be here in two weeks' time."

He looked surprised. "I guess progress has been made." When she didn't reply, he mopped his brow. "It's hot." He lifted his eyes, and she read the question in his eyes.

"At least the wind's not blowing." Her gaze inadvertently dropped to his mouth before turning to check on Matthew's schoolwork.

Matthew gave her a knowing look and grinned. She fervently hoped that the grin meant he'd finally finished his lessons, and that the look he gave them had nothing to do with the heated signals passing between her and Luke.

"Did you finish your arithmetic?" she asked. She had spent the greater portion of the afternoon trying to keep cool and quizzing Matthew on his multiplication tables.

He nodded listlessly and pointed to his slate, which was on the bed. His face was flushed with the heat.

She sat down on the bed and checked over his work. "I do believe your son is gifted in arithmetic."

Luke tightened his jaw. "Something else that runs in the family. I read in the newspaper that after my father was hung, they discovered the walls of his cell covered in mathematical problems."

She let the slate drop to her lap. "Don't," she pleaded. "Don't keep doing this, Luke."

Luke walked out to the barn after supper, intent on starting on the slates for Maddie's students. By ten, he had cut the wood into strips for the frames and applied the first coat of linseed oil.

He doused the lantern and stepped outside. Overhead the sky was a mass of bright stars. But other than a quick glance upward, his attention was riveted on the tipi. He couldn't help himself.

Maddie was moving about inside, but it wasn't clear what she was doing until she lifted her arms and pulled her dress over her head. He'd seen her undress before and had managed to maintain his distance. But not to-night. For tonight the memory of her lovely firm breasts in his hand was too momentous, the memory of her lips too real.

A little knowledge may be a dangerous thing, but never had it been so defeating as it was at that moment. He could no longer resist her silent call.

Like a man being guided by something out of his control, he walked to the tipi and unfastened the flap. He could see her clearly now. She was naked from the waist up, and the sight of her took his breath away.

She looked at him with a softness that made him shiver with anticipation. She made no attempt to cover her nakedness, and he knew for the first time in his life what it meant to be trusted by someone. He stepped inside the tent and felt her lovely essence close around him. He was shaking now. He wanted to do right by her, to be deserving of the trust and love he saw in her eyes. He struggled to put the self-doubts behind him, but it was a difficult chore.

"I'm sorry, Maddie. I shouldn't be here . . . I have no right . . ."

As she rose to her feet and let the last of her garments fall away, it occurred to him that nothing could be more beautiful.

Accustomed to women who feared physical closeness, he was overcome with awe by the raw desire in her eyes.

"Oh, God, Maddie!"

He cleared the distance between them in one motion and swooped her into his arms. But even as he touched her, he was conscious of his actions. He never wanted to hear her cry out in pain again. He forced himself to touch her gently, reminding himself that she was still inexperienced in such matters. But when she pressed against him, his best intentions were quickly undermined.

*Be careful.* The words came from some deeply

buried memory, and he squeezed his eyes shut, not wanting anything to interfere this time. But interfere they did, the warnings, the memory of who he was, who his father was.

Anger rose within him. Not this time. Nothing was going to prevent him from showing Maddie the full extent of his love for her. Nothing!

He tightened his arms around her, but a lifetime of holding back proved a powerful force to overcome.

She pushed him away, and he quickly opened his eyes. Had he been mortally wounded he could not have felt worse. "Maddie?"

"You're doing it again, Luke." She looked close to tears, and he knew that despite his vow he had caused her pain.

"What? What am I doing?"

"Treating me as if I'm nothing more than a fragile teacup!" She was angry and hurt, and her eyes flashed with green fire. She grabbed her nightgown and pulled it in front of her. It was only a piece of flimsy fabric, but to him it seemed like a solid wall.

He didn't want walls between them. And in that moment, he knew there was something that Maddie needed to know.

"My father . . . hurt my mother."

Her eyes widened as if she didn't understand. "Hurt her? You mean physically?"

"I mean he raped her." A look of horror crossed her face, and he let the full knowledge of what he was telling her sink in before he continued. "I'm the result."

"Oh, Luke . . ." She spoke in a husky whisper. "It must be awful to know such a thing about your father." Her eyes filled with tears, and he could see his misery mirrored in their watery green depths. A lifetime of holding back had prevented him from giving in to tears, and he envied her the ability to express her feelings so openly and honestly.

"Is that why you pulled away from me our first night together? Because of your father?"

He nodded. "When you cried out . . . I realized I was just like him."

Her tear-filled eyes widened. "Oh, Luke," she gasped, "you could never be like him."

He lifted his hand to her face and captured a tear on the tip of his finger. No one had ever shed tears for him. The tear shimmered on his finger like a clear, pure diamond, and he thought of all the tears he'd seen on his mother's face—tears of pain, tears of shame, tears of anger. Never once had he known that tears could also be shed for love.

"I wanted you to know, Maddie. You have the right to know."

"I don't understand," she said. She wrapped her hand around his, and the tear he held was crushed between their fingers. "There have been other women in your life. Catherine-Anne. Didn't any of this affect your marriage?"

He shook his head. "Catherine-Anne hated the physical part of marriage. She . . . she'd had a hard life. I knew that from the start. I'm afraid that's one of the reasons I married her—I felt safe with her."

"Safe?" A frown settled on her forehead. "Is that what you want? To feel safe?"

He shook his head. "Not anymore. Do you still want me . . . knowing how I came to be?"

"You make it sound like you're the one who did something wrong."

"Can you blame me? The son of a rapist, a murderer!"

Her face grew still as she gazed at him. "Why are you so willing to believe you're like your father?"

"It's not that I'm willing," he protested.

"Isn't it? You're willing to believe you killed that doctor. I let out a little cry, and you jump to all the wrong conclusions."

"It's not just who my father was ... it's how everyone treated me ... as if I were a criminal or about to become one. Even my mother ..." His voice grew husky. "After a while I guess I started believing it myself. I'm sorry, Maddie. If you still want me, I swear that I'll try to put all this behind me."

"I still want you," she whispered. "But not if you intend to keep treating me like some fragile doll that's going to break if you press too hard."

"I've never thought of you as fragile," he said.

"I'm glad." She gave him a smoky look, then slowly let her gown fall away. He sucked in his breath. She moved her body seductively, and he could hold back no longer.

With one sweeping motion he crushed her to him. Like a man suddenly set free, he ran his hands up and down her silky flesh. He covered her mouth hungrily, his lips hard and searching.

His movements were swift and intense, but were no more demanding than hers. Passion exploded between them as he tugged and she pulled at his clothes until nothing prevented their bodies from melting together like overheated metal.

They fell on the bedroll, him on top of her. Her hands were all over his body, caressing and urging, pressing and demanding.

In a frenzied moment of uncontrollable desire, he plunged inside her. Her soft, slick warmth welcomed him and almost immediately spastic waves of ecstasy ripped through him. Answering tremors rippled through her body, as if they'd both been struck by the same bolt of lightning. It was over so quickly, he hardly had time to breathe.

Shaken by the sheer power of what they had shared, he rolled off her and lay stunned by her side. Never before had he allowed himself to lose himself so completely in the moment. He hadn't dared.

He was filled with wonder. He might be capable of violence, but Lord Almighty, it filled him with the greatest relief to know that he was also capable of expressing love in its purest form. He wanted to shout with the joy of discovery. More than that, he wanted to lose himself again.

He rolled toward her and cupped her face in his hands, her beautiful, loving face. "It was all right, Maddie, wasn't it? I held nothing back. I didn't think about anything but the moment, and it was all right . . . Tell me if it wasn't. Tell me, please, you've got to tell me."

She took his hand and pressed her mouth against his fingers. "Oh, Luke. It was wonderful. It was . . . ecstasy."

"And I didn't frighten you?"

"Of course not," she declared. "What a notion."

"Maddie, you must tell me the truth. Did I hurt you?"

She gave him a shy look that surprised him. Maddie Percy, shy?

"I was afraid I might have hurt *you*," she said softly.

His heart did a somersault, and for a moment he couldn't speak. He pulled her into his arms and buried his nose in the soft fragrance of her flesh. Suddenly, it was all so clear. Only in freeing himself, had he given Maddie the freedom to express her own needs.

If he had anything to regret at that moment, it was the speed with which he'd taken her. She deserved so much more from him. Yet when he lifted his head to look into the soft glow of her eyes, he saw nothing that suggested he'd failed her. "I've wanted that for so long. I'm sorry I was so . . ."

"Expeditious?"

He had to laugh. "What a word."

It surprised him when she rubbed the palms of her hands across his damp chest.

The fact that Maddie looked, well . . . downright determined to explore every part of him filled him with wonder and joy, and thanksgiving.

He moaned when she took a daring dive down his belly. "What are you doing to me?"

She laughed softly, and he slipped his arms around her waist, easing her body on top of his. It amazed him how their bodies seemed so perfectly suited to each other.

He brushed his fingers over the lovely mounds of her breasts and marveled at the pleasure he felt when desire, slow and sweet this time, began to rise again.

Without the frantic urge that had previously driven him, he was able to explore every lovely curve of her body at leisure. It gave him such pleasure to know he didn't have to hide his passion, that he could experience love in its many forms. And now, having sated the lust that had stolen his self-control, he now intended to linger over her until dawn's light.

# Chapter 32

Maddie awoke with a start, vaguely aware of feeling warm and protected—and very much loved. The light of dawn shone through the bleached buffalo hides that were the walls of the tipi. Luke's sturdy arm was flung across her waist, and one powerful leg lay protectively across her thigh. Thinking back over the events of the glorious night, she smiled. It hadn't been a dream after all.

As if sensing her watching him, he stirred. His warm gaze found hers immediately, as if waking up in her arms was the most natural thing in the world.

"Good morning," she whispered.

A shadow of a smile touched his mouth, followed by a frown. "Don't tell me it's morning already!" He moaned. "I've got to go before Matthew awakens." He sat up and ran his fingers through his tousled hair. "I'm not sure I'm ready to explain the birds and the bees to him."

She ran a finger up his strong back. "He's not due to wake for another hour or so."

"It'll be my luck that he wakes up early today. Besides, isn't Lefty due to make his early-morning inquiry as to what day of the week it is? What does he call it? The Great Father's Day. And let's not forget Picking Bones. Oh, no!"

Maddie caught her breath. "What's the matter?"

"What's Picking Bones going to say when she learns that your virtue is no longer intact?"

"I won't tell her if you won't." Maddie flattened her palm against him, and he collapsed against her.

"Now look what you're doing."

She giggled. "I do believe it is the Great Father's Day."

He took a playful dive for her neck and ran his tongue across the lobe of her ear. "You're shameless, you know that?" She rolled out from under him and tossed him his pants. "What you need is some good old-fashioned exercise."

"What do you call what we were doing all night long?"

Ignoring the question, she dressed quickly. "Last one outside is a one-legged frog!"

She beat him by seconds, but he dashed after her and caught her by the barn. She ducked beneath his arms and ran along the track she'd worn into the ground with her daily runs. "You can't catch me."

Grinning, he chased after her, and their laughter filled the air as they ran around the soddy, carefree as children. When they reached the woodpile, he pulled her into his arms and kissed her soundly.

Lord, it felt so good to hold her, to kiss her, to touch her without reservation or fear. How could he have let anyone convince him that such feelings were wrong?

"Are you feeling less tense?" she asked with feigned innocence.

"I'm afraid running is not going to help my problem," he whispered in her ear. He looked up and cursed. Picking Bones was heading toward them. It wasn't until she came closer that he realized that, for once, she had a smile on her face.

The normally reticent woman suddenly had a lot to say, though he couldn't for the life of him figure out what it was. But whatever had happened this morning had brought a sparkle to her faded eyes and a flush to her weathered cheeks.

"What do you suppose she's trying to tell us?" he asked. The woman nodded her head up and down and pounded her chest with her hand.

"I think it has something to do with the heart," Maddie said, looking worried.

"You don't suppose she's having a heart seizure?"

Maddie creased her forehead. "She wouldn't be smiling if she was having a medical problem, would she?"

"Maybe she's not smiling. Maybe she's having digestion problems."

Maddie grabbed Luke's arm. "I think she's talking about our hearts, yours and mine."

"We're not having heart seizures," Luke explained to the woman. He exaggerated his words to make himself more easily understood. But the woman continued to speak rapidly and pound her chest. Nodding in what could only be approval, she walked away, heading for the Cheyenne encampment.

Watching her, Luke burst out laughing.

Maddie looked up at him as if he had lost his mind. "What's so funny?"

"I think the old woman was trying to tell us she approves of us. You and me. Our closeness . . . Now that you and I are together, she no longer sees you as a threat. She thinks her daughter's future is no longer in jeopardy."

"You mean because you and I . . . She thinks Shooting Star will marry White Blossom?"

He grinned and slipped his arms around her. "Now I understand why Picking Bones was so angry with me. She couldn't understand why it took me so long to discover what apparently was obvious to her—how much I love you and want to be with you." He kissed her on the lips, then rested his forehead against hers. "Maddie, last night was the most memorable night of my life. But ... it doesn't change anything."

"Maybe not for you."

"I'm still the same person I was before. A possible murderer. I can't forget that."

"I'll never believe that's true."

He took her hand in his and drew it to his lips. He loved her for the faith she had in him. If only he had that same faith in himself. Things would be different. "I never thought I'd ever see anyone look at me like you look at me. The love I see in your eyes ..." He touched her on the lips. "I want so much to be deserving of that love."

She gazed up at him. "Oh, Luke ... I never knew that love could be this way."

The two of them were so caught up in the wonder of each other that it took a moment for the sound of gunfire in the distance to register.

Luke frowned at the cloud of dust that rose to meet the sky. "Looks like we have company."

She tightened her hold on him at the sound of more gunfire. "Who?"

"I don't know. Hunters. Probably shooting rabbit." He gazed into her eyes and brushed his lips against hers. "It wouldn't by any chance be your Smithsonian people, would it now?"

"I wouldn't know."

The gunfire increased, as did the dust and the dirt. "I think I'll go and have a look." He headed for his horse. Moments later he thundered past her, throwing her a kiss, which she caught in her hands and clutched to her breast.

She watched him gallop across the prairie until she could no longer see him. Even then she was reluctant to turn away, as if doing so would break some invisible bond between them. What a glorious, wonderful feeling it was to be in love.

She whirled about in a circle, holding her face up to the sky as she twirled. Her hair fell freely around her shoulders. *Love.* What a wonderful word that was! What a wonderful place to be in love, for the landscape around her was as boundless as her feelings.

She hummed softly to herself as she walked back to the house to check on Matthew. He apparently had heard the gunfire, for he was standing on a box, looking out the window. He was still dressed in his nightshirt.

"Hunters," she said lightly. She rested her chin on his shoulder and peered out the window. A wall of dust swept from east to west. Usually only the wind could whip up so much dry ground, but today the air was perfectly still, with not even a breeze rippling the grass.

She felt a moment of apprehension but quickly chose to disregard it. For once, she was not going to allow her imagination to spoil the joy she felt inside. She drew Matthew away from the window. "We'd better start breakfast. Your father's likely to be hungry when he gets back."

Despite her best efforts, her apprehension increased. She wondered what had happened to Lefty. He was late and that was not like him. As soon as he arrived, she would send him to look for Luke.

She held breakfast for as long as she could, but when Luke hadn't returned by nine, she fed Matthew and sipped a cup of steaming hot coffee.

As the morning wore on, the cloud in the distance faded, but still there was no sign of Luke. She walked back and forth between the barn and the house and, for Matthew's sake, made a pretense of doing chores.

Lefty had not made his customary morning appearance, and she wondered why he and the others had failed to show up for their calisthenics class.

As she and Matthew carried feed to the chickens, Matthew noticed that Picking Bones was not in her usual place. "I don't think Picking Bones will be coming around anymore," she explained, surprised to find herself missing the woman.

Matthew looked puzzled by this, but since it was difficult to explain, she shrugged. "We'll tell Lefty that we miss her. Maybe she'll come back and visit us."

At eleven, the sound of a horse galloping toward the house made her pulse jump in anticipation. She ran outside to greet Luke. Her smile died as Luke's riderless horse drew near.

Fear gripped her heart. Where was he? Where was Luke?

She lay a hand on Matthew's shoulder. "Stay here."

He slipped his hand in hers and looked at her with tear-filled eyes. She squeezed his hand and brushed away the hair from his forehead. "I'm worried too, Matthew. But you can help me . . . You can help your father by going inside and writing your feelings on your slate." She knelt down in front of him. "That's what will help us."

He nodded and started toward the house. She waited until he was safely inside before mounting Luke's horse.

Luke's horse was larger than hers, and it was all she could do to keep from slipping out of the saddle, but Luke's horse was faster than Rutabaga.

She rode the horse as hard as she dared through the buffalo grass, picking up speed upon reaching one of the trails. Birds circled ahead, their ravenous cries filling her with cold dread. Turkey buzzards.

She tugged on the reins, and the horse reared on its

hind legs before coming to a halt. Nearby, a buffalo lay on its side, blood trickling from its mouth. She pulled her eyes away from the sight, only to find another lifeless body a few feet from the first.

Further on, the buzzards had descended on a woolly bull. A flock of the birds suddenly rose from the ground and took to the sky in squawking protest. Rising in her saddle, she scanned the prairie beneath the circling birds and, much to her relief and joy, spotted Luke walking toward her.

An almost unbearable excitement filled her as she galloped to meet him. She slid from the saddle and ran into his arms. "I was so worried about you," she cried. "I thought . . ."

He crushed her to him, and it felt as if he never meant to let her go. "I know," he whispered in her hair. "My horse reared and threw me. Fortunately I was only stunned."

His eyes darkened as he looked down at the dead buffalo at their feet. Releasing her, he pulled off his hat and held it respectfully to his chest. Her heart filled with tenderness as she counted yet another thing to love about him.

She dropped down to her knees to stroke the animal's rough coat. "I don't understand. Who did this and why?"

"Without the buffalo, the Indians can't survive."

She searched his face, not wanting to believe what he was saying. "This . . . this awful crime was done against the Indians?" The Cheyennes were her friends. She thought of Lefty and his eagerness to learn, of Picking Bones, who put the welfare of her daughter above her own needs and comfort. She thought of Flying Hawk and all the others she had grown to care about. How could anyone wish these people harm?

"It's not only a crime against the Indians, Maddie. It was done against all of us."

"It's such a beautiful animal," she whispered. Tears blurred her eyes.

"I'm afraid it's an animal close to extinction." He lay his hand on her shoulder. "Come on, my love. Let's go home."

She thrilled to the term of endearment that fell so easily from his lips, but nothing could soften the horrible crime that had been committed that day. She stared down at the dead buffalo and felt a deep and abiding sadness.

"Luke, do you think I could take one of these animals back to the house? If what you say is true, I want the world to know what a magnificent animal once roamed this prairie. I want future generations to know how they were senselessly slaughtered, and the only way I can do that is through my museum."

"Lordy sakes, Maddie. You're not thinking of preserving one of these animals are you? One of these beasts would fill up the soddy. Have you any idea how much these animals weigh?"

"But . . ."

"Absolutely not!"

The following morning, Lefty came galloping up the road toward the soddy. Although it was nearly time for the morning calisthenics class, he was alone.

Maddie waited for him by the windmill. "Lefty, where have you been? I missed you yesterday."

Lefty slipped from the bare back of his pony. "Picking Bones say no exorcist . . ."

"Why wouldn't we exercise?"

"She say you doing courting dance."

"Courting . . . ?" Maddie laughed. "Is that what

Picking Bones told you? Well, we'll just have to work twice as hard today. Go and tell the others to hurry."

He stayed her with his hand. "I come to warn you. Things are not good with my people. The buffalo ..." He glanced toward the distant skies to the still circling flocks of scavengers.

Sickened by the memory of the senseless killing, Maddie nodded sadly. "It was a terrible thing. If I ever get my hands on whoever was ..." Something in his face chilled her heart. "Your people ... They don't think Luke or I had anything to do with that slaughter, do they?"

"Red Feather blames all white people."

"Then you must convince him otherwise. You must tell him that some white people are outraged by this slaughter. Tell him that for me. Please, Lefty, you must."

"I tell him. But Red Feather not listen."

"Make him listen, Lefty. You must make him listen."

Lefty mounted his pony and rode off. In the distance came the sound of drums. Their slow cadence was far different from the usual joyous sounds that celebrated a birth or marriage.

Gooseflesh rose along her arms, and not even the hot morning sun could chase away the cold chill.

# Chapter 33

Late that afternoon, a thunderstorm rolled across the plains. Blue-white lightning flickered against the sky, followed by the low rumble of thunder.

At the first sign of the storm, Luke hurried outside to watch for any sign of fire on the prairie. Maddie finished putting the clean dishes away and, after telling Matthew to stay in the house, rushed outside to join him.

They stood hand in hand next to the windmill, looking across the grasslands for smoke.

As each zigzagging line of lightning streaked across the sky, Maddie held her breath until enough time passed to assure them that none of the dry grass had been torched.

At last the rains came, and the immediate danger passed. But it was only a short reprieve, for this was no quick thundershower. The three of them spent the remainder of the day watching the roof of the soddy for leaks or cave-ins.

"I can't believe what a boring existence I had in Washington," Maddie declared. "Here, it's one thing after another."

Luke feigned surprise. "You mean you didn't have to worry about being washed away in the rain in Washington?"

"Nor did we have to worry about snakes, buffalo stampedes, fires . . . or hunters."

"What did you do with your time?"

She laughed. "We sat around all day and drank tea and made polite gossip."

He shook his head and slipped his arm around her waist. "That must have been a sight. You drinking tea and making polite gossip."

"Actually, I was the *subject* of the polite gossip."

He laughed and nuzzled her neck with his nose. "I bet you were." He captured her lips, unmindful of Matthew, who watched them with a smile.

The storm left as suddenly as it had arrived. Maddie walked outside with an empty bucket. The rain-washed air smelled fresh with the odor of damp grass. Already patches of clear blue sky could be seen breaking through the storm clouds.

She tied the pail to the well just as the beating of the drums broke the serenity that had followed the storm. The tempo was fast—too fast, she thought, to be beating out the rhythm of a new life or new love.

Luke joined her at the well, and together they stood looking in the direction of the Cheyenne village.

She squeezed his hand over hers. "Do you suppose the drums mean trouble?"

"I don't know, Maddie." He slipped his arm around her shoulders. "I'd feel a lot better if you were somewhere far from here."

She looked up at him and felt her heart swell anew with the depth of her love for this man. "I won't leave you."

He studied her face. "We don't know what's going to happen."

"Whatever happens, Lefty won't let his people harm us."

Luke folded her in his arms and held her close. "Sometimes things happen despite our best efforts."

She sensed that he was not referring to the current situation with the Indians, not entirely. She brushed a wayward lock of hair from his forehead, but it was the worry for her that she wanted to push away.

"Luke, I mean it when I say I have no intention of leaving you. It took us so long to find each other." She flung her arms around his neck and planted a kiss on his lips. It was a crushing blow when her show of love for him was met with resistance, no matter how fleeting, before he kissed her back.

She pulled away from the circle of his arms.

"I'm sorry, Maddie . . . I . . ."

"You don't trust me."

"Of course I trust you. You have to understand, Maddie, I'm not used to people who express their feelings so openly and easily. I was taught that showing love . . . wasn't something that was done." He drew her into his arms and held her close. "Do you think I like this any more than you do? I want to feel free to show my love to you . . . to Matthew . . . in every way possible."

"You can do that," she whispered. "You have so much love to give."

"But what I said . . . about my father . . ."

She drew back, fists at her waist, eyes flashing with green fire. "I don't care a fig about your father. I love you, Luke Tyler, and as far as I'm concerned, your father may have led a wretched life, but he was responsible for one very good thing. He had a son who turned out to be good and kind and all the things I ever wanted in a man."

Something deep inside melted, the last part of himself, perhaps, that had been afraid to acknowledge his love for her. "God, Maddie. No one ever said anything like that to me before."

"Well, it's true."

"Even so, Maddie, there's a lot about me you don't know. There's a lot about myself I don't know."

"There's a lot about me I don't know either," she said. "I never knew until I met you how it felt to be in love."

"But you never had reason to think yourself a criminal. All my life I feared that I might be like the man who fathered me. I tried so hard not to be. I purposely kept myself from doing anything that might bring out my worst side, including . . . loving someone." He grimaced as if in pain. "That's why I originally jumped at the chance to come to Kansas. I thought I would be safe here, safe from the legacy of my father, safe from that part of myself that I don't even know. There's no escape for me, it seems."

"The doctor . . . that was an accident, Luke."

"I keep trying to tell myself that." He dropped her hands and turned, his back to her. "If I ever cause you harm . . ."

She lay her head against his strong, powerful back. "I don't believe you're capable of harming anyone. Last night when we made love . . . it was the most wonderful night."

"It was wonderful for me too. You'll never know how wonderful. And I'm trying, Maddie. I don't want to pull away from you. I'm just so afraid that as long as I have these doubts about myself, I will always have to battle the urge to hold back when I'm with you."

She bit back the tears that stung her eyes. It hurt her that her love and faith in him weren't enough to relieve him of his doubts. "There's got to be a way to find out the truth . . . Maybe . . . Maybe Matthew can remember something . . ."

"I told you, Maddie. I won't have Matthew put through that. He was so traumatized that he may never be the same again. I can't take a chance ..."

"Has it ever occurred to you that talking about that day might help him regain his speech?"

He turned and took her hands in his. "It's too risky."

She drew back. "Is that really what worries you, Luke? Or are you afraid that Matthew might confirm everyone's belief that you purposely murdered the doctor?"

"Of course not, Maddie. I want Matthew to speak!" His face twisted in denial, but she knew that whether or not he admitted it, even to himself, she had hit upon more of the truth than she could ever have guessed.

She slipped her arms ever so slowly around his waist so as not to alarm him. At that moment she didn't think she could handle further rejection, however much he might battle it. She lay her head against his chest and squeezed her burning eyes tight. What a complicated mess. She loved and cherished this man, and she wanted him to find peace more than she'd wanted anything in her life. Somehow there had to be a way to free him from his shadowy past.

The drums ceased after dark, but the silence that followed seemed strangely unnatural, much like the calm that preceded a storm.

After supper Luke stood guard at the open doorway. "I want you to sleep inside tonight. You can have the bed. I'll take the floor."

"That's not necessary."

"Please, Maddie. Don't fight me on this."

"And don't fight me," she pleaded.

The drums continued for the next week. Maddie hated the sense of foreboding that seemed to settle upon the prairie, the unnatural quiet and stillness. Even the prairie dogs remained underground. To make matters worse, it was so hot that waves of arid air shimmered over the heat-wilted grass.

Lordy be, she thought, as she peered across the sweltering plains. Where was Lefty? Why hadn't he made his usual morning runs to inquire as to the day of the week? She hoped it was the oppressive heat that kept Lefty and his friends away. But in her heart she doubted it. She was standing by the windmill when Luke joined her.

"I think maybe someone should ride to the fort," he said. "Let them know that trouble is brewing."

"The army might make matters worse. Lefty and the others could be killed."

"It's more likely that the Cheyennes will be forced to return to Indian Territory. I don't think the army will purposely kill anyone."

Maddie recalled the many times she had watched Lefty and Flying Hawk race their ponies across the prairie, as free as the wind. "There are many ways to kill someone."

"What choices do we have, Maddie? If something happens to you or . . ."

"Nothing's going to happen. I trust Lefty and Flying Hawk and the others."

"They're not the ones I'm worried about."

"Do you think Red Feather will cause trouble?"

"I don't know. He might. That's why I want you to leave the area. Go to Hays . . ."

"I won't go back to Hays."

"Then go to Washington."

She searched his face. "You want me to leave you?"

"I want to know you're safe."

"But . . ."

"Please, Maddie. If you do this one thing for me, I'll ask Sheriff Beckleworth to meet with Red Feather.

He's good at that kind of thing. He talked a whole town out of lynching me. One angry Indian should be a cinch for him."

"You would do that? Ask the sheriff to talk with Red Feather?"

"So you'll go to Washington?"

"Only for a short while."

"And you'll take Matthew with you?"

"If you want me to."

"I'll feel better knowing that you and Matthew are safe."

"Thank you," she whispered. Her impulse was to throw her arms around him in gratitude and love, but she held herself rigid, not wanting anything to come between them—yet knowing all the while that the very act of holding back was barrier enough. "Thank you for wanting to help the Indians. I know it's going to work, Luke. I just know that once someone sits down with Red Feather, the problem will be resolved."

She awoke early the next morning to the smell of smoke. Praying that it wasn't a prairie fire, she scrambled out of her bedroll on the floor of the soddy and raced outside.

A column of smoke rose from the direction of the newly rebuilt town of Colton. She called to Luke. "Hurry!"

Luke came on the run, followed by Matthew.

She clutched at his arm. "It's Colton, isn't it?"

"I'm not sure. It looks too far to the left."

The lines on his forehead deepened, and she could guess why. A fire, any fire, in the prairie could be disastrous. If Colton was not yet in danger, it soon would be.

"We'd better go. Every hand will be needed to put it out. Besides, I don't want to leave you and Matthew here alone."

It was the newly built Eldridge barn that was afire. Lucy had had her way, and the sod house had been abandoned. With the help of several families, the house, a fine dwelling with wood siding and a wrap-around porch, had been built, along with a wood barn. The house was still unpainted, but lace curtains hung at the windows and a thin stream of smoke rose from its stone chimney.

Luke grabbed a shovel from the back of the wagon and rushed toward the barn, where dozens of men were already at work. Maddie and Matthew followed close behind. Maddie picked up two empty buckets, and she and Matthew raced to the stream. She filled up a bucket and handed it to him.

"Hurry, Matthew, take the bucket to your father."

The wind had picked up slightly in the last hour. Fiery sparks began to float through the air. A small portion of prairie grass caught fire, but the recent invasion of grasshoppers had thinned the vegetation, which kept the fire from spreading as quickly as it might have. It took the men only a few minutes to stomp out the flames with their boots. But no sooner had they put out the one fire than three more began to blaze.

Everyone was too occupied to notice that the flames had leaped from the barn to the bare wood house. It was little Caroline Eldridge who called the alarm. A mad scramble ensued as the men grabbed buckets of water and dashed to the house.

Already the dry wooden shingles of the roof had burst into flames. A fireball exploded from inside, followed by the sound of shattering glass. Peter grabbed hold of Luke's arm. "Lucy and the baby . . ."

Luke's face turned ashen. "Lucy's in there . . . ?" Luke dropped his spade and raced to the house.

"Luke, no!" Maddie screamed, but Luke kept running. Maddie clutched Matthew to her and watched in horror as Luke took a flying leap over the flames and through the front door.

She spun around to face Peter, who stood frozen by her side. "Don't just stand there. Help him!"

Peter's face was drained of color. His glazed eyes appeared not to see her. It was obvious that he was in no condition to help.

"Stay here, Matthew." She raced to the house, issuing orders to the others, who seemed to be working in slow motion. Wood crackled as the flames consumed the roof.

She raised her arms to protect her face from the searing heat. She screamed Luke's name, but her voice was drowned out by the roar of the fire.

Mayor Mettle shouted for water, but it was a futile gesture at best. By now the house was already engulfed in flames. Seconds seemed to stretch into minutes, minutes into eternity.

Something snapped inside her. She started forward. Someone grabbed her by the arm. In the red glow of flames, she recognized the man who held her as Max Weedler.

Then a shadow dashed from the house. Maddie pulled away from Weedler and battled her way through the circle of men who rushed to help Luke.

Upon reaching safety, Luke discarded the gray woolen blanket he had thrown over his head. Lucy was flung over his shoulder and the baby tucked into the crook of his arm.

The sheriff and mayor took Lucy from him and stretched her out upon the ground. She appeared to be dazed and she was coughing furiously.

Maddie took the baby from Luke's arms. "You crazy fool. You could have been killed." Her eyes filled with tears of thanksgiving for his safety, for the safety of mother and child.

A crooked smile showed from beneath his soot-covered face. He dropped down on his haunches to give his son a hug before rushing off to fight the still raging fire.

Lucy called out for her baby, and Maddie quickly moved to her side. Lucy's hand flew to her mouth upon seeing her child safe in Maddie's arms. "I thought . . ."

"I know," Maddie whispered. She lay the tiny infant in her mother's arms.

Lucy looked up her. "Caroline and Jamie . . ."

"They're safe." Caroline and Jamie were racing back and forth to the stream to fill buckets of water for the men.

"And Peter . . . ?"

"Your whole family is safe."

Suddenly Lucy's expression changed. "No thanks to those awful savages. I wish they were dead. Every one of them."

Shocked by Lucy's hateful voice, Maddie thought she might have misunderstood. "Are you talking about the Cheyennes?"

"Of course she's talking about the Indians," Weedler snarled. "Who else would she be talking about?"

"They're not savages."

Weedler wagged a finger in her face. "Don't you go telling me what they are and are not!"

Maddie took a step backward. "I know the Cheyennes."

"Know them?" He barked an ugly laugh. "Do you also know that a few years ago those savages raided many of the homesteads, killing men, women, and children—including my parents and three sisters?"

Maddie was so stunned that she could hardly find her voice, "I'm sorry . . ."

"Sorry doesn't mean a hill o' beans."

"You're right," she said. "But neither does blaming a whole race for the deeds of a few."

"I don't know which of those savages is responsible. I don't care. All I know is I'm not resting until every last one is gone."

It was the hard, raw edge of hatred on his face that made her realize something. "You!" she sputtered in outrage. "You're the one responsible for slaughtering those buffalo!"

His dark eyes glittered hatefully. "When the buffalo are gone, there won't be any reason for the savages to stick around."

"What you're doing is unjust and unfair."

"Do you think that what happened to my family was just and fair?"

"No, I don't think that." As much as she disliked the man, she could hardly blame him for wanting some sort of vengeance for his family's death. "Mr. Weedler, please. There's got to be a way to handle this without innocent people being hurt. Maybe the army . . ."

"The army? What good does the army do? The soldiers round them up, take them down south, and then what? The savages keep coming back. My way is best. I aim to make sure that those savages ain't never coming back." He tipped his hat to Lucy and walked away.

"Poor man," Lucy said to Maddie. "Imagine losing your family like that." She shuddered. "It's horrible to think about. I don't know how you can continue to defend those awful savages."

"They're my friends . . ."

"They're the ones who set the barn on fire. I wager you'd feel differently if it was your house that lay in ruins."

"The . . . the Cheyennes did this?"

"I saw it with my own eyes. There were five of

them. One of the savages was all dressed up with a red feather in his hair."

"His name is Red Feather. Not every Cheyenne thinks as he does."

"How do you know what those savages think? Why do you feel you have to defend people like this Red Feather and Luke?"

Maddie's temper flared. "Luke risked his life to save you and the baby."

Lucy sniffed in disbelief. "Peter saved us."

"Peter couldn't save a man from drowning in a desert!" Maddie immediately regretted her harsh words. Lucy had just lost her home, and it was obvious she was still in shock. "I'm sorry, Lucy. Forget what I said."

"It's true," Peter said from behind her. Neither woman had noticed Peter's presence.

Lucy looked up at her husband. "What's true?"

"I'm a coward." Peter glanced at Maddie. "That's what you meant to say, wasn't it?"

"I had no right to criticize you," Maddie said.

Lucy concurred. "Considering the company you keep."

"That's enough!" Peter said sharply.

"Enough?" Lucy frowned at her husband. "Why do you insist upon defending Luke? He wasn't even man enough to fight in the war. But you did. You fought for your country and lost a leg because of your bravery."

"I lost a leg because of my cowardliness!"

Both women stared at Peter.

"How can you say that?" Lucy stammered at last.

"I panicked, Lucy. My company was waiting in ambush, and I panicked and ran. That's when I was shot. Many men died that day because I gave away our location."

"You were a hero that day," Lucy protested. "Everyone knows that Luke was the coward. Refusing to fight."

"Luke fought the war in his own way. He donated almost every penny of the profits from his business to support the war effort."

"I don't believe it, Peter. Why are you saying these things?"

"Because they're true, Lucy. I wasn't even man enough to stay around for Annie-May's birth."

"You were there all the time. I know you were." Lucy looked up at Maddie for confirmation. "You told me he was."

"She was protecting me," Peter said. "And today, I . . ." Tears formed in his eyes. "I almost lost you and the baby, and there wasn't a damned thing I could do about it but watch." He adjusted his crutches. "Oh, Lucy. Will you ever forgive me?"

Lucy stared at him but offered nothing in the way of encouragement or forgiveness. Peter waited, and then, when no response was forthcoming, he walked away as quickly as his crutches would allow.

Maddie waited until Peter was out of earshot. "He's a good man, and he deserves your support."

Lucy's eyes blazed, full of hurt and confusion. "How can you say that? He almost let me die."

"It took courage for him to admit the truth."

Lucy's eyes filled with tears. "He was so different when I married him. Before that awful war. He came back a broken man. I tried so hard to make him feel like a hero . . . but nothing I say or do seems to make a difference."

"Maybe the problem is that he doesn't feel that you love him for himself."

"A coward, you mean."

"Not a coward, Lucy. A man who did nothing more than act out of fear."

Lucy slumped back as if in defeat. "I wanted to believe that Peter was a hero not because I would love him any less if he wasn't one but because it made me feel a whole lot safer to think of him as such." She gave Maddie a beseeching look. "This land terrifies me, Maddie. I'm not like you. The Indians, the animals, the isolation, it all terrifies me. Telling myself that Peter could save us from anything—it was the only way I could get through the days and nights."

Maddie squeezed Lucy's hand. "In the short time that I've known you, you've come through some trying times. It wasn't heroics that got you through those times, it was courage and fortitude."

"So what are you saying, Maddie? That I don't need protection? That I have what I need to get me through whatever lies ahead?"

"That's exactly what I'm saying. You're strong, Lucy. I think once you accept that fact, Peter will rediscover his own strengths."

Lucy stared down at the baby in her arms. After a moment she looked up. "Would you hold Annie-May for me? I need to find Peter."

"Of course." Maddie lifted the sleeping infant from Lucy's arms.

Lucy hesitated a moment. "Maddie ... what you said ... it makes sense. Thank you."

# Chapter 34

It was late that afternoon by the time the fire had been fully contained. The train had long left Colton and there was nothing to do but return home.

Neither Maddie nor Luke felt like talking much during the drive home. Matthew fell asleep between them, his head on Maddie's lap.

She waited until Luke unharnessed the horse before she asked him to confirm Peter's story.

"Is it true what Peter said? Did you donate money for the war?"

She walked by his side as he led the horse to the water trough. He looked surprised by the question. "When did you talk to Peter about the war?"

"Today."

He stopped and looked at her in surprise. "Today? While we were fighting the fire?"

"I know it seems like a strange time to be talking of the past . . . Actually, it was Lucy he told."

"Lucy?" He looked more puzzled than ever. "I can't imagine why the subject came up. The war is over. What difference does it make at this point?"

"It makes a difference to me. It further proves that I'm right about the kind of man you are."

He frowned. "It proves nothing, Maddie. I hated slavery. I always have, but my modest efforts did little to change things. It was men like Peter who made the real difference."

"According to Peter, he did nothing."

"He made the effort, Maddie. He put his life on the line."

"So did you, Luke. Today I watched you put your life in jeopardy to save the life of a woman who despises you. As far as I'm concerned, this just confirms what I've been saying all along. Whatever happened to that doctor was an accident. I know that as surely as I know how much I love you."

Later that afternoon, when Maddie was busy preparing supper, Shooting Star appeared at the door asking to speak to Luke. Her initial alarm upon seeing the Cheyenne was soon dispelled.

Shooting Star was alone, and he didn't appear to be hostile. If anything, he seemed overfriendly. He kept smiling at her and pointing to his potbelly, apparently thinking she approved.

Maddie sent Matthew to the barn to fetch his father. While they waited for Luke, she invited Shooting Star into the soddy, which was considerably cooler than the outside.

Shooting Star stepped across the threshold, dropped to the floor, and pulled out a knife.

Startled, Maddie cried out. Then she realized it was the mounted bobcat that Shooting Star was about to attack.

"It's all right. It won't hurt you. See?" She reached up to stroke the animal.

Shooting Star stood, glanced around at the other mounted animals, and his eyes filled with distrust and suspicion. Although he slid the knife into the shield at his waist, the wariness remained on his weather-carved face.

Maddie tried to take his mind off his surroundings. "Where's Lefty? Why hasn't he come?"

Shooting Star didn't seem to understand. "Lefty." She repeated. She lifted her left arm to demonstrate, but before she could convey her meaning, Luke walked in the door and greeted the Indian with a solemn nod.

"For you," Shooting Star motioned outside to three spotted ponies that were tethered there.

"Why are you giving me your ponies?"

"You don't like?"

"I like very much, but I don't know why you're giving them to me."

"Fair trade."

Luke considered this for a moment. "What are we trading?" When the Indian looked puzzled, he elaborated. "What do you want me to give you in return?"

Shooting Star indicated with his hands that he understood. "You give me Ostrich."

Luke drew back in puzzlement. "Ostrich?"

Maddie suddenly felt sick. "I think he means me. The Cheyennes think I look like an ostrich."

Luke's eyebrows flew to his hairline in utter astonishment. "Do they have any idea what an ostrich looks like?"

Obviously misunderstanding the conversation, Shooting Star pounded his chest. "Me want Ostrich!"

Lines creased Luke's forehead as he tried to make sense out of what Shooting Star was saying. "Let me see if I understand. You want to trade those ponies—" he pointed outside—"for Maddie."

Shooting Star grinned. "Fair trade."

"No fair trade."

"Fair trade!" Shooting Star insisted. He was no longer smiling. "Shooting Star's squaw safe from harm."

Luke narrowed his eyes. "You think your people want to harm Maddie?"

"Red Feather not harm Shooting Star's squaw."

"I'm most grateful for your concern," Maddie began tactfully, "but I cannot be your squaw."

"No squaw?"

"White Blossom will make a much better squaw for you."

"No want White Blossom!" Shooting Star thundered. "Me want Ostrich."

"You can't have Ostrich . . . ah, Maddie!" Luke thundered back.

Shooting Star looked ready to argue further, but the mounted animals seemed to make him nervous. He kept glancing toward the bobcat as if he expected it to attack. Finally he stormed outside.

After Shooting Star rode away, taking the ponies with him, Luke poured himself a drink and slumped down at the table. "Maybe you'll listen to me now. If Shooting Star thinks your life is in danger, than I guarantee it is."

Their gazes locked for a moment before he lifted his glass to his mouth and took a long, hard drink. "I wish we didn't have to wait until tomorrow before I can put you and Matthew on the train."

"Come with us."

"I'm not leaving, Maddie. This is my home, my land."

"You'll only be gone for a while, Luke. Once the trouble dies down, we can come back."

"If I leave, it might be a violation of my homesteading agreement. The government could take back my land. I could lose everything I've worked for for the last four years."

"Please, Luke. Your life could be in danger. If anything happened to you ... If you really care for me ..."

"I do care, Maddie. You've got to believe that. But what kind of husband would I make if I don't even know what kind of a man I am? And I'm never going to find out if I continue to run at the first sign of trouble."

"I know what kind of man you are. You're good and kind ..."

He leaned forward and touched his fingers to her lips. "I hope to God you never see me any other way."

"You're not a murderer, Luke. You'll never make me believe otherwise."

"I don't know whether I am or not, Maddie. Maybe I'll never know."

"Luke, if you really were a murderer, it wouldn't haunt you so. Do you think your father sat in prison thinking about what he'd done?"

"No, I don't think that."

"Then how can you possibly think you're like him?"

"The problem is, I don't really know who I am. I've been afraid to let myself feel. I look in your eyes, and I see love, pure and simple, without any restrictions or limitations or doubts, and it hurts me so to think that I can't return that same kind of spontaneous love. Every time I put my arms around you, I must fight a little voice inside that reminds me of the past."

He framed her face with his hands. "I don't want anything to keep me from expressing my love for you as fully and completely as you deserve to be loved."

"And you think that staying here with trouble brewing is going to make that little voice go away?"

"I don't know, Maddie. Maybe the voice will never go away. I was afraid to fight in the war, afraid to find out what kind of man I really was. Loving you has given me the courage to seek out the truth."

She started to speak, but once again he touched her lips, silencing her even as he beseeched her to understand. "I've walked away from far too many battles in my life. This is one battle I mean to fight."

# Chapter 35

The following morning, Luke watched Maddie pack Matthew's few things along with her own into the wooden trunk she'd brought to Kansas with her.

He handed her a roll of money. "I've been saving this. I want you to have it."

It was far more than she needed. "I can't take all this."

He wrapped his fingers around her hand. "I want you to take Matthew to a doctor. Travel to Boston if you must. But please, Maddie, find someone that can help him."

Her lips parted as she looked up at him. So at last he was ready to face whatever it was that Matthew might be able to tell him about that long ago day. "I'll do whatever I can, Luke. You have my promise."

"Maddie, you do understand why I have to stay . . . ?"

It sounded crazy, but she did understand. He needed to learn about himself. "Just as long as you know you don't have to prove anything to me."

He sighed and pulled her into his arms. The pain of watching her pack was too much to bear. He lowered his head and kissed her. Even something as simple as a kiss required his complete concentration, for he feared that something would rise from his past to spoil it. Old habits die slowly, it seemed—he was beginning to wonder if they ever died at all. He released her and grabbed his straw hat. "I'll be back in time to take you to the train."

Outside, it was quiet, with no sound of Indian drums to mar the early-morning stillness. Nor was there any sign of smoke. He hoped this meant the worst trouble was over.

He saddled his horse and rode aimlessly across the prairie. He was a man in search of himself, and it appeared that if he wanted answers he was obliged to sift through the ashes of his past.

Voices rose up from the past, ugly voices, accusatory voices. He tried to fight back; he thought of Maddie, imagined her as she looked at him, her eyes soft and filled with love.

He tried to hold on to that vision, but despite his best efforts, it faded away, replaced by the memory of the cold eyes that had dogged him all his life.

*Murderer. Your father was a rapist. Some people are born with the devil in them. You're nothing but a wicked boy. Mustn't show your feelings . . .*

He pressed his legs against his horse's flanks and thundered across the plains until the voices could no longer keep up. The sun rose higher in the sky until it was directly overhead, and he knew it was time to head back.

Time to take Maddie and Matthew to the train station.

Time to say good-bye.

He tugged at the reins and took a shortcut along a narrow buffalo trail. His heart felt so heavy, it was all he could do to stay astride the horse.

The trail was partially blocked by a dead buffalo. He dismounted and stooped on his haunches to check the cause of death. It was a bullet wound between the eyes. *What a waste,* he thought.

He was startled out of his reverie by a bloodcurdling

cry. Acting on instinct, he spun on his heel. Shooting Star raced toward him, the deadly blade of a tomahawk held high above his head.

Luke diverted the blow, and the two men rolled in the dirt. "Dammit!" Luke shouted. "What's the matter with you?"

"Me want Ostrich."

Shooting Star's fist slammed into Luke's jaw. Luke brought his knees up, then kicked the Indian off him with a violent thrust of his feet.

Luke jumped to his feet and barely managed to duck the tomahawk that flew straight at him. He escaped the weapon but not the warrior. With a savage cry, Shooting Star rammed into Luke headfirst.

Winded and dazed, Luke staggered backward, but Shooting Star followed in relentless pursuit. This time he held a knife.

The sun danced upon the blade as the shiny metal sliced through the air. Luke backed away. "Let's talk about this."

"No talk." Shooting Star kept coming, hacking at the space between them with his weapon.

Sucking in his breath, Luke caught his foe by the wrist and wrestled the knife from his hand. A wild scramble ensued. Shooting Star was strong, but Luke's hand closed around the knife handle first. After a tug-of-war, Luke gained the advantage.

Dagger in hand, Luke raised his arm over Shooting Star's prone body. The warrior froze, his face drained of color as he eyed the lethal blade.

Poised for the kill, Luke held the knife an arm's length from Shooting Star's bare chest.

With an anguished moan, Luke dropped his arm to his side and dragged himself upright.

Surprised by the sudden reprieve, Shooting Star stared up in disbelief.

Luke wiped the blood away from his mouth with the back of his free hand. He felt dazed and light-headed. But even the fogginess of his mind failed to blot out the one thing that was suddenly crystal clear to him: he could not kill Shooting Star; he was not a killer. Whatever had happened that long ago day between him and the doctor could only have been an accident.

Maddie was right. Dear God, she was right!

Overcome by relief and gratitude, he felt what had been an unbearable burden lift from his shoulders. For the first time in his memory, he felt free enough to embrace the feelings of love and happiness that flooded through him and opened his heart.

And the voices, those persistent voices from the past had finally been silenced. He wanted to shout at the top of his lungs. But more than anything, he wanted to rush home to tell Maddie.

Just thinking her name brought a flush to his already heated body. She had never believed he could kill. She was right . . . Lord, she was right . . . just as she was right about Matthew's temper tantrums.

He realized he was still holding the knife. He tossed it away, and it disappeared somewhere in the tall prairie grass, hopefully never to be found again. Grabbing his foe by the hand, he shook it like a man who'd just met a long-lost brother. "I'm not a killer!" he shouted with glee, "I'm not a killer."

At another time, the astonishment on the warrior's face might well have made him laugh. But now his only thought was of Maddie.

Heaving himself into the saddle of his horse, he turned until he faced Shooting Star, who still lay on the ground looking dazed and bewildered.

It was then that Luke noticed Picking Bones standing a short distance away. He wondered how long she had been there. How much had she seen and understood?

She looked at him with undeniable approval, and lifted her hand in what Luke recognized as a gesture of friendship. He then recalled that Shooting Star was the reason the old woman had spent all those days in front of Maddie's tipi.

He touched his finger to the brim of his hat in a salute and watched as she descended upon the still dazed Indian. Luke deduced from Picking Bones's sharp, rasping voice that Shooting Star was receiving a thorough tongue-lashing.

Despite his aching jaw and sore muscles, Luke rode away laughing. He'd never seen a woman so determined. Well, almost never, he corrected himself, thinking of Maddie. If Shooting Star had any sense, he'd forget about Maddie, marry Picking Bones's daughter, and be done with it.

He dug his heels into the side of his horse and raced in the direction of home, feeling free as the wind as his horse sped along the buffalo trail.

The happiness in his heart turned to cold dread when he saw several Indians on horseback ahead. One of them held a flaming torch. In the distance Luke saw a thin column of smoke rising upward.

Luke pulled sharply on the reins, and his horse reared before coming to a standstill. He recognized one of the Indians as Red Feather.

"Don't do this," Luke shouted. "Work with us. Together we can find the men responsible for killing the buffalo. Believe me, I hate what they're doing as much as you."

Without a word, the Indian raised his hand and dropped it. It was the signal for attack. Cursing beneath his breath, Luke swung his horse around and took off like lightning. He didn't know sign language, but he knew an act of aggression when he saw it— knew that Maddie and Matthew were in danger.

It took him a moment to realize that the searing pain that flashed through his shoulder was an arrow. With one hand on the rein, he tried to pull the rigid shaft from between his shoulder blades, but the arrow was embedded too deeply.

His head grew heavy and the sun seemed to dim.

Maddie.

He held on to her name with all his heart and soul. His only hope was that she had already left for the train.

He looked up at the sky and tried to make sense of the two yellow globes that floated over his head. Then he heard a high-pitched sound and recognized it as Maddie's godawful whistle. A surge of energy blazed through him, and his vision cleared.

Clinging to the sound of the shrill whistle that bonded him to the woman he loved, he reached over his shoulder and pulled the arrow out of his back. The effort cost him dearly in strength. He tried for Maddie's sake to hold on, but the light slipped away completely as he tumbled from his horse.

Maddie pulled her fingers out of her mouth. She had whistled off and on for the last twenty minutes, but still there was no sign of Luke. The loud, shrill sound of her whistle had sent countless meadowlarks, blue jays, and swallows skyward in a wild flutter of feathers and screeching protests. But there was still no Luke, and she finally gave up and headed back to the house.

When Luke failed to return to the soddy in time to

take her and Matthew to the train, Maddie lugged her trunk out to the wagon.

"It's time to leave, Matthew." Matthew looked at her with worried eyes, and she did her best to comfort him. "Your father could be waiting for us at the train station," she said. She knew he wouldn't have gone to the station without them, but it gave her some measure of comfort to voice the possibility, no matter how remote. "Don't forget your slate, Matthew." She had a feeling that Matthew was going to need it—that they were both going to need it.

It wasn't until she turned the wagon onto the main road that she noticed the smoke rising from the area around Colton. Thinking that the fire explained Luke's absence, she snapped the whip over the horse's head.

Although she had known it was only a slight possibility that Luke would be waiting at the train station, she was nonetheless devastated when she pulled the horse and wagon alongside the deserted platform. To add to her dismay, they had missed the train by minutes, despite the frantic race to the station.

She had only herself to blame. She had waited until the last possible moment before leaving the soddy, hoping beyond hope that Luke would return.

She was furious with Luke. Furious at herself. She couldn't believe he had let her and Matthew go without saying good-bye. Then her anger dissolved into guilt. Luke was risking his life to save Colton, and all she could think about was herself!

Her eyes blurred with tears, she turned the wagon around and headed back. It was because of the tears that she failed to spot another cloud of smoke, this one further south, until Matthew tugged on her arm and pointed it out to her.

She slowed the wagon and shaded her eyes against the bright afternoon sun. Anger turned to worry as she noticed a third column of smoke rising from yet another direction.

# Chapter 36

Snapping the whip over the horse's head, Maddie raced homeward. Sensing her urgency, Matthew tried to write something on his slate, but the jostling of the wagon made it impossible.

"Your father will be all right," Maddie shouted, trying to be heard over the loud rumble of wagon wheels. "He's probably fighting the fires." She glanced at Matthew and felt a tug at her heartstrings. "Don't look so worried. Your father's going to be all right." *Oh, God, please let it be true!*

She pulled the wagon up in front of the soddy and searched for Luke's horse. In the distance birds circled overhead. *More slaughtered buffalo,* she thought. Would the senseless killing ever stop?

Luke's horse was nowhere in sight, but even so, she dashed inside, hoping to find him. The room was empty, and there was no indication that he had returned in her absence.

She slumped into a chair, trying to decide what to do.

She could smell smoke in the air and decided to check on the progress of the fires. The sky overhead was clear and the blades of the windmill stood motionless. Standing in a narrow strip of shadow cast by the windmill, she scanned the prairie in every direction.

More smoke filled the horizon, this time from the north.

But it wasn't the smoke that made her hold her breath. It was something in the distance. Luke's horse, she thought, her heart skipping a beat, but it was still too far away to know for certain. Shading her eyes against the bright sun, she squinted to get a better look.

Lord, if it was Luke's horse, it was certainly taking its own sweet time!

Matthew emerged from the soddy and ran to join her by the windmill. He slipped his hand into hers. "Does it look like your father's horse?"

Matthew's gaze followed her pointed finger. After a moment he nodded.

Apprehension gripped her, but it was the sight of the two turkey buzzards that began to circle over the horse that filled her with cold dread.

"Stay here, Matthew!" She tore through the knee-high prairie grass, mindless of the dangers posed by rattlesnakes and the numerous prairie dog holes. She ran until she gasped for air and thought she could run no more—and still she ran.

Luke was slumped in the saddle when she reached him, barely conscious, her name trembling on his dry, pale lips. "Maddie," he whispered. "I almost couldn't get back ... on ... the ... horse."

"Hold on, Luke. Hold on!"

Gasping for air, she managed to keep him from falling off the saddle as she mounted behind him and rode the horse back to the soddy. The back of his shirt was covered in blood, and it rubbed off on her clothes. Dear God, he'd been shot!

She motioned to Matthew with her arm. "Hurry!"

Luke groaned. "Maddie?"

She tightened her grip on him. "Hold on, Luke. We're almost there."

Matthew came running toward her, his face filling with horror when he saw his father. "Help me hold him. Don't let him fall."

Maddie slid off the horse. Luke groaned again, and his eyes flickered open. "Maddie."

"We're home, Luke. But you have to help me. Come on now, hold on."

She tugged on his limp arm, and he practically fell on top of her. "Matthew! Quick!" Matthew ran to his father's side and pulled at his other arm. She slipped one arm around Luke's waist and pulled his arm around her shoulder. "Steady now." He was heavy, but she was strong, and for once in her life, her height proved an advantage. "Luke, stay with me. It's only a short walk."

Barely conscious, he stumbled and nearly fell. "Open the door, Matthew!" Somehow she managed to half-drag, half-carry Luke into the soddy and to the bed, where he fell face down. "Matthew! Quick! Bring me some water."

She grabbed her scissors and cut his blood-soaked shirt away from his body. His eyes flickered open, and his parched lips moved, but his voice was so weak that she could hardly make out what he was saying.

"Don't talk, Luke. You've got to save your strength."

"Red Fea . . . ther."

Straining to catch his urgent words, she touched a finger to the open cut above his lip. "Red Feather did this?"

"Arrow."

He grabbed her wrist, and at first she was gratified by the strength of his grip. But alarm soon took precedence as she felt his energy drain away.

"Luke!"

"Go," he whispered. "Red . . . Fea . . ."

She leaned closer. "What about Red Feather?"

"He'll be here . . . soon. Take Matthew . . ." His eyes closed.

"Luke! Stay with me. Please, Luke."

Matthew hurried into the soddy, lugging a bucket of water.

She grabbed the bucket from him and washed Luke's wound with a clean rag. It was an arrow, not a gunshot wound, so there was no bullet to worry about. But he'd lost a lot of blood, and that was cause enough for alarm. "Bring me that bottle of whiskey."

Matthew, looking wide-eyed and pale, stood motionless. "Matthew!" she said sharply. He lifted his eyes to hers. Her heart went out to him. Poor boy. First his mother and now . . . this. "It's all right, Matthew. The bleeding has stopped. Bring me that bottle."

This time Matthew did as she asked, but the fear in his face was evident as he watched her dump the contents onto Luke's back. "That'll help to stop infection."

She cut strips of clean flour sacks to use for bandages. She worked feverishly, and after she had tended the wound she sponged off his face, being careful to wipe around the bruises on his cheek and forehead.

Matthew tugged on her arm.

"Don't bother me, now, Matthew. Please."

He tugged on her arm again. This time he was more insistent.

"What is it, Matthew?" she snapped, and immediately regretted her impatience. "All right. Show me what you want."

Matthew led her to the door and pointed. A wall of smoke rose, close enough to smell. The creak of the windmill indicated that the wind was picking up. That meant they were directly in the path of the fast-spreading fire.

She swept her gaze up and down the soddy walls. The walls would protect them from fire, but they could not keep Red Feather and his men from harming them if that were truly his intent.

She pulled Matthew back inside and bolted the door after them. She shook Luke, but got no response. Frantically, she reached for his pulse. Her fingers trembled so much that she had trouble finding one at first. At last she felt a slight flutter. He was still alive, thank God, but for how much longer?

Matthew stood stock still, looking pale and frightened. "It's all right, dear one." She hugged him and knew she had no choice but to leave Luke. Matthew's safety had to be her first concern. There was nothing she could do for Luke. Nothing but protect the son he loved so much.

She leaned over Luke and kissed him on the forehead. His skin was cold to the touch, a sickly ash color. She pulled her head back, leaving a teardrop in the wake of her kiss.

How she loved this man. How she hated to leave him. If it weren't for Matthew, she would stay to the bitter end. "I won't let anything happen to Matthew," she whispered. Her promise was all that she had to give him, and she prayed that by some miracle he heard her.

Brushing aside the tears, she moved away. Her heart ached. She would never have guessed such pain and anguish were possible. Lord, if anything happened to Luke, if she lost him ... What would she do? "Come on, Matthew."

Luke's horse was the faster of the two, but it had wandered away from the soddy and was grazing in the grass a distance away. She took Matthew by the hand and ran.

A cloud of dust rose a short ways off, and a small

band of horsemen could be seen heading toward them. Red Feather! He was still a mile or two away, but it was close enough. Feeling trapped, she spun around to consider her options.

As soon as she hit the road, Red Feather would spot her. It would do her no good to run in any other direction. They'd never get through the spreading fire, which now cut off their escape on three sides.

She jerked Matthew by the hand and ran back to the soddy. She searched frantically for the gun she had given Luke for safekeeping. It wasn't much, but it was something. Lord Almighty, what had he done with it? In her anguish, she knocked over Matthew's little cardinal, and the bird fell to the floor with a thud.

She stared down at the bird ... maybe there was a another way. A way to save both Matthew and Luke.

Her heart fluttering, she dashed around the room. "Quick, Matthew! Help me carry the animals outside."

She wrapped an arm around a mounted groundhog and grabbed a jackrabbit in her free hand. "Hurry!" She raced out the door, keeping her body low to the ground so as not to be seen by the fast-approaching Indians. Matthew followed close behind, a badger cradled in his arms.

She set the prairie dog and jackrabbit in front of the soddy and took the badger from Matthew. It took two more trips to gather up the remaining animals. "Hurry, Matthew. Back inside. I'll be there in a minute."

Crouching to the ground, she quickly arranged the bobcat. A raucous sound filled the air as hundreds of birds left the refuge of the tall grass and took flight to escape the advancing Indians.

She could hear the horses, and she knew that she was now in range of Red Feather's vision. It was too late to run back inside. Her only hope was to take advantage of the Indians' superstitious beliefs. Still on her knees, she froze in place.

Her heart pounded so fast, it almost drowned out the sound of horses as the Cheyennes rode past the windmill. She could see them now out of the corner of her eye.

Red Feather signaled his band of men to halt. Though their ponies stood at the edge of the clearing, Maddie could hear the men's voices. She couldn't make out the words, but it was obvious that they were arguing among themselves.

The sun was so hot, beads of sweat formed on her forehead and ran down the side of her face.

The argument continued. At last, one brave rode away, followed by another. She felt a surge of hope. Maybe her crazy plan would work. Maybe the Indians would be afraid to cross the circle of death. Another Indian left and finally a fourth. Just one more . . . Lord, one more.

But Red Feather was not so easily fooled.

# Chapter 37

*Go, dear God, please go!*, she pleaded silently. Don't let this be the end. A dozen thoughts tumbled through her mind like spinning wheels. She thought of her father and all the dangers he'd survived, of her mother back home, peacefully filling her days with social teas. And Luke, oh, Lordy be, Luke—lying inside, most surely dead, lost to her. The last thought would have been enough to make her surrender to Red Feather had it not been for Matthew.

But she had promised Luke she'd save his son. No matter what it took or what it cost her, she would protect Matthew.

Determination flowed through her, and her earlier resolve was restored, only to be shattered a moment later when Red Feather dismounted.

With pounding heart, she watched Red Feather walk up to the nearest animal, a jackrabbit, one of her best works.

Red Feather examined the rabbit closely, then checked the prairie dog next to it.

The sun was so hot, Maddie felt as if she were going to faint or melt, or both. Her mouth felt stiff and dry, her tongue swollen. Rivers of sweat ran down her back.

It was the sweat that was bound to give her away. As soon as he reached her, he would know . . .

His dark skin glistened with war paint, and his whole appearance was formidable. His eyes glinted dangerously as he gave the soddy a cursory glance. He then followed the circle of animals toward Maddie.

There was something menacing in the way he walked, his moccasins soundless against the hardened sod, his body tense and alert.

Maddie's mind raced. There was nowhere to run. Nowhere to hide. What a stupid thing for her to do, putting herself in such danger. She should have taken Matthew and run. Anything would have been better than waiting here to be slaughtered.

Red Feather stopped some two feet in front of her.

For a moment it seemed as if the world stood still. Not even the sound of a bird broke the silence.

*He knew it was a trick.* The others in his tribe might be fooled, but not Red Feather.

She was shaking so hard, she was sure he could hear her bones rattle. She thought of Matthew and Luke and forced herself to hold on for their sakes. She held her eyes still, refusing to blink, and they burned from lack of moisture. She held her breath until her chest felt as if it were about to explode. She grew dizzy, and the ground seemed to waver.

Desperate for air, she inhaled. Almost at once, Red Feather grabbed her, his lip curled in an ugly, hateful sneer.

A high, shrill sound that was neither human or animal but a combination of both pierced the air.

Startled, Red Feather released her. She flew backwards and scrambled madly to her feet. Red Feather had hold of Matthew and was shaking him.

Snapping into action, Maddie attacked the Indian like a wildcat. "Take your hands off him!" she screamed. She surprised Red Feather with a well-aimed kick, and in the instant it took him to recover, she pulled Matthew away.

"Run, Matthew. Run!"

Red Feather grabbed Maddie's arm and pushed her to the ground. He raised his tomahawk. "White woman die!"

Fear gripped her like steel chains. The metallic taste of terror filled her mouth.

At first, she thought she'd imagined the woman's voice. It wasn't until Red Feather drew back that she realized the crackling, high-pitched voice was real.

Picking Bones stood only a few feet away, confronting Red Feather. She looked like an angry magpie protecting her nest as she pointed her finger at Maddie and gave free rein to her displeasure.

Red Feather tried to argue with the woman, but anything he said only made Picking Bones raise her voice that much more. He finally turned on his heel and angrily stomped away. The old woman continued to scream after him until he had mounted his horse and ridden away.

Completely drained, Maddie tried to still her quivering heart. It wasn't until Matthew threw his arms around her neck that she could find her voice.

"Matthew, was that you who cried out?" He nodded, and she squeezed her eyes tight. She held him at arm's length. "Can you say something? Try. You must try."

Matthew's lips quivered as he struggled to make a sound and failed.

"From the throat, Matthew." She touched him on the throat. "You can do it."

Matthew strained. "I . . ."

She inhaled. "That's it. Don't stop. *I* what, Matthew? Tell me."

"I . . ." His face turned red as if to speak required

the use of every muscle in his body. "I ... was ... scared."

"Oh, Matthew." She hugged him close, her eyes filling with tears. "Your father will be so ..." *Luke!* Fearing the worst, she looked for Picking Bones, but the woman was already some distance away. "Wait!" She jumped to her feet and ran after her. "Picking Bones. Wait!"

The fire was so close that she could actually see the flames. A buffalo bull was running in circles as if confused. Upon closer observation, however, Maddie realized it must be injured. A short distance from it a small herd of buffalo stood grazing, oblivious to the two elk who bounded by in an attempt to escape the advancing fire.

"Picking Bones. Please. You must help me!"

Maddie wasn't certain that the old woman could hear her. Feeling desperate, Maddie shoved her fingers into her mouth and whistled. The shrill sound carried across the prairie.

The injured bull threw his head back and bellowed loudly, startling the rest of the herd and creating a chain reaction.

In seconds, the peacefully grazing herd became a surging mass. Picking up speed, the herd trampled everything in its path. The ground shook and the air vibrated with the sounds of thundering hoofs and echoing cries. The animals raced blindly toward the fire, kicking up dust until they were all but invisible.

Maddie watched in horror, but there was nothing she could do to divert the panicked animals.

Picking Bones had stopped to watch the stampede. After the loud, rumbling sound had faded away, Picking Bones surprised Maddie by turning back toward the soddy. Apparently the old woman had decided that between the stampeding buffalo and the fast-spreading fire, she had best postpone her departure.

"Hurry!" Maddie motioned with her hand. Lord, don't let it be too late. In her impatience, she grabbed hold of the woman's arms and literally pulled her the distance to the soddy.

Protesting loudly, the woman's contentious voice grew more intense when they neared the mounted animals. "They won't hurt you."

She guided the woman through the door and to the bed. "Red Feather ... arrow ..." She cupped her left hand near her breast. With her right hand, she made the motion of drawing an arrow from her left hand.

Lefty had taught Maddie well. Picking Bones nodded and leaned over Luke's still body. She spread her arms over him and said something in her native tongue.

Without another word, she scurried away from the bed like a little rodent and dashed out the door.

Thinking that Picking Bones's quick departure meant Luke was dead or nearly so, Maddie raced to his side and anxiously felt for his pulse. He was still alive—but barely. "Luke!" She shook him. "Please don't leave me, Luke!"

"Pa ..."

Matthew's plaintive cry made her fight back her panic. She swallowed hard, fighting for control. For Matthew's sake, she must be strong.

She drew Matthew to her side. "Say something to your father." Her voice shook, but it was the best she could do. "It'll help. I know it will."

Matthew leaned over his father. It was difficult for him to get the words out, and at first his voice was so hoarse that she couldn't decipher the words. But she encouraged him to keep trying, and at last he managed to make his meaning clear. "Papa. I don't want you to die like Mama."

Maddie slipped her arm around the boy's shoulder. As much as it pained her to hear the boy's plaintive cry, it was important for him to let his feelings out. "Keep talking, Matthew. I know your father can hear you."

Matthew continued to talk, his words hesitant and punctuated by long silences. Maddie nodded encouragement whenever he looked frustrated or seemed about to give up altogether. "Keep talking, Matthew. The more you talk, the easier it will become."

For the rest of the day and all through the seemingly endless night, Maddie sponged Luke's head with cool water. He felt feverish, and she feared that infection had set into his wound.

It was nearly dawn when the sound of a horse sent her flying to the door. It was Lefty. Never had she been so glad to see anyone in her life. She cried out in relief and ran out to greet him.

"Luke is hurt. Is there anything you can do? Picking Bones . . . heavens to Betsy, what's taking you so long?"

Lefty frowned. "Animals . . ."

"The animals won't hurt you. They're for my museum. Now come. You must hurry." She grabbed him by the arm and practically dragged him to the soddy. He insisted upon knocking at the door before entering. He had never forgiven her for requiring him to knock, and today he glared at her as he did so. "Like woodpecker."

"Forget about knocking, Lefty. Please hurry!"

She waited impatiently for him to examine Luke's wound. "There must be something we can do?"

Lefty held up a buckskin bag. "Picking Bones heap big medicine."

"Picking Bones sent that?"

He nodded and set to work covering Luke's wound with what appeared to be wild mushrooms. He pointed to the stove. "Hot water. Drink." She poured some hot water into a cup and handed it to him. He crushed dried leaves in his hand and dumped them into the steaming water.

"Him drink."

Lefty slipped an arm beneath Luke's shoulders and held him upright while she ladled the hot liquid down his throat, a teaspoon at a time, until the cup was empty.

Lefty nodded in satisfaction. "I go. My people wait for me."

"Wait?"

He looked defeated. "We go to government land."

She lay her hand on his arm. Her heart went out to him, to all his people. "I'm going to miss you, Lefty."

He patted his stomach. "Me do exorcists."

"I hope so, Lefty."

"Eat green stuff."

"Vegetables."

"And always remember Great Father's Day."

She glanced at Luke. "Is he going to be all right?"

Lefty made a circle with his hand. "You do. Me do. Now Great Spirit . . ." He corrected himself . . . "Great Father do."

She surprised Lefty by throwing her arms around his thick torso. "You're right, Lefty. It is in God's hands." She drew back. "Is this what you want? To live on government land?"

"We keep fighting or we live in peace."

"What about Red Feather?"

"He go with us."

She thought about this. She supposed there would be those who considered it a victory. But she couldn't help but feel that something wonderful and precious was about to be taken away from this land known as Kansas.

"Be careful, Lefty. The fires . . ." She stopped. She had been so concerned about Luke, she'd completely forgotten about the fires.

"No fire," Lefty said.

"No fire?"

"Picking Bones say white woman talk to buffalo and buffalo put out fire."

"Talk?" Maddie tried to make sense out of what Lefty said. "You mean the buffalo . . . when they stampeded . . . they put out the fire?"

"Wildfire Ostrich make whistle, buffalo put out fire."

Maddie couldn't believe what she heard. It appeared that her father's influence had made her more resourceful than even she suspected. "Please tell Picking Bones how much I appreciate the medicine."

"She joyful squaw. Shooting Star and White Blossom . . ." He held a finger of each hand together.

"Marry?"

He grinned. "Shooting Star and White Blossom marry."

Maddie couldn't help but smile back. "I don't think Shooting Star had much choice in the matter."

She walked Lefty to the door. He knocked furiously on the door before stepping outside, scowling fiercely at the perceived indignity.

She watched him ride away on his pony. He looked as free and graceful as the wind. "May your spirit always be as free as the wind," she said softly.

She hastened back to Luke's side. There was still no visible change.

"He can't hear me," Matthew said.

"He can hear you," she whispered, and she believed

with all her heart that what she said was true. "When you couldn't talk, you could still hear, couldn't you?"

Later that night, after Matthew had fallen asleep on the bed she'd made for him on the floor, she sat in a chair by Luke's side, exhausted and frustrated. Why wasn't Luke responding to the medicine?

She had spent the day spooning the hot water and crushed leaves that Lefty gave her down Luke's throat, but there was still no improvement.

At midnight, she touched his head and was shocked at how hot he felt. She frantically sponged him off and then forced more liquid down his throat.

It was almost dawn by the time she collapsed into the chair by his side and fell into a troubled sleep.

She awoke to the sound of a voice. She wasn't accustomed to hearing Matthew's voice. He was talking with none of his earlier hesitation or hoarseness. It was as if talking was the most natural thing in the world to him.

"Maddie pretended like she was a mounted animal," he was saying in that all-too-bright way children his age spoke when relaying bigger-than-life adventures. "Those Indians were scared."

It wasn't until she heard a deep-toned response that she let her eyes fly open. Even then, she could do nothing but fully absorb the wondrous sight in front of her. Finally she pushed herself forward in the chair. "Luke?"

Luke turned his head on his pillow to look at her. His face was still pallid, but the corner of his mouth lifted in that special half-smile of his that never failed to bring a full smile to her own lips.

"Oh, Luke!" With a cry of delight, she dropped to his side and grabbed his hands in hers. "Oh, my dear, sweet, wonderful Luke, I was so afraid for you." She showered his face with kisses. Matthew, happy but embarrassed, went outside.

He laughed and captured her face between his hands. The loving look he gave her filled her already bursting heart with the most profound joy.

"If I'm to believe what Matthew's been telling me— and I know I have you to thank for that miracle—I don't know how you had time to be afraid for me. What's this about you stampeding the buffalo to put out the fire?"

"Somebody had to put the fire out," she said without the least bit of modesty.

"And Red Feather? Is it true that you used those damned mounted animals to frighten him and his friends away?"

She gave him a smug smile. "Now don't you regret all the times you complained about my animals?"

"I don't know that I would go that far," he said.

She pushed a lock of hair off his forehead. "I love you, Luke Tyler, and if you ever scare me like that again, I won't be responsible for what I do!"

The look of pleasure her words brought to his face took her breath away. The sparkling blue color in his eyes more than made up for the lack of color on his face. "Maddie, I never killed that doctor, not on purpose."

"I never thought you did."

His eyes glowed softly. "I know that. But I couldn't think of us having a future together as long as I doubted myself."

Not sure what he was trying to say, she sat back on her heels.

"Don't look so worried," he said, brushing the shadow away from her brow. "I know now that you were right. It was an accident. George's death . . . it was an accident."

"How . . . how do you know . . . did Matthew . . . ?"

"Matthew wasn't there. He told me about finding his mother, but he knows nothing about what happened with George. But *I* know, Maddie. Shooting Star attacked me . . ."

"Shooting Star!" She tried to make sense of what he was saying. "But I thought it was Red Feather who attacked you."

"It was. But that came later. Shooting Star and I fought, and I had a chance to kill him, Maddie. I had the knife in my hand and I held it over his heart and I knew then that I could never take a man's life. Not willingly."

"Oh, Luke." She lay her head on his chest. "Does this mean that . . ."

"Yes."

Her head snapped up. "Yes, what?"

"Yes, we have a future together. That is, if you'll agree to be my wife."

The words were music to her ears. She was so overcome by the uncensored love she saw in his eyes, she couldn't speak.

Luke looked worried. "I thought you'd be happy, Maddie. I thought it's what you wanted. If you'll agree to be my wife, I'll . . ."

She simply couldn't resist teasing him a bit. Trying to keep from giving herself away, she crossed her arms in front of her and forced a formidable scowl. "Continue. What is it you'll do?"

"I'll never again complain about your strange hobby of mounting animals."

He fell silent and waited.

"What else do you promise?" she asked. She was beginning to enjoy herself. Maybe she was better at these male-female games than she thought.

"I'll never again complain about your calisthenics or

that godawful whistle of yours or the dandelion greens or the petticoats on the ceiling or your habit of . . ."

Before he had a chance to finish listing all the things that he was never again going to complain about, she had brazenly planted her mouth squarely on his and proceeded to do the most startling and unladylike things with her tongue. Then shockingly she slid her hand beneath the covers and . . .

Moaning in pleasure, he mentally added one more thing to his list that he would not complain about.

ANNOUNCING THE

# TOPAZ FREQUENT READERS CLUB
## COMMEMORATING TOPAZ'S 1 YEAR ANNIVERSARY!

### THE MORE YOU BUY, THE MORE YOU GET

Redeem coupons found here and in the back of all new Topaz titles for FREE Topaz gifts:

Send in:

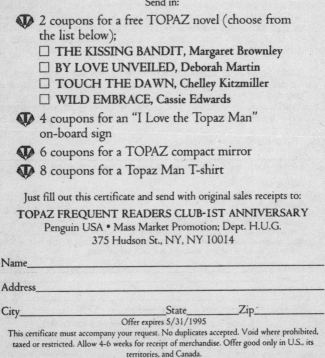

- 2 coupons for a free TOPAZ novel (choose from the list below);
  - ☐ THE KISSING BANDIT, Margaret Brownley
  - ☐ BY LOVE UNVEILED, Deborah Martin
  - ☐ TOUCH THE DAWN, Chelley Kitzmiller
  - ☐ WILD EMBRACE, Cassie Edwards
- 4 coupons for an "I Love the Topaz Man" on-board sign
- 6 coupons for a TOPAZ compact mirror
- 8 coupons for a Topaz Man T-shirt

Just fill out this certificate and send with original sales receipts to:

**TOPAZ FREQUENT READERS CLUB-1ST ANNIVERSARY**
Penguin USA • Mass Market Promotion; Dept. H.U.G.
375 Hudson St., NY, NY 10014

Name_____

Address_____

City_____ State_____ Zip_____

Offer expires 5/31/1995

This certificate must accompany your request. No duplicates accepted. Void where prohibited, taxed or restricted. Allow 4-6 weeks for receipt of merchandise. Offer good only in U.S., its territories, and Canada.